FIRE & RESCUE SHIFTERS COLLECTION 1

※

ZOE CHANT

Copyright Zoe Chant 2017
All Rights Reserved

Created with Vellum

ALSO BY ZOE CHANT

Fire & Rescue Shifters

Firefighter Dragon
Firefighter Pegasus
Firefighter Griffin
Firefighter Sea Dragon
The Master Shark's Mate
Firefighter Unicorn
Firefighter Phoenix

Fire & Rescue Shifters: Collection 1 (Books 1-3)
Fire & Rescue Shifters: Collection 2 (Books 4-7)

Fire & Rescue Shifters: Wildfire Crew

Wildfire Griffin
Wildfire Unicorn
Wildfire Sea Dragon
Wildfire Pegasus
Wildfire Hellhound

Wildfire Shifters: Collection 1 (Books 1-3)

Fae Mates

(set in the same world as Fire & Rescue Shifters)

Tithed to the Fae

… and many more!

All books are standalone romances, each focusing on a new couple. However,

characters from previous books reappear in later stories, so reading in series order is recommended for maximum enjoyment!

FIREFIGHTER DRAGON

FIRE & RESCUE SHIFTERS 1

CHAPTER 1

The first thing Virginia Jones had learned in her very first lecture as a college student was that *real* archaeology was nothing like archaeology in the movies. "We do not," her professor had declared as he swept the rows of eager young faces with a withering stare, "break into foreign locations with crowbars and dodge deadly traps in order to find lost golden treasures."

If he could see me now, Virginia thought with black humor as she levered the crowbar, *the old man would have an aneurysm.*

Admittedly, the foreign location was a construction site in the south of England, and the deadly traps were a couple of CCTV cameras, but Virginia was pretty sure her old professor would still have disapproved. Particularly as she was technically—OK, *very definitely*—breaking the law. Along with the site's side gate. If she could manage to get the stupid thing open.

Next time I have to break and enter in order to protect a site of major historical interest, I'm bringing an angle grinder. Virginia threw her full weight against the crowbar, and was rewarded by the creak of complaining metal as the gate twisted on its hinges. Taking a firm grip on both her nerves and her metal detector, Virginia wriggled through the gap.

In the green static of her rented night vision goggles, the construction site looked like a lunar landscape, with deep ruts and craters where the bulldozers had already scraped back the topsoil. Virginia scowled, anger flooding through her at the sight. Whatever vestigial burial mound might have remained would have been thoroughly destroyed, and precious information along with it. She could only hope that she wasn't already too late to save priceless artifacts from being crushed and desecrated beyond hope of recovery by the uncaring machines.

Checking the compass on her cell phone, Virginia rotated to orient herself. Far below her to the south, she could see the distant lights of Brighton, strung out along the seaside. Up here on the rolling chalk hills of the South Downs, the city looked like a glittering handful of jewels in a cupped palm.

An image of what it would have looked like over a thousand years ago flashed through her head—just a few tiny sparks from the hearths of the Saxon settlers, surrounded by vast, forested darkness. Had one of those settlers looked up at the looming hills where she now stood, and planned how he would be buried there so that he could watch over his descendants as they multiplied in the new home they had named after him...?

"I hope so," Virginia muttered to herself.

Unslinging her metal detector, she set to work. The chalky soil slid under her boots as she methodically quartered the site, swinging the metal detector with a steady rhythm. For the moment, she kept out of view of the CCTV cameras that guarded the scattered bulldozers parked at the center of the site. Her heart leapt at every squeal and click in her headphones, only to plummet again as her searching fingers uncovered nothing more than a stray nail or discarded Coke can.

"Come on, Brithelm," she coaxed under her breath, as though a warrior who'd been dead for over fifteen hundred years could obligingly shift his grave into a more discoverable position. "Don't be shy."

Unfortunately, Brithelm continued to be a coy corpse, as her sweep of the perimeter turned up not even as much as a bent copper coin. Virginia eyed the CCTV cameras, wishing that she'd taken a few electronics or computing courses alongside her archaeology major as an undergrad. As it was, her extensive and detailed knowledge of Anglo-Saxon Migrations (AD 400-900) did not provide her with any particular insights as to how to disable a modern security camera. With a shrug, she started sweeping her way across the monitored area anyway. Having spent the better part of three months single-handedly examining every other square inch of the hills above Brighton, she could hardly turn back now.

"Come *on*, Brithelm," she pleaded, each foot of ground covered eroding her hope.

Four years of research, three preliminary papers, two trips to Europe and one nearly-exhausted grant all led to this tiny bit of churned mud. She'd staked her reputation on this find. If there was nothing here—

The metal detector squealed.

Virginia's heart leaped into her mouth, and she dropped to her knees. Carefully locating the source of the signal, she pulled her trowel from her tool belt and started digging. She methodically passed the metal detector from deepening hole to growing pile of earth and back again, testing each shovelful as she dug. Nothing. Nothing. Nothing.

Signal!

Virginia gently sifted the soil through her shaking hands. Her bare fingers brushed metal, and a peculiar, very unscientific thrill shot through her veins. Even before she rubbed off the dirt, she was strangely certain that this, *this* was what she'd been looking for, and that somehow it had been looking for her too.

Though exactly what it was she had found wasn't immediately apparent. The gently-curving piece of metal was as wide as two of her fingers, and about five inches long. Cradling it in one hand, Virginia fumbled with her night vision goggles with her free hand, pushing them up onto her forehead. She took her penlight from her tool belt, clicking on the narrow beam of light, and directed it onto the piece.

"Oh, you beauty," she breathed, as the light illuminated the unmistakable gleam of pure gold.

She turned the piece over. The concave side was smooth, but the convex side was chased in intricately worked patterns. Even through the concealing grime, Virginia could see that the workmanship was exquisite. An enormous domed gem glinted up at her from the center of the piece, the shifting highlight trapped in its heart making it look like the slitted eye of some fabulous beast.

Like...a dragon? Virginia's heart skipped a beat.

"*Brave Brithelm, with the dragon's eye,*" she said aloud in Old English, quoting one of the few handful of surviving texts from the period that referred to the warrior.

Suddenly what she was looking at clicked into place. "The nose guard of a helmet."

She imagined how it would have looked complete, how the jewels and gold work would have crowned the head of the warrior who wore it in a dazzling display of wealth and power. "A bright helm. *Brithelm*."

"Ah, the indefatigable Virginia," drawled a familiar, amused male voice from behind her, nearly making Virginia drop the precious artifact. She just managed to shove the nose-guard into her pocket before she was pinned in the beam of a flashlight. "Why am I not surprised?"

"Bertram." Virginia stood and turned, her eyes watering in the sudden glare. Even though her heart was hammering in her mouth, she would rather have died on the spot than given her nemesis the satisfaction of knowing he'd startled her.

"What, slumming it out in the field? I thought you liked to leave that sort of thing to us," she made air quotes with her fingers, "'less intellectual dirt-diggers.'"

"Unintellectual dirt-diggers, my dear," Bertram said, his aristocratic British accent making each syllable ring like cut glass. "Do learn to quote sources accurately. It would improve your papers immensely."

He sauntered forward, delicately picking his way over the churned ground. As ever, he was impeccably dressed in a slim-cut pale grey suit that had probably cost as much as Virginia's entire research grant.

He twitched the flashlight's beam down to the hole at her feet, then back up to her face. "My, haven't you been a busy girl."

I didn't hear a car, Virginia realized uneasily.

Bertram looked as freshly-pressed and crisp as if he'd just dropped out of the sky, but she could only assume that he'd been lurking in the shadows the whole time. Had he seen the nose-guard?

She forced herself to keep her hand away from her coat pocket, and her voice light and even. "Have you been following me, or just hanging round here in the hopes I'd turn up?"

"I had a feeling your little wild goose chase might lead you to do something rash." Bertram inclined his head in the direction of the CCTV camera. "I thought it prudent to keep an eye on my father's investment. After all, I did recommend this site to him as an ideal location for his latest hotel. *Such* charming views, after all."

"You knew," Virginia spat, fury making her fists clench. "You knew all my research pointed to this being Brithelm's grave. You aren't fit to call yourself an archaeologist, you, you *vandal*."

"And yet, somehow, all our peers look up to me, and consider you a laughingstock." Bertram brushed a nonexistent speck of dirt off his sleeve, his heavy gold signet ring flashing as he did so. "If I may offer you a bit of free professional advice? Give up this ridiculous love affair of yours with this entirely mythical warrior. Perhaps you could take up a nice, quiet position in a local history museum? You'd make a simply splendid tour guide for schoolchildren."

"I am so looking forward to seeing your face when I present my findings," Virginia said. "I'll make sure the conference organizers reserve you a front-row seat."

Bertram sighed. "Alas, the academic world is so prejudiced. Criminals are rarely invited to give keynote speeches. Are you aware of the maximum sentence for breaking and entering?"

"Are you aware of the maximum sentence for corruption and bribery?" Virginia shot back. "Because I know you signed off on the paperwork for this site, saying that it was of no historic interest and so suitable for building. And there is no way in *hell* you actually did that survey."

Bertram went suddenly very still. "You found something."

I am alone at midnight in the middle of nowhere with a man who has despised me for nearly a decade, with something in my pocket that is both going to professionally ruin him and incidentally cost his family a very, very large sum of money.

"No," Virginia said, unconvincingly.

"You found something," Bertram repeated. His eyes narrowed. "What? A mere trifle, no doubt. A coin, or an arrowhead. Nothing of significance."

"Hah! You wish." Virginia couldn't help the grin that spread over her face. "Oh, you are so busted, Bertram. This isn't just any old burial mound. This is *Brithelm's* burial mound, and I can prove it."

"You found proof?" Strangely, he sounded exultant. "You must have found...*it*." A hungry expression spread over his face as he took a step closer. "Give it to me. Now."

Virginia backed away, fumbling for her crowbar. "Lay one finger on me and I swear I will brain you."

"Are you threatening me?" Bertram chuckled. "How entertaining. I think that I would very much like to see you try it." He kept coming forward, and Virginia kept retreating. "Come on, my dear delectable Virginia. Don't be ridiculous. You have never been able to win against me, and you certainly won't now. Just give me Brithelm's gem."

Virginia's palm was sweating on the handle of the crowbar. "You'll have to prize it out of my cold, dead fingers, you bastard."

Bertram's eyes glittered oddly in the light. "Excellent."

He lunged, and Virginia hurled the crowbar at him. Without waiting to see if it had connected, she whirled and ran, her boots pounding over the rutted ground. Over her own panicked breathing, she heard Bertram laugh, then a strange noise like an enormous tarpaulin flapping in a storm. Then—nothing.

As she wriggled back through the broken gate, Virginia risked a glance behind her. All was dark. Had Bertram switched off his flashlight, the better to stalk her through the night? She half-slid down the sloping hill to where she'd left her Range Rover parked next to the road, dropping her crowbar in order to fumble frantically for the keys. Expecting at any moment to feel Bertram's hands grabbing at her, she flung herself into the vehicle.

Only when she was finally barreling back down the twisting countryside roads at a thoroughly unsafe forty miles per hour did her galloping heart begin to slow. She drew in a deep, shuddering breath, checking her rear view mirror. No sign of pursuit. Maybe he hadn't had a car. Maybe he'd given up. Maybe he was just—her racing mind scrabbled for ways that rich, evil English aristocrats might deal with people who'd crossed them—on the phone, calmly placing a hit on her.

Okay, now you're just being ridiculous. Giving herself a mental shake, Virginia returned her attention to the road ahead.

There was a dragon in the middle of it.

Virginia had barely even registered the impossible shape when her reflexes took over, stomping hard on the brake and jerking the steering wheel. She had a brief impression of a wall of ice-white scales shooting past the side windows as the Range Rover fishtailed wildly, spinning almost out of control. With all her strength, she clung onto the wheel. In a stench of burning rubber, the car screeched to a halt, facing back the way she'd come. Virginia stared through the steam rising from the hood, her knuckles white on the steering wheel.

There's a dragon in the middle of the road.
There's a dragon.
In the middle of the road.
It's a dragon.
That can't be right.

Shock gave her a strange sense of detachment, as if she was just watching a movie. Everything seemed to go into slow motion, every last detail of the beast searing into her retinas. It was sitting upright like a cat, long white tail wrapped primly around its front—paws? Feet? Huge taloned things? Its horned head was at least twenty feet off the ground. The glowing orange eyes met hers, and the dragon's jaw dropped open slightly, forked tongue lolling out. It looked for all the world as if it was smirking at her.

The dragon unfurled its wings. The lean muscles of its back legs tensed, then it sprang into the air, its wings sweeping downward with a *boom*.

The sound broke her paralysis. She fumbled for the keys in the ignition, her nerveless fingers slipping. Before she could restart the engine, the entire car shook as the dragon thumped into the ground right next to it.

Virginia screamed as the passenger-side window shattered. She hurled herself out of the driver-side door as two sharp ivory talons thrust into the compartment. Then she was sprinting, running faster than she had ever run before in her life, away from the sounds of tortured metal as the dragon tore her vehicle apart behind her.

The loud *boom* rang out again. Virginia whimpered in terror, knowing that the dragon had once more taken to the air. Her night vision goggles chafed her sweating forehead; without breaking stride, she yanked them down over her eyes. Darkness gave way to a flat, monochrome green world. She was in an overgrown field, weeds catching at her jeans as she ran.

A whistle of wind at the back of her neck gave her the barest hint of warning. Virginia flung herself flat as the dragon's talons snapped shut inches above her. Being so large, it couldn't immediately turn back and grab her. It sailed onwards and upwards, the wake of its passing blowing a heavy, animal reek into Virginia's face.

Virginia cast around wildly for any sort of shelter. There was a cluster of barns at the far end of the field—clearly dark and unoccupied, but better than nothing. Virginia ran for them, the downdraft from the dragon's wings cold on her back and neck. She just managed to fling herself into the nearest barn just as the dragon swooped down for another pass. She heard a hiss of frustration as it was forced to veer off again, wings beating hard to avoid crashing into the roof. She slammed the door that she'd come through shut, forcing rusted bolts home.

Got to find somewhere to hide.

To her relief, the barn was an old but sturdy structure, made out of thick wooden beams and metal cladding. She couldn't imagine that even a dragon would be able to easily demolish it. Virginia stumbled between looming, mysterious machinery and piles of boxes, trying to quiet her panicked gasps. A thump reverberated through the ground, as if something very large had just landed outside. Virginia pictured it circling the cluster of buildings, trying to sniff her out.

Trembling, she sank down in the shadows behind a stack of crates. *I've got a moment before it works out where I am. Long enough to call for help.*

She pulled her cell phone out of her pocket, and nearly sobbed in relief when she saw that it had signal. By sheer reflex, she nearly dialed 911 before correcting herself.

"999," said a calm, professional voice in her ear. "What is the nature of your emergency?"

Virginia's mind went completely blank. "Dragon," she blurted out.

There was a momentary pause from the emergency call handler. "Pardon?"

"There's a dragon outside," Virginia whispered. She could

hear it pacing outside the barn. It paused, and there was an odd sucking sound, as if it was drawing in its breath. "It's trying to get in."

Another, longer pause. "Do you require fire, ambulance, or police for that, ma'am?"

Outside, the dragon exhaled, and the edges of the barn door lit up with a dazzling orange glow.

"Fire," said Virginia.

CHAPTER 2

*D*ai Drake beat his wings hard, hovering on the night wind for a moment as he scrutinized the South Downs far below. His searching eyes caught on a flickering orange spark near the crest of the tallest hill.

Well, there's definitely a fire, at least, he sent telepathically to Ash. *Can't tell if it's dragonfire unless I get a lot closer.*

Proceed with caution, the Fire Crew Commander sent back. As always, his mental voice was tightly controlled, but from long experience Dai could detect the growing concern under the calm surface of his thoughts. *Dispatch reports we just lost contact.*

Dai hissed under his breath, forked tongue flickering. That meant that the woman who'd made the call, saying she was trapped by a dragon in a burning building, had either hung up or lost consciousness. The rest of his fire crew wasn't far behind, but even with Chase's reckless driving there was no way they could reach the scene as fast as he could.

See you there, Dai sent to Ash, then broke contact. He swept his wings back into a dive, arrowing toward the fire.

Even before he saw the other dragon, Dai knew it was no ordinary blaze. The wooden barn was burning with the white-hot ferocity that could only be sparked by dragonfire. The leaping flames silhouetted a lean, pale form hunched in front of the barn door like a cat in front of a mouse hole.

Anger rose in Dai's chest, and he had to swallow his own dragonfire. He roared instead, hurling a thought into the stranger's mind like a javelin. *Stop!*

The white dragon leapt, wings twitching open and head snapping round. The stranger's startlement lasted barely an instant, however, before his wings and tail settled into a posture of offended dignity.

How dare you! His mental tone was as rich as gold, and imbued with an absolute sense of his own power and righteousness. His snout turned upwards disdainfully at the sight of Dai's own crimson scales. *Some peasant Welsh red, interfering in my business? Who do you think you are?*

Firefighter Daifydd Drake, of the East Sussex Fire and Rescue Service, Dai shot back as he backwinged in to land. He drew himself up to his full height, glaring down at the white dragon. *Stand aside, now!*

You can't possibly challenge me. The other dragon's head spines bristled in indignation. *Don't you know who I am?*

Yes, Dai replied. The other dragon squawked as Dai lashed out with his muscular tail, knocking the smaller dragon clean off his feet. *You're in my way.*

Before the other dragon could recover, Dai shoved past him. Much as his own inner dragon wanted to formally challenge the arrogant bastard, there was no time for it. He appraised the burning barn with a single practiced glance. There was no way he could enter in dragon form without bringing the whole lot down on the heads of both himself and whoever was in there.

He shifted back into human form. Even as the other

FIREFIGHTER DRAGON

dragon struggled back upright, hissing with outrage, Dai ducked through the burning door.

Immediately flames surrounded him, licking at his skin—but the only fire a dragon-shifter needed to fear, even when in human form, was that which came directly from the jaws of a rival. This blaze had been started by dragonfire, but now the flames were just fueled by ordinary wood and air, and so couldn't harm him. Dai still wore the standard protective gear of a firefighter, but it was more for the look of the thing than any real need.

He drew in a breath, the heavy smoke passing easily through his lungs, guiltily savoring the tang of it like an ex-smoker sneaking just one puff from a friend's cigarette. The fire called to his dragon, beguiling in its beauty and power.

Pushing down the instinctive urge to luxuriate in the flames, Dai ducked to peer through the thinner smoke near the floor. "Fire and Rescue," he shouted. "Can anyone hear me?"

That woman is my rightful prey! The other dragon shoved his head through the door, the burning wall disintegrating around him. *She's stolen from my hoard. I demand—*

"Get back before you bring the building down!" Dai yelled back as beams snapped and popped warningly overhead. He couldn't burn or suffocate, but even a dragon could be hurt by a collapsing building. Not to mention the fact that there was a human trapped in here. "Or so help me God, I will find your hoard and personally melt it into slag!"

The other dragon narrowed his orange eyes, but grudgingly retreated. Fresh air sucked in through the hole it had made in the wall, making the flames roar greedily. Dai calculated he had barely a minute before the whole thing came down anyway.

Bits of falling debris clattered off his helmet as he searched through the swirling smoke. According to Griff—

the dispatcher who'd taken the call—she'd taken refuge near the back of the building, away from the worst of the flames...

Just as he was giving up hope, he found her. She was unconscious, lying full-length on the floor with her face pressed against a crack in the wall. She must have been desperately trying to suck in fresh air from outside as the smoke overwhelmed the building. She wasn't a small woman, but Dai easily lifted her, cradling her limp form against his chest. He hunched over, trying to shield her from the falling embers as he ran for the door.

He burst out into clean air just as the central support beam in the roof gave way with a cataclysmic groan. There was no time to shift—Dai could only hurl himself to the ground, covering the woman's body completely under his own as burning debris sprayed in all directions. Pain pierced his shoulder as a foot-long splinter of wood hit him with enough force to get through his protective gear. Dai didn't flinch. He kept his body between the woman and the collapsing building until the last strut had crashed to the ground.

A sharp talon prodded him on his wounded shoulder. *As I was saying before I was so rudely interrupted—*

Dai had never been so glad to hear the sing-song wail of the approaching fire engine. "If you have a legitimate grievance, you can either take it to the Parliament of Shifters, or have it out with my commander right now." The post-adrenaline surge crash was starting to catch up with him. His shoulder throbbed, and a dozen lesser pains were clamoring for his attention. "If you're feeling *very* brave. He's not very sympathetic to arsonists."

The dragon hesitated, glancing uncertainly in the direction of the siren. He backed up, opening his white wings. *Just remember, the treasure is mine. And I will be back to claim it.*

FIREFIGHTER DRAGON

"Now there's something to look forward to," Dai muttered as the dragon took to the air.

Dai pushed himself up, wincing as the wooden splinter dug deeper into his muscle. With a bitten-off curse, he reached over his shoulder and yanked it out, tossing the red-stained wood away. He could feel blood trickling down his back, but the wound clearly wasn't life-threatening so he dismissed it from his mind. He was far more worried about the woman he'd rescued from the blaze.

She was still sprawled bonelessly, her eyes closed and her rich brown skin flecked with pale ash. Dai crouched over her, checking to see if her airway was clear. To his relief, she stirred at his touch, coughing.

"It's all right," Dai said, slipping an arm under her shoulders to support her in a more upright position as she fought to clear her lungs. "You're safe. Everything's all right now."

The woman opened her eyes. Dai looked into their warm, dark amber depths, and suddenly, for the first time in his entire life, everything *was* all right.

"Dragon," the woman whispered.

"Yes," Dai said, voice cracking as delight and awe spread through him. Of course, of course his mate would be able to see straight into his soul, recognizing his hidden nature at a glance. Then her eyes flicked away from his, her gaze skittering over the surroundings as a look of panic spread across her face, and he belatedly realized that she'd meant the *other* dragon. "I mean, no! It's all right, the dragon's gone. You're safe with me now."

She clutched at his hand. "You...saw?" Her voice sounded like she was having to drag words out of her throat on rusty barbed wire.

"Don't try to talk." Dai scooped her up, unable to help noticing her stunning, lush curves as he did so. She fit into his arms so perfectly, he never wanted to put her down again.

Cradling her with infinite care, he carried her further away from the fire, out of range of any further debris. He could feel the way she had to fight for every breath, and his own chest tightened in anxious response.

Where ARE you? he sent to Chase, the driver. *I need the crew here right NOW!*

Astonishment rippled back down the mental link. *You want* me *to go faster?* Chase's gleeful laugh echoed in Dai's head. *Well, if you* insist...*

Barely seconds later, the fire engine screeched into the farmyard in a blaze of noise and color. Dai could have sworn that the madman actually managed to get the fifteen-ton vehicle to travel sideways round the corner. He had to duck to protect the woman yet again as the truck screeched to a stop in a spray of sharp gravel and dirt. The driver door flung open, and Chase bounced out, his tousled black hair nearly as wild as his grin.

"And it's a neeeew woooorld record!" Chase announced to the world in general, raising his clasped hands above his head as if posing on a podium.

"Out of the way, featherhead," John rumbled as he squeezed his seven-foot bulk out of the rear seats with some difficulty. He crossed the distance to Dai in two long strides, holding out his enormous hands. "Are you hurt, kin-cousin? Shall I take her?"

"I'm fine," Dai replied, reflexively holding the woman closer as his inner dragon snarled at the thought of someone taking her away from him. "I'll look after her. Where's Hugh?"

"Setting up on the other side," said Fire Commander Ash, jumping lithely down from the fire engine. "He's not geared up, so I want him to stay back."

The Fire Commander's dark, calm eyes swept the scene, taking in every detail at a glance. "Daifydd, get the casualty to Hugh. Chase, stay on the radio, warn us when the police are about to arrive. John, let's take advantage of our lack of mundane onlookers. I'll contain the fire. Can you call the rain?"

The other shifter nodded, the charms woven into his long blue braids clinking. "The clouds are melancholy tonight. I shall sing their tears down."

"Good. Let's get to it, then, gentlemen." Turning to face the burning ruins of the barn, Ash flung his arms wide as if to embrace the fire. It leaped unnaturally in response, stretching out to the Fire Commander as if straining to reach a long-lost lover.

Ash slowly brought his hands together, and the fire grudgingly concentrated itself into a white-hot circle. John tilted his head back, beginning a droning hum in his own language as Ash chivvied stray flames back into the herd.

Dai was happy to leave them to it. His own talents lent themselves more to the "Rescue" side of the work, and it always made him feel inappropriately morose to have to put out a perfectly good fire.

"Hugh!" he called, striding round the truck. "I have a casualty for you!"

"Put her down here." Hugh's distinctive silver hair gleamed in contrast to the red fire engine behind him. He'd already unrolled a blanket and opened up a first aid kit.

Dai carefully lowered her down to the ground and stepped back to give Hugh access to the patient, though his inner dragon growled at having to move even an inch from his mate. He forced down the dragon's possessive instinct as Hugh crouched next to the woman, his intense blue eyes narrowed in assessment.

"Hello," Hugh said to the woman. "I'm a paramedic. Can I

help you?" His clipped, upper-class English accent made it sound like he was merely making polite conversation, but Dai knew he was assessing the woman's ability to respond.

"Throat," rasped the woman. "Hurts."

A tiny crease appeared in Hugh's forehead at her tone, and Dai's heart missed a beat. His dragon rose up, desperate to fight whatever threatened his mate.

She's in good hands, he told his inner dragon as Hugh tugged off one of his disposable plastic gloves with a smooth, practiced motion.

Hugh touched the woman's neck lightly. As his bare skin brushed hers, she winced—and so did Hugh. His mouth twisted in a distinct grimace of pain as he slowly slid his hand down from jaw to collarbone. After a moment, he drew back his hand, flexing his fingers as if shaking out pins and needles.

"Can you tell me your name?" he asked the woman.

"Virginia." She looked startled at her own voice, which was much clearer than before. She drew in a deep breath. "Virginia Jones. Wow, that feels better." She rubbed her own throat, staring at the paramedic in wonder. "How on earth did you do that?"

"Mild irritation from smoke often clears up quickly," Hugh said, his curt tone dissuading any further inquiry. He snapped his glove back on before taking her pulse, expression back to his customary reserve. "Can you tell me what happened, Virginia?"

"Uh." Virginia's brown eyes went from Hugh to Dai and back again. "It's all a bit...confused."

"He knows about dragons too," Dai said. "He won't think that you're crazy."

Virginia let out a brief bark of half-hysterical laughter. "*I* think I'm crazy." She wrapped her arms around her knees, hugging them to her chest. "That monster...it can't have been real. *Dragons* aren't real!"

"Alas, if only that were true." Hugh murmured as he checked her for any further injuries. Catching Dai's dirty look, he added, "You can't deny we'd all be a lot less busy." He sat back on his heels. "Virginia, you don't have any burns, and you don't have a concussion. However, you've gone through a lot of trauma tonight. For safety, I would like to call an ambulance to take you into hospital for observation and any further treatment."

Virginia's hand suddenly flew to her coat pocket, gripping something through the fabric. "No. I want to go home. I feel fine. Can I just go home?"

Hugh sighed. "One day, one of my patients will actually *want* to go to the marvelous temple of modern medicine. Yes, you can go home, *if*," he raised one long finger forbiddingly, "you can call someone to both take you there and take care of you tonight."

Virginia's face fell. "Oh." She rubbed her forehead. "I'll...think of someone."

Can you give us a minute? Dai sent to Hugh.

The paramedic's pale eyebrows rose, but he got to his feet. "I'll go report to Commander Ash. Let me know when you decide what to do." Flashing Dai a curious glance, he left.

"Please, allow me to watch over you tonight," Dai said to Virginia, as casually as he could with his inner dragon roaring in eagerness. "It's not safe for you to be alone, and not just for medical reasons. The dragon threatened to return."

That bothered him. If she'd never seen a dragon before—and clearly she hadn't—how could she have taken something from one's hoard? Had the other dragon been lying? He pushed the thought away; there were much more important matters to deal with now.

Virginia's eyes widened. "It—what?"

"Shh, shh!" Dai grabbed her shoulders as her breathing started to go shallow and panicky. "It's all right. I'm here to protect you."

"From *dragons*?"

"Yes. It's, ah, sort of my specialty."

She stared at him, apparently taking in his uniform. "But you're a firefighter," she said blankly.

"Yes. But I'm also a dragon..."

That monster, she had said.

"...hunter," Dai finished.

It *was* true. Just not...the whole truth.

"A dragon hunter." Virginia made a choked hiccup of strangled laughter. "I managed to call a firefighter who's also a dragon hunter. Boy, is it my lucky day. Apart from the dragon, of course."

"Well, it wasn't exactly luck," Dai said, rubbing his thumbs over her shoulders soothingly. She was still looking rather wild-eyed, but at least no longer on the verge of a panic attack. "Our dispatchers know to send the, ah, unusual calls to our crew. We're used to handling this sort of thing. I really can protect you from the dragon."

Virginia bit her lip. She seemed to waver for a moment, then shook her head. "This is crazy. Everything is crazy. I don't even know your name."

"Dai. Daifydd Drake." Dai exaggerated the soft *th* sound of the *dd*—from her accent, she was American, and they always seemed to have difficulty pronouncing Welsh names.

He stuck out his hand. "East Sussex Fire and Rescue. At your service."

Now, and forever.

CHAPTER 3

This is crazy.
Of course, compared to all the crazy things that had happened this evening—finding Brithelm's burial mound, the confrontation with Bertram, the *motherfucking dragon*—inviting a strange man to stay the night seemed positively sensible. Nonetheless, the taxi ride back to her rented apartment was long enough for some of Virginia's shock to wear off, allowing second thoughts to creep in.

Am I being stupid, trusting a man I've only just met?

Virginia knew that she should have meekly gone to the hospital and let the doctors take care of her. But that would mean delaying investigating her find. Virginia once again touched the thrilling weight of the gold nose-guard safely hidden in her pocket and shook her head. She couldn't afford to wait—and it wasn't just to satisfy her own burning curiosity. She doubted that it was mere coincidence that the dragon had appeared after she'd found the artifact.

Virginia was familiar with many dragon legends from across Europe, and a common factor in them all was the great wyrms' lust for gold. Somehow the beast must have sensed her removing the treasure from its hiding place, and come to retrieve it. But how? Virginia mentally added it to the long list of questions to ask Dai later.

She cast a sideways glance at Dai's profile, half-seen in the dim, strobing glow of the streetlights passing by outside the taxi's window. She hadn't even gotten a good look at his face yet, with all the smoke and confusion at the site of the fire.

I don't know anything about this man. Apart from the fact that he'd pulled her out of a burning building, which anyone would have had to admit was a pretty excellent character recommendation.

However, there was still something about the set of his powerful shoulders that projected an aura of danger. Even his tiniest movements seemed controlled, deliberate, as if he had to keep himself tightly in check at all times. He'd opened the taxi door for her as carefully as if he'd been worried he might absentmindedly tear it off its hinges.

Yet despite all that contained strength, Virginia didn't feel the slightest bit uneasy around him. Sitting next to Dai was like huddling next to a roaring campfire—something fierce and dangerous that nonetheless provided life-giving warmth, and protection against the encircling dark.

Virginia shook her head again, more ruefully. *If the paramedic hadn't given me a clean bill of health, I would suspect that I have a concussion.*

The taxi slowed to a crawl, pulling into a street of close-packed Victorian townhouses, and stopped outside her building. Dai was out of the car and opening her door even before Virginia had managed to get her seat belt unbuckled.

"I'll pay the driver," he said, in that lilting Welsh accent that seemed incongruously gentle coming from such a big man. Virginia could feel the calluses on his long, strong fingers as he offered her a steadying hand out of the car. "Do you need help up the stairs?"

"I'm fine," Virginia said, though in truth she had to haul herself up the few steps to the front door.

Her legs had definitely had enough tonight, and were threatening to mutiny from her body. She surreptitiously leaned on the wrought-iron banister as she fumbled for her keys, grateful that she had the ground-floor apartment.

She let herself into the high-ceilinged lounge, and some of the lingering tightness in her chest eased. Even though it was only a temporary rental rather than a home, it was comforting to be in a space of her own. The research papers scattered over the worn sofa were just as she'd left them this morning, back when the world had been a rational place. It felt like an aeon ago now.

Virginia took the nose-guard out of her pocket, eager to see it in decent light. For the second time that evening, she found herself unable to breathe. It made every piece of Saxon gold work she'd ever seen before—even the famous Sutton Hoo helmet—look like cheap costume jewelry.

Down the length of the nose-guard, the thick gold was chased with exquisitely carved spiraling dragons, writhing round small cabochon rubies. A much larger cabochon ruby took pride of place at the top of the piece, which would have placed it centrally on the forehead of the warrior wearing the helmet. The ruby seemed to glow through the dirt veiling it, a rich blood-red with a dazzling six-pointed star captured within its depths.

Virginia bit her lip, glancing out the bay window. The taxi was just pulling away, which meant that Dai would be entering the apartment at any moment. Where he would find her standing with a king's ransom in the palm of her hand...

And I really don't know anything about this guy.

Even if Dai wasn't the sort to be personally tempted by a hunk of solid gold set with precious gems, there was still the fact that he worked in emergency services, alongside the police. Who would already want to be asking searching questions about how the fire started, and why she'd been up on the Downs in the middle of the night in the first place.

If Dai found out about the artifact, he'd probably feel obliged to inform the police, and then they'd find out that she'd been illegally metal-detecting without the permission of the landowner. In the best case, they'd confiscate the artifact, and she'd lose all chance to work on the find.

In the worst case, it would end up in Bertram's hands.

Best if Dai just doesn't find out about this.

Cradling the treasure, Virginia glanced around. Her tools and specimen boxes were set out on the small dining table, where she'd been working on some coins and minor finds from other sites, but that didn't feel like a safe enough hiding place.

Hearing boots coming down the hall, she dashed into her bedroom and yanked open the drawer of her bedside cabinet. She tucked the nose-guard carefully out of sight behind a packet of tissues, a tube of hand cream, and a box of aspirin. As an extra deterrent to casual snooping, she made sure her favorite vibrator was right at the front.

There. That ought to do it.

"Virginia?" Dai called from the lounge. Virginia heard him shut the door behind himself. "Are you all right?"

"Be out in a sec!" Virginia called back.

She tiptoed into the en suite bathroom and flushed the toilet, just in case he was wondering at her absence. Catching sight of herself in the mirror, she wrinkled her nose at her charred hair and soot-smeared face. Shower battled sleep on her list of priorities...but neither was as important as finally getting some answers. She pulled off her ruined coat, dropping it in a corner as she left the bedroom.

"Dai," she said as she reentered the lounge. "I want to know—"

The words died in her throat.

Okay. I have not just invited a strange man over to stay the night. I have invited an incredibly attractive *strange man round to stay the night.*

Dai had his helmet under one arm, revealing a strong, square-jawed face that made Virginia's tongue stick to the roof of her mouth. A streak of ash cut across his smooth tanned skin, highlighting the perfect planes of his cheekbones. He absently ran a hand through his short, red-gold hair, tousling the loose curls even further as he looked around.

His bright green eyes seemed to take in every detail at a glance, with the casual but sweeping appraisal of some large predator scanning its surroundings for prey. That assessing gaze snagged on the smoke alarm set into the ceiling. He reached up to it, not even having to stretch onto his toes to push the test button.

"Sorry," Dai said sheepishly, as a loud beeping filled the small room. "Professional habit. You wouldn't believe how many people take the batteries out of these." He jabbed the button again to shut the alarm up. He cocked his head to one side, looking down at her. "What were you saying?"

Virginia belatedly realized that she'd just been staring slack-jawed at him. She struggled to recapture her previous train of thought despite the looming distraction occupying a sizable fraction of her lounge.

"Uh. Dragons. Yes. That was it." She cleared her throat. *Down, girl. So the firefighter is hot like burning. He's here in a professional capacity only. His* other *professional capacity.* "Do dragons come into cities?"

The corner of Dai's mouth twisted wryly. "Yes. But we're safer here than out in the middle of the countryside with no witnesses, at least. We—they normally try to avoid attracting attention."

"I should think it's damn hard for a fifty-foot dragon to avoid attracting attention!"

"You'd be surprised. Many dragons can do a sort of mind trick, which stops people from being able to see them."

"Oh good." Virginia collapsed into the nearest chair. She rubbed the bridge of her nose. "Fifty-foot *invisible* dragons."

"Don't worry, it only works on ordinary people." Dai navigated his way gingerly around the furniture to her side, having some difficulty finding space for his large, heavy boots amidst the scattered books.

He made a short, abortive gesture, as if he'd started to put a reassuring hand on her shoulder but had stopped himself. "I can see them. He can't hide from me."

"But it can make itself invisible to me? Even if I'm standing right in front of it?" Virginia shivered. Despite the warmth of Dai's reassuring presence, the thought of something being able to make her *not notice it* made her blood run cold. "Do you learn to resist dragon mind tricks as part of being a dragon hunter? Can you teach me how to do it too?"

Dai shook his head. "It's something you're born with, I'm afraid." He hesitated, shifting his weight from foot to foot. "You have to be…part-dragon. Descended from them."

"Are you telling me that the fifty-foot invisible dragons can," Virginia groped for a politer word than the first that had sprung to mind, "*interbreed* with people?"

"Ah, yes." Dai avoided her eyes, busying himself unfastening his uniform jacket. "Dragons don't always look like dragons."

With a slight wince, he shrugged off the protective jacket. Underneath he was wearing a simple black T-shirt which strained against his upper arms. Braces ran over his shoulders, holding up his fire-resistant pants and emphasizing the hard lines of his muscled chest. He adjusted one of the straps as he spoke. "Dragons are shifters, you see. Most of the time, they *are* people."

Virginia stared at him, for more than one reason. "Let me get this straight. You're saying that dragons can turn into people."

Dai fidgeted, rubbing at one shoulder. "I'm saying some people can turn into dragons."

Virginia did not feel that this was the time to argue semantics. "Whatever. And they sometimes...*mate* with people."

The tips of Dai's ears were turning red. "Quite often. Ah, that is, I mean, often dragons take *a* mate, not that they often mate with lots of—"

Virginia held up both hands to stop him, shuddering in revulsion. "*Please* do not tell me about the sex lives of dragons. I don't even want to think about it."

Dai's mouth opened, then shut again. He looked desperately uncomfortable. "It's not—"

"Seriously, this is the one area where I really don't need details." Something was nagging at Virginia. She frowned, thinking back over the night. She abruptly sat bolt upright. "Bertram!"

Dai looked taken aback. "Pardon?"

"Bertram. Bertram Russell. He's a...sort of professional rival of mine."

Dai glanced down at the maps and papers scattered around his feet, then at the small brushes and magnifying glasses laid out on the dining table. "You're an archaeologist?"

Virginia liked the rather reverent way he said the word. It made a nice change from the raised eyebrows she usually got when she mentioned her profession. "Yes. I specialize in the early Saxon period, particularly tracking migrations across Europe. Anyway, earlier tonight I ran into Bertram at a building site his family owns, up on the Downs. I ended up running away because I thought he was going to attack me, but when I looked back he'd vanished. And then..."

Her stomach clenched at the memory of bone-white claws stabbing at her, and she had to pause for a moment to regain her composure. "Then the dragon appeared."

Dai's mouth tightened into a grim line. "He's the shifter, then."

He fell silent, studying her. Virginia had the uncomfortable feeling that those clear green eyes could read her like an open book. She was certain that he'd noticed the way she hadn't mentioned just why she'd been up on the Downs in the first place. She was mentally scrabbling for an excuse for her night time hike that *didn't* involve a fortune in gold, when Dai spoke again. "Dragons are incredibly possessive."

It was Virginia's turn to blink at the apparent non sequitur. "What do you mean?"

"A dragon always has a hoard. Gold and jewels are irresistibly attractive, especially anything unique or significant in some way. But taking even the smallest coin from a dragon's hoard is like kidnapping one of their children. He'd stop at nothing to get it back."

"I didn't take anything that belongs to Bertram,' Virginia said firmly.

It was technically true, she told herself. The nose-guard, and anything else that remained in Brithelm's burial mound, was part of Britain's cultural heritage. By law, it belonged to the nation, not to whoever happened to own the land it was found on.

Dai let out his breath, looking relieved. "That's good." Virginia felt a twinge of guilt at the way he just took her words on trust, without asking for any details. "It avoids certain...complications with draconic law."

Implying that if she *had* stolen something, Dai wouldn't

have been able to stop the dragon from taking it back. It was a good thing Bertram hadn't managed to find the artifact first. Virginia felt physically ill at the thought of the artifacts that must be gathering dust in the dragon's hoard. The noseguard's true value did not lie in mere gold or jewels, but in the hidden stories it contained, waiting to be unlocked by careful study. The thought of Bertram hoarding it away to privately gloat over was unbearable.

"You know, this does explain a lot about Bertram," she mused aloud. "Now I know why he's such a nasty, controlling, sneering bastard. Suddenly, it makes perfect sense. It's because he's a dragon."

All the relief fled from Dai's face, chased away by dismay. "He *could* just be a bastard."

Is he defending dragons? Virginia was momentarily puzzled, until she remembered something he'd said earlier. "Wait. You're a dragon hunter."

"It's something I do, yes," Dai said, cautiously. "But if you're asking me to kill this Bertram—"

Virginia cut him off with a shake of her head. "Tempting, but not where I was going." Her eyes narrowed as she studied him from head to toe. "You said you had to be part-dragon in order to hunt them, right?"

Every muscle in Dai's shoulders tensed. "Yes."

"So *you've* got dragon blood."

Dai looked like a man staring down a firing squad. "Yes."

"Which you're bleeding all over my carpet."

Dai blinked. "What?"

"You're bleeding, Dai!" Virginia launched herself out of her chair as yet more crimson drops joined the spreading stain on the beige carpet. All other thoughts fled her mind at a sudden urgent, instinctive need to make sure he was all right. "Did you get hurt in the fire?"

"Oh, that. It's just a scratch." Dai rubbed at his shoulder

again, then looked at the palm of his hand, which was now covered in blood. "Ah. Hm."

"Let me see," Virginia demanded, pulling at his arm.

Dai was so tall, he had to go down on one knee to let her get a good look at his shoulder. His T-shirt was wet with blood, clinging to the curves of his back like a second skin.

Virginia gingerly peeled the shredded fabric away, and sucked in her breath at the sight of the puncture wound in the thick muscle of his left shoulder. "Dai, I think you need to go to the hospital."

Dai rolled his shoulder experimentally. His jaw clenched, but he shook his head. "It's all right. I can still use it."

"Yes, because my only concern about the giant bloody hole in your shoulder was that it might affect your dragon-fighting ability." Virginia cast around for something to staunch the bleeding, but everything she was wearing was covered in dirt and ash. For lack of any better option, she grabbed a cushion and pressed it to the wound. "I left my phone in the bedroom. Hold this in place while I go call an ambulance."

"No!" Dai caught her wrist. Despite the speed and suddenness of the movement, his fingers closed gently, just a feather-light touch on her skin. His green eyes blazed with intensity. "I am not leaving you unprotected."

With him on his knees, their faces were only inches apart. This close, she could see all the shades of color in his irises, from dark emerald to leaf-green, with a thin band of burning gold right around the pupil.

Dragon eyes.

She remembered other eyes—orange instead of green, but with that same hidden fire—and couldn't help flinching.

Dai must have felt her movement, because those brilliant eyes darkened. He looked away abruptly.

"I'll be fine, truly," he said, a rough catch in his voice. "I heal quickly."

"Dragon blood?" Virginia guessed, and sighed at Dai's nod. "Fine, have it your way. But at least let me clean that and put a bandage on it."

She twisted out of his grasp, catching his wrist instead. Feeling rather like a tug boat guiding a battle cruiser, she pulled him to his feet, towing him in the direction of the bathroom. "Before any more dragon blood completely ruins my chance of getting my deposit back on this apartment."

CHAPTER 4

Dai had charged into collapsing apartment blocks to rescue children trapped on the top floor, climbing metal staircases even as the treads melted and twisted under his feet. He'd hauled workers out of a blazing chemical factory, holding his breath for agonizing minutes as he ran through clouds of acidic gases. He'd shielded his crew from dragonfire with his own scaled hide, and had the scars to prove it.

The hardest thing he'd ever done was to sit absolutely motionless under Virginia's gentle touch.

The bathroom was so small, he had to kneel practically between her thighs while she dressed his wound. Every accidental brush of her leg or hip against him burned like dragonfire. His inner dragon writhed in ecstatic agony, demanding that he turn and seize her, to carry her away to his hoard and complete the mating ritual. Dai's fingers dug into his knees as he fought for control. He had long practice at containing the dragon's fiery nature, but all his tricks of focus and distraction were useless in the presence of his mate.

The problem was, he didn't *want* to control the dragon. He too wanted nothing more than to explore Virginia's perfect curves, to taste the softness of her lips. The dragon's desire and his own matched and amplified, until every brush of her fingertips against his back was exquisite torture. Only one thing kept him from turning and claiming his mate.

She hates dragons.

Considering all that she'd been through, it was a perfectly understandable reaction. Dai wouldn't have blamed her for being a sobbing wreck. But Virginia seemed to take all the trauma and convert it into an unbreakable inner strength, like a diamond formed under intense pressure. There had been no fear in her face when she'd spoken of the dragon—just revulsion.

If she knew what I was...

Dai hadn't missed Virginia's tiny flinch when she'd looked into his eyes. Subconsciously, the mate-bond attraction blazing between them had given her a glimpse of his inner dragon. And it had revolted her.

I can't tell her. Not yet. Not until she's had a chance to get to know me, see that I'm not like that other dragon. I have to be patient.

His inner dragon thought that this was a terrible idea. His dragon was much more in favor of sweeping away Virginia's objections to dragons by bringing her to peaks of ecstasy, and provided detailed mental images of exactly how this might be accomplished. Dai breathed slowly, counted wall tiles, and was deeply grateful for the triple-layered material of his fire-resistant trousers.

"Okay, I'm done," Virginia said at last, taping the final corner of bandage into place. She tapped his tense shoulder. "I'm sorry, I could tell that wasn't great for you." She sighed. "It's been too long since I last did remote fieldwork. I'm out of practice with my first aid."

Dai wished he could reassure her that his knotted muscles had nothing to do with pain, and everything to do with her proximity. "It felt good," he forced out through the raw need tightening his throat. "I mean, it feels good. Better. My shoulder. Thank you."

"Anytime." He felt her lean back a little, inspecting her handiwork. She ran her hand over the edges of the dressing, checking it was all secure. "I think this will hold for now. But you should get your doctor friend with the magic hands to look at it later." Her fingers absently continued down the line of his spine. "I like your tats, by the way."

Dai's breath froze in his chest. Even if he'd been able to speak, he could hardly have explained that the scarlet scale patterns that ran down his back were natural, not tattoos. Or that they were so exquisitely sensitive to touch, she might as well have just run her fingers directly over his cock.

He shot to his feet, bashing his head against the light fitting and nearly knocking Virginia from her perch on the edge of the bath.

"Sorry," she said, holding up her hands. Her deep brown skin hid any blush, but Dai could tell she was embarrassed. "That was, um, inappropriate of me."

"No, no," Dai managed to gasp out. He unconvincingly rubbed one leg. "Just, uh, cramp. Anyway. You should get cleaned up yourself." Virginia looked down at her charred clothes, a mortified expression crossing her face, and Dai could have kicked himself. "I mean, it's been a long, tough night. You must want to wash and get some rest."

Virginia smiled wryly. "I could say the same to you." She bit her lip. "Um, not to be inappropriate again, but I don't think you should get that bandage wet. Before I kick you out to get cleaned up myself, did you want some, uh, help in the shower?"

His dragon thought that this was an *excellent* idea.

"No," Dai yelped, hitting his head again on the light fitting in his haste to back out the door. "I'll just go—elsewhere. Now."

He caught a glimpse of amusement battling embarrassment on Virginia's face before the door swung closed between them. A moment later, he heard the shower running. Firmly repressing a mental image of water running over her lush curves, Dai went into the kitchen.

A couple of gallons of icy cold water later, he was at least somewhat cleaner, and in better control of himself. His dragon sulked at the back of his mind, coiled sullenly under iron chains of self-discipline once more. Dai ran his fingers through his wet hair, shaking himself like a dog. Virginia was still showering next door, and he would rather have disemboweled himself than knock on the door to ask for a towel.

What about clothes? his dragon muttered snidely.

Dai looked down at his bare chest and fire-resistant trousers, cursing himself as he belatedly remembered that he was only wearing boxers underneath--he'd been on call tonight rather than at the station, and had been asleep in bed when the alarm had gone out to summon his crew. For a moment, he debated just continuing to wear his turnout gear, but he had the feeling Virginia might not appreciate the aroma of sweat and smoke that permeated the uniform.

I'm never going to hear the end of this, he thought in resignation, as he mentally reached out. **Chase? Are you up?**

As always, came the cheerfully lascivious response. **Where are you, my man? We've all been shitting kittens, waiting to hear from you. Who is this mysterious lady friend you ran off with? Is it true she's taken you home? Have you fu—**

Will you please shut up and listen for once? I need your help.

Did your parents not sit you down for the birds and the bees talk? Chase inquired solicitously. **Don't worry, I'm here to hold your hand all the way through. Metaphorically speaking. Of*

FIREFIGHTER DRAGON

course, if your lady friend is into that sort of thing, I'd be happy to help out non-metaphorically too—

CHASE! Dai blasted him with a mental roar, cutting off the torrent. *Seriously. I need some clothes.*

There was a brief mental pause. *Sorry, could you repeat that?*

I need some clothes. I didn't bring anything with me.

So sorry, terrible psychic static tonight. Maybe you're going through a tunnel. One more time?

Dai ground his teeth. *How many times have I rescued you from drunken escapades gone terribly wrong?*

About the same number of times that you've lectured me about my wild ways, Chase responded cheerfully. *Hey, do you think you could call me and repeat this conversation? I want to record it on my phone to savor later. I might make it my ringtone.*

Dai rubbed his forehead, wondering whether to try one of the other members of his crew. Unfortunately, John was probably asleep underwater by now, and just the thought of trying to explain his predicament to Commander Ash made him wince. *Are you going to help me or not?*

Not only am I going to help you, I am going to remind you that I helped you every single day for the next year or so. And I'm already on my way. Dai had an impression of wind whistling past Chase's ears as he stretched into a gallop. *Go outside.*

"Virginia?" Dai called. The sound of running water had stopped, and he could hear her moving around the bedroom. "I'm just going outside. A friend is dropping off some things for me. I'll only be a moment."

Without waiting for a response, he let himself out of the apartment, leaving the door ajar behind him.

Whatever Chase's flaws—and they were many—at least he was fast. Dai barely had to wait five minutes before a duffel bag thudded out of the sky like a meteor, narrowly missing hitting him. He glanced up, catching a brief flicker of Chase's black wings occluding the stars.

Thanks, he sent to the other shifter. **I owe you one. Unfortunately.**

The only response was an amused whinny, drifting down from the sky as Chase shot away again. Dropping the mental connection and picking up the duffel bag, Dai went back inside. Virginia was sitting on a chair in the lounge, wrapped in a fluffy bathrobe, drying her hair with a towel.

"I put a blanket and a pillow on the sofa for you," she said, slightly muffled from the depths of the towel. She flipped it back over her shoulder, scrunching her fingers into her glorious halo of dark hair. "Was that your friend? Didn't he want to come in?"

"Just a flying visit." Dai had to look away from the sight of her flushed, damp skin as his dragon reared up again, fighting his self-control.

He busied himself unzipping the duffel bag, and discovered that Chase had thoughtfully packed him a box of forty-eight condoms, prominently displayed on top of the folded clothes. He thrust them into the depths of the bag. "You should go get some rest."

Virginia yawned, getting to her feet. "No kidding. I feel like I could sleep for a week." Nonetheless, she hesitated at the door to her bedroom. "Are you sure you're going to be all right?"

He caught her gaze with his—and this time, she didn't flinch as she met his eyes. "I've got everything I need," he said. A slow smile spread over his face. "You go sleep. I'll keep guard here."

See? he told his dragon. *Patience. Everything's going to be fine.*

CHAPTER 5

The dragon pinned her down. The bone-white claws dug into her chest, the weight of the beast pressing all the air out of her lungs. She could taste the reek of its breath, a foul mixture of carrion and ash. Its glowing orange eyes were filled with cruel delight at her helpless struggles. The dragon's nostrils dilated as it inhaled; the smirking jaw dropped open. Virginia looked into the gaping maw, and saw the burning flames rushing up the dragon's throat, right into her face—

"Virginia! VIRGINIA!"

Virginia fought like a mad thing against the hot weight pinning her to the bed. She raked her fingernails down—skin? Not scales? She gasped for breath, and tasted clean air rather than smoke.

"It was a dream. Just a dream." Dai's soft Welsh voice in her ear brought her fully out of the nightmare. He was lying across her, on top of the bedclothes. "You're safe. You're safe now."

"The dragon." Virginia swallowed a sob, her breathing

still harsh and ragged. Tears streaked her face. "I thought it had me—"

"Shh. I know. Just a dream." He eased his weight off her, releasing her wrists. He pulled her up to a sitting position in the bed, steadying her with an arm around her shoulders. "I'm sorry I scared you. I ran in when you screamed. You were thrashing around so much, I was afraid you would hurt yourself."

Virginia leaned gratefully against his chest. She could hear the deep, reassuring beat of his heart. Her own racing heartbeat started to slow in response.

"I should be apologizing to you." She leaned back a little, tilting her head to look up at Dai. The dim light of early dawn filtering through the blinds was enough to show her the red scratches she'd cut into his cheek and neck. Without thinking, she reached up to trace the marks. "As if you haven't already been injured enough in the course of protecting me."

Dai went perfectly motionless as her fingertips brushed his face. Against her side, Virginia felt the hard muscles of his chest tense, although his grip on her shoulder stayed featherlight. Virginia could hear his strong heartbeat speed up, even as the rest of him went utterly still. Heat radiated from him like a bonfire—but it was a good sort of heat, clean and protective.

That heat kindled an answering fire in Virginia's own body. She'd never had such a strong reaction to a man before. Every fiber of her being yearned for him, like a moth drawn to a flame. She wanted to bury her face in the junction of his neck and shoulder, to drive away the memory of smoke in her lungs with his scent. She craved his skin on hers, his body in hers, burning away her nightmares.

Consumed by that desire, she twisted upright to face Dai, and kissed him.

His lips were motionless under hers for the barest moment. Then he made a low moan, deep in his throat. He flung himself into the kiss like a parched man finally finding water after uncounted days alone in a desert. His strong hands twined in her hair. Virginia ran her own hands down his chest, feeling the hot, solid lines of his muscles through the softness of his T-shirt. She tugged up the hem of the shirt, slipping her hands underneath, glorying in the intoxicating heat of his skin. Her fingers traced the line of his spine, over the tattoos she'd seen earlier.

Dai gasped, jerking his head backwards and breaking the kiss. His eyes were wide and dark, just a thin rim of gold and green showing around the edge of his dilated pupils.

"Virginia," he said hoarsely. "We—first—I should tell you—"

"What?" That brief taste of him had only fanned the flames of her desire. She traced the line of his jaw with her mouth, exploring and nibbling, the slight friction of stubble teasing her lips.

"I—" He shuddered as she bit lightly at his neck. His hands clenched in the thin material of her own nightshirt. "Oh God. Later. Virginia, oh, *Virginia.*"

With a quick jerk, he ripped her shirt from her body—literally, as she heard the fabric tear. She would have laughed in surprised disbelief, except that he'd already dipped his head down to her freed breasts. Virginia arched her back at the unbelievable sensation of Dai's tongue spiraling over her nipples.

His fingers slid under her panties, caressing her slick folds. She pulled at his T-shirt, desperate for more of him. He backed off just long enough for her to pull the shirt over his head, exposing his bronzed chest and hard nipples, then bent back to tease her breasts once more. His tongue left trails of fire over her skin. Virginia ran her palms over the taut curves of his shoulders, savoring both the feel of the solid muscles under her hands and the way Dai's breath hitched at her touch.

His strong fingers circled her clit. Somehow, without any guidance, he seemed to know exactly how to caress her. Virginia's hips jerked as her orgasm built into an unstoppable wave. She clung to him as her climax shook her, biting down on his sweat-slicked shoulder to stifle her cries.

"Please," she gasped as the waves of pleasure subsided. Her pussy ached to be filled. She fumbled with the buttons of his jeans, shoving them down over his hips. "Please, now."

Dai groaned, his mouth open and hot on her breast as her hand closed around his thick, hard shaft. "My Virginia." His voice was a deep growl, shaking with his need and desire. "Mine."

He slid his hands underneath her, cupping her ass. His powerful arms flexed as he lifted her, seemingly without effort, and threw her back onto the bed. He jerked off his jeans and boxers. Virginia had only a brief, glorious glimpse of his full naked body before he was on her, his mouth hungrily finding hers as his cock pressed between her legs. She spread willingly for him, thrusting her hips upward.

The broad head of his cock pushed tantalizingly against her opening—and then stopped. Virginia made a wordless sound of protest, but Dai drew back a little. His chest heaved with barely-restrained need as he raised himself up on his arms above her.

"Condoms," he gasped, glancing toward the door.

She couldn't bear the thought of delaying for even a second. "I've got an IUD." She shifted her hips, rubbing her swollen clit against his thick cock as she spoke. "I'll trust you if you'll trust me."

With a groan, Dai seized her hips, thrusting deep into her. Virginia cried out in ecstasy as his rock-hard cock slid into her slick pussy. She raked her nails down his back, wordlessly urging him to pound her faster, deeper. Dai threw his head back, jaw clenched. She could feel him struggling to contain his own climax as his thick cock caressed her most sensitive inner area over and over, again and again, until she clenched tight around him. Virginia's wordless cry as she came was echoed by Dai's own; his fingers dug into her hips, pulling her hard against his thrusting hips as he finally spent.

They both collapsed back on the bed, still joined. Despite Dai's weight on top of her, Virginia felt as light and weightless as ash on the wind, utterly consumed by pleasure.

After a moment, Dai let out a long sigh. "I never want to move." Nonetheless, he rolled, sliding out of her. He spooned her against his chest, curling around her protectively. "But my shoulder's seizing up. Sorry."

"I'll forgive you," Virginia said, without opening her eyes. "Just this once."

He smelled of clean sweat and wood smoke, the heat of his body against her back as comforting as a log fire in the depths of winter. Something snagged at her slowing mind.

"Hey," she mumbled drowsily. "What was it you wanted to tell me?"

If he answered, Virginia didn't hear. She fell into a deep, contented sleep, and didn't dream of dragons.

CHAPTER 6

When Dai had been a young kid still getting to grips with his dragon, he'd been expressly forbidden to practice fire-breathing. Naturally, this had meant he'd regularly snuck out of the house when his parents were asleep to do so. Whenever his experiments had gone terribly wrong—as they had more often than not—he'd always tried to preemptively put his parents in a good mood by bringing them breakfast in bed the following morning. The bigger the field he'd accidentally torched, the more lavish the breakfast he'd prepare. His mother claimed that to this day, the sight of a plate of bacon and eggs brought her out in a cold sweat of dread.

Dai was currently wishing that Virginia owned a bigger frying pan.

He cursed himself as he flipped the bacon. All his good intentions, all his practiced control—it had all gone up in smoke when she'd touched him.

Yes, his inner dragon agreed happily.

In contrast to Dai's grim mood, his dragon sprawled in

luxurious contentment, as smug as a cat in a sunbeam. As far as the dragon was concerned, the only thing that was wrong was that he was out here instead of still in his mate's bed. Even now he could be awakening her with kisses, running his hands over the lush curves of her hips—

Dai shook his head, forcibly thrusting the alluring daydream out of his mind. The dragon was a creature of instinct, unable to think beyond seizing what it wanted, but his human half was not so fortunate. He felt like a little kid again, waking up to the consequences of his nighttime transgressions in the cold, harsh light of day.

I should have stopped. I should have told her what I am. She wouldn't have wanted me if she'd known. I betrayed her trust. I betrayed her.

Dai sighed, steeling himself for what he knew he had to do. *I have to tell her. Straight away, as soon as she wakes up. No matter what the consequences.*

He stared down at the frying pan. *Maybe I should make some pancakes too.*

He could tell the instant Virginia awoke by the way his inner dragon was suddenly on full alert, straining eagerly like a dog on a short leash. He heard the bed creak as she stretched, then the sound of her bare feet on the floorboards. He didn't look round, delaying the inevitable moment by as long as possible.

Virginia's hands slipped around his hips, rucking up his T-shirt. All of his stomach-churning dread melted away at the simple warmth of her skin against his.

"I had this crazy dream that I was rescued from a dragon by a hot firefighter who's amazing in bed." Despite her bold words, her touch was a little hesitant, as if she doubted her welcome. "And now it turns out he can cook, too. I hope I never wake up."

"Good morning," Dai said, turning around in her embrace

to catch her in his own arms.

With a tiny sigh of relief, Virginia melted against him. For a moment, all he could think about was how right she felt, how perfectly their bodies fit together.

Then his guilt reared up again. *I'm not worthy to hold her. I shouldn't even touch her.*

Nonetheless, Dai didn't release her. He couldn't bear her to think for even one second that he didn't want her, or that she was just some casual one-night stand to him.

"I hope you're hungry," he said into her ear.

"Ravenous," said Virginia. She leaned round him to peer into the pan. "Okay. Let me clarify that 'ravenous' doesn't mean I can eat six eggs. I hope *you're* hungry."

"Actually, yes," Dai said apologetically, releasing her.

Turning back to his cooking, he slid two eggs onto Virginia's plate, and the rest onto his own. Shifting burned a lot of energy. He added the bacon to the plates, having some difficulty finding space for it next to the eggs, fried bread, sausage, and grilled tomatoes. "It was a busy night."

Virginia raised her eyebrows, a teasing smile tugging at her lips. "Due to the fire or the dragon?"

Dai put a finger under her chin, tilting her face up for a long, deep kiss. "Neither," he breathed.

Releasing her again, he picked up the plates. He tilted his head in the direction of the dining table, which was still piled with papers and archaeology tools. "I didn't want to move anything you were working on, so I didn't set the table. Where do you want to eat?"

"Oh, don't worry, there's nothing important out here." Virginia cleared a space by the simple expedient of sweeping an arm across the table, jumbling papers into haphazard drifts. They sat down, and for a few moments were both fully occupied shoveling food.

"Dai," Virginia said, when they'd both taken some of the

edge off their hunger. She kept her eyes on her plate. "I have to tell you something. I haven't been entirely honest with you."

Dai, who'd finally worked up his nerve and opened his mouth to say the exact same thing, found himself totally nonplussed. He blinked at her across the table. "Oh?" he managed to say.

Virginia toyed with her fork. "You know last night, when I told you I hadn't taken anything from Bertram?"

It took Dai a moment to cast his mind back to their earlier conversation, what with the much more significant events that had occurred later. "The dragon? Yes. Though he thinks that you did." Virginia looked at him quizzically, and Dai clarified, "I talked to him last night, at the scene. He was, ah, angry." He reached over the table to put his hand on hers in reassurance. "Don't worry, I'll sort it out with him. I'm sure he'll be back in control of his dragon by now, and able to realize he made a terrible mistake."

Virginia bit her lip. "The problem is, I kind of did take something."

Dai sucked in his breath. "Something valuable?"

She nodded. "Not directly from his hoard, mind. But...I found a valuable historic artifact on land that his family owns. Under British law, they'd be entitled to half the value of the find." She paused, then added, reluctantly, "Actually, in this case, probably the total value. I didn't have their permission to be metal-detecting there. Anyway, I was thinking about what you said, that if I'd taken something it would cause 'complications with draconic law.'" She made air quotes with her fingers. "Is this a complication?"

Dai leaned his chair back on two legs, frowning as he thought. The situation wasn't clear-cut. If Virginia had directly stolen from Bertram's hoard, technically Dai would have had to return the treasure or risk being declared a rogue and hunted down by other dragons.

But since the treasure had just been on Bertram's land...it could be argued that the other dragon hadn't actually claimed the treasure itself, leaving it fair game for anyone else, human or dragon. Of course, it could also be argued that the land included any artifacts hidden within it.

Dai had a nasty feeling he knew which way Bertram would argue.

He sighed. "Unfortunately, yes. Possibly." Catching sight of Virginia's frightened eyes, he thumped the chair back down again, leaning across the table to catch her hand. "*No. No, it's not a complication*, in that I am not going to let any dragon lay so much as a single claw on you. I am going to keep you safe, Virginia. I swear to you, I will keep you safe."

Virginia squeezed his fingers. "I know you want to. But safety isn't everything." Her jaw set in determination, though her eyes still betrayed her apprehension. "I'm not giving Bertram my find, even if it means he's going to come after me. But I don't want to put you in danger too."

"Danger is just a standard day at the office, as far as I'm concerned," Dai said with a wry smile. "Don't worry about me. You take care of your job, and I'll take care of mine." Letting go of her hand, he picked up his fork again. "Which is to protect you from dragons."

Virginia pushed bacon around on her plate, frowning a little in thought. "About that. Is Bertram going to keep trying to steal the artifact back, even after I've handed it in to the proper authorities? A find like this is legally classed as Treasure, so it belongs to the nation. Would he try to break into a museum collection?"

"No, I doubt he'd be that foolish. This Bertram might be

willing to risk snatching something from you in a deserted field at midnight, but he'd be in serious trouble if he tried to steal from a museum."

Virginia looked relieved. "You have no idea how glad I am to hear you say that. I was starting to wonder how good the British Museum's anti-dragon defenses are."

"Oh, anything in there belongs to the Queen," Dai said around a mouthful of breakfast. "No one is going to interfere with *her* hoard."

Virginia's fork froze halfway to her mouth. "The Queen is a dragon?"

"Um. Probably best if you forget I said that," Dai said. He waved a hand. "Anyway, the point is, dragons aren't allowed to go around smashing their way into museums—or banks or shops, for that matter. The Parliament of Shifters—a sort of government—comes down very hard on that sort of thing. Dragons are too powerful and dangerous to be allowed to run riot."

"So once I've reported my find and had the site properly declared an area of historic interest, Bertram will have to give up?" Virginia asked.

"Unless he wants to find himself branded a rogue. And trust me, he won't want that. My team would have free license to hunt him down, as would all the other dragon-hunters nationwide. He'd have to flee the British Isles entirely."

Virginia beamed. "Then all I have to do is make a few phone calls, and—oh, damn." Her face fell. "It's Sunday. I won't be able to get hold of anyone until tomorrow morning." For some reason, she cast a worried glance in the direction of the bedroom. "That gives Bertram a whole day."

"Then I won't leave your side for a single moment," Dai said firmly. "If Bertram wants your find, he'll have to get through me."

Abruptly, Dai's dragon reared up in his mind, roaring a challenge. At the same instant, the front door flew back on its hinges with an ear-splitting crash, revealing a tall, slender figure in a pale grey suit.

"That could be arranged," said the other dragon shifter.

CHAPTER 7

"Bertram," Virginia spat. Dai was already on his feet, interposing his body between her and the dragon shifter. "What are you doing here?"

"Mainly, being appalled." Bertram came through the doorway as though forced to step into a swamp, glancing around her small apartment with a look of disdain. His nose wrinkled as his gaze fell on Dai. "Really, Virginia? I had such low expectations of your taste, and yet you still manage to disappoint me."

"You are trespassing," Dai said. His voice had dropped into a deep growl, with a distinct feral edge. He stalked toward Bertram, every muscle in his shoulders and arms tense and ready. "I think you should leave now."

Even though Bertram was at least four inches shorter and a good deal lighter than Dai, he didn't back down. Then again, he could turn into a fifty-foot dragon, after all, so Virginia supposed he had no particular reason to be intimidated by the firefighter's greater size. He met Dai's eyes coolly, lifting his chin a little.

"I possess a flawless four carat princess-cut diamond,"

Bertram said, his own voice holding a hint of contained snarl.

Virginia blinked, but Dai halted as abruptly as if he'd just run into an invisible wall. His back straightened. "I possess an unworked nugget of Gwynfynydd gold, exceedingly fine."

Bertram's lip curled. "Hah. I possess *four* ingots of pure gold, each one a kilogram in weight."

"What's going on?" Virginia asked, looking back and forth between them.

The two men ignored her. They circled each other like cats preparing to fight, eyes fixed on each other.

"I possess a choker containing a dozen matched rubies of exceptional quality, set in platinum," Bertram declared.

"I possess a flawless five carat cushion-cut emerald, surrounded by twenty diamonds, set in gold," Dai countered.

Okay, Virginia thought in bemusement. *Either firefighters in Britain are paid* much *better than they are back home in the States, or there's a lot Dai hasn't told me yet about his family.*

She didn't dare interrupt again. The mounting menace between the two men was almost visible, like a heat haze in the air between them.

Bertram sniffed. "I possess a flawless *eight* carat emerald, mounted in platinum. Are we going to continue to trade mere baubles, or do you have even a single item of *real* worth?"

Dai set his shoulders like a boxer entering the ring. "I possess a silver chalice, set with cabochon rubies and worked with gold, over six hundred years old."

Bertram waved dismissively. "I possess a complete set of ten nested golden bowls, exquisitely chased, which I took myself from the burial chamber of King Cynewulf of Wessex."

"You do?" Virginia exclaimed.

Dai's jaw tightened. "I possess...the torc of Dafydd ap Llewelyn, first Prince of Wales."

"You *do?*" Virginia said again.

"I see." Bertram's eyes narrowed. "And that is your greatest treasure?" His lean form angled forward, poised for Dai's answer.

Dai's own shoulders relaxed slightly, as though he felt he had the upper hand at last. "It is."

"Oh, well then." All the tension went out of Bertram's body. He threw back his head, letting out a disdainful laugh. "I've barely even got started. I have *nineteen* gold torcs, some worn by kings so old their names are barely remembered. I have so many gold and silver coins from barrows, I can sleep on the pile full-length without even having to curl the tip of my tail. Little red, you could not even begin to *imagine* the scale of my hoard. Do you concede?"

Dai's face was rigid. "I concede."

"What on earth is going on here?" Virginia tugged at Dai's arm. He felt like an iron statue. "Dai?"

Dai breathed out, looking down at her. Though his expression was still tightly controlled, some sixth sense told Virginia that he was mentally cursing himself. "You know the way that a lot of animals don't usually straight-up fight each other, because there's too much risk of getting seriously hurt? Like, say, sheep."

"Sheep," Bertram said. "*Really?*"

"In mating season, rams show off their horns to each other," Dai said to Virginia, ignoring the interruption. "The ram with the biggest, most impressive horns gains dominance over all the others. Rams are big, strong animals who could seriously hurt each other in a real fight. Comparing horns lets them avoid that." He gestured from himself to Bertram. "Dragons do something similar, except instead of comparing horns, they compare hoards."

"Thankfully," Bertram murmured, idly turning a hand so that the light flashed from his heavy gold signet ring.

"So the dragon with the biggest, most valuable hoard is the boss?" Virginia said, looking from Dai's unhappy expression to Bertram's smug one and back again. "But...you just have dragon blood, because of your ancestor. Surely this doesn't apply to you?"

"Oh?" Bertram looked sharply at Dai, who glowered back. Virginia had an odd impression of some unspoken communication flashing between them. Abruptly, Bertram laughed again. "Indeed. Dragon...ancestry." A smile tugged at the corner of his mouth. "My. Well, I suppose that *is* true. And you certainly aren't a *proper* dragon."

"Dragons have *very* strong instincts about dominance and submission rituals," Dai said tightly. "They have to, otherwise they'd all have killed each other off long ago. I can't help having those instincts too."

Virginia's heart sank. "Which means?"

"Which means that I am dominant over him, and he is thus bound to obey me," Bertram said. His smile widened. "For example, I could order him to leave the city, right now."

"Go ahead and try it," Dai growled. He took a step closer to Virginia. "You'll find that there are some instincts even stronger."

"Mm." Bertram's gaze flicked from Dai to Virginia and back again. His lips pursed as if he'd bitten into a lemon. "How tiresome. But it is an inconvenience rather than an obstruction." He tapped his forefinger thoughtfully against his chin. "Ah, I have it." He pointed at Dai, his tone turning formal. "Daifydd Drake, by right of dominance I lay this restriction on you—while you are in my territory, you must appear as you do now."

"What? Wearing jeans and a T-shirt?" For a moment, Virginia was perplexed—then she realized that Dai probably didn't usually fight dragons with his bare hands. "Bertram, you can't do that!"

"I can, and indeed, I have." Bertram cocked his head at Dai. "Haven't I?"

Dai's face was expressionless, but his green eyes blazed with fury. "You are dominant over me. Don't think that means I won't punch you in the face."

Bertram raised an eyebrow at him. "A threat, from someone who *isn't* a dragon shifter? I suggest it would be wise to keep silent, little red, and let me talk." He cast a sideways glance at Virginia. "Unless you want me to...talk."

Virginia had the nagging feeling that she was missing about half of the conversation. "What's that supposed to mean?"

Dai folded his arms across his chest, fists clenched as though he was having to physically restrain himself from taking a swing at Bertram. "It means we have to hear him out."

"Good boy. I'm so glad we had this little chat." Bertram dismissed Dai entirely with a flip of his hand, turning instead to Virginia. "It may surprise you to hear that I have come to make you a very gracious and generous offer."

"You can shove it up your English *arse*," Virginia said hotly. "No matter what you've done to Dai, you've lost, Bertram. Soon the whole world will know that I discovered Brithelm's burial mound, and that *you* tried to hide it. Your professional reputation will be ruined."

"That is, of course, assuming that the burial mound is still there," Bertram said.

Virginia sucked in her breath. "You *wouldn't*."

"Oh, believe me, I would." Diamonds glittered as Bertram ostentatiously checked his watch. "It is now...11:23 on Sunday morning, which by my reckoning gives me at least twenty hours before you could possibly hope to report your find to the relevant authorities. Meanwhile, I have an entire construction team who is just *delighted* at the prospect of triple pay for working on a Sunday." He gazed contemplatively at the ceiling. "My. How much concrete could they could lay in twenty hours, I wonder?"

"And if Virginia gives you the artifact she found?" Dai said. "That's what this is about, isn't it?"

"Of course." Bertram smiled condescendingly at Virginia. "I am prepared to be magnanimous. I shall trade you the artifact for the rest of the site."

"What?" Virginia stared at him. "You mean, you'd give me permission to investigate it properly?"

"I would immediately halt construction work, and as the landowner give you full access to the land." Bertram spread his hands. "I'll even help you secure the site. We'd announce the discovery of the site together. My reputation will give you at least some degree of credibility, enough to make sure that you secure funding for a full dig."

"In other words, you want to steal the credit," Virginia said. "And no doubt any other valuable artifacts too. Dai's told me how greedy you dragons are."

"Has he now," said Bertram. "How amusing. No doubt that's true when one only has a pitiful excuse for a hoard." He cast a withering glance at Dai. "I, on the other hand, possess so many treasures already, I would be hard-pressed to even *notice* the addition of one more paltry pile of golden grave goods. I merely have a personal interest in the particular piece you removed. It belonged to an ancestor of mine, and has great sentimental value to my family."

"Sentimental value." Virginia snorted. "Right. Nothing to do with the fact that it's a big chunk of—"

"Ah!" Bertram raised a finger. "If I may offer some advice. It would be wise not to discuss the piece in detail in front of your little...friend here."

"Why are you so sure I haven't already shown it to him?" Virginia asked.

Bertram smiled. "Because he did not list it in his hoard when we dueled. And believe me, if he'd seen the artifact, it would be in his possession right now. He's dragon enough for *that*." He straightened, turning to the door. "You have two hours to accept my offer," he said over his shoulder as he left. "I shall look forward to hearing from you."

Virginia looked at Dai, expecting him to indignantly deny Bertram's parting accusation, but he avoided meeting her eyes. A tiny worm of doubt squirmed in the pit of her stomach. Bertram was a liar and a thief, and she knew she should ignore every word he said...but Dai *did* seem to have a lot of dragon instincts. She was starting to suspect that he was trying to hide the full extent of his dragon heritage from her.

She knew with bone-deep certainty that she could trust him with her life...but could she trust him with her gold?

CHAPTER 8

"I don't know, Dai. Maybe I should just accept Bertram's deal," Virginia said. Even though Dai was careful to check his pace to match her shorter stride, she still kept dropping behind, as though having second thoughts about following him at all. "One artifact isn't worth the destruction of an entire site. And it shouldn't matter who gets the credit for the discovery, as long as the site is preserved for study."

Dai wished with all his soul that he could smooth the worry from her beautiful face, but he didn't know how to close the distance that had opened up between them since Bertram's visit. She'd been quiet and reserved since the other dragon shifter had left. The new doubt in her eyes when she looked at him tore his heart in half.

"It does matter," he said firmly. With a light touch on her elbow, he guided her down an alleyway so narrow that the eaves of the houses on each side almost met overhead.

They were in the heart of the Brighton Lanes, a warren of ancient, cobbled back streets. The narrow alleys were packed with an eclectic range of tiny shops catering to a range of specialist interests. Everything from antiquarian maps to fetish wear could be found in the Lanes.

And there were a few very private, very discreet businesses for a *very* select group of customers—shifters.

"It's your discovery," he said to Virginia as he guided her through the maze of streets. It was a route so familiar, he could have found his way in pitch darkness. "I'm not going to let Bertram steal either the artifact or your credit."

Virginia shook her head doubtfully, her face shadowed. "But Bertram's made it clear he's top dog. Top dragon." She blew out her breath. "No offense, but your dragon ancestry seems to be more problematic than helpful at the moment."

"Can't disagree with you there," Dai muttered, making his inner dragon lash an indignant tail.

The beast was as agitated as Virginia was subdued. Bertram's command not to shift weighed on the dragon like iron shackles. It writhed against the restraints, but couldn't overcome its own instinctive respect for a more dominant male. The dragon's helpless rage felt like scales scratching the underside of Dai's skin.

"I know you want to help, and I appreciate everything you've already done," Virginia continued. "But I don't see what you can do now. Bertram's got your hands tied."

"I know," Dai stopped in front of a black, iron-banded door, set uninvitingly in an otherwise blank wall. "Which is why I've brought you here."

Virginia looked up at the grimy sign above the door. It was so thick with dust that the full moon painted on it was only barely visible. "To...a pub?"

"Not just any pub," Dai said. He rapped on the door with his knuckles.

"We're closed!" yelled a woman's voice from inside.

"No you're not," Dai called back. It wasn't much of a password, but it sufficed to keep out random passers-by.

The door opened, revealing the round, smiling face of Rose, the pub owner. "Ah, there you are at last," she said, beckoning them in.

In contrast to the plain, forbidding exterior, the interior of the pub was a snug, comfortable haven of polished wood tables and plush velvet chairs.

"All the other lads beat you here. They're waiting upstairs." Rose's kindly gaze fell on Virginia, who was looking around with a startled expression. "And you must be Virginia."

Although Dai hadn't told her anything more than Virginia's name, there was no hiding anything from Rose. She scrutinized both their faces for a mere second, then clasped her plump hands together. "Oh, Dai, I'm so pleased for you."

"Why?" Virginia asked, a perplexed crease appearing in her forehead.

Dai shot Rose a warning look, but she just laughed. "Because our Dai's never brought a lady friend in with him before," she said to Virginia. "And I can already tell you're not one to put up with any of his nonsense."

It was Dai's turn to frown. "What nonsense?"

"Now that would be telling." Rose winked at Virginia. "Which I shall do later, my dear, when you have time. Our Dai is a lovely lad, but he does tie himself up into knots through overthinking things."

"I do not!" Dai protested.

"Ah, you sweet summer child." Rose patted his arm, then gestured at the back of the pub. "The lads are up in the Fire room, of course. Give me a shout if anyone wants another drink." Rose headed off toward the bar, calling back over her shoulder, "*Except Chase!*"

Virginia flashed Dai a wry grin as she followed him through the bar area and up the staircase toward the private rooms. Dai's heart leapt. It was the first time she'd smiled at him since Bertram's visit.

"I take it this isn't an ordinary pub," she said.

"No," said Dai, smiling back at her. He ducked his head to avoid the heavy oak beams. For a shifter pub, The Full Moon had inconveniently low ceilings. "It's for people like me."

"Dragon hunters?" Virginia asked.

"Amongst other things," Dai said. "Dragons aren't the only type of shifter." He opened the door to the Fire room. "And I want you to meet some of them."

CHAPTER 9

My God, Virginia thought in bemusement. *It's full of muscles.*

The small room was decorated in rich shades of red and gold, creating a warm and snug space that would have been perfect for an intimate private dinner. It was entirely unsuited to the sheer volume of rippling beefcake that currently occupied it. Five men were crammed around a circular table, their broad shoulders hunched over their drinks. The moment Virginia stepped into the room, she was pinned by five sets of interested eyes. She froze under the weight of so much focused attention.

"Dai!" A man with black curly hair sprang from his chair, nearly upsetting his drink into the lap of the blond man sitting next to him. He punched Dai playfully in the shoulder, flashing him the widest grin Virginia had ever seen.

"What took you so long?" the man asked in a strong Irish brogue. His bright, dark glance flitted to Virginia, and his smile widened even further. "Forget it, my question is answered." He made an elaborate bow in her direction. "Lovely lady of mystery, it's a joy to lay eyes on you at last. If you ever need any more midnight supplies, consider me forever at your service. I hope you enjoyed the—"

"*Chase,*" Dai rumbled forbiddingly, and the smaller man shut up, still grinning.

Dai turned to Virginia. "This is my fire crew," he explained. There was something oddly shy in his expression, as if he was introducing her to his family. "My fellow fire fighters. Virginia, this is Chase, our driver. He's the one who brought me the clothes last night."

"In that case, thank you," Virginia said to Chase, shaking his hand. Under any other circumstances, she would have thought him tall and muscular, but standing next to Dai he appeared practically lithe. "And thank you for getting the crew to me so fast last night. Any later and I would have been in big trouble."

Chase's eyes brightened. "My pleasure. Always nice to meet someone who appreciates speed. Tell me, have you ever wanted to take a ride in a fire engine?"

Dai took a firm grip on Chase's arm, dragging him away. "*Do not* get into any form of vehicle with him. Ever."

"Spoilsport," Chase said, as Dai deposited him firmly back in his chair. He folded his arms in mock-petulance. "It was only *one* little crash."

Dai ignored this, gesturing to another man, who was sitting in a corner of the room a little apart from all the others. "You've already met Hugh, of course."

"How could I forget?" Virginia said, recognizing the silver-haired paramedic.

Now that she could see him properly, rather than in the confusion after the fire, she realized that he couldn't be any older than Dai. His fine, elegant features were young and unlined despite his prematurely white hair.

"I'm glad to have a chance to meet you in better circumstances." Crossing the room, she held out her hand to him. "Thank you for, well, saving my life."

"You are most welcome," Hugh said, leaning back a little. His tone was polite enough, but his upper-class English accent couldn't help reminding Virginia unpleasantly of Bertram. He made no move to take her hand.

Dai gently tapped her wrist. "It's nothing personal. Hugh's not really a hands-on sort of person."

"But I am, so let me make up for my colleague's rudeness," said one of the other men, rising. He was stocky, with a mane of shaggy blond hair framing a square, kind face.

His broad, calloused hand enfolded Virginia's in a warm grip. "Griff MacCormick," he introduced himself. "We *have* already met, in a way, though I'll be astonished if you remember me."

There *was* something familiar about that reassuring voice with its light Scottish burr.

"It was you on the phone!" Virginia exclaimed, realizing. "When I called the fire services!" She squeezed his hand gratefully before she released it. "You talked me through what to do, and kept me calm while I was waiting for rescue."

"Ah, wasn't much work for me, what with a brave lassie like you on the other end of the line." Griff smiled at her, laughter lines crinkling around his golden-brown eyes. "I've never heard anyone describe a dragon so thoroughly."

"I think I was in shock," Virginia admitted.

"And this is John Doe," Dai said, continuing the introductions.

Virginia turned, and took an involuntary step backward as she was confronted by a solid wall of muscle. Dai might have made Chase look slender, but the man who'd just stood up made *Dai* look small.

"John Doe?" she said inanely, the man's sheer size temporarily stunning her brain. "Really?"

"I am told it is traditional use-name amongst your people." The giant's voice was so deep, it practically vibrated Virginia's bones. He had to keep his head bent to even fit in the room. Despite his size, he had a handsome, intelligent face, with deep blue eyes that perfectly matched the shade of his long, braided hair. "I fear you would find my true name unpronounceable."

Virginia couldn't help rising to the bait. "I speak seven languages, four of them extinct. Try me."

"Actually, even John can't pronounce his own name," Dai said. "Not above water, anyway." Before Virginia could ask what he meant by that, Dai gestured at the final man, who had been sitting quietly observing all the other introductions. "And last but no means least, this is Commander Ash."

Now I know what they mean when they talk about people being "old souls."

A shiver ran down Virginia's spine as she met the Commander's calm, assessing gaze. Ash couldn't have been more than ten years older than she was, but she had the sense of something ancient behind those dark eyes. He made her feel oddly small, even more than John had.

"Sir," she said respectfully. She looked around at the five men—all different, yet all powerful in their own way. "So...are you all dragon hunters too?"

All five men stared at her for a moment. Then, in perfect unison, they looked at Dai.

CHAPTER 10

"Dragon...hunters?" said John.

Just go with it? Dai sent to them all. Normally he couldn't make five mental connections simultaneously, but panic gave him the strength. *I know it's an oversimplification, but—*

Chase snorted. "Oversimplification is kind of the understatement of the century."

"You mean it's more complicated?" Virginia said, understandably under the impression that he was responding to her. "Do you hunt other shifters as well, then? Dai did mention something about that a moment ago."

Griff was shaking his head. "I don't know what Dai's said, but—"

PLEASE! Dai's psychic shout made the other five men wince. *Don't scare her off. She's my mate!*

There was a momentary pause.

Then Chase let out a whoop. "Uh, sorry," he said, as Virginia stared at him. "I just thought of something funny."

"O...kay," Virginia said, edging away from him a little. She turned back to Griff. "What were you saying?"

"I, uh." Griff flashed Dai a glance that said he had a *lot* of explaining to do later. "I...wouldn't exactly call us hunters." He cleared his throat, recovering some of his usual aplomb. "But we do specialize in handling incidents relating to shifters."

"I am curious," Hugh said to Virginia. His pale blue eyes were narrowed. "What exactly *has* Dai told you about shifters?"

"Not that much," Virginia said. "We've mainly talked about dragons, for obvious reasons. About how they're vicious and greedy, driven by animal instincts."

"Yes," Chase said solemnly, clearly fighting a grin. "Yes, they definitely are. Utter bastards, the lot of them." John made a noise somewhere between a cough and a growl, and Chase quickly added, "Just fire dragons, though, of course. *Sea* dragons are majestic and noble and incidentally would never ever even think about punching someone smaller."

"Um, right." Virginia had clearly given up on making sense of anything Chase said, which Dai felt showed her to be an excellent judge of character. "Unfortunately, my problem is definitely with a fire dragon. The one who started the fire that you rescued me from." Her mouth twisted. "I've come to *really* dislike dragons."

Five fascinated stares fell on Dai again. He fidgeted uncomfortably in his chair.

She doesn't know I'm a shifter, he sent, in a very small mental voice.

"What?!" Griff exclaimed out loud. John said something in his own language which was probably the equivalent.

"As I thought," Hugh murmured into his drink.

My friend, you are totally fucked, Chase sent. *And not in the good way. What were you* thinking?*

"Uh," Virginia said, obviously baffled by the way everyone's expressions had just changed. "Did...I say something wrong?"

"No," Commander Ash said. "*You* did not." Dai shrank down, feeling about two inches tall as Ash leaned forward, folding his hands on the table. "But it seems Daifydd has neglected to tell you some important facts. Firstly, that *we* are shifters."

"Real shifters?" Virginia flinched back a little. "Not just descended from them, like Dai?"

What in the name of sweet green apples did you tell her? Chase mentally demanded of Dai. *If I'd known you were lying to get laid, I would not have helped you out.* For once, he actually sounded completely serious.

Kin-cousin, this is both unwise and dishonorable. John's sonorous psychic voice undercut Chase's. His face was set in a mask of disapproval. *I cannot take part in your deception.*

The overlapping telepathic communication made Dai's head hurt. "I *was* going to tell her, when I found the right moment," he said, having trouble keeping all the conversations straight. He gestured at John, hoping to forestall any more awkward questions. "John here is another dragon shifter, but a different type of dragon. He's a sea dragon."

"Oh," said Virginia, her usual boldness subdued. She looked John up and down, or rather up and further up. "Um. Majestic and noble, huh?"

A small smile cracked John's stern face. "We like to think so," he said. He tilted his head, the gold hoops that ran up the edge of his left ear glinting. "Although, from my perspective, I am actually a human shifter. My people live in the depths of the oceans. We are born as dragons, and we die as dragons. Very few of us ever walk the land."

As Dai had hoped, Virginia's curiosity overcame her apprehension. She leaned forward eagerly, her brown eyes alight with professional interest. "You have your own culture? Entirely separate from any human culture? How—"

"I'm sure John would love to tell you all about his people, but it'll have to wait for another time," Dai said. Inwardly, a glimmer of hope grew to a flicker. If she was warming to dragons, maybe she wouldn't hate him when he revealed he was one. "In any case, you see now that dragons aren't all bad? Despite Bertram?"

"Hm." Virginia didn't sound convinced. "Sea dragons, maybe." She looked around the table again. "Somehow I'm guessing that you aren't all sea dragons."

"No," said Griff, smiling. "My mother is an eagle shifter." Virginia opened her mouth, but Griff was already moving smoothly on, leaving no opportunity for questions. "Commander Ash is the phoenix. And Chase is—"

"Ooh, ooh, let me," Chase said, bouncing from his seat. He struck a dramatic pose, as if about to recite a Shakespearean soliloquy. "After all, how can mere words convey my full glory?"

"Not in here, Chase!" Dai yelled...but it was already too late.

The room had been crowded enough before. Adding a stallion did not improve matters.

John grabbed for the table, stopping it from overturning, while Hugh and Griff squashed themselves flat against the wall. Dai encircled Virginia in his arms, trying to keep her away from Chase's hooves.

"My God," Virginia breathed. She reached out to stroke Chase's gleaming blue-black neck. He flirted his head, ears pricked, clearly delighted with himself. "You're a horse."

Chase gave an indignant snort. Virginia's jaw dropped open as he spread his wings.

"Enough!" Dai slapped Chase on the withers. "She gets the point, you're a pretty, pretty pony. Now shift back before you destroy the place."

The air shimmered, and the room abruptly seemed a lot bigger. Chase straightened his suit jacket, an unrepentant grin on his face. He winked at Virginia as he sat down again.

Virginia sank back into her own chair as if her knees had given way. "And...you're a phoenix?" she said to Ash, her voice wavering a bit.

"*The* phoenix," Ash corrected, his tone mild. "Forgive me if I do not demonstrate."

"Uh, right. Of course." Shaking her head as if still in disbelief about what she'd just seen, Virginia turned to Hugh. "And you are...?"

"Private," Hugh said flatly.

Dai cleared his throat, breaking the awkward pause. "Anyway, everyone here has special talents. Between us, I'm certain we can deal with Bertram."

He quickly outlined the events of the last day—well, *most* of the events—to the rest of the crew, filling them in on the details of Bertram's threat. "So you see, the first thing we have to do is protect the site, so that Bertram can't destroy it," he finished. He turned to John. "How are the clouds feeling today?"

"Clouds?" Virginia said.

"I have a kinship with water in all its forms," John said to her. He held out a hand, humming a short phrase under his breath. Virginia gasped, jerking her fingers back as a pint of beer ran up the side of its glass and snaked across the table to curl up like a kitten in the sea dragon's palm.

Griff looked mournfully into his now-empty glass. "I was drinking that."

"My apologies, oath-brother." John flicked his fingers, arcing the liquid sphere neatly back into Griff's glass. He looked back at Dai. "In answer to your question, kin-cousin, when I sing the sky your tale, not a single droplet shall fail to grow fat with rage."

"You can control the *weather*?" Virginia said, sounding awestruck.

"No. I merely talk to it." John shrugged one massive shoulder. "But clouds are just water stricken with wanderlust, and are often pleased to hear a voice from home." His teeth gleamed in a feral grin. "You may expect it to become very, *very* wet indeed."

"Which should stop Bertram's builders, at least for today," Dai said. He looked at Virginia. "You said that you could report the find tomorrow?"

She nodded. "As soon as my colleagues in London are back at work. A find of this magnitude needs to go straight to the top, to the Head of the Portable Antiquities Scheme at the British Museum. I've met him before, so he should take me seriously. He'll have the authority to shut down Bertram's building works."

"Why wait until tomorrow?" Chase asked. "Why not send him a message now?"

"I don't know him *that* well," Virginia said. "It's not like I have his private phone number or anything."

Chase grinned lazily. "I wasn't thinking of a phone call. More like a personal courier." He cocked an eyebrow at Commander Ash. "If you can spare me?"

"You're not on call until Tuesday, anyway," Ash replied. "Can you find him?"

"I can find *anyone*," Chase said, with complete confidence. He inclined his head at Virginia. "If the lovely lady would care to write a note, I will personally put it in the hands of the Chief-Digger-Upper by dinnertime."

A corner of Virginia's mouth curved upward. "Okay, now I know what to put as my title on my next business card. Virginia Jones, Digger-Upper."

She took a notepad and pen out of her jacket pocket and started scribbling away, still looking amused. For once, Dai was grateful for Chase's clowning, if it could put a smile on Virginia's face.

"Griff," he said, turning to the dispatcher. "Can you talk to some of your contacts, see if anyone knows anything useful about the dragon shifter? I'd really like to keep track of where he is and what he's doing."

Griff nodded. "I know some shifters in the police. If I drop a few hints that he was involved in the fire last night, we might even be able to get him brought in. What was the name again?"

"Bertram Russell," Virginia supplied, tearing off her note and handing it to Chase. "But be careful. His family's rich enough to buy him out of trouble, and powerful enough to *cause* trouble. They own Russell Development Group, you see."

Chase whistled. "RDG? That isn't small potatoes. No wonder he trumped your hoard, Dai."

"Thanks for bringing that up," Dai muttered, as his inner dragon snarled at the memory. "But it does bring me to the final part of my plan." He took a deep breath, his dragon's shame at having been forced to submit amplifying his own shame at having to ask for this sort of help.

"Commander," Dai said, not quite able to meet Ash's eyes. "This isn't like our usual rogue dragons, the ones I can freely fight. He challenged me in accordance with dragon custom. And..." His throat clenched on the words, but he forced them out. "He won."

"It wasn't a fair fight," Virginia said, and some small part of Dai's anguish was eased by her defense of him. She folded her arms over her chest, scowling. "His family just bought him a lot of trinkets, and he flat-out stole the rest from archaeological sites. It shouldn't give him any power over you, Dai."

"Unfortunately, by dragon law, it does," Ash said quietly.

He considered Dai in silence for a moment, his expression unreadable. "You know that my freedom to intervene is tightly constrained."

"Bertram attacked a mundane and committed arson in the process," Dai said. "Doesn't that put him into your domain?"

Ash steepled his fingers. "In the heat of the moment, yes," he said. Dai couldn't tell whether the pun was deliberate. He'd never quite been able to decide whether or not the Commander had a sense of humor. "But the event has passed, and there does not appear to be immediate threat. I cannot trespass into the jurisdiction of the dragons."

Virginia was looking from Dai to Ash, trying to follow what was going on. "So you can't do anything about Bertram?"

Ash shook his head slowly. "Not while he keeps the peace. If he physically attacks you again, however, it will be a different matter. Let us hope it does not come to that." He looked at Dai. "But if it does, I shall be there."

"We all will," rumbled John, to general murmurs of assent.

"Is there anything in particular you need of me?" Hugh asked Dai.

Dai shook his head. "Not at the moment."

"Wait, yes there is!" Virginia interrupted, sitting up straighter. She poked Dai in the arm, glowering at him. "Or have you forgotten the enormous hole in your shoulder?"

"It's nothing," Dai said hastily, as Commander Ash raised an eyebrow in his direction. "She's exaggerating. I'm fine, honestly."

Hugh sighed. "One day," he said, addressing the ceiling, "one, just *one* of my colleagues might finally grasp the subtle distinction between stoicism and stupidity." He rose gracefully from his chair, taking a sealed packet out of his inside jacket pocket. Ripping it open, he extracted a pair of surgical gloves, pulling them onto his hands. "Let me see it, then."

Dai pulled his T-shirt over his head, and was more than a little pleased by Virginia's soft, involuntary intake of breath. He turned his back on Hugh so that the paramedic could peel back the bandages.

"Mm," Hugh said. Dai winced as the paramedic's gloved fingers lightly probed the wound. "For your future reference, Dai, 'fine' is an appropriate descriptor when one does *not* have a severe puncture in the supraspinatus muscle." There was a rustle as Hugh pulled off one of his gloves. "Now hold still."

Dai felt the paramedic's palm brush his skin—but only for the briefest moment. Hugh snatched his hand back with a bitten-off curse.

"Something wrong?" Dai asked, twisting round in concern. Hugh had shown discomfort when healing him before, but never as vehemently.

"Just caught by surprise," Hugh said through gritted teeth. He was gripping his wrist as if he'd put his hand down on a hot stove. His pained gaze flicked briefly to Virginia. "Though I should have guessed." Clenching his jaw, he placed his palm back over Dai's wound. "Now hold *still*."

A familiar warmth spread through Dai's muscles as Hugh did...whatever it was he did. Despite their years working together, Dai still had no idea how Hugh's talent worked, or even what type of shifter he was. Still, however mysterious it was, it was certainly effective. In less than a minute, the dull, painful throb of the fresh wound had faded to nothing more than a slight twinge.

"That will have to do," Hugh said, sounding dissatisfied. He stepped back, taking out a small packet of disinfectant wipes and starting to clean his hands. "Please try not to injure yourself more seriously, for my sake."

Virginia touched Dai's shoulder herself, sending a very different sort of warmth spreading through his body. "It's almost completely healed." She turned to Hugh, her eyes wide with wonder. "What *are*—"

"Gentlemen, you have your tasks," Ash interrupted, rising. Chairs scraped as the rest of the team reflexively stood up as well, Dai included. "Let us all be about them." His penetrating eyes rested on Dai for a moment longer than was comfortable. "And Daifydd, see that you do not neglect yours." With a small nod to Virginia, he left.

"What did he mean by that?" Virginia asked Dai, as the others filed out after Ash.

Guilt coiled in Dai's gut. He knew *exactly* what Ash had meant. But Virginia was looking so happy, at last reassured that everything would be well...he couldn't bear to snuff out the light in her face so soon.

"My job is to look after you," he said, hating himself for yet another half-truth. "We still have to get through today. I'm not leaving your side."

"Well." Virginia's gaze dropped to his bare torso, and her soft lips curled in a wicked smile. "I'm sure we'll think of *something* to do."

CHAPTER 11

When I said we'd have to find something to do, Virginia thought, sea-smoothed pebbles shifting under her feet as she trudged after Dai, *I didn't exactly mean a trip to the seaside.*

At any other time, Virginia would have enjoyed the walk along the promenade. She hadn't spent much time in the city itself over the past few weeks, being far too busy hiking the nearby countryside looking for Brithelm's burial site. The sea front was well worth a visit, with the faded grandeur of the old Victorian buildings making a stately backdrop to the cheerfully kitsch stalls and fairground rides that lined the pebbled beach. And, unfortunately, Dai seemed hell-bent on a long, leisurely stroll.

If someone had told me a few days ago that I was going to be given a personal tour of Brighton's top tourist attractions by an incredibly attractive man, I wouldn't have believed them.

Virginia sighed. She watched the play of muscles in Dai's upper arm as he gestured at the pier, only half-listening to his lecture about its history. The breeze blowing in from the grey-green sea rippled the fabric of his T-shirt, flattening it against the hard planes of his chest.

And if they'd told me that I wouldn't be having a good time, I would have laughed in their face.

The problem was, Dai didn't seem to be enjoying himself either. His stride was just a little too quick, constantly hurrying her along, while his continual monologue never gave her a chance to get a word in edgewise. Virginia had a sinking feeling that Dai was taking her on this walk not because he wanted to share his city with her...but because he didn't want to be alone in private together.

After Dai's fire crew had offered their help in thwarting Bertram, Virginia had felt as if a huge weight had been lifted off her shoulders. She'd even dared to start thinking beyond the next few days. In the cozy pub, with Dai at her side, she'd felt so at home that she'd had a brief, crazy, shining daydream that maybe this could be the start of something more.

If they stopped Bertram from destroying the site and she got funding for a proper dig, she could be based in Brighton for months to come. Years, even, if the site was as significant as she suspected. She and Dai could get to know each other properly. And if she played her cards right, she might be able to use the academic renown from this find to get her dream job at the British Museum. And if she did *that*...maybe she and Dai could have a future together.

Sure, there were a lot of ifs there, but for a moment it had all seemed so possible. And then she'd tried to take Dai's hand, and he'd jumped for the door as fast as if she'd tried to taser him. Since then, Virginia had tried a couple of times to casually touch his arm, but he'd always evaded her, not-quite-casually moving away in order to point out an interesting building, charming view, or (in one case) a passing seagull. For whatever reason, he very definitely wanted to keep his distance.

Virginia forced herself to look away from Dai's strong profile. There was no point tormenting herself with memories of running her hands through that red-gold hair, or the feel of those lips on hers.

Last night didn't necessarily mean anything. We were both high on adrenaline and stress hormones. It was just post-traumatic comfort-sex, that's all.

She stared down at the beach, scuffing the sea-worn pebbles with the toe of her boot.

I bet it happens to him all the time. He must rescue a lot of women, from both fires and dragons. No doubt loads of them get overly attached to him. He's a good guy, he must always try to shake them off without hurting their feelings too much.

Well, she wasn't going to cling to him like some stupid damsel in distress, weeping and begging him to love her. She had her pride. Virginia straightened her back, ruthlessly crushing down her disappointment.

I'm about to announce the biggest find since the Sutton Hoo treasure hoard. I don't have time to moon after some firefighter-slash-dragon-hunter, no matter how hot he is. Or sweet, or brave, or kind, or...

A rumble of thunder broke her rather unhelpful train of thought. The sky was darkening with ominous black clouds, rolling in from the sea so quickly that it looked like a cheap special effect.

"Huh," said Virginia, interrupting Dai's monologue about coastal erosion. She shielded her eyes as the wind picked up. All along the beach, people were hurriedly folding deckchairs and packing up picnics. "That storm sure is coming in fast."

"Ah," said Dai, looking up. "John." He seized her hand, and all of Virginia's determination not to let herself fall for him went up in smoke at the heat of his touch. "Run!"

"Why—" Virginia started—and then the rain came.

It was as if someone had scooped up half the sea in a bucket and tipped it out over the city. The raindrops came down so hard and fast they stung like hail. She staggered under the impact, pebbles shifting and rattling under her feet.

Without even a grunt of effort, Dai scooped her up in his arms, hunching over her in a futile attempt to protect her from the downpour. Virginia clung to his neck as Dai sprinted up the beach toward the promenade. The steps up to the top were thronged with people trying to get off the beach; rather than try to force his way through, Dai found shelter at the base of the wall, under one of the high vaulted brick arches.

"Best to wait for a moment for the rush to die down," he said, his breath warm in Virginia's ear. He lowered her to her feet, though his arms still kept her pressed against him, his broad back sheltering her from the worst of the storm. He let out a short, rueful laugh. "I should have brought an umbrella."

"I'm not sure it would have helped." Virginia laughed too, giddy from their wild dash through the storm. "Bertram's goons certainly won't be able to work through *this*."

She was soaked to the skin. She nestled against Dai's muscular body, his closeness warming her to the core. Despite the heat radiating from him, he trembled a little as he held her, as if he himself felt chilled. His breathing was deep and even, but against her cheek she could feel his heart hammering in his broad chest.

Virginia leaned back a little, tilting her head to meet his eyes, and found them wide and dark, the irises a thin green band around his dilated pupils. Emboldened by the suppressed fire in his gaze, Virginia reached up to brush his wet hair back from his forehead, her fingertips continuing down to trace the line of his cheekbone. His breath hitched. He caught her hand in his, pressing her palm to the side of his face, his eyes closing as if to better concentrate on the feel of her skin on his.

"Virginia," he breathed.

The rain made a silver curtain across the archway, enclosing them in their own private world. She captured his face between her hands, drawing him down for a long, deep kiss. Fire shot through her blood as his arms tightened around her, his tongue exploring her mouth with hungry desire.

Virginia drew back a little, breaking the kiss, though she kept hold of his head. "Why were you pushing me away this afternoon?"

Dai let out his breath in a long sigh. "Because I've been very, very stupid." He leaned his forehead against hers, eyes still closed. "And I'm terrified that you're going to run away when you find that out."

"I'm not going anywhere. Not if you don't want me to." Virginia slipped her hands down, lacing her fingers behind the back of his neck. "So yes, you *have* been stupid."

"No, that's not it." Dai raised his head, opening his eyes at last. His jaw set, as if he was bracing himself to face something. "I mean, I haven't told you something about myself. Something very important."

Virginia raised her eyebrows. "You mean, that you've been deliberately vague about your 'shifter ancestry' because you didn't want me to figure out just how much of a dragon you really are?" She couldn't help laughing at his utterly floored expression. "Dai, I figured *that* out a long time ago."

He gaped at her, his mouth working as if he was having trouble finding words. "When?" he said at last.

"Oh, round about the time Bertram started playing dominance games. The strength of your dragon side became pretty obvious." She tilted her head at him. "Does it come from your mother or your father?"

"Father," Dai said weakly. He stared at her. "It doesn't bother you? Really?"

Virginia shrugged. "Well, it would if you were a dragon like Bertram." She might have wondered if he *was* actually a full dragon, but Bertram's barbed insults about 'not being a proper dragon' had made it very clear that Dai wasn't a shifter. "But you aren't."

"My bloodline isn't even related to his," Dai said, with great finality. "I can promise you, I am *nothing* like Bertram."

"So." Virginia relaxed against him. "This is me, not running away."

She glanced up at him, a little shyly. He was looking at her as if she was some long-lost, priceless artifact that he'd just unexpectedly pulled out of the ground. The heat in his eyes made her stomach flutter. "What happens now?"

Dai stepped back, taking her hand. "Now," he said firmly, "we get extremely wet. There's something at my house I want to show you."

Laughing, Virginia let him pull her out into the rain. The feel of his strong fingers interlaced through hers was enough to warm her whole body. She felt light with relief, as if only Dai's firm grip kept her from floating away into the clouds.

How could he have thought I'd be frightened if I found out he's half-dragon? As he said, he's not like Bertram, after all.

He's not a dragon shifter.

CHAPTER 12

Dai felt oddly shy as he led Virginia up the stairs to his bedroom. He rarely had visitors to his house—his dragon's possessive instincts meant he couldn't relax with anyone else in his private space. Now, however, his inner dragon was coiling itself into eager, anxious knots, desperate to see if their territory would please their mate.

"Oh!" Virginia exclaimed in surprise as they entered the bedroom.

Dai's anxiety eased as she looked approvingly around the light, airy room. Dai's house was small, but he'd converted the entire top floor into one big open space, lit by large skylights set above the bed.

"This is nice," Virginia said. To his amusement, she went straight to the floor-to-ceiling bookcases along one wall, being careful not to drip on the leather-bound volumes as she read their spines. "Vintage atlases and travelogues?"

"They're not particularly valuable, but I like them. Most dragons have some sort of personal collection. My father loved science fiction B-movie posters." His mouth quirked in bittersweet nostalgia. "My mother always claimed to hate them, but she still has them all on display."

He took her hand. "But I wanted to show you something else."

Virginia's eyes sparkled as he drew her over to the bed. "I was hoping you—"

Dai put his thumb on the fingerprint sensor hidden in the headboard. With a click and hiss of pneumatics, glass-topped steel drawers slid out from under the bed, display lights switching on.

"...did," Virginia finished weakly. Glittering reflections from the hoard sparkled over her stunned face. "Okay. I have to admit, that wasn't quite what I was expecting."

"Dragons like to sleep on their treasures, so I had the safe built into the bed. It's a bit more comfortable than a literal pile of gold." Dai fidgeted, trying to gauge Virginia's expression as she knelt to inspect his treasures. "Do you like it? I know it's not much, but—"

"Not much?" Virginia cast him a half-amused, half-shocked glance over her shoulder. "If this is what a dragon considers *not much*, I'm terrified to think of what Bertram's hoard must be like."

She laid a careful finger on the bulletproof glass, over the exquisitely-worked gold torc that took pride of place at the heart of his collection. "Is that what I think it is?"

"The torc of Prince Dafydd ap Llewelyn, yes. A distant ancestor." Dai swallowed, his mouth dry. "Would you...wear it?"

"Oh, no, no, I couldn't." Virginia recoiled, looking as guilty as a child caught eying up a forbidden cake. "An artifact like that shouldn't be handled too much. It should be in a museum, not under a bed!"

Dai had been afraid she'd say something like that. "I know. But...I couldn't give up any of the hoard. It's more than just my dragon's possessiveness, though that's a factor of course." He spread his hands. "These are family heirlooms, collected by generations of my ancestors. They're part of my heritage. Part of who I am."

Virginia bit her lip. "Well...it's not like you personally stole artifacts, like Bertram. And you can't help your dragon instincts." A slow smile crept back onto her face as she shot a sideways look at the torc. "Can I really touch it?"

Dai let out his breath in relief. "I want you to touch it. I want you to touch everything." He drew her to her feet, clasping her tight in his arms. "You have no idea how much."

Virginia's hips pressed against his. "Oh, I have *some* idea." She plucked at his soaking t-shirt. "Shall we get out of these wet things?"

Dai put his hands on her shoulders, taking a half-step back even though he could hardly bear to tear himself away from her deliciously soft curves. "Before we do, there's something else I need to tell you about dragons."

"Oh." All flirtation slid from Virginia's expression, replaced by a distinct wariness. "Uh-oh."

"This one's actually a good thing." *I hope you'll think it is, at least.* Dai took a deep breath. "You remember I mentioned that dragons sometimes take a mate?"

From the perplexed crease between Virginia's eyes, she didn't. "A...mate?"

"Yes. All dragons have one true mate, just one person in all the world who's their perfect partner. The mate bond is unmistakable, and unbreakable. Many dragons never even meet their mate, but those who do recognize them immediately."

He gestured at his own heart. "It's...just a bone-deep knowledge, as simple and instinctive as breathing. Just suddenly being totally sure that you've found her. The one."

Virginia had gone very still. Her wide, dark eyes never

left his. "You sound like you're speaking from personal experience," she said slowly.

"I am." Dai took both her hands in his own, holding them as carefully as if cradling a bird. "You're my mate, Virginia. There isn't anyone for me but you, and there never will be. I know this must all sound bizarre to you, and I swear it doesn't bind you in any way—"

"Just one question," Virginia interrupted. She looked down at their joined hands. "This mate bond. Does the dragon's mate feel it too?"

"I—" Caught off-guard, Dai hesitated. He couldn't remember his mother ever mentioning how she'd felt when she'd met his father. He sent a mental query to his own inner dragon, but was met with unhelpful silence. "Actually, I don't know."

"Well." Virginia met his eyes. Slowly, the corners of her mouth curled upward. "I do."

Dai's heart missed a beat. *Does she...can she really mean...?*

Virginia laughed ruefully, shaking her head. "It's kind of a relief to know that I'm not going crazy. I never believed in love at first sight before."

"And now?" Dai breathed, drawing her close again.

"Now I believe in dragons. And you." She smiled up at him. "And us."

"If you really mean that, then there's something I'd like to do." He brushed her hair back from her face, still hardly able to believe that this was really happening. His inner dragon radiated smugness, mixed with both anticipation and a touch of exasperation that it had taken him so long to get to this point. "It's a sort of ritual that seals the mate bond."

Virginia's eyes brightened with interest at the word "ritual." "So your father raised you to be familiar with his culture? I'd love to—"

He bent to capture her mouth, cutting her off. He felt

FIREFIGHTER DRAGON

Virginia's lips curve under his own, then she kissed him back, abandoning her academic curiosity for now. His hands went to the front of her blouse. His inner dragon wanted to just rip it off, but he made himself take his time, kissing her with luxurious thoroughness as he carefully undid each tiny button. By the time he slid the garment off her lush shoulders, he was shaking with barely-controlled desire. His trembling fingers skimmed Virginia's glorious curves as he unfastened her bra and let it drop to the ground.

Virginia reached for the hem of his t-shirt, but he intercepted her hands. "Please, let me undress you first," he said, his voice so low it was almost a growl. "I want to do this right, and I won't be able to restrain myself long enough if you touch me."

Virginia nodded wordlessly. With the lightest of touches, he guided her down to the edge of the bed. He drew off her shoes and socks, his thumbs caressing the elegant arch of her instep as he did so. There was no graceful way to deal with the soaking wet jeans that clung to the ample curves of her legs; Virginia stifled a giggle, wriggling her hips to help him as he carefully worked the tight material down her thighs and calves. With the same slow deliberation, he slid her panties off as well.

Virginia ran her tongue over her upper lip. Never breaking eye contact, she leaned back on the bed, letting him feast his eyes on every inch of her.

"And now?" she said, her voice husky.

"Now I want to adorn you." Dai opened the cases as he spoke, filling his hands with gold and gems. "I want to adorn you, and adore you."

He straightened, turning back to offer her the very best of his hoard. "Virginia," he said formally. "I show you my hoard, so that you may judge whether I am worthy of you. Do my treasures please you? Will you accept me as your mate?"

She didn't hesitate for even a second. "I will."

Carefully, he fastened the torc around Virginia's neck. The gold gleamed against her dark skin, lovely and precious--but not as precious as her soft sigh of pleasure, or as lovely as the beat of her pulse in the soft hollow of her throat.

"My Virginia," he said hoarsely, crowning her with diamonds and draping her shoulders with pearls. She held perfectly still for him, allowing him to wind emeralds around her wrists and encircle her fingers with rings of gold and platinum. "My mate." He knelt to slip bangles over her feet, until she glittered from head to toe. He sat back on his heels, breathless at the sight of her, adorned like the goddess she was. "My greatest treasure."

He spread her thighs apart, bending his head to worship her with his tongue. She wound her fingers into his hair, wrapping her legs around him. He licked her with slow, circling strokes until her heels pressed deliciously into his back, her thighs clenching as she shuddered with pleasure.

"Dai," Virginia gasped, when she could speak again. "Oh, please." Her fists knotted in his T-shirt, urging him upward. "Please, I need you now."

He didn't need to be invited twice. Virginia lay back, watching him with desire-filled eyes as he stripped his own clothes off. The sight of her spread-eagled, undone with pleasure and gleaming with gold, drove him out of his mind with desire.

Virginia threw back her head, welcoming him with a wordless cry of ecstasy as he sheathed himself in her with one deep thrust. Her fingers raked down the dragon marks on his back, setting his blood aflame. He moved urgently in her, fast and hard, driven by her mounting moans and his own deep need. Her inner walls tightened around him.

"My mate," he gasped as he lost himself utterly. *My mate!*

And at last, she truly was.

∾

"Dai," Virginia said hesitantly some time later, as they lay bonelessly together in the afterglow. "I feel...something strange, in my head."

Hello, he said down the mate-bond, and grinned as she jumped. He propped himself up on his elbows.

"Sorry," he said out loud. "I forgot to warn you."

"I didn't imagine that, then? I heard you in my mind?"

"It's a dragon thing. We can communicate mind-to-mind with other dragons, and some other types of shifters as well." He ran a finger over the torc around her neck. It had warmed to the exact temperature of her skin, as if the gold had become part of her. It was intensely erotic. "Now that you're truly my mate, in a way you're part dragon too. So I can send to you now."

He'd been concerned Virginia might find all this alarming, but her muscles stayed loose and relaxed underneath him. She hesitantly touched his forehead, a look of wonder in her eyes. "I think...I think I can sense how you're feeling."

"Well, I hope you don't need psychic powers for that." He turned his head to kiss the inside of her wrist. "But yes, the mate-bond gives us a sense of each other." The warmth of her mind was stronger than a summer sun. He wanted to lie there and bask in it forever. "You should be able to talk to me when you want, too."

Why don't you try it? Dai sent.

Virginia got a peculiar expression, as if she was attempting complicated mental arithmetic. Dai could feel her fumbling with the mate-bond, sending waves of random, unformed sensations at him. It was rather like being subjected to a kid trying out an unfamiliar musical instrument for the first time.

After a moment she gave up, shaking her head. "That's *very* strange."

"It'll become second nature before too long." Sensing that she was beginning to find him rather heavy, he reluctantly rolled off her, tucking her close against his side. He buried his face in the curve of her neck, breathing in her delicious scent. "My Virginia. My mate."

Virginia giggled, impishly shifting her glorious backside against his stiffening cock. "You've got to be kidding me. Again? Already?"

"I can't help it." He traced the gold and emerald chains looping her arms. "I'm wild for you even when you're fully clothed. You have no idea what seeing you properly adorned does for me."

"Hmm." To his surprise, Virginia wriggled away from him. He would have been dismayed, but the mate-bond reassured him that nothing was wrong—she'd just made up her mind about something. "Wait here a minute?"

Dai crossed his arms behind his head, all the breath sighing out of him at the enticing sway of her breasts as she got up. "Any longer and I'm coming looking for you."

True to her word, she was back in moments, slipping into the room with a shy expression and something concealed in one palm.

"You showed me yours." A mixture of pride tinged with a hint of nervousness radiated down the mate-bond as she held out her hand, opening her fingers. "It seems only fair that I show you mine."

Dai bolted upright. "*Fuck me!*"

Virginia burst out laughing. "That *was* my general intention, yes."

"No—I mean yes, but—" Dai clutched at his own head,

nearly deafened by the roars of his inner dragon. The beast was a storm of flame and goldlust, wings beating frantically.

The jewel, the lost jewel, the Dragon's Eye! Jewel of kings!

A torrent of mental images flooded his mind's eye. Warriors in crimson cloaks, dragon-headed ships plunging across a storm-lashed sea, swords and shields and a dragon-eyed man crowned with gold and rubies...

"Dai?" Virginia touched his bare shoulder. "What is it?"

Dai became aware that he'd hunched over as if hurricane winds were howling around his ears. He made himself uncurl, clamping down on his inner dragon's agitation. He stared at the massive star ruby in Virginia's hand in disbelief. "That's the artifact you found? It's called the Dragon's Eye, and it's important. It belonged to...a king?"

Virginia's eyebrows shot up. "I'm pretty certain it's from the helmet of King Brithelm. He was a Saxon warrior who founded the first settlement here, which eventually became Brighton."

"He was also a dragon shifter." Dai rubbed his forehead, trying to sort through the sudden influx of racial memories. "Maybe the first white dragon in the British Isles. Red dragons are native here, but the white dragons came over from Europe along with the Saxon invaders. No wonder Bertram's desperate to get it. Any dragon who claimed that gem would gain incredible dominance."

Virginia's fingers closed reflexively over the artifact. "Dai, if I could give it to you I would, but—"

"No, no." Dai shook his head emphatically. "It's yours. I won't let my dragon try to steal it from you."

His dragon lashed an indignant tail. *Our mate's hoard is as wondrous as she is. We would never seek to diminish it.* It paused for a moment, looking wistfully through his eyes at the ruby. *Unless she wished to trade...?*

Despite his headache, Dai chuckled under his breath. *I*

don't think so, he told it. "Actually, my dragon is very impressed with you. That piece is a spectacular hoard all on its own. You'd have a lot of power and status, if you were a shifter."

Virginia sat down cross-legged on the bed opposite him, turning the artifact over in her hands thoughtfully. "You talk like your dragon half is a separate being to yourself."

"Well, it is and it isn't." Dai hesitated. "If you really want to have a serious discussion about the metaphysical nature of shifters right now, do you mind if we put on some clothes?" He gestured sheepishly at his groin. "It's really hard for me to think straight when most of my blood isn't making it as far as my brain."

Virginia's expression clouded with dismay. "I'm sorry, I killed the moment." She held up the Dragon's Eye. "I intended to ask if you'd like it if I adorned *you.*"

"Oh," Dai breathed, as his inner dragon surged up. "Oh, yes. I would like that." From Virginia's brief downward glance and sudden smug smile, she could see exactly how *much* he would like it. Nonetheless, he got up. "But later."

"Why later?" Virginia asked, pouting a little.

He kissed her as he started removing his hoard from her gorgeous body, piece by piece. "Because our bond tells me that you're hungry."

"I am?" Virginia's eyebrows drew down, then she let out a surprised laugh. "I am. And so are you."

"So we'll eat, and talk about dragons, and then..." He kissed her again, more lingeringly.

Despite the temptation to decide that neither of them was *that* hungry, they got dressed, though it took rather longer than strictly necessary. Virginia's clothes were still soaking; she rummaged through his wardrobe, finally settling on one of his dress shirts, which drowned her from neck to knees.

"I feel like a reverse Cinderella," she said ruefully, rolling up the sleeves. "From princess to rags."

"You look adorable," Dai told her, holding out his bathrobe for her. She shot him a dry, disbelieving look as she shrugged into it. He spread his hands, smiling. "Just check the mate-bond if you don't bel—"

DANGER!

His inner dragon's shriek came barely in time. Dai flung himself on top of Virginia as the skylight above them blazed with incandescent flame. The glass barely withstood a second before exploding in a hail of shards, but it was enough time for Dai to make the fastest shift of his life, basic self-preservation instinct overriding Bertram's restriction. Dragonfire washed over his back, scorched his armored scales.

The space was much too small for his dragon form. His sides and tail squeezed agonizingly against the walls for a moment before the brickwork crumbled. The floor gave way, unable to support his sudden weight. All Dai could do was curl in a tight ball of wings and scales around Virginia, desperately trying to shield her as they plummeted.

The impact of hitting the ground made him black out for a moment. When he came to, the first thing he was aware of was Virginia writhing in his grip, her hands shoving futilely at his scaled chest. The second was the crushing weight of the collapsed house. With tremendous effort, Dai forced his wings open, bricks and beams sliding off his back.

He twisted his neck, rain running over his spines and into his eyes as he scanned the sky. Since there was no sign of another imminent attack from above, he painfully uncurled, his tail sweeping through burning debris. He managed to roll to one side just far enough to allow Virginia to wriggle free from his grasp.

Heedless of the wreckage all around, Virginia stumbled

back, her huge eyes fixed on him. Her terror and panic beat at him down the mate-bond.

"Dai!" she screamed, looking around wildly. "*Dai!*"

His heart froze in his chest. *Impossible. She knew, she told me she knew!* Yet there was no trace of recognition in Virginia's expression.

I'm here, he sent urgently to her. He tried to get to his own feet, but fallen beams still pinned his hindquarters to the ground. **Virginia, it's me!**

Virginia shook her head in mute denial, still backing away from him—and then Dai saw what was lurking, invisible to non-shifter eyes, right behind her.

VIRGINIA! he roared, both physically and psychically. He made a desperate lunge, but couldn't reach her. **NO!**

Virginia broke and fled—running straight into Bertram's waiting, outstretched claws.

CHAPTER 13

Virginia struggled back to consciousness in a cold, muddy field. Her first thought was: *He's a dragon. Dai's a dragon shifter.*

Her second thought was: *I really wish he were here now.*

The white dragon crouched opposite her, legs and wings folded neatly. With an involuntary whimper, Virginia scrabbled away from it, her back hitting a wall before she'd gone more than a foot. The great burning eyes stayed fixed on her with unblinking fascination, like a cat watching a trapped mouse. The tip of the dragon's tail twitched slightly.

Virginia swallowed hard. "I know that's you, Bertram," she said, her voice trembling despite her best efforts. Her legs had turned to rubber. "And you aren't impressing anyone, so you might as well knock it off. I know you aren't actually going to eat me."

The white dragon yawned expansively, giving her a fine view of teeth as long as her forearm. *What makes you so sure?*

Virginia skin crawled at the oily, slick feel of Bertram's voice in her head. She made herself sit up straighter at least, trying to pull together what dignity she could while barefoot and in a bathrobe. "Because you'd be in a hell of a lot of trouble with the other shifters."

The Parliament of Shifters? Bertram's black, forked tongue lolled out in amusement. *My dear delectable Virginia, shifter politicians are much like politicians anywhere—concerned only with keeping their supporters happy. And my family have been* extremely *generous supporters.*

"I didn't mean the shifter government," Virginia said, hoping she sounded a lot more courageous than she actually felt. "If you don't let me go right now, you aren't going to last long enough to face any formal court of justice. Dai will tear you apart."

Bertram rustled one wing in an unconcerned shrug. *The last time I checked, the little red was occupied with more pressing matters. Such as the house on top of him.*

Virginia's blood ran cold as she remembered her last sight of Dai—his sinuous dragon's body pinned under bricks and beams, battered and broken. Even now, he could be bleeding to death, trapped in the rubble...but the mate-bond was a steadfast, warm presence in the center of her chest. Even though she was too far away from Dai to tell what he was thinking or where he was, she knew that he wasn't badly hurt.

Hugh, she thought in relief, remembering the silver-haired healer with the magic hands. *Hugh and the rest of the crew must have helped him.*

"He's fine," she said defiantly. "And I bet he's already on his way here."

What touching faith. You always did have a knack for rejecting the facts. Bertram cocked his head to one side, still looking amused. *How exactly do you think he's going to find you?*

Virginia risked taking her eyes off Bertram long enough

to glance around. She'd blacked out during the terrifying flight, so she had no idea where he'd taken her. They seemed to be in a paddock—behind Bertram, she could see a small group of horses huddling at the far end as far away from the dragon as they could get, though curiously they didn't seem totally panic-stricken by his presence. The wall behind her looked like part of some sort of stable building.

Dusk had fallen, but it wasn't yet fully night, so she must have been unconscious for about an hour. It wasn't raining anymore, so either John had called off the storm or—more likely—Bertram had carried her well away from Brighton.

How is Dai going to find me?

"He'll find me," she said, and was rather surprised to find that she *did* believe that he would, with absolute faith. "He's my mate, and he'll find me."

Bertram flipped his tail dismissively. *Then I'll kill him.* His jaw dropped in an unmistakable feral grin. *I am still dominant over him, thanks to his pathetic hoard. I can stop him from shifting.* His head snaked down so that they were eye to eye, his slitted pupil the size of her entire head. *Tell me, my dear Virginia, how much of a chance do you think a human stands against a dragon?*

Virginia had a horrible certainty that Dai *would* take on a fully-grown dragon with his bare hands, if it was standing between him and her. *The fire crew,* she reminded herself. *They'll help him. He won't be alone.* "I think, if it comes to you or Dai, I'm betting on him."

Bertram's orange eyes narrowed a little. *Give me the artifact,* he demanded abruptly. *Now.*

Virginia's mind raced. She wrapped Dai's robe tighter around herself, mustering as withering a look as she could manage under the circumstances. "Bertram, I'm wearing a *bathrobe.* Do you honestly think I've got a fragile, priceless artifact in my pocket?"

Twin jets of smoke hissed from Bertram's nostrils. *Where is it?*

Virginia took a deep breath, steeling herself. "Dai has it."

Bertram reared back as if she'd slashed him across the snout with a sword. He roared in outrage, the blast of his reptilian breath flattening her against the wall. *WHAT?!*

"I showed it to him, and he recognized what it was. Like you warned me, he wanted it for himself." She folded her arms across her chest, tucking her hands into her armpits so that Bertram couldn't see how they were shaking. "You're too late, Bertram. With the Dragon's Eye, Dai's got a more valuable hoard than you. *You'll* have to submit to *him*. Just give up now, while you still can."

Bertram growled. Without warning, he snatched her up in one of his front feet, the white claws closing around her so tightly Virginia couldn't even draw breath to scream.

Hobbling awkwardly on three legs, Bertram carried her out of the paddock and into a courtyard surrounded by stable buildings. The complex was dominated by a huge structure, big enough for even a dragon to enter, which Virginia assumed had to be a covered riding arena—until Bertram nosed open the door, and her eyes were blinded by dazzling gold.

My God. And I thought Dai's *bed was over the top.*

Bertram hadn't been kidding about being able to sleep full-length on top of his hoard. The plain exterior of the barn concealed an enormous mound of jumbled gold, silver and gems. An almost physical pain shot through Virginia's chest at the sight of so many artifacts so casually tumbled together. It was a far cry from Dai's meticulously stored and treasured collection.

Bertram's claws raked carelessly through the pile as he clambered over coins and cups to the center of the room. Stretching on his back legs, he dropped Virginia onto one of the steel girders supporting the high A-frame roof. Heart hammering, Virginia clutched at the dusty metal, fighting vertigo at the sight of the floor so far below. There was no question of jumping down, and nowhere to go. She was trapped.

Virginia forced her breathing to slow. Carefully, she straddled the beam, trying not to look down. She concentrated instead on the steady beacon of the mate-bond in her mind.

"Dai *is* coming for me," she said out loud.

The white dragon shimmered, shrinking into human shape. "Indeed." Bertram smirked up at her as he took his cell phone out of his pocket. "In fact, I'm counting on it."

CHAPTER 14

"I don't have time for this," Dai snarled at Ash. "I have to find Virginia!"

"If you move again, I will personally break your other bloody leg," Hugh snapped. His bare fingers dug into Dai's calf as his healing talent knit bone and muscle back together. "Do you want to have to crawl to your mate's rescue?"

"If I have to, yes!"

"You don't know where he took her," Ash said. Dai could have throttled the Commander for his level voice and calm expression.

Behind the Commander, another fire crew worked to put out the smoldering remains of Dai's house. Thanks to John's rain and Ash's prompt arrival, the blaze hadn't had the chance to spread to neighboring properties. The police were cordoning off the street, keeping curious onlookers well back.

"Chase is on his way back from London as fast as he can fly," Ash said. "As soon as he's here, he'll be able to lead us to her."

"I can't wait that long!" Dai tried to push himself up, but

John's enormous hands on his shoulders kept him firmly seated on the ground. "I can't sit here doing nothing. Virginia needs me *now*." Her fear sawed at his soul through the mate-bond. "If you'd ever met *your* mate, you'd understand!"

Ash looked at him. Though his expression never changed, even Dai's inner dragon recoiled from the brief glimpse of the inferno concealed behind those black eyes.

"I understand very well," the Commander said quietly. "But it does not change the fact that you can do nothing to help her right now."

Dai was saved from saying something potentially career-limiting to his commander by Ash's phone beeping. Ash touched his hand to his earpiece, listening. His eyebrows rose fractionally.

"I see," Ash said. Unclipping the phone, he passed it to Dai. "It's Griff."

"Dai?" Griff's Scottish burr was more pronounced than usual, a sure sign of agitation. "We just got the oddest emergency call here. He called 999 and then asked for you personally. He won't give his own name or location, but I'm certain it's your dragon shifter."

Adrenaline surged through Dai's blood. "Can you trace the call?"

"I'm working on it, but he's on a mobile phone so it's not easy." Dai could hear the rapid rattle of computer keys in the background. "Do you want me to keep stalling him, or put him through to you?"

"Put him through," Dai growled. There was a click as Griff did so. "Bertram?"

"I will offer you this trade once, and once only." Bertram's icy tones struck Dai like a blow. He could practically taste dragonfire rising in his throat in response. "Your mate for the Dragon's Eye."

"I don't have it." Dai glanced over his shoulder at the pile of wreckage that had been his house. "Even if it's still intact, it's buried under a ton of bricks."

Bertram's scornful laugh rang in his ear. "Do you think me a fool? I know she gave it to you, so it must be on your person right this moment. No dragon would have put down such a treasure for even a second. You have thirty minutes to bring it to the site of Brithelm's burial mound. Come alone. If you try to trick me, your mate will burn."

"Wait—!" Dai found himself talking to a dead line. He lowered the phone, his forehead furrowing. He looked up to find the rest of the crew watching him in concern. "Did you all catch that?"

John nodded. "Do you actually have this treasure the crawling worm seeks, kin-cousin?"

"No," Dai said slowly. "And now I'm trying to remember if *Virginia* ever put it down."

CHAPTER 15

⁂

Virginia's feet were freezing, and she had a cramp in one hand from clinging to the cold metal beam. Bertram seemed to have been gone for hours. With childish malice, he'd flicked the lights off when he'd left, leaving her stranded in pitch darkness.

Virginia buried her face in the soft, worn material of Dai's robe, breathing in the faint trace of his wood-smoke scent to keep herself calm. She knew that he was getting closer. The mate-bond was growing steadily brighter, flaring from a mere ember to a roaring bonfire in her soul. Through it, she could sense Dai's fierce rage and his determination—and also how terribly afraid he was for her.

Just come to me, she tried to send down the mate-bond, over and over. She didn't know whether her words were reaching him. All she could do was concentrate on radiating encouragement and reassurance down their mental link. *Trust me. Come.*

The huge door rattled open again. Virginia squinted as the lights came on again, blinding after the total darkness.

Her heart leapt at the sight of Dai's tall form in the

doorway—but Bertram, back in dragon form, was right behind him, prodding him along with vicious jabs of his ivory talons. From Dai's windswept hair and ripped shirt, Bertram must have carried him through the air rather than allowing him to shift and fly himself.

"Dai!" Virginia called out to him. "Up here!"

"Virginia!" Dai rushed forward, but had to halt as Bertram whipped his tail forward to bar his way. Dai struck his fist impatiently against the white scales. "I need to get closer to talk to her, since you've forbidden me to mindspeak anyone," he said, glaring up at the fanged head towering above him. "I'm not giving you the Dragon's Eye until I'm absolutely satisfied she's unharmed."

Bertram hissed, but reluctantly raised his tail to allow Dai past. The firefighter's eyes stayed fixed on Virginia, without even a glance at the gold coins crunching under his boots or the fantastic hoard all around.

Perfect trust in her poured down the mate-bond as he stopped directly underneath her. "I'm here, Virginia."

Virginia met his eyes, reflecting the faith and love straight back at him, the mate-bond so incandescent she could almost see it in the air between them. "Daifydd Drake, my mate."

She took her hand out of her pocket, opening her fingers. Gold and rubies gleamed as they fell. "I give you the Dragon's Eye for your hoard."

Bertram lunged with a shriek of rage, but Dai was faster. He leapt, snatching the Dragon's Eye out of midair. Before his feet hit the ground again, they had shimmered into talons.

The red dragon spread his wings, green eyes blazing with rage and triumph. White-hot flame spilled from his jaws as he roared. *Bertram Russell, I challenge you!*

The white dragon twisted awkwardly as he aborted his charge. He eyed up the red dragon for a second, then his spines lowered submissively. *Your hoard is superior. I concede your dominance.*

I reject your submission! The red dragon lunged, claws flashing.

Bertram barely managed to twist away in time. *You—you can't do that!* He backpedalled rapidly, nearly tripping over his own tail. *I've submitted. You can't hurt me. You'd be outlawed!*

And you'd be dead. Dai's snarl made Bertram flatten to the floor in terror. *I'll kill you for touching my mate!*

"Dai, wait!" Virginia called down, but the red dragon ignored her, intent on stalking Bertram. Virginia danced from foot to foot, nearly toppling off the beam. She didn't know what happened to outlawed shifters, but she was betting it wasn't good. "No, he's not worth it!"

The white dragon made a break for the door, but the red shot a blast of fire that forced him away from it again. Bertram shrieked in pain as Dai's teeth closed with a sickening *crunch* on his throat. The white dragon writhed, futilely trying to claw at Dai, but the larger dragon pinned him down. Virginia could see the thick muscles of Dai's jaws strain, striving to choke the life out of Bertram.

If Dai killed him...Virginia took a deep breath, closing her eyes. Concentrating on the mate-bond, she threw her heart and soul into reaching her mate.

CHAPTER 16

DAI! STOP!

Dai jerked as Virginia's voice echoed in his mind. Her mental shout broke his dragon's bloodlust, leaving room for human reason to take over. He could feel Bertram's jugular pulsing under his teeth. It would be so easy to bite down...but then he'd be declared rogue. His own fire team would have to hunt him down.

A moment of revenge is not worth a lifetime with our mate, he told his inner dragon. The dragon's rage boiled in his blood...and then slowly, grudgingly, began to subside.

Dai opened his jaws, allowing Bertram to squirm free. He stared disdainfully down at the cowering white dragon for a moment, then turned his back. Stretching upward, he held out one forefoot to Virginia, claws open.

She stepped into his grasp without hesitation, and Dai carefully lowered her to the ground. She let out a relieved sigh as her bare feet touched the piled gold of Bertram's hoard. She swayed, and Dai quickly shifted, supporting her.

"Are you all right?" he asked.

Virginia leaned her head against his arm. "Never better."

She reached up to his face, tracing the bruises and cuts Hugh hadn't had time to heal. "You?"

"I'm fine." He kissed her fingertips, overcome with relief. "Virginia. My mate."

Belatedly, he realized he still clutched the Dragon's Eye, now that he'd shifted back to human. He chuckled as he pocketed it, freeing his hands to embrace her tightly. "My clever, clever mate. Figuring out how to break Bertram's dominance over me."

"I wasn't sure it would work," Virginia said, slightly muffled against his chest. "But I thought, if the Dragon's Eye is *that* valuable..." She trailed off, and Dai felt her shoulders move in a small sigh, a twinge of regret passing down the mate-bond. Before he could ask her why, she pulled back a little, looking at Bertram. "What about *him*?"

The white dragon glared balefully at them both. Dai sent a wordless command to Bertram, exerting his dominance in order to force the other shifter to revert to human form.

Bertram struggled to sit upright, blood staining the front of his suit. "You won't get away with this." His voice was hoarse but outraged. Already his shoulders were settling into their usual arrogant lines. He pointed an accusing finger at Dai. "You attacked me after I submitted. I'll see you dragged before the Parliament and outlawed." His trembling finger jabbed at Virginia. "And as for *you*—"

Exactly what Bertram planned to do to Virginia, they never found out. A fiery, winged shape soared through the open doors, so incandescently bright that Dai instinctively squeezed his eyes tight shut. When he opened them again, Commander Ash stood in front of Bertram, hands clasped behind his back.

"Bertram Russell?" the Commander asked, perfectly composed.

Bertram stared at him. "Who the bloody hell are you?"

"Fire Commander Ash, of the East Sussex Fire and Rescue Service." Wisps of smoke rose around Ash's feet. Behind him, the wooden floorboards were scorched black in the outline of feathered wings. "I am the phoenix eternal, and you are in my jurisdiction."

"I don't have to answer to some jumped-up bird shifter," Bertram spat. "I am a dragon, of the line of kings! You have no authority over me."

"By birth, by blood, and by order of the Parliament of Shifters, I do. All wildfires are mine, and those who light them. You have committed arson and assault by flame, and so put yourself into my power." Holding Bertram's eyes, Ash crouched so that their faces were level. "As you have sought to burn others, so shall you yourself burn."

Bertram seemed hypnotized, frozen in place. His expression still betrayed his utter incomprehension, but his breathing sped up with primal, instinctive fear. "You—you can't burn me. I'm a dragon. I'm fireproof."

"I am the phoenix. There is nothing I cannot burn." Very gently, Ash placed one fingertip on the exact center of Bertram's forehead. "From the ashes, you will rise anew."

White light flared. Dai pressed Virginia against his chest, turning to shield her from the wash of intense heat.

"What was *that?*" Virginia exclaimed, as the blaze faded. She looked at Bertram, who was now slumped vacant-eyed and slack-jawed, but otherwise unharmed. She turned to Ash. "What did you do to him?"

The Commander rose, his expression as impassive as ever as he gazed down at Bertram. "I burned away his dragon."

CHAPTER 17

"What's going to happen to him?" Virginia said, watching the uniformed paramedics escort Bertram to the ambulance.

The former dragon shifter stumbled docilely between the muscular assistants. His face was still as blank and wondering as a newborn baby's.

"They'll look after him at the psych ward. It'll take him a while to adjust to the loss of his dragon." Dai wrapped an arm round her shoulders, holding her close. "I've seen this before. He'll be all right in the end. Just...very different."

Virginia shivered, huddling up against Dai's side. She was glad Commander Ash was fully occupied talking to the other emergency service workers that he'd summoned. She was grateful to him, of course...but right now, she'd rather be grateful from a distance. There was something deeply unnerving about a creature who could so fundamentally change people against their will.

"Is it over now?" she said hopefully. "Can we go home?"

Dai tilted his head, presumably communicating telepathically with his commander. Across the courtyard, Ash never glanced round from his conversation, but after a second Dai nodded.

"He says we should slip away now." With a touch on her elbow, Dai guided her away. "The Commander will handle the police and Bertram's relatives. It's best if we stay out of the way."

"No kidding." Virginia realized that they were headed further into the field. "Uh, Dai, the road is back that way."

He flashed her a wry grin. "I don't usually go places by road. And I noticed that there's a lovely park behind your house. Perfect for landing." He hesitated, expression turning somber. "Unless you'd rather I called a taxi. I'd understand if you've had enough of dragons for one night. Or lifetime."

Virginia laced her fingers through his. "There's one dragon I can never get enough of." She squeezed his hand, then released him, stepping back. "And I want to look at you properly, now that I'm not in terror for both of our lives. Go on."

Dai's outline rippled. Light distorted strangely around him—and then the red dragon stood in his place, posed like some heraldic beast. All the breath sighed out of Virginia's lungs. She cast a glance over her shoulder, but the police and paramedics were still going unconcernedly about their business, completely unaware of the wonder behind them.

Flashing lights from the emergency vehicles washed over Dai's scaled hide, striking gleaming red highlights from his jewel-like scales. The dragon's horned head curved downward, luminous green-gold eyes tracking her anxiously as she circled him. Virginia tentatively ran her hand across the vast shoulder, feeling the furnace-like heat emanating through the plated armor. The dragon rumbled, leaning into her palm a little. With a rustle, he spread his wings, one foreleg bending to offer her a way up to his back.

Feeling as though she'd stepped into a fairytale, Virginia climbed up. She fit herself between the crimson spines that ran down his spine, straddling the base of his neck. She felt Dai's enormous muscles shift and bunch under her thighs. Then, with a mighty leap, they were airborne.

It was nothing like her abduction by Bertram—Dai bore her up smoothly, with utmost care. His steady wingbeats rocked her as gently as if she was floating on the surface of the ocean. Virginia leaned into the motion, exhilarated by the wind rushing past and the sight of the ground falling away beneath them. She whooped, and Dai roared, echoing her delight.

All too soon, they reached the city. The lights of Brighton spread out like a shining constellation underneath them. Virginia braced herself against the spines before and behind her as Dai spiraled downward. Despite his bulk, he landed so lightly she didn't even realize he'd touched the ground until his wings folded closed. She slid off his back, wind-swept and laughing, stepping back to let him return to human form.

"Oh, that was wonderful!" She couldn't stop grinning like a loon as they walked the short distance from the park to her apartment. "Can we really do that whenever we like?"

"You'll never have to take a train again," Dai promised, his eyes gleaming with satisfaction at her reaction. "I'm afraid you're still stuck with planes for trans-Atlantic flights though." He hesitated on her doorstep. "Ah. You know, with Bertram gone, you don't need me by your side constantly anymore. If you'd prefer some privacy, I could go to—"

Virginia stretched on her toes to kiss him, cutting him off mid-sentence. "Rose was right," she said when she'd finished. She took his hand. "You really *do* overthink things."

He smiled ruefully as she led him to the bedroom. "I did make rather a hash of this, didn't I?" He caught her in his arms, tucking the top of her head under his chin. "My beautiful, brave mate. I'm sorry I didn't tell you everything straightaway."

"I didn't exactly make it easy for you." Virginia leaned against him. Even in human form, he retained that draconic heat. She snuggled closer to his chest, enjoying his more-than-human warmth against her wind-chilled skin. "I'm sorry too."

Dai was silent a moment. She had a sense of him diffidently questing at the edges of her mind, trying to untangle her mood.

"You're still sad about something," he said at last.

"No, not sad." Virginia sighed, still pressed against him. "Just a little regretful. I would have liked to examine the Dragon's Eye."

Though she couldn't see his face, she felt his puzzlement down the mate-bond. "Why can't you?"

"I'll appreciate it if you'll let me look at it, of course. But it won't be the same as being able to study it properly." She sighed again. "And it would have made a *spectacular* centerpiece to a museum exhibit."

Unexpectedly, Dai laughed under his breath. "Oh." His long, strong fingers circled her wrist, turning her hand over. "Virginia," he said, taking the Dragon's Eye out of his pocket. Without the slightest hint of hesitation or doubt, he placed the priceless artifact in her palm. "You didn't think I meant to *keep* it, did you?"

"B-But—" Virginia stammered. She stared down at the ruby-studded gold, then up into his warm, dancing green eyes. "I gave it to you, freely. It's part of your hoard. I thought dragons never gave away anything from their hoards."

"We don't." He tilted her chin up, bending his face down to hers. "But we do trade. So you'll have to give me something of equal value."

He kissed her, long and deep and slow. Virginia melted against his strong body, sweet fire singing through her veins. She could sense answering heat rising in Dai, their mutual desire echoing and amplifying along the mate-bond into an inferno of passion. That fire swept away all thought, all time, everything in the world except the two of them. She floated in a perfect, endless moment, aware of nothing except the blissful sensation of his mouth on hers.

Dai drew back fractionally. "There," he said, his lips brushing hers. He cupped her face in his palms, his thumb reverently stroking across her cheek. "That seems like a fair trade to me."

"Oh, no." Virginia pushed at his chest, guiding him down to sit on the bed. She stood in front of him, between his sprawled legs, and held up the Dragon's Eye so that the massive cabochon ruby caught the light. The hidden six-pointed star in its heart flared.

"I wouldn't want the other dragons to think I cheated you." She shook her head solemnly. "This is worth much more than just one kiss."

Dai's green eyes gleamed wickedly as he allowed her to push him back onto his elbows. His feet were still on the floor, his long, muscled body stretched across the bed. "Is it worth two kisses, then?"

"I'll show you what it's worth." Virginia let her robe slip off her shoulders. She still wore nothing but panties and one of his dress shirts underneath.

He watched hungrily as she slowly undid each button until the shirt hung open. She shrugged it off, and was rewarded by Dai's long sigh. His need pulled at her down the mate-bond as she slowly slid her panties down. She could feel how badly he wanted to touch her, to worship her.

Wait, she told him silently.

After all her recent fear and helplessness, she wanted to

reclaim power in at least one small area of her life. From the gentle glow of acceptance and love that washed over her, she knew that Dai had sensed her need to take control, and understood it. He settled back onto his elbows obediently, though his eyes tracked her every movement with intense desire.

Virginia straddled him, feeling the thick swell of his erection even through his jeans. His hips jerked involuntarily, the friction sending delicious waves of pleasure through her.

"Wait," she said again, out loud this time. She brushed his lips with her fingertips, forestalling his protest. "It's my turn to adorn you."

"Yes," Dai said hoarsely. His eyes had gone to thin rims of gold around the wide, dark pupils. His strong hands clenched in the bedcover. "Oh, *yes*."

Raising herself up a little on her knees, she freed the hem of his t-shirt. His abs bunched in hard ridges as he leaned forward to let her pull it over his head. Pushing him down flat again, she sat back on her heels, for a moment just admiring the gorgeous lines of his body.

Mine, she thought wonderingly, and didn't even realize she'd sent the thought to him until she felt the wave of wholehearted assent coming back down the mate-bond. He was hers; all of him, always, hers and hers alone.

Very carefully, Virginia placed the Dragon's Eye in the center of Dai's chest, right over his heart. The gold and gems sparkled at his sharp intake of breath. The star at the center of the largest ruby danced with his heartbeat.

"Daifydd Drake, I adorn you." She tapped the artifact with one finger, shooting him a mischievous smile. "Now *stay* adorned. If you can."

Virginia bent to kiss the hollow of his throat. Her breasts brushed deliciously against the hard planes of his chest as she traced the line of his collarbone with her tongue. She ached to feel him inside her, but forced herself to stay slow and unhurried, relishing the way his breathing quickened as she worked her way down to his tight nipple.

He groaned as she grazed his nipple with her teeth, every muscle tightening. "Virginia—!"

"Careful," Virginia murmured against his tanned skin. She tapped the Dragon's Eye with one finger. "Don't let it slip."

He subsided again, though she could feel what exquisite torment it was to him to have to hold still. To have such a powerful man willingly placing himself entirely at her command was as exhilarating as flying on dragonback. Her own heartbeat sped, matching his as she worked her way yet lower, licking along his hard abs.

"Virginia," Dai gasped as she unbuttoned his jeans. His head was raised, watching her over the gold glittering between them. Awe and agony mingled in his face. He lifted his hips a little to allow her to work his jeans down. "Oh God. Virginia."

His hands fisted as she ran her tongue along the enticing grooves leading from hipbone to the base of his rigid cock. "Please. I can't take much more of this."

In response, Virginia opened her mouth and enveloped the straining head of his cock. He threw his head back with a cry, the cords of his neck standing out. Virginia swirled her tongue around him, savoring his helpless moans as she explored every inch of his thick cock. She relished filling her mouth with him, in a tantalizing preview of being filled by that rock-hard shaft. Even taking in as much as she could, he was so long she still had room to wrap her fist around the base, working him with her hand as well as her mouth.

She could feel the way she was driving him to the very edge. His intense pleasure washed over her down the mate-bond, every stroke of her tongue or hand on him echoed in her own body.

She knew the point when he could take no more, because his urgency was her own. She reared up, straddling him again. His hands coming up to intertwine with hers, his strong arms bracing her as she finally, finally slid down onto his cock.

She was so ready that the first exquisite thrust tipped her over the edge. Waves of pleasure washed over her. She rode him in a strong, swift rhythm, his hips urging her on. They mounted to higher and higher peaks of ecstasy like a dragon spiraling up into the sky, and when Dai finally arched up underneath her, calling out her name as she gasped his, it was as if they flew together into the very heart of the sun.

Sweat-drenched and satisfied in every fiber of her being, Virginia collapsed down onto Dai's broad chest. For a long, luxurious moment, she just lay there as their heartbeats slowed in unison. Then she fidgeted. The Dragon's Eye was digging into her breast. She fished it out from between their bodies.

"Well," she said ruefully, placing the artifact onto the bed beside them. "My old archaeology professor would *really* not have approved of that."

Dai's laughter rumbled deep in his chest. "I did, though." His fingers traced wondering, tender paths down her bare back. "Even my dragon thinks we got the better deal in that trade."

Virginia propped herself up on her elbows, gazing down at him. "Oh, no, no. The Dragon's Eye is worth *much* more than that." She tried to school her face into a serious expression, but one corner of her mouth tugged up despite her best efforts. "That was just the first installment of my payment plan."

"Oh?" Dai smiled up at her. His love for her was a radiant beacon in her mind. "And exactly how long does this payment plan last?"

"Well, it *is* a priceless artifact." Virginia leaned down to claim his mouth again. "How about forever?"

FIREFIGHTER PEGASUS

FIRE & RESCUE SHIFTERS 2

CHAPTER 1

Connie West was an excellent navigator. She could find her way through a fog bank at thirty thousand feet with nothing more than an altimeter and a compass. She could plot a course across three states with just a paper map, and beat pilots flying planes with the latest GPS computers. She could navigate back to an unfamiliar landing field at night with nothing more than her own two eyes.

And she could also, unfortunately, always find her way to the roughest, dirtiest gambling den in any city in the world. She'd had a lot of practice at *that* one.

She'd never been to the English seaside city of Brighton before, but it only took her an hour of searching its narrow back streets before she found the sort of bar she was looking for. She knew she'd come to the right place by the way the room fell absolutely silent the moment she opened the door.

The only patrons in the place were a small group of hard-eyed men, their glasses frozen halfway to their mouths. Connie flinched as their suspicious stares assessed every inch of her ample body.

As one, the bar patrons seemed to silently conclude that a

lone, plump, nervous-looking young woman in khakis and a flight jacket was unlikely to be an undercover cop. The low buzz of muttered conversations resumed as the men turned back to their drinks and cards.

Breathing a sigh of relief, Connie edged her way to the bar. "Excuse me? Sir?"

"Well, you certainly aren't from around here." The shaven-headed bartender didn't look up from the shot glasses he was cleaning, if that was the right word for what he was doing with his gray, greasy dishcloth. "I think you've taken a wrong turn, Yankee girl."

"I'm looking for someone." Connie showed him the well-worn photo she always carried with her. "Very tall, very loud, very Irish?"

The bartender's eyes flicked from the photo to her face momentarily. "No idea."

Connie fumbled through the unfamiliar bills in her wallet, pulling out a twenty. "You sure about that?"

The bartender gave her a long, thoughtful look. Connie put the twenty down on the bar, keeping her finger on it.

With a shrug, the bartender jerked his head in the direction of a door at the back of the bar. "You could try in there. Though if I were you, I'd go straight back home instead."

Connie sighed. "Boy, do I wish I could."

Leaving the money on the bar, she headed for the indicated door. It opened into a narrow, dirty stairway that sloped steeply down into darkness. As Connie gingerly descended, a familiar Irish voice floated up the stairs.

"—the most beautiful plane you'll ever have the pleasure of laying eyes on, my hand to God. If you won't take my word for it then you can all come and see her in action at the race next week. In fact, would any of you fine gentlemen care for a little side bet…?"

"Not again," Connie groaned. She hastened down the last few steps so fast she ran straight into the door at the bottom.

"What was that?" said a man sharply.

The door opened, and an enormous hand grabbed Connie's shoulder. She stumbled as she was yanked forward into a small, smoky room.

A small group of men were seated around a green-topped table, cards and cigarettes in their hands. They started at Connie's intrusion, their cards reflexively jerking closer to their chests.

All except one man. *He* greeted her arrival with a dazzling smile—and not the slightest hint of repentance.

"Darlin'!" Connie's dad exclaimed with evident delight.

The huge man holding Connie's shoulder brandished her in her father's general direction. "This yours, West?"

"You'll not be speaking of my daughter like that, thank you," her dad said indignantly. "Or else I'll be having to ask you to step outside."

Connie twisted her shoulder free from the giant. "Dad, you *promised*!"

"Ah, now, don't be like that." Connie's dad flung his arms wide, regardless of the other men's scowls. "It's just a friendly little game."

Connie looked at the not inconsiderable pile of money already stacked in the center of the table. Even with her unfamiliarity with British currency, she could recognize they were mostly high-value bills. "A friendly game? Dad, you know we can't afford this right now!"

One of the other men at the table folded his cards, casting a level look over them at Connie's dad. "Is that so?"

"I said I'd be good for it, and I will be." Her dad gestured extravagantly at her. "With my lovely daughter copiloting my plane with me, we're a dead cert for winning the air race next week. The prize money is as good as in my pocket."

"It is *not*," hissed Connie. She cast a weak, apologetic smile around at the seated men. "We really have to go now. Sorry for any misunderstanding."

"But I'm winning!" her dad protested as she tried to tug him to his feet.

"Yeah, you can't go yet, West," said a man whose skinny, supple fingers seemed oddly out of proportion with the rest of his hands. Connie mentally nicknamed him Longfingers. "Have to give us a chance to win back our money."

"That's only fair," said another man.

A general rumble of agreement ran around the table. There was an ominous undertone to the sound that made Connie think of a pack of wolves, growling low in their throats as they closed in on their prey.

No matter how infuriatingly impulsive Connie's dad was, at least he wasn't stupid. "Ah, well," he said, starting to gather bills toward him. "Better call it a night. Sorry, lads."

Longfingers caught his sleeve. "No. You said you'd play, so you play to the end."

Connie's hand closed on the pepper spray she always carried in her pocket. It wouldn't be the first time she'd had to use it to buy them a quick escape.

Connie's dad flashed his trademark disarming, charming smile as he brushed off the man's clinging fingers. "I wish I could, my friend, but I daren't cross my daughter here. No man can change her course when she's got the bit between her teeth. Women, eh?"

Out of the corner of her eye, she noticed the giant man cast a swift, questioning glance at Longfingers. The smaller man jerked his chin in an almost imperceptible nod.

"He's been cheating," the giant announced. "I saw him. He's got cards up his sleeve."

"Now, no one likes a poor loser—" Connie's dad started.

A large man to his right grabbed his wrist, twisting it

viciously. Connie's dad's protests fell on deaf ears as the thug ripped back his jacket sleeve.

A card fluttered out, landing softly on the tabletop. The black ace stared up like an accusing eye.

Connie's dad's mouth hung open for a moment. "I honestly don't know how that got there," he said weakly.

"Cheat!" roared the thug.

"Dad!" yelled Connie.

"Run, Connie!" Her dad ducked the first punch, toppling off his chair. *"Run!"*

The table overturned as men shot to their feet, shouting and pushing. Cards flurried into the air. Her dad disappeared into the middle of a mob of angry muscle.

Connie took aim and maced the nearest man. He screeched, dropping his cigarette to claw at his eyes. But that still left five, and her action hadn't gone unnoticed.

"Don't get in the way," growled the giant. "Ain't none of your business."

Connie tried to get him with her pepper spray, but he was too fast for her. The giant shoved her aside, kicking her feet out from under her with a casual movement. Leaving her sprawled on the ground, he waded into the fight.

Pushing herself up to her hands and knees, Connie saw her dad for moment between the angry, shoving bodies. Most of the men were just taking outraged, imprecise swings at him, but not the giant. *He* moved with complete control, cutting through the crowd like a shark through water.

Connie's blood ran cold. In a flash, she knew her dad had been set up. And she had a bone-deep certainty that he was in terrible danger.

She desperately cast around for some way to distract the mob. Her eye fell on her dropped pepper spray... and the still-lit cigarette beside it.

I can't believe I'm doing this, but...

Connie grabbed the cigarette and a handful of fallen bills. She'd never wondered how well money would burn, but the answer turned out to be 'surprisingly fast.' Connie yelped, involuntarily dropping the bills as flames licked at her fingers. They landed in a puddle of spilled alcohol and cards.

The result was considerably more impressive than she'd intended.

"Fire," Connie yelled, as loud as she could. "*Fire!*"

"What?"

"Where?"

"Hey, there *is* a fire!"

Longfingers glanced back over his shoulder. His face froze as he noticed the flames. Even though the fire wasn't *that* big yet, he suddenly looked utterly terrified.

"Oh no," he moaned. "Hammer!"

"What?" The giant's head appeared above the crowd. His expression changed to horror too as he saw the fire. "Oh, *shit.*"

The other men had lost interest in Connie's dad by now, more concerned with rescuing their money before it was caught by the rapidly-spreading flames. The giant hesitated, one meaty hand still wrapped around her dad's throat. "What about—?"

"We'll finish the job outside!" Longfingers was already bolting for the door. "Come on, we gotta get out of here! Before *they* come!"

"No!" Connie threw herself in their path. She grabbed for her dad's dangling legs, trying to wrestle his limp body away from the giant. "*No!*"

"Out of the way, girl," the giant snarled.

Connie didn't even see his fist coming. The last thing she heard as darkness closed over her was the fire's greedy, triumphant roar.

CHAPTER 2

Chase Tiernach barreled gleefully at sixty miles per hour the wrong way down a twenty mph street. He lived for this—the thrill of speed, the urgency of the mission, the horrified looks on other drivers' faces as they found themselves unexpectedly confronted by a wall of bright red steel hurtling toward them.

His inner pegasus shared his elation. Driving wasn't as good as flying, but it still made his stallion prance and snort with fierce joy. Like all pegasi, his stallion was intensely competitive. There was nothing that gave it as much satisfaction as matching speed and strength against a rival, and *winning*.

To Chase's delight, an oncoming Lexus convertible tried to play chicken with twenty tons of oncoming truck. Whooping, Chase slammed the accelerator to the floor. The truck roared like an animal. Chase laughed out loud as the sports car was forced to veer off the street, ruining its shiny chrome hubcaps.

"Bastard!" the Lexus driver yelled.

Chase gave him a cheery wave out the side window as he hurtled past. "Just doing my job!"

"Alpha unit checking in," Commander Ash said calmly into the radio. The Fire Commander balanced easily in the passenger seat, barely swaying despite the fire truck's wild, bouncing motion. "Any update on the situation?"

"Observers say there's a lot of smoke," Griff's voice crackled out of the speaker. Concern thickened the dispatcher's Scottish accent. "The buildings around are close-packed, and not in good repair. High danger of the fire spreading."

"Alpha unit ETA three minutes," Ash said. "Currently proceeding east down Montgomery Street."

"Correction!" Chase spun the wheel. "Currently proceeding north up Stewart Street!"

"Please note correction," Commander Ash said into the radio. He gave Chase a level look. "Chase, *why* are we proceeding north up Stewart Street?"

"I can get us there in a minute this way," Chase yelled over the sing-song wail of the fire truck's siren. "Trust me!"

"Just when I thought I couldn't get any more nervous," muttered Hugh. The paramedic was strapped in behind Ash, and had a death-grip on his safety restraints. "Chase, are you *sure* you can get to Green Street this way?"

"Positive." Chase threaded the fire truck neatly through a slalom course of parked cars. "Up here, then nip down that little alley, and we'll pop out in just the right place."

"What little alley?" Hugh's face went nearly as white as his hair. "Chase, that's a pedestrian cut-through!"

"It's fine. There's no one in it." Chase knew that for a fact —his pegasus gave him an innate sense of where people were. It was what let him drive so fast in perfect confidence.

Ash eyed the rapidly approaching alleyway. His eyebrows drew together slightly, just the tiniest crack in his otherwise unflappable expression. "We will not fit."

"Yes we will!" Chase gunned the accelerator.

There was a horrible crunching sound.

"Mostly!" Chase added.

"Alpha Team proceeding east down Green Street," Commander Ash said into the radio. "Without side mirrors."

"May I ask if we are there yet?" John Doe said plaintively from his seat next to Hugh.

In the rear-view mirror, Chase could see that John had his eyes tightly closed. He was faintly green, which was not a good combination with his long, indigo hair.

Chase stomped on the brake, spinning the steering wheel at the same time. The fire truck lurched on two wheels, sliding sideways round the corner as it decelerated. The smell of burning rubber from the truck's tires mixed with the thicker tang of smoke.

"And here we are," Chase announced brightly.

Ash had the side door open even before the truck had fully come to a halt. He jumped down with a smooth, practiced leap. The rest of the fire team disembarked more slowly as Ash's intense, dark eyes swept the scene.

To Chase, it all just looked a mess. Thick black smoke was billowing out of the door of a shabby bar, while a small crowd milled uncertainly on the opposite side of the road. From the clouded windows, it looked like the entire building was filled with smoke. A man was collapsed on the sidewalk out front, but no one seemed to want to go to his aid.

Chase couldn't even begin to guess where the fire had started, or the best way to go about putting it out. His talents were suited to making instinctive, split-second decisions when driving, not to this sort of tactical stuff.

Fortunately, that wasn't his job.

Commander Ash gave the building the barest glance before turning back to his fire team. "Basement. There must have been a great deal of paper debris."

That was the advantage of being led by the Phoenix. He always knew *exactly* where the fire was.

"I am keeping the fire from spreading further, but we must work quickly," Ash continued. He had the slightly abstracted look that meant he was focusing on using his special talent to control the flames. "Hugh, attend to the casualties. Chase, is there anyone in the building?"

Chase concentrated. His stallion raised its head, sniffing the wind. Its ears pricked up sharply. There *was* a scent under the smoke. Something compelling, and familiar...

Chase shivered, suddenly feeling oddly on edge. "Yes. One person. A woman, I think."

"In which case, John and I will go in." Ash looked up at the enormous shifter. None of the fire team were small men, but John still loomed over them all. "We will need respiratory gear."

John nodded, heading back to the truck to unpack the breathing masks. Normally, they didn't need such equipment —Dai, their fire dragon shifter and the last member of the team, would have just strolled straight into the smoke without any protective gear at all. But he was off duty today, and miles away in London with his mate. The fire team would have to carry out the rescue the old-fashioned way... and just hope that they could reach the trapped woman in time.

Chase stared into the swirling smoke darkening the windows of the bar.

Why do I really, really wish that Dai was here right now?

"Chase. *Chase.*" He started, Commander Ash's voice finally getting through to him. "I said, get the hose ready."

"What? Oh." Chase shook himself, forcing himself to concentrate on the job instead of his strange, rising sense of urgency. "Right."

He tried to turn toward the truck, but his stallion reared

up and *screamed* at him. His pegasus was frantic, hooves flashing and wings beating with agitation.

Run! Go! Now!

And abruptly Chase knew exactly who was trapped in the burning building.

"*Chase!*" Ash's shout followed him as he plunged into the smoke.

Immediately, Chase's eyes started to burn. He closed them, relying on his stallion to guide him as he charged blindly through the bar. He could feel the heat of the floor even through the thick soles of his boots.

Commander Ash's telepathic voice abruptly crashed into his head. **What are you DOING?**

Trust me! Chase sent back.

He couldn't spare the time to explain further. All of his concentration was focused on sound and touch, tiny cues that told him how to navigate safely through the burning building.

His lungs burned in his chest, but he didn't dare draw in a breath. He could taste how thick the smoke was, bitter and acrid on his tongue. Even a single lungful would put him helpless on the floor, coughing his guts out.

Holding his breath, he charged down a flight of stairs, leaping the ones that had already fallen in. Embers swirled around him. His uniform jacket and trousers protected him from most of them, but some still burned the bare skin of his neck and face. Chase barely felt the pain. His stallion danced in agitation, urging him on.

There. There!

Chase scooped her up, cradling her protectively against his chest. There was no time to check whether she was breathing. His own lungs were burning, every instinct in his body desperate to draw in air. White spots danced behind his closed eyes as he blindly raced back up the stairs.

His chest felt like he was being squeezed by iron bands. Chase stumbled, strength draining out of his legs as his body cried out to breathe. Only the weight in his arms kept him moving forward. His entire world narrowed to the single desperate need to get his precious burden to safety.

Just one more step. Just one more. One more—

He stumbled out into light and cool air. Chase collapsed to his knees, still cradling her tightly in his arms. Clean air had never tasted so good. For a moment, all he could do was blink his streaming eyes, and breathe.

Ash seized him under the arms. The phoenix shifter dragged both Chase and the woman he'd rescued further away from the burning building. "Hugh!" he shouted.

A second later, Chase felt Hugh's bare hand on his neck. A familiar, comforting warmth spread out from the paramedic's touch. The pain from his burns eased as Hugh's healing talent took effect.

"I'm okay," Chase said, jerking away. "Concentrate on *her*. Please, now!"

Hugh shot him a curious look, but transferred his focus to the rescued woman instead. Chase watched anxiously as the paramedic ran his bare hands over her throat and face. She was pale and motionless, limp in Chase's arms. Terror filled him, as thick and deadly as smoke in his lungs.

When she finally took a breath, all the air rushed out of him. He sagged in relief.

"That's it," he said to her, stroking her singed red hair back from her beautiful face. "There you are. There you are at last."

"Chase. Explain yourself." Chase had never heard Ash so coldly furious. A faint heat-haze shimmered in the air around his shoulders, in the shape of burning wings. "What is going on here?"

"Commander Ash, allow me to introduce Constance

West." Chase never took his eyes off Connie's face. A broad grin spread across his own face as she started to stir. "That's it. You're okay, Connie. Everything's going to be okay."

Connie's eyelids fluttered open. She looked straight up at Chase. Her eyes widened with recognition.

"Oh, *no*," she croaked, and promptly fainted again.

Chase beamed up at the rest of the fire team. "She's my mate."

CHAPTER 3

Connie drifted up into consciousness to the reassuring sound of beeping equipment. A faint scent of roses mingled oddly with a stronger smell of disinfectant.

Hospital. I'm in a hospital. I think.
How did I get here?

She had a confused, dreamlike memory of being pulled out of a burning building. But she must have been hallucinating from smoke inhalation, because she could have sworn she'd been rescued by—

"Hello, Connie," said an impossible, Irish voice.

Connie opened her dry, scratchy eyes, blinking. The vague blur of color next to her bedside resolved into an instantly familiar, infuriatingly handsome figure. The ghost from her past grinned down at her, as cocky and charismatic as ever.

Connie groaned aloud, closing her eyes again. "Chase Tiernach, *go away.*"

"All right," Chase said, unexpectedly.

Connie reopened one suspicious eye. She couldn't see him anymore.

"Is this better?" Chase inquired solicitously from the foot of the bed.

"I mean go away entirely. Out of my room. Out of my life. Again." Connie sank lower down in the bed, pulling the sheets over her head as if she could hide from her past under the covers. "What are you even doing here?"

"The rest of my team had the fire well under control and didn't really need me any more, so my Commander very kindly agreed that I should accompany you in the ambulance." The mattress dipped as Chase sat down on the edge of the bed.

She was acutely aware of the warmth of his hip through the bedclothes. "What?" she said blankly.

She felt him shrug. "Well, actually, I didn't bother to ask him until we'd arrived at the hospital, and his response was more along the lines of 'Chase, it is a very good thing you are already five miles away from me,' but I think that counts as agreement, don't you?"

"None of that," Connie mumbled into her sheet, "made the slightest bit of sense."

"How about this, then." Chase shifted on the bed. Even without looking, Connie knew he was leaning over earnestly, his brilliant, lying black eyes full of sincerity. "I've missed you desperately. I'm overjoyed to find you again. Will you marry me?"

Connie pushed herself up on her elbows to stare at him in disbelief. "Are you completely out of your—"

She stopped mid-sentence as more of her surroundings came into focus. Every flat surface in the small private room was covered in roses. For a moment she had a mad thought that perhaps Chase had bribed the paramedics to bring her to a florist rather than a hospital. It was exactly the sort of thing he'd do.

Chase himself was set off by a background of glorious white roses that made the perfect contrast to his dark good looks. His shoulders were broader than she remembered. His long, muscled arms bore unfamiliar scars, the barely-visible traces of old burns. Instead of a custom-made designer suit, he wore a smoke-stained fire-resistant uniform. His thick black hair, once so carefully cut and styled, was now tousled and singed.

But his face was exactly the same, unchanged even after three years.

She should know. Despite her best efforts, that face had haunted her dreams every night.

Connie tore herself away from those bright, compelling eyes. *Remember what he did*, she reminded herself. *He's a lying, womanizing cheater.*

Don't fall for him again.

"Okay," she said firmly. "First things first: No. I am absolutely not marrying you."

Chase's hopeful expression fell. "So you're still mad at me."

"I caught you naked in bed with two other women, Chase!"

On the night I'd finally decided to sleep with you, Connie didn't add aloud. Chase didn't need to know *that* little detail.

She glared at him. "Of course I'm still mad at you."

"But you never even gave me a chance to explain," Chase said, so rapidly that his strong Irish accent made his words run together. "You see, I went to the club for a drink, and the next thing I knew-"

"I wasn't interested in excuses then, and I'm definitely not interested now," Connie interrupted. She pushed the old hurt back down into the bottom of her heart. "It was a long time ago, anyway. It doesn't matter anymore."

"Yes, it *does*," Chase insisted. "Please, Connie. You have to believe me, I never meant to hurt you. I don't even know what happened!"

"I said I'm not interested." Connie rubbed at the bridge of her nose, feeling the start of the familiar headache that prolonged exposure to Chase tended to inspire. "Why are you wearing a firefighter's uniform? Why is this room full of roses?"

Chase spread his quick, agile hands. "The room is full of roses because you like roses. I'm wearing a firefighter's uniform because I'm a firefighter."

None of *that* made any sense, either, but Connie let it go as a far more urgent question finally occurred to her.

She sat bolt upright in the bed, panic seizing her. "*Where is my dad?*"

"He's fine," Chase said, and Connie's heart started beating again. "We found him outside the bar. He's been pretty badly roughed up, but he'll be okay. He's here in the hospital, too."

"I have to see him." Connie threw back the sheet, struggling to her feet. "Take me to him, now!"

Chase caught her as she swayed. His gaze flicked downward. Connie belatedly realized that she was wearing nothing except a backless hospital gown. *Literally* nothing.

"Here." Chase shrugged out of his firefighter jacket, offering it to her. His lips quirked teasingly. "Not that I don't like what you're wearing…"

With what dignity she could muster, Connie put the jacket on over the hospital gown. It was streaked with soot and reeked of smoke, but it was better than wandering the corridors bare-assed. She pulled it closed around her ample hips as best she could. "Thanks. Now take me to my dad."

∼

"Dad!" Forgetting her own aches and bruises, Connie rushed to his bedside.

Connie's dad gave her a pale shadow of his usual wide grin. "Hello, pumpkin. We've both had better days, eh?"

She would have squeezed his hand, but both his arms were encased in plaster casts and suspended in traction. "Are you okay? How did you get away from those goons?"

"Ah, once they broke my arms, they lost interest." Despite his light-hearted tone, Connie could tell that he was deeply upset. "Connie, I was trying to get back in to you, I swear. But they kicked me in the head as they ran away, and I couldn't get up, and—"

"Shh. I know, Dad. It's okay." She sat down on the chair next to his bed. "You'd never have left me."

"It's all my fault." Her dad blinked rapidly, his eyes suspiciously damp. Connie pretended not to notice. "The nurses said you were all right, though?"

"I'm fine." It was, surprisingly, true. For someone who'd been unconscious in a burning building, Connie felt pretty good. "I was lucky. I guess the firefighters managed to get me out before I breathed in too much smoke."

Chase, who was hanging back in the doorway, made a small, choked sound, like a hastily stifled laugh.

Her dad's gaze moved to him. For a moment, he just stared blankly... and then his jaw dropped. "Good God. That's never young Tiernach, is it?"

"It's good to see you again, Mr. West," Chase said, coming forward. His black eyes danced. "Just to let you know, I still haven't crashed. Well, at least not a plane."

"You are still the most god-awful student I've ever had the misfortune of teaching to fly," her dad informed him. His brow creased. "What in the name of all that's holy are you doing wearing a firefighter's uniform?"

"Why do people keep asking me that?" Chase said to the ceiling.

"Apparently, he's playing at being a firefighter," Connie said to her dad. "Don't ask me why."

"I am not *playing*," Chase said indignantly. "I happen to be a very respected and valuable member of my crew. Just ask..." He trailed off, apparently searching for a name. "Hmm. Actually, perhaps it would be best if you didn't."

"Chase Tiernach, a productive member of society. Now I really have seen it all." Connie's dad shook his head. "Well, if you did rescue my daughter, I'm eternally in your debt, sir."

"Excellent!" Chase said brightly. "In that case, may I ask for your blessing?"

Connie's dad looked across at her in a wordless request for interpretation.

"Ignore him," Connie said firmly. "He's leaving now, anyway."

"Oh, I don't have to be anywhere else," Chase assured her. "I already told Commander Ash that I'm taking an indefinite leave of absence. He thought it was an excellent idea." He paused, a slightly worried expression briefly flashing across his face. "I *think* I still have a job. Though I might have to persuade him on that point, later."

Connie glared at Chase. "My dad needs peace and quiet to recover. He doesn't need you. *I* don't need you. Go *away*, Chase."

Her dad shifted uneasily, despite his broken arms. "Ah. Well. I hate to say it, but there might actually be something he could help us with."

Connie threw up her hands. "Dad! Don't encourage him!"

"I can be *excessively* helpful," Chase assured him earnestly. "What do you need?"

Her dad cleared his throat. "You know the big air race next week, over at Shoreham Airfield?"

"The Rydon Cup? Of course!" Chase's eyes brightened. "I've been looking forward to it ever since they announced it was going to be flown here this year."

"We were going to enter our plane. Me flying, Connie navigating—we were sure to win. But now…" Her dad made a helpless little motion with his head, indicating his broken arms. "I, ah, was kind of counting on winning that race."

"We're not going to ask the Tiernachs for money, dad," Connie said sharply. "Don't worry about the race. We'll just have to pull out. Things will be a little tight, but I'll manage."

Already she was making mental lists of air shows where she could display her plane, places she could advertise for passengers, evening jobs she could take… It wouldn't be the first time she'd had to hustle to cover her dad's debts. No doubt it wouldn't be the last.

It's not a disaster. I can get us through this. I always have.

Her dad dropped his head. "It's about more than the prize money," he mumbled.

With a sinking sensation of dread, Connie recognized that guilty, hangdog expression. "Dad, *what did you do?*"

Her dad's eyes shifted from side to side, as if seeking an escape route. "You know the money we used to transport the plane here from America?" he said reluctantly.

"So *that's* where you were," Chase said. He scowled. "I have to sack my private detectives. Apparently they've been chasing wild geese all over Europe."

He hired private detectives to find me?

Connie brushed away the thought. There were more important things to deal with right now.

"You didn't want to tell me where the money came from, so I assumed you won it gambling," she said to her dad.

"I did! In... a manner of speaking." He fidgeted. "I just haven't *quite* won the bet yet."

Connie groaned, burying her face in her hands. "Let me guess. You bet that you could win the Rydon Cup."

"It was a sure thing!" her dad protested. "Hardly a gamble at all! More like a, a loan. And we did need the money to get out of the country right away."

"Oh?" Chase said, cocking his head to one side with interest.

"He got deported," Connie said grimly. "My mom was American, so I'm a U.S. citizen, but he isn't. Let's just say that in future, *I'm* handling all his immigration paperwork. Not to mention our taxes." She sighed. "Okay, Dad. How much do you owe *this* time?"

Her dad avoided her eyes. "Well...I didn't really bet money, as such. Sammy wasn't interested in that."

"Sammy?" Connie sucked in her breath. "Not Sammy Smiles. Dad, tell me you didn't make another deal with him. Not after last time."

"Sammy Smiles?" Chase said, his eyebrows shooting up. "The shark?"

"How on earth do you know Sammy Smiles?" Connie said, momentarily distracted. She couldn't imagine that Chase, the son of a billionaire, had ever had need of a loan shark.

"We move in some of the same social circles, shall we say." All the good humor had slid away from Chase's expression, leaving him looking uncharacteristically grim. "He's pretty notorious. Well, that explains why you're lying there with two broken arms, Mr. West."

"I knew his reputation, but I thought..." Connie's dad trailed off, hanging his head in shame again.

He thought he could talk his way out. He always *thinks he can talk his way out.*

Connie shook her head in despair. "Dad. What deal did you cut with Sammy Smiles?"

"He offered money. A lot of money. Enough to pay for our move. Tickets, shipping the plane, an apartment, everything. And all I had to do was win the Rydon Cup, and he'd write off the entire debt." Her dad peered up at her sidelong. "It *was* a good deal, Connie."

Cold dread closed around Connie's heart like a fist. "And if you lost?"

Her dad swallowed hard. "Then he got our plane."

Connie was struck literally speechless. She stared at her dad, overcome by the sheer scale of the betrayal.

"Wait," Chase said, looking from one to the other. "*The* plane? Connie's plane? You gambled *Connie's airplane?*"

"Technically it's half my plane," Connie's dad said defensively. "And it *was* a sure thing."

Chase looked like he would have loved to break Connie's dad's arms himself. He took three quick, agitated paces back and forth, running his hands through his hair as though physically unable to keep still. Connie still couldn't move, frozen in disbelief.

The plane. He gambled my mother's *airplane. The only thing we have left of her, and he staked it in a* bet.

"Right," Chase said, swinging round. There was a determined set to his jaw that Connie had never seen before. "I'm going to fix this. Mr. West, I'm going to need to talk to Sammy. I presume you've met him?"

"Yes, I met him in the Marina a few days ago," Connie's dad said. He was looking at Chase with the sort of hopeful, ingratiating expression he usually turned on Connie when he wanted *her* to clean up his messes for him. "He's in town for the race. I think he's staying on his yacht, though. Do you think you'll be able to find him?"

"If he's within my range," Chase said, mysteriously. He

stared at her dad in an oddly intent way. "Can you describe him for me? And the men who attacked you, too."

"Well, they were about—" Connie's dad began.

"That'll do," Chase interrupted, his smile reappearing. "Yes, I can find them. Connie, don't worry. Everything's going to be fine."

"No it won't," Connie said numbly. She gestured at her dad. "Sammy Smiles wants my plane badly enough to do *this*. There's no way he'll listen to you."

"Oh, I think he will," Chase said, flashing a grin that was rather more feral than usual. "I can be *very* persuasive."

CHAPTER 4

"Why did I let you talk me into this?" Griff shouted into Chase's ear.

Chase snorted. *You've been sitting behind a desk for too long. You said you wanted to get out into the fresh air.*

"I didn't say I wanted to fall into fresh air!" Griff clung onto Chase's mane for dear life. "Do you have to go so high?"

High? This isn't high! He beat his wings harder. *Look, you can still see the boats on the water below."

Chase felt Griff's weight shift on his back as the dispatcher peered down.

They're those tiny little specks, Chase pointed out helpfully.

Griff let out a low moan, burying his face again in Chase's neck. "Oh, this was a bad idea."

You're afraid of heights? Really? Chase let out a whinny of laugher. *You can't be afraid of heights! You're half eagle shifter!*

"And no doubt I wouldn't be afraid of heights," Griff snarled, his knees squeezing Chase's flanks hard enough to bruise, "if I could actually shift!"

I've always wondered about that. Chase curved his neck to

look back at Griff thoughtfully. *Maybe you just need proper motivation?*

"Chase, you bastard, don't you daaaaaaare—!"

Griff's last word turned into a drawn-out yell as Chase folded his wings, arrowing down out of the sky. Chase was tempted to do a barrel roll, just to see what other interesting noises the dispatcher might make, but there wasn't time for horsing around. A long, sleek white yacht cut through the waves below, and Chase's pegasus senses told him that their quarry was aboard.

A couple of crew members looked up as he soared overhead, pointing out his black-winged shape to each other. They had to be shifters; no ordinary human could see a mythic shifter who didn't want to be noticed. But unfortunately, Chase's 'don't see me' mind trick didn't work on other shifters, not even those who turned into ordinary animals rather than legendary beasts.

Well, he hadn't counted on having the element of surprise. Chase beat his wings, landing neatly on the raised deck at the rear of the superyacht.

Griff slid off Chase's back. He pushed his wind-swept, tawny hair back from his face, eying the crew members who were rapidly converging on them.

"I hope you know what you're doing, Chase," he muttered.

Chase shifted back to human form. "Trust me."

"This is private property," a uniformed crew member yelled at them. From the man's thick neck and beefy arms, Chase was pretty sure his role on board wasn't just to serve drinks. "You need to leave!"

Chase flashed the thug his most dazzling smile, along with his firefighter badge. As a mythic shifter, his clothes and any small items in his pockets came with him when he shifted, which came in handy for situations like this. "We're here to see Sammy Smiles. Official business."

The thug paused at the sight of the metal shield. "Uh…"

Chase flipped the leather wallet shut before the man could realize it wasn't actually a police badge. "I suggest you fetch him right away."

The thug dithered for a moment, then snapped his fingers at a smaller man. "Go get the boss."

Well? Chase sent silently to Griff as the crew member ran off.

Griff's piercing golden eyes swept the ring of men surrounding them. Even though he couldn't shift, he still had an eagle shifter's ability to see tiny details that others would miss.

"Mako sharks, mostly," Griff murmured. "The big one is a tiger shark."

Chase's smile widened. *No one in our league, then.*

Griff shot him a sidelong, exasperated look. "Will you at least *try* not to tempt fate?"

"Now, I'm fairly certain I would have heard about a pegasus shifter joining the police," said a new voice, sounding amused. The crowd of shark shifters parted to let the speaker through. "So I'm guessing Chase Tiernach has dropped by for a visit."

What was that about tempting fate? Chase sent to Griff.

Sammy Smiles towered a good foot over both of them. His bald head seemed to slope directly into his wide shoulders, which were as thickly muscled as a body-builder's. He was not so much clothed as upholstered in a brilliant white suit.

His wide smile showed way, *way* too many teeth.

"Well now," drawled the Great White shark shifter in a strong Texan accent. "No fires here, boys. Aren't you a little out of your jurisdiction?"

Chase matched his shit-eating grin with one of his own. "I'm here on behalf of a friend. Shane West."

"Ah, good old West. Great pilot. Great gambler, too." Sammy's brilliant smile didn't touch his flat, cold eyes. "I'm so looking forward to seeing him fly in the Rydon Cup in a few days. Should be quite the race."

"Sadly not," Chase said lightly. "Seeing as he has two broken arms."

"Really." Sammy's expression didn't change. "What a pity."

Chase held the shark shifter's stare. "Naturally that means all bets are off."

Sammy sighed regretfully, his teeth sharp and gleaming. "Ah, no can do, boys. I've got my reputation to consider. West bet me his plane, and, well, a deal's a deal."

"Do you cheat on a deal?" Chase countered. "Because I know for a fact you were responsible for landing West in hospital."

Sammy's smile never wavered. "That's a mighty rude accusation, son. Folks could take offence."

Chase raised an eyebrow. "Are you claiming you knew nothing about it?"

Sammy spread his stubby-fingered hands. "Nothing whatsoever."

"Lying," Griff said, very softly.

Sammy looked at the dispatcher, his smile turning just a shade less friendly. "Excuse me?"

"I'm sorry, I should have introduced you," said Chase. "This is Griff MacCormick. Have you heard of the MacCormicks? They're a Highland eagle clan. They are remarkably good at spotting things. Prey. Body language. Lies. That sort of thing."

"We know that two of your people started that bar fight," Griff said. "And that bar fight turned into a fire. And *that* puts it under the jurisdiction of Commander Ash."

"You may have heard of him," Chase added.

"The Phoenix," Sammy said. His smile was still fixed in place, though it was looking more and more like a predator baring its teeth rather than any sort of human gesture. "Well now, that's all mighty fine, but I have to say I don't know why you think my boys were involved in any bar fight. Let alone a fire."

Chase gazed contemplatively up at the clear blue sky. "There's an interesting legend about pegasus shifters. Says that we were created by Hermes, the God of Messengers. Do you know what a messenger needs to be able to do, above all else?"

"Fly real fast away from bad situations?" suggested Sammy.

Chase looked the shark shifter straight in his black, dead eyes. "Find people."

"West saw his attackers," Griff said. "Chase picked their faces right out of West's mind. And so he knows they're right here on this boat, right now."

"Still claim you know nothing about the attack, Sammy?" asked Chase.

Sammy held Chase's stare for a long, long moment.

Then the shark shifter tilted his head. "Rusty," he said to one of his henchmen. "Ask Hammer and Eights to step up here, would you?"

I told you this would work, Chase sent psychically to Griff, as the henchman disappeared off below decks.

"Don't count your chickens too early," Griff muttered grimly. "Or your sharks. He's up to something."

A few uncomfortable minutes passed, during which Sammy and Chase continued to smile at each other. Chase's jaw was starting to ache by the time the henchman hurried back, escorting two other men.

"Hammerhead and... octopus, I think," Griff informed Chase under his breath.

He didn't have to point out which was which. The hammerhead shark shifter was nearly as big as Sammy, while the octopus shifter had uncannily long, supple fingers. Both looked incredibly edgy.

"Pay attention, Mr. Eagle," Sammy said to Griff. He switched his attention to his two fidgeting thugs. "Boys, you remember I mentioned a certain Mr. West the other day?"

"Yes boss," rumbled the hammerhead shifter.

"What exactly did I say?" Sammy asked, glancing over at Griff.

The octopus shifter twined his hands together nervously. "That he was such a good pilot, the only way he'd lose the Rydon Cup was if he broke both his arms."

"Did I *tell* you to break both his arms?" Sammy pressed.

Both shifters shook their heads.

"Was I, in fact, laughing and smiling in such a way that might indicate I was just joking around?"

The hammerhead and the octopus shifter nodded silently.

Sammy swung back to Griff. "Seems to me that my boys had what you might call an excess of initiative. A bit of high spirits that just got a little out of hand. Don't you agree, Mr. Eagle?"

Griff mouth set in a thin line. "He's telling the truth. As far as it goes."

Damn! Chase thought. He maintained his smile, though it took all his willpower. He wasn't going to give the shark shifter the satisfaction of seeing him wrong-footed.

Sammy put his hands in his suit pockets, rocking a little on his heels as he contemplated his cowering henchmen. "Now, boys, from what these nice folks tell me, the Phoenix is very upset about that fire."

"It wasn't us!" the octopus shifter blurted out.

"It was the girl," said the hammerhead. "She started it."

"Yeah." The octopus shifter nodded vigorously. "If the Phoenix is gonna burn anyone, it should be her."

"Thank you, Hammer, Eights." Sammy dismissed them with a flick of his hand, and they scuttled off gratefully.

"Don't you worry, boys," Sammy said, turning back to Chase and Griff. "I'll make sure my men learn a real good lesson from this little incident. It won't be happening again in future, you have my word. Thank you for bringing the matter to my attention, and please do give the Phoenix my very *warmest* regards."

"But what about the plane?" Chase's mind raced frantically. "What about the bet?"

Sammy shrugged. "West already took my money. I intend to collect the payment."

"I'll pay the money back myself," Chase said, his fists clenching. "Double. Triple. Whatever you want, just name your price."

"Now, that's a mighty fine offer. I know your family has deep pockets. But, see, here's the thing." Sammy gestured around at his luxurious yacht. "So do I. Keep your money, boy. I don't want it. But I *do* want that plane for my collection. And I intend to have it."

"Wait!" Chase called, as the shark shifter started to stroll away. "You can't take Connie's plane!"

"If West's plane doesn't win the Rydon Cup, then it's mine," Sammy said over his shoulder. "That was the bet."

Chase paused.

If the plane *doesn't win...?*

He threw back his head and laughed, long and loud. Griff stared at him as if he'd started barking. Sammy paused mid-step.

"Oh, Sammy." Chase chuckled. "You have no idea how glad I am you said that."

Sammy turned around again, folding his arms across his broad chest. "And why might that be, son?"

"You just said that the bet is on the plane, not the pilot." Chase grinned at him. "West's plane *is* going to race. I'm going to fly it."

Sammy's eyes narrowed. He didn't otherwise move, but the group of shark shifters surrounding Chase and Griff started to circle them, drifting closer.

"And if you think West is good," Chase added, "you should see *me* fly."

"Now why," Sammy said softly, as the circle of shark shifters closed in like a trap, "do you think you're going to be flying anywhere? This is the open sea, boys. You're a long way from the Phoenix, or the Parliament of Shifters, or any of your dry-lander laws. We have our own rules out here. And you two are *way* out of your depth."

Chase's grin widened. "Funny you should say that."

The yacht tipped to one side as a massive, scaled head erupted from the water. Sammy's shark shifters scattered in panic as a long, sinuous neck arched into the air, dwarfing the boat. Seawater streamed from indigo scales, falling like rain onto the yacht's deck.

"I think that you'll agree that *he* is very much *not* out of his depth," Griff murmured.

Sammy lost all traces of his smile at last. "Ah," he said, looking up.

"That," Chase said conversationally, "is the Walker-Above-Waves, Emissary to the Land from the Pearl Throne, Oath-Sworn Seeker of the Emperor-in-Absence, Anointed Knight-Poet of the First Water, and… you know, it's so tricky to remember all these titles. What was the last one, Griff?"

"Firefighter for the East Sussex Fire and Rescue Service," Griff supplied, grinning himself.

"Oh, yes, that was it." Chase turned back to Sammy, who

had gone as pale as his suit. "His real name is a little tricky to pronounce above water, so we just call him John Doe. Say hello, John."

The sea dragon rumbled, with a sound like continents colliding. The shadow of his great, fanged head fell over the shark shifter.

"So you see, Sammy, I *will* be flying West's plane in the race," Chase said. "And I'm going to *win*."

CHAPTER 5

*C*onnie stared numbly out of the bedroom window of her cheap rented apartment. From up here, she could just about make out the colored lights of Shoreham Airfield. Even in the dark, she knew exactly which speck of light marked the location of the small hanger that housed her plane.

Her *mother's* plane.

Connie had only been twelve when her mom died. But she remembered her mother's strong hands, wrapped over hers on the handle of a wrench, showing her how to disassemble a wheel assembly. She remembered the comforting smell of engine oil mingling with her mother's floral perfume. She remembered her mother's delighted laugh when a repair went well, and her inventive cursing when it didn't.

And she had a distant, dreamlike memory of being very small, small enough to curl on her mother's lap as she worked on restoring the plane's controls. Small enough to be perfectly happy, cocooned in the cockpit with her mom, utterly secure and safe. Because mom could fix *anything*.

"I wish you were here, mom," Connie said softly to the distant, hidden plane.

She drew in a deep breath, scrubbing the back of her hand across her face. There was no time for tears. For a long time now, she'd had to be the one who fixed things. She would fix this now.

She wouldn't let anyone touch her plane.

Chase's head appeared, upside down, at the top of the open window. "Good news!" he announced cheerfully. "I'm going to fly your plane!"

Connie leaped backward with a strangled yelp. "Chase, what are you *doing*?"

"Hanging by my knees from the guttering." He flashed her an inverted grin. "It was the fastest way down from the roof."

Connie rubbed her forehead. "Do I even want to know what you were doing on the roof?"

His devil-may-care smile faltered. "Probably, but that's one of those things I'm not allowed to talk about. Sorry."

Oh. One of those *things.*

She'd frequently run into *those things* with Chase, during the brief summer they'd spent together three years ago. There had been certain topics that made him go uncharacteristically silent if they came up in conversation. Some of them were silly, innocuous things, like his favorite type of animal or why his whole family seemed to treat his desire to fly airplanes as somehow perverse.

But there were more significant things he wouldn't discuss either. Things like why a rich playboy who was notorious for countless flings with supermodels would abruptly become obsessed with the plain, dumpy daughter of his flight instructor. Things like why he'd pursued her so relentlessly, despite her initial refusals. Things like why someone like Chase would want someone like her.

Compared to *that*, his habit of turning up on rooftops

seemed positively normal.

Connie knew from experience that questioning him further would only result in him doing something astonishingly random, and usually quite dangerous, in order to force a change of subject. "If I don't let you in, you're going to hang there all night, aren't you."

Chase's trademark grin reappeared. "How well you know me, my love."

"I'm not your love." Nonetheless, she stood back from the window, gesturing him in.

Chase flipped himself neatly through the window, landing on his feet. Connie's heart, which was still hammering after the shock of his abrupt appearance, gave an odd little skip. He'd changed out of his firefighter uniform into black jeans and a slim-cut button-down shirt, sleeves rolled up to show off his tanned forearms. The neck of the shirt hung open a little, displaying the strong lines of his throat and a hint of muscled chest.

Remember. Remember all the things he is. Womanizing, dishonest, fickle, flighty, unreliable...

Unfortunately, there was one other thing that he undeniably was:

Gorgeous.

Connie folded her arms, trying to conceal the traitorous rise of her hormones by giving Chase a withering glare. "Why are you here, Chase?"

"I told you." Chase plopped himself down her bed, lounging back against the headboard and looking infuriatingly at home. "I'm going to fly your plane."

Connie stared at him. "No, you most definitely are not."

Chase spread his hands, palm up. "Well, if you want I could co-pilot while you fly it, but to be honest I think we've got better chances the other way round. You're a much better navigator than I am, after all. I haven't had a lot of experience in doing that sort of thing. And I bet you've been studying the race course for at least a month already—"

"*Chase,*" Connie cut across the babble. "Start at the beginning. What on earth are you talking about?"

"I talked to Sammy. He wouldn't drop the bet entirely, but I made him stick to the literal words of the agreement he made with your dad." Chase's white teeth flashed in his feral smile. "The bet's on the plane, not specifically on your dad flying it, you see. So now everything will be fine. We just have to win the Rydon Cup together, flying your plane."

Shoving Chase's feet out of the way, Connie sat down heavily on the end of the bed. "We *just* have to win the Rydon Cup. Right. One question. Are you completely insane?"

"What?" Chase looked wounded. "You know how I fly."

"Like God Himself gave you the wings of an eagle," Connie said through gritted teeth. "And the brains of a hummingbird."

"That's the nicest thing you've ever said to me," Chase said, grinning. "Well? Come on, Connie. You and me. We can do it. Together."

Connie pinched the bridge of her nose, thinking it over. Much as every fiber of her being screamed *NOOOOOO!* at the thought of Chase even sitting in her mother's plane, let alone flinging it across the sky, she had to admit that he *was* a ridiculously fast pilot. Not a *good* one—he was far too cavalier about little things like 'air traffic control' and 'the ground' for that—but she'd be sitting right behind him in the co-pilot's cockpit. She'd be able to take over control if he got too reckless.

Maybe they really could do this together.

"All right," she said reluctantly. "It's a terrible, crazy, ridiculous idea. But I don't have a better one. Are you up to date with your license? How often do you fly?"

Chase's mouth quirked. "You'd be surprised. But the type

of piloting you mean... pretty frequently. I fly the service helicopter when we need air support putting out fires. And I've got a plane of my own that I try to take up on a regular basis. Every week or so, usually."

Connie eyed him suspiciously, but couldn't tell if he was lying. "I'm surprised you find time, what with the firefighting as well."

Chase's eyes darkened, his expression turning uncharacteristically serious. "Whenever I flew, it made me feel closer to you. Knowing that you were up in the same sky, even if I didn't know where."

I am not *going to fall for him.*

"Well, I'm glad to hear you've been practicing," Connie said, determinedly ignoring his intense gaze. "We'll go up in the plane together tomorrow. I'll teach you the quirks of the controls. I warn you, it won't be like anything you've ever flown before."

A quick, private look of amusement flashed across Chase's face. "I think you'll find I'm a fast learner."

"I know you are. When you actually decide to listen." She jabbed his muscular leg with her finger. "I'm serious, Chase. If you're going to get behind the controls of my mother's plane, then you'd better be serious, too."

"When it comes to you," Chase said, all traces of laughter sliding away, "I am *entirely* serious."

The heat in his dark, intent eyes made an answering warmth spread through her. It was like he was a magnet, pulling the compass of her soul out of alignment. She knew, *knew,* that he was a cheating playboy, and yet she couldn't help but want to throw caution away and fly straight into his arms.

She stood up abruptly. "Good. In that case, I'll see you tomorrow. Good night, Chase."

He remained sprawled across her bed.

"I said, *good night*, Chase." She glared at him. "That means it's time for you to leave. Now."

"Ah, well." Chase folded his arms comfortably behind his head. "I'm afraid I can't do that."

Connie rolled her eyes. "Chase, you live in this city. There is no possible way you are going to convince me that you don't have somewhere to go."

"I do. A very nice place. Much nicer than this, if you don't mind me saying so." He sat up, swinging his feet off the bed. "In fact, why don't we go back there now? I'd like to show you my roof garden. You can sit in the hot tub and look out at the sea, and—"

"I am *not* going anywhere with you. And you are leaving. Now."

"I really, really can't," Chase said firmly. "Considering that Sammy Smiles has already put your father in hospital, I can't take the risk of leaving you alone."

Connie folded her arms across her chest. "I can take care of myself."

Chase's jaw set. "I mean it, Connie. I'm not leaving your side."

"And I'm not having you *staying* at my side every moment until the race," Connie retorted.

Chase's roguish grin flashed again. "Good. Because actually, I'm planning on sticking with you for a lot longer than that. Something like forever."

Connie threw up her hands in despair. "Look, if I have sex with you, will you finally agree to just leave me alone?"

The words slipped out from her unbidden, fuelled by a combination of exasperation and attraction. She hadn't meant to say it.

But it did mean she had the pleasure of finally seeing Chase Tiernach completely, utterly, and absolutely lost for words.

"Well?" Emboldened by his stunned silence, Connie took three steps back toward him, planting herself right between his knees. "Come on, Chase. You and me, right here, right now. Get it out of your system, so you can finally get over me."

So I can finally get over you.

Chase swallowed, hard. "Connie, we... please don't tease me. You don't understand what you mean to me."

"I'm not teasing." Throwing common sense to the wind, Connie ran her fingertips up Chase's bare forearm, tracing the rock-hard swells of his muscles. "Don't tell me a playboy like you doesn't always carry around a condom or two."

"Actually, I don't." Chase said hoarsely. "So—"

"Well, I'm on birth control anyway, so as long as you'll take my word for it, it's not really a problem. In your line of work I assume you have to have a clean bill of health, right?"

Chase couldn't have looked more stunned if she'd walloped him across the back of the head with a two by four. "Yes, of course, but.... you can't actually be serious?"

"Why not? We're both consenting adults. There's unfinished business between us, so lets finish it, for once and for all." Connie started undoing the buttons of her top. "Then we can both move on with our lives."

Chase's hand closed around her wrist, stopping her mid-motion. Connie could feel the contained strength in the grip. He was shaking, ever so slightly, as if it was taking immense force of will to hold himself back.

It felt *wonderful* to make someone else be the sensible one for once.

"Don't do that," he said, something dark and primal roughening his voice. "Not unless you really mean it."

Connie met his black, heat-filled eyes, and discovered that she really *did*.

"This is a one-time offer, Chase," she said. "Take it or

leave it."

With a low moan, Chase pulled her down to him. The last vestiges of Connie's better judgment burned away at the first touch of his lips on hers. Chase kissed her desperately, as if she was the air he needed to breathe. Connie kissed him back with equal fervor, three years' worth of pent-up desire finally bursting free.

Chase's hands skimmed her thighs and hips, exploring her curves. Connie abruptly needed to feel those agile, sensitive hands on her bare skin. Breaking the kiss, she tugged her top over her head in one swift, impatient movement.

Chase's breath hissed between his teeth. His arms tensed, holding her away from him so that his hungry gaze could devour her, savoring every curve of her exposed body.

Then he actually closed his eyes.

"Connie," he said hoarsely. "If you want me to take this slowly, I'm going to need a second."

"You've never in your entire life taken *anything* slowly." Connie tried to press closer to him, but his rigid arms were like iron bars. "And for God's sake, Chase, don't start now!"

Chase let out a sound that was half-laugh, half-growl. Then, before Connie had even registered the movement, he had her bra off. She gasped as his mouth closed fiercely over one breast, even as his hands flashed downward to undo the button of her jeans. She closed her eyes, surrendering herself to the glorious sensation of Chase's tongue flicking and circling her nipple.

Chase yanked down her jeans and panties. He made a low, feral sound, deep in his throat, as his strong fingers grasped her butt. Then, somehow, she was on her back on the bed, the last of her clothes falling away. Chase's agile hands and expert mouth seemed to be everywhere at once— teasing her nipples, sucking at her neck, exploring her wet, eager folds.

"Oh," she gasped, as his long fingers slid into her. "*Oh.*"

She threw back her head, fiery pleasure sparking through her. His mouth was hot on her breasts, his teeth nipping at her skin with barely-contained passion. She wound her limbs around him, her hands tangling in his shirt, his jeans rough against her bare legs as climax overtook her.

"More," she demanded, when she could speak again. She tugged at his shirt, desperate for his body naked on her, in her. "Now, Chase!"

She felt his lips curve against her breast. Then he was gone, the air suddenly cold on her flushed, sweaty skin. She propped herself up on her elbows to watch greedily as he unbuttoned his shirt.

Though they'd briefly dated, all those years ago, she'd never let him get this far before. Now she was finding out what she'd been missing.

Her breath caught at the sight of his broad chest and lithe abdomen as he pulled off his shirt. Every muscle in his body was sharply defined, shaped and honed to perfection by the tough, physical nature of his job.

Chase bent over to strip off his jeans, revealing his slim hips and tight ass. Then he straightened, turning.

"Holy shit," Connie couldn't help yelping.

He was hung like a fucking *horse*.

From the quick, pained smile he flashed her, she guessed she wasn't the first woman to have second thoughts when confronted with his frankly intimidating erection.

"Do you want to stop?" he said, his voice shaking with raw desire. The swollen head of his enormous cock was already glistening with eagerness.

Connie very nearly said "Yes," but her body had its own ideas. No matter how much her brain screamed that he was just too big, her pussy demanded that long, wide shaft.

Powerless to resist, she spread her legs wide.

Chase needed no further invitation. Before she had time for second thoughts, his hard body was on her, his mouth capturing hers. His tongue slid between her lips, claiming and possessing her even as the thick head of his cock pressed at her entrance.

She gasped at the incredible feeling of his shaft stretching her wide. He slid slowly but unstoppably into her. She'd never imagined that she could take so much.

His rock-hard girth simultaneously caressed every part of her most sensitive inner areas. Her entire world narrowed to nothing except him as he thrust steadily, relentlessly into her.

Chase paused. Connie could feel him shaking, fighting to control himself. He filled her more than she could have dreamed possible. She balanced on the very brink of orgasm, only needing one last push to fly away.

His dark eyes were filled with raw, animal need, but he held himself still. "Connie," he said huskily.

The way he said her name held an unspoken question. In answer, she clenched around his impaling shaft.

With a heartfelt groan, Chase thrust forward a last incredible inch, finally filling her utterly. Connie was pushed over the edge, free-falling into waves of pleasure.

His strong hands seized her hips as she writhed. He withdrew and thrust, again and again, harder and harder. His breath came in great ragged gasps as he lost all control at last. He strained, burying himself deeper in her than ever, as if he was trying to make them one body, one soul.

Connie dug her fingers into his hard, muscled back... but even as she pressed against him, a tiny part of her kept a wary distance. In the middle of the storm of ecstasy, a single, simple thought remained at the center of her mind, like the calm eye of a hurricane.

I am not going to fall for him.

CHAPTER 6

Chase came back to himself slowly, as if spiraling down out of the sky to land. He could feel Connie's heartbeat against his chest, her pulse beating in perfect time with his own.

Our mate! In contrast to his own lassitude, his pegasus pranced in triumph, unable to keep still. *Our mate! We pleased her, we won her, she chose us! Our mate!*

Chase let out a soft, amused huff of laughter at the stallion's shameless pride in their own prowess. He pressed his face into the junction of Connie's neck and shoulder, inhaling deeply. Her flushed skin held an intoxicating trace of his own scent now. She smelled like the sky, like sex, like everything good. He could have lain there forever, breathing her in.

His stallion snorted impatiently, flicking its tail. *Up, up, swiftly! Back to the nest! Finish it, mark her, make her ours forever, ours alone. Our mate!*

"So." Connie shifted underneath him, pushing at his shoulder. "That happened."

"Mmm," Chase agreed. He reluctantly rolled onto his back to let her up. "It certainly did."

She wriggled out from under him. Chase put his arms behind his head, admiring her lush, glorious body with lazy pleasure as she started to hunt for her clothes.

"And now we've got it out of our system." Connie's voice was muffled as she pulled her top back over her head. "So we can forget this and move on."

Chase laughed. Then, abruptly, he stopped. "Wait. You're serious?"

Connie turned to face him, hands on her hips. "I told you. One-time sex, just to settle things. And now that you've gotten what you wanted, you have to go."

All his languid contentment slid away as he sat bolt upright. "Connie, no!"

"Leave, Chase!" She threw his clothes at him. "That was the deal, remember?"

He raked his hand through his sweaty hair, staring at her in utter dismay. "Yes, but—I thought—"

"You thought one taste of you would have me begging for more." Connie folded her arms over her chest, glaring at him. "Well, sorry to puncture your massive ego, but sleeping with you hasn't made me fall for you. Now leave me alone—unless you're going to break *another* promise to me?"

He'd had his mouth open to protest, but at her last words it snapped shut again. He groped for an explanation, excuses… but she was right.

Three years ago, he'd promised to be faithful to her. He'd thought it would be easy. Sure, before he'd met Connie, he'd enjoyed the billionaire playboy lifestyle, but as soon as he'd laid eyes on her he'd known that he'd never again so much as look at another woman. He'd *promised* her that.

And then, somehow, in a night that he couldn't even remember, he'd broken that promise.

If he broke another one now, she'd walk straight out of his life. Again.

No no NO! His stallion raged, hooves stamping, trying to force him to stand his ground.

For once, Chase bridled the beast, forcing it down. He could still feel it beating its wings furiously at the back of his mind as he slowly, reluctantly pulled on his clothes.

Connie held up a hand as he stumbled toward the door. "Oh, and Chase?"

He spun round so fast, he nearly lost his balance. "Yes?"

There was not the slightest hint of regret or indecision in her expression as she met his eyes. "I'll see you at the airfield tomorrow. What we... what happened doesn't change anything. We've still got a race to win."

She shut the apartment door in his face. Chase stared blindly at it. He wanted nothing more than to kick it down again, to demand that she love him as fervently and passionately as he loved her.

Because that worked so well for you last time, didn't it?

He knew he was overwhelming and impetuous and generally an all-round massive pain in the ass. Enough people had told him so, on a daily basis, pretty much his entire life.

But he'd always assumed that his fated mate would *like* that about him. Growing up, he'd just thought one day that he'd meet his mate, sweep her off her feet, and carry her off triumphantly into the sunset.

Three years ago, he'd met Connie. And she'd taken one look at him, and run away as fast as her legs could carry her.

Admittedly, in retrospect it *might* have been the wrong tactic to propose to her before even asking her name.

Chase had spent an entire month hanging round Kilkenny Airport every single day, under the excuse of taking flying lessons from her father, just for the chance to be near her. When she'd finally spoken to him again at last, her words —"Pass me that torque wrench"—were the most beautiful poetry he'd ever heard.

A month to get her to talk to him. Another month of slowly, so slowly winning her trust, persuading her that he wasn't just some flighty playboy trying to get into her pants.

She'd finally, *finally* let him take her out on a date. One date turned into two, three, more...

They'd spent a single, glorious month together as a couple. Even though she'd never let him get further than a few stolen kisses, it had been the best month of his entire life.

And then, just when she'd seemed ready to fully let him into her heart at last, he'd thrown it all away.

He still didn't know what had happened. Connie had called him to invite him round to her apartment that night 'for dinner', with a shyness that had made the subtext clear. He'd been so jubilant and nervous that the hours until the evening had seemed endless. He'd gone out to his club for a drink, just one, to pass the time.

The next thing he knew, he'd woken up in bed with two women he'd never met before, and Connie staring at him from the doorway with shocked, hurt eyes.

And then she'd turned on her heel, and walked out of his life.

Not again. Not this time.

Chase took a deep breath, straightening his shoulders. Much as he longed to charge back immediately, trying to explain things to her right now would be like running a race while wearing shackles. He was hobbled by the fact that there was so much he wasn't allowed to tell her. If only she understood that he was a shifter, and she was his mate... but that was impossible.

But that was about to change.

Connie's roof turned out to have excellent cellphone reception. Chase sat cross-legged on the tiles, impatiently hitting *Redial* over and over again. Happily, it took a mere eighteen attempts before someone picked up.

"Chase," growled his cousin's irate Irish voice. "It is *one o'clock* in the *fucking morning.*"

"Killian?" Chase blinked. "That you? What are you doing with my father's phone?"

"Handling his business calls for him while he's on vacation. And it took me and your mom eight solid months of arguing with him to persuade him to take this break, so no, I am *not* putting you through. Whatever crisis you're having this time can wait."

"No, it really can't." Unable to sit still, Chase bounced to his feet, pacing back and forth along the ridgeline. "Killian, you'll never believe it. Connie's here!"

There was a moment of stunned silence from the other end of the line. "Your *mate?*"

"Yes!" Words poured out of him uncontrollably at being able to talk to someone who would understand. "And she's talking to me again, and I proposed, and her dad's in hospital, and I saved her from a fire, and—your detectives were wrong, she was in America, by the way—anyway, she's back now with her plane for the Rydon Cup air race, and there's this shark shifter called Sammy Smiles who wants to kill her because he doesn't want her to win it, but I'm going to make sure she does, so he's probably going to come after me, too."

"What?" Killian said, as if none of that had made any sense whatsoever.

"Never mind, that's not the important part," Chase said impatiently. "We had sex!"

"You did *what?*" Killian sounded utterly appalled.

"And then I messed everything up," Chase admitted.

Killian heaved a deep, heartfelt sigh. "Of course you did."

"Which is why I need to talk to my father. The only way I'm going to be able to fix this is if I can tell Connie that I'm a shifter. Once she understands about mates, she'll—"

"Chase, we went through this before, three years ago," Killian interrupted. "You can tell her once you're married. That's the way it's been for hundreds of years."

"But I can't persuade her to marry me *unless* I tell her." Chase clenched his fist. "Father's the pegasus alpha. I have to persuade him to relax the rules, just this once."

"You may be the apple of your father's eye—God knows why—but he's not going to put all of our kind at risk. Not even for you. The rules of secrecy are there for a reason, Chase. We can't risk ordinary people finding out about us. Unless you're willing to issue a formal challenge, you can't change our laws."

His stallion bared its teeth, ears flattening. *Fight the alpha. Take the herd. Win our mate!*

Chase mentally recoiled from the thought. He loved his father, and wouldn't dream of challenging him. For pegasus shifters, dominance fights were always to the death. Murdering his own father would *not* be a good start to a long-term relationship with Connie.

Plus, of course, Chase would immediately inherit the entire family business. He'd spent almost his entire life running away at top speed from *that* responsibility.

"Look," Killian said more gently, interpreting Chase's glum silence. "I know how much this means to you. Tell you what, I've got a few business things to sort out up here, but I'll come down as soon as I can and talk to her myself, okay? I think she likes me."

Chase perked up a little. Connie *had* gotten along well with Killian, on the few occasions they'd met. His older cousin was just the sort of person Connie admired—steady, reliable, serious. As the CFO of Tiernach Enterprises, he'd gained a lot of respect in both the business and shifter communities, which added to his natural air of authority. Connie would listen to him.

"Thanks, Killian," he said gratefully, sinking back down. "I owe you one. Again."

Another deep sigh. "That's me. Rescuing you from responsibility, every time." Killian paused a moment. "If you *do* win her, does that mean you'll come back? Last time you were dating her, you were full of plans to settle down. Will you finally take your place in the family business, like your father's always wanted?"

Chase shuddered, shying away from the idea like a horse from a saddle. But still... "Maybe. I like being a firefighter, I really do. But it's a dangerous job. I wouldn't want Connie to be fretting every time I went to work."

"Come to the Dark Side." Killian deepened his voice. "We have *spreadsheets*."

"Only you could make finance sound even more boring than it actually is." Chase kicked his feet, gazing up at the stars. "I suppose I'll have to. That's how it goes, isn't it? Find your mate, get married, become responsible…"

"Some of us skip straight to the last one," Killian murmured.

"I'm grateful to you for that," Chase said, meaning it. "You say I'm the golden boy, but you're the one who's my dad's right-hand man. I should be more like you."

"I don't recommend it," Killian said, sounding rather wistful. "I haven't found *my* mate, after all."

"When you do, I bet you won't have half the trouble I've had." Beneath him, he could feel Connie's exact location. It was physically painful to resist the way she pulled at him, a throbbing ache deep in his bones. "You've always been able to control your stallion. Not like me. I can't even sit still right now."

"I'll be down to help as soon as I can. Just don't make things worse, okay? Listen. Why don't you go out, find a club? Drink and dance and distract yourself from all this."

"No clubs," Chase said sharply. "No drinking. Not after last time."

"I'm sorry, I wasn't thinking. That was tactless." Killian paused. "But Chase, you *should* go find something to keep yourself busy. Otherwise you'll be singing under her window or setting fire to the place or some other harebrained scheme, five minutes after I hang up. I know you."

Killian *did* know him. Chase drummed his fingertips on the roof, thinking. He couldn't leave Connie unprotected, but he really would go out of his mind with restlessness if he had nothing to do except stare wistfully at the roof between them. Maybe, if he asked one of the other members of his fire crew to stand guard for him for a short time...

A slow smile spread across his face. "There *is* something I need to do. But I'm going to need some money."

"What have I done," Killian muttered under his breath. "Chase, you asked for an extra two million just six months ago. What happened to that?"

"I spent it," Chase said. "Obviously. Can I have some more?"

Killian sighed yet again. "How much do you need?"

"Tell you what." Chase's grin widened. "I'll just send you the check."

CHAPTER 7

Connie stretched as she woke, sleepily reaching out across the bed. Her questing fingers found nothing but air. The mattress next to her was empty.

A jolt of panic raced through her. She sat bolt upright, and had a confusing few seconds staring blankly at the empty space on the bed before her brain fully woke up and overruled her irrational heart.

Of course Chase isn't there. I kicked him out.

I can't believe he actually left.

She realized that part of her had been utterly convinced that he would find some way to sneak back in. At some deep level, she'd been expecting to wake up to his cocky, unrepentant grin and a torrent of nonsense explaining why he'd simply *had* to spend the night with her after all.

Connie checked under the bed. Still no Chase.

He really is honoring our deal. I slept with him, so now he'll leave me alone.

Just like I wanted.

I should feel happy about this.

Then she heard someone moving around quietly in the

second room of the apartment, on the other side of the bedroom door.

Her heart skipped a beat, even as she buried her face in her hands and groaned. Of course he hadn't actually left. No doubt he was filling her tiny combined kitchen/living room with roses or iguanas or God only knew what he considered to be a romantic gesture.

Without bothering to pull on her robe, Connie marched over to the bedroom door and yanked it open. "Chase, I told you—"

It wasn't Chase.

Connie recoiled so hard she bruised her naked butt against the door handle. "Who the hell are you?"

The man turned quickly at her shout. He was tall and muscled, with short brown hair in a vaguely military cut. There was something about his dark eyes that made some deep, primal part of Connie's psyche cower back in instinctive fear. Whoever he was, this man was *dangerous*.

"Chase!" Connie grabbed the first thing that came to hand —a pillow—and flung it at the intruder. "*Help!*"

The man ducked the pillow, but Connie had already seized her bedside lamp. Brandishing it like a baseball bat, she charged him, swinging for his head with her full strength.

Reflexively, the man flung up one hand, seizing the body of the lamp. White fire flared. Connie yelped, dropping the lamp as the suddenly hot metal bit her skin.

"Please," the man said quickly, holding up both hands. "Do not be alarmed. I mean you no harm."

Wide-eyed, Connie stared at the scorched lamp now lying on the carpet, then back at the man. "What *are* you?"

"A friend of Chase." The man sighed, rubbing his face. "I am very sorry, but I am afraid I have no choice but to start this conversation again. Please forgive me."

Connie would have backed away from him, but she was abruptly frozen by his burning eyes. Terror-stricken, she could do nothing to resist as he reached out to touch her forehead.

Fire flared.

Connie blinked. There was a strange man in her front room.

However, he was kneeling on the ground with his eyes closed and his hands in the air. He looked more like a hostage than an intruder.

"Chase asked me to guard you while he ran an errand," the man said, very rapidly, as she drew in her breath to yell. "He was worried that Sammy Smiles might attack you in your sleep. I am Fire Commander Ash, of the East Sussex Fire and Rescue Service. May I show you my identification?"

Connie eyed him warily, casting around for a weapon. For some reason, her bedside lamp was lying in the middle of the floor. She picked it up. The metal was oddly warm in her hand as she held the lamp high, ready to bring it down on the man's head if he was lying. "Okay. But slowly."

Connie tensed as the man reached into his jacket, but true to his word he just pulled out a leather wallet. He flipped it open, silently displaying the metal shield inside.

Feeling a little silly, she lowered her impromptu weapon. "Oh. Um. Nice to meet you, Commander Ash. I'm sorry if I startled you. Chase didn't tell me you were coming."

"So I gathered," Commander Ash said, a touch grimly. "I believe I shall have words with him about that."

He was still on his knees, although he'd lowered his hands. "Uh, you can get up now, if you want," Connie offered. "I promise I won't try to brain you. Would you like some coffee?"

Ash cleared his throat, eyes still closed. "Ah. Perhaps you would care to put on some clothes first?"

Connie looked down at herself.

"Yes," she said, her voice going rather higher-pitched. "Yes, that would be a good idea."

∽

Even with clothes on, conversation with Ash proved to be an uphill struggle. The Fire Commander was perfectly polite, but so blandly noncommittal that Connie gave up on questioning him at all. He seemed content to sit in utter silence, gazing thoughtfully into the depths of the coffee she'd offered him. He exuded such an intimidating aura of reserve, Connie found herself involuntarily edging backward in her chair.

Ash abruptly looked up from his contemplation of his untouched coffee, his head turning toward the door. A moment later it slammed back on its hinges, and Chase bounced into the room.

"Oh good, you're up!" he said cheerfully to Connie. "I see you've met my Commander."

"Twice," Ash said under his breath. He looked hard at Chase.

Chase's grin slid off his face. Connie had an odd sense of some unspoken communication going on between the two men for a moment.

"Oh," Chase said in a small voice. He turned to Connie. "I'm sorry about that. Next time I'll remember to warn you."

"Next time?" Connie rolled her eyes. "Next time I throw you out of my apartment, don't take that as meaning I need you to provide someone to replace you."

Chase's grin reappeared. "Ah, so there *will* be a next time?"

"Next time is about to be right now, if you don't stop smirking at me," Connie informed him.

Commander Ash got to his feet. "I believe that my presence is no longer required."

"It was, uh, nice meeting you," Connie told him, with as much sincerity as she could muster. "Thank you for watching over me, anyway. Sorry for threatening you with a lamp."

"Please accept my sincere apologies as well," Commander Ash said, which was rather weird given that *she'd* been the one threatening *him*. With a last inscrutable look at Chase, he left.

"You tried to hit Commander Ash with a lamp?" Chase sounded utterly tickled.

Connie glared at him as she gathered up the coffee cups. "You're lucky I didn't actually take a swing at him. Honestly, Chase, what were you *thinking?*"

"I didn't mean to surprise you. I thought you'd never even know he'd been here."

Connie dumped the coffee cups into the sink with a loud clatter. "Really not helping your case, you know."

"That came out a little different to how I intended," Chase admitted. "I only meant, I planned to get back before you woke up. But I got delayed."

"Delayed doing what?" Connie said suspiciously, her back to him as she rinsed out the cups.

"Shopping," Chase said, as if this was a perfectly reasonable thing to have been doing before dawn.

"Shopping?" Connie turned around to stare at him. "What were you—"

She stopped mid-sentence. Chase was down on one knee, holding up an engagement ring with an enormous solitaire diamond.

"Constance West, will you marry me?" he said, utterly seriously.

Connie threw up her hands. "Chase, I've turned you

down twice already. What on earth makes you think I've changed my mind?"

Well, apart from the absolutely incredible sex...

Connie stomped down on the traitorous thought. Fantastic sex couldn't make up for Chase's reckless, unreliable behavior. They couldn't spend *all* their time in bed.

"I didn't really ask properly before. Now I am." He held up one hand, forestalling her interruption. "Please, just hear me out. I love you, Connie. I always have, from the moment we first met, and I always will. I know you think that's crazy, but it's true. And there's a very good reason why I *know* it's true… but unfortunately, I can't tell you what that is until after we're married. So: Will you marry me?"

Connie stared at him.

"I also chartered a jet to Vegas," Chase added. "So we can get married today, I can tell you everything, and then we can still be back well in time for the race."

"You," Connie said slowly, "are *certifiably insane*."

He didn't move. "If you don't like what I tell you, then we can get an annulment straight away. Please, Connie. Marry me, and I swear this will all make sense. Trust me."

Connie pinched the bridge of her nose, taking deep breaths until she could trust herself to speak without yelling. "No. I am not marrying you. For God's sake, Chase, we've barely even spent any time together!"

"We've known each other for three years," he argued. "Lots of people get married in less time than that."

"Three months over three years! The time when we weren't in contact doesn't count!"

"It does to me," Chase said softly. "I thought of you every day."

And I thought of you every night...

"Fantasies of some idealized versions of each other don't mean anything," she said ruthlessly. "You don't know me,

Chase. No matter how much you think you do, you don't. I mean, you didn't even know that I don't like diamonds."

Chase's expression inexplicably brightened. Carelessly tossing the diamond ring aside, he rummaged in his pocket.

"Constance West," he said, pulling out a vintage gold ring set with three fabulous fire opals, "will you marry me?"

Connie's mouth hung open.

"I *did* remember that you'd mentioned once that you didn't care much for diamonds," Chase explained, offering her the ring. "But I know you also like traditions, so I thought I'd better try a very traditional ring first. Anyway, this one reminded me of that pendant you used to wear, so I thought you might like it."

"You bought *two* engagement rings," Connie said weakly. "In the middle of the night."

"Well, I found a jeweler who lived above her shop, so then it was just a case of shouting loud enough to wake her up. And then convincing her that it would be worth her while to open up." He looked a little sheepish. "I, um, actually bought five rings. I also have one with your birthstone, one with emeralds to match your eyes, and an Irish Claddagh ring."

Connie stared at him yet again.

"I have difficulty saying no to pretty things," Chase admitted.

Connie folded her arms. "Well, we both know *that's* certainly true."

Chase winced, but didn't back down. "Connie, I'm deadly serious about this. I need to marry you. Please?"

For a mad moment, Connie entertained the idea of actually going through with it, just to finally get an insight into his peculiar head. Maybe there *was* some great secret that would explain everything…

Her common sense ruthlessly crushed the silly thought. Of course there was no so-called secret, no rational reason for his erratic behavior. If he wasn't genuinely mentally ill, then he had to be just playing her, in some private, twisted joke.

"No," she repeated, hoping he hadn't noticed her hesitation. "Now get up. We have a plane to fly."

CHAPTER 8

*C*hase fought to contain the grin that wanted to spread across his face as he followed Connie to the airplane hanger.

She hesitated! She definitely hesitated before she said no. I'm making progress!

His stallion flicked its tail sullenly. *Slow progress. Too slow.*

It wasn't in the pegasus's nature to be patient. Or, if he was honest with himself, his own. Even though he treasured any tiny hint of Connie softening toward him, he couldn't help but want to accelerate the process.

Fortunately, he had the perfect opportunity.

Don't worry, he told his stallion, as Connie unlocked the hanger doors. *We're going to fly for her. That's sure to impress her.*

His pegasus perked up, prancing on the spot. *Yes! No one is faster, no one swifter, no one stronger than us! Show our mate! Shift, shift, now!*

Chase's lips quirked at the stallion's rampant enthusiasm. *Not* that *sort of flying.*

"Here she is," Connie said, rolling the big sliding door back.

Chase let out a long, low whistle of appreciation.

The vintage Spitfire gleamed like a work of art. Even parked in the hanger, the venerable WWII warplane looked ready to leap up into the air at any moment. It sat back on its wheels like a crouching beast, its single propeller pointed toward the sky, eternally keeping watch for Nazi planes.

"Hello, baby," Connie said to her plane, her voice soft.

Chase would have given anything to have her speak to *him* that way. "She's even more beautiful than I remember. New paint job?"

Connie nodded, stroking the plane's gleaming olive-green hide. "Battle of Britain squadron colors. It's not historically accurate, given that she's a Mark IX, but I flew her at a big World War II memorial event a few months back and they wanted the classic camouflage colors on her. I think it suits her, anyway."

"She's stunning." Chase noticed the way that Connie stiffened slightly as he approached the plane. He carefully kept his hands behind his back as he circled the vintage warbird. "You've kept her in absolutely perfect condition."

"And I want her to stay that way." Connie turned to face him, putting her hands on her hips. "Chase, I'm taking a huge risk here. I need to hear you say that you understand what's at stake. Do you even know how much a plane like this is worth?"

"About two and a half million dollars," Chase said absently, still admiring the plane. "Not including brokers fees."

Connie's eyebrows shot up. "How did you know that?"

"I kept an eye out for any news about Spitfires, looking for clues about where you were." Chase shrugged. "One was up for auction a little while ago. Though that one was a standard single-seater Mark IX. I suspect yours would be worth more."

"A lot more, actually." Connie pointed up at the two glass bubbles of the cockpits, one behind the other on top of the plane. "There are fewer than ten of these trainer Mark IXs still in the sky, and they're the only way a non-pilot can ever experience the thrill of flying in a Spitfire. People will pay a *lot* of money for a ride. Dad might get the occasional win from air racing, but the vast bulk of our income comes from passenger flights. This is my livelihood I'm trusting you with, Chase."

And it's your mother's plane. The one she restored from a twisted wreck, by hand, over decades. It's not just your livelihood, Connie. It's your heart.

But Chase knew that Connie would never say that out loud. She was so determinedly pragmatic, she hated to admit to being influenced by emotion.

"I know what you're trusting me with," Chase said gently. "And you can trust me. I promise."

He regretted saying it the instant the words were out of his mouth. Connie's lips compressed, as she no doubt remembered just how badly he'd kept the last promise he'd made to her, three years ago.

"I'll be in the flight instructor's cockpit," Connie said, pointing to the rear cockpit. "Both cockpits have full controls, so either one of us can fly the plane, but only I'll have the switch which toggles between the two cockpits. If I think that you're being at all reckless, I *will* throw that switch and take control back from you."

"Understood." Chase moved toward the front cockpit, ready to swing himself up.

Connie stopped him with a hand flat against his chest. "Let me make this crystal clear. If you value your balls, do not make me throw that switch."

"I won't. I hope to have a lot of future use for them, after all." He cocked a grin at her, which she did not return. "Can I get into the plane now?"

Connie hesitated, clearly searching for any other excuse to keep him out of the cockpit.

She really, really doesn't want me to do this. Maybe I should suggest she flies, and I navigate...

His pegasus pawed at the ground, snorting angry denial. *No! She must see our strength, our speed! We* must *fly, or we will not win our mate!*

His stallion had a point. Chase was pretty sure that no hero had ever won a fair maiden with an impressive feat of map reading.

He lightly pushed Connie's hand aside. "It's going to be pretty difficult for me to win the race for you if you won't even let me into the plane, you know."

Connie grudgingly stepped to one side. "All right. I'll take her up, and then once we're in level flight I'll hand over control to you. Don't make me regret this."

∽

It was a beautiful day for flying. The old warbird soared like an eagle over the sparkling sea, its wings cleanly cutting through the air. The land was just a distant smudge behind them. Clear blue sky spread out before them, open, inviting.

The plane was a living thing, all around him, every tiny shiver and tilt transmitted directly to his awareness. He could feel it flex underneath him, leaping eagerly in response to every minuscule movement of his hands. It was like the Spitfire's body had become his own.

It was *exactly* like shifting.

The plane even had a mind of its own, just like his own stallion. This was a perfectly-honed weapon of war, with a proud history of defending Britain's skies from evil. It didn't want to cruise sedately in level flight. It wanted to swoop and dive and dogfight. It may have had the form of a machine, but it had the soul of a pegasus.

His own pegasus spread its wings, sharing the plane's exhilaration. Flying with Connie in a plane wasn't *quite* the same as carrying her in the pegasus mating ritual, but it was close enough that the stallion found it intensely arousing. Chase gritted his teeth, trying to ignore his raging erection and concentrate on the controls.

"You're doing good." Even through the tinny earpiece, the surprise in Connie's voice was obvious. "Nice and steady. How does it feel?"

"I don't think I can describe it," Chase said into his headset, wishing he'd worn looser pants. "I'm getting it under control now, though. Talk me through the race circuit, while I keep getting a feel for how she handles. Then we'll try a practice run."

"Okay," Connie said. "How much do you know about the Rydon Cup?"

"I've never seen it flown, but I've read a little about it," Chase replied, as he eased the Spitfire through a sequence of elegant banking turns. "It's a handicap race, right?"

"Right. The planes start the circuit at different times, set by the race organizers. The idea is that if everyone flew perfectly, they'd all finish together. That way it's more a test of who's the best pilot rather than just who's got the best plane."

Chase gave the Spitfire a bit more throttle, and grinned as the engine's deep snarl kicked up a notch. "And we've got the best of both. The other planes aren't going to know what hit them."

He was pretty sure Connie was glaring at the back of his head from the rear cockpit. "Don't get cocky. Our handicap is pretty substantial. The race organizers have never had a WWII warplane enter before—all the other planes are modern light aircraft. The judges spent a lot of time debating a fair starting position. They've erred on the side of caution, and put us about halfway down the line-up. You're going to have to fly extremely well to make up for the handicap."

"No problem." The Spitfire was as responsive as his own wings. "She may be a grand old lady, but she's raring to go. I bet she'll fly rings round those young upstarts."

"Just remember that we have to stay within the race corridor, otherwise we're eliminated. That's where I come in. I'll be keeping us on course. If I give you a heading, you have to respond *instantly*, understand? No arguing, no messing around, no improvisation."

"You're the boss," Chase said. "How tight are the course turns?"

"To stick to the ideal line, pretty tight. We can expect to be pulling two, maybe three Gs on the turns. There's also the notorious hairpin corner, near the end of the race."

"I've heard of that," Chase said. "Last year a couple of planes crashed trying to make that one, right?"

"Yes, it's a dangerous maneuver. Fortunately, it's been enough of a problem that the organizers have decided pilots can circle round counter-clockwise there this year, if they don't want to risk the hairpin turn. We will *definitely* be circling."

"What?" Chase protested. "Where's the fun in that?"

"The fun of not ripping the wings off a priceless antique plane," Connie retorted tartly. "The turn's technically within the Spitfire's capabilities, but I'm not risking it. I mean it, Chase. Don't even think about it."

Chase silently patted the Spitfire's instrument panel. *Don't worry, girl. I won't hold you back. We'll show her what you can do.*

"Chase," Connie said suspiciously. "You're thinking about it, aren't you?"

Chase let out a rueful laugh. "You may think that I don't know you, but you *definitely* know me."

"Unfortunately," Connie muttered. "Listen to me very carefully, Chase Tiernach. I *will* take back control of the plane from you if I think you aren't going to be sensible on the hairpin. And then I will rip off your balls and wear them as earrings."

"Earmuffs," Chase corrected cheerfully. "They're too big for earrings. You should know."

"Chase," Connie growled.

"Fine, fine. I promise, no hairpin. I'll make sure that we're well in the lead by that point, so we can do the turn the slow way. No problem." Chase took a firmer grip on the steering column. "Shall we do a practice run?"

"Okay. The actual course is half over the sea, half over the land, starting and ending at Shoreham Airport. But we'll do the whole thing over the sea for now, just in case..." Connie trailed off.

"Just in case I crash," Chase finished for her. He rolled his eyes. "Stop being so nervous, Connie. I've never crashed a plane."

"What *have* you crashed?" Connie asked suspiciously.

"Never you mind." Chase gunned the engine to drown out any further discussion on the matter. "Let's go."

Connie gave him the first heading, and Chase obediently turned the plane, pitching the nose upward as he did so.

Show me what you've got, old girl...

The Spitfire climbed like a homesick angel. Chase laughed out loud in sheer delight. Connie muttered a soft curse in his earpiece, but didn't tell him to be more cautious. She too knew that the best strategy for the race would be to gain as much height as possible at the start, so that they'd be able to dive if they needed to get a speed boost later on.

Connie called the first turn point. Chase tipped the Spitfire up on one wing, banking while still climbing. The harness straps cut into his chest as the plane whipped through the turn, as fast and deadly as a hunting falcon.

His pegasus spread its wings and soared along with the plane, filled with fierce delight. *Faster!* it urged him. *Show our speed, win our mate!*

A distant speck in the sky caught Chase's eye as he banked through the next turn under Connie's direction. He craned his neck, peering through the glass bubble of the cockpit.

"Connie," he said. "You cleared our flight path, right?"

"Of course I did. Air traffic control are keeping this area free for us. Why?"

"No reason," Chase said, his forehead creasing as he stared hard at the rapidly-approaching speck.

A rival! His pegasus bared its teeth. *Overfly him, swoop, strike!*

Hush, Chase told the aggressive stallion absently as he tried to identify the other flyer. *Of course it isn't a rival.*

Even from a distance, the bat-wing silhouette clearly wasn't a pegasus. He would have said it was a dragon, except that it was much too small. He knew all the dragon shifters living in Brighton—including his own teammate, Daifydd Drake—and all of them were at least the length of a bus.

This dragon, if dragon it was, looked to be about the size of a large horse. About the size of his own pegasus, in fact, which explained why his own stallion had mistaken it for a challenger. It was a poisonous emerald-green, which wasn't a dragon color Chase had ever seen before. There was something not quite right about its tail, too...

"Chase!" He jumped at Connie's shout. "I gave you the heading twice! Why aren't you turning?"

"Sorry." Chase hastily changed course, the plane lurching as he jerked it roughly round. "I got distracted."

"Distracted by what? It's empty sky out there."

"That's what you think," Chase muttered, too quietly to be picked up by the microphone.

The other shifter was approaching swiftly now, on an intercept course with the Spitfire. Chase couldn't imagine that it could possibly have failed to notice them. The Spitfire was loud enough that the shifter would have to be stone deaf not to have heard the plane.

Maybe it's just having some fun? It probably doesn't realize I can see it.

Chase had occasionally buzzed light aircraft himself, just for the challenge of matching speed and course with them. A normal human pilot wouldn't be able to see a mythic shifter like a dragon or a pegasus, not if it didn't want to be seen.

Deliberately, he tipped the Spitfire first to one side, then the other, waggling the wings in hello.

"What are you doing?" Connie demanded.

"Just, uh, a little crosswind," he lied, still watching the other shifter.

It hadn't responded to his impromptu greeting. Chase tried to mind-speak it, but it was like shouting at a closed door. The other shifter was deliberately blocking all psychic communication.

I'm starting to get a bad feeling about this.

It was close enough now that he could see that it *was* roughly dragon-shaped, with a long neck and wedge-shaped reptilian head. But it only had two legs, not four. Its curved, muscular tail ended in a scorpion's barb, the needle-sharp point at least two feet long.

Bloody hell, it's a wyvern!

Chase had never seen one before. He'd never *heard* of someone who'd actually seen one before. They were so rare, they bordered on legendary, even amongst mythic shifters. They were bogeymen in the stories shifter kids told around campfires: *Stone heart, poison blood, acid breath...*

The wyvern opened its jaws, and spat out a fine, dense cloud of mist.

Chase slammed the plane into a near-vertical climb. The plane shrieked in protest, threatening to stall, but Chase forced it upward. The cloud of acid missed them by inches.

"What are you *doing*?" Connie screamed in his ear as the plane hurtled straight up toward the sun.

"Sudden emergency!" Chase desperately craned his neck, trying to see where the wyvern had gone. "No time to explain!"

He caught sight of the wyvern, only a dozen feet off their tail. Its wings cut through the air like knives. Even with the Spitfire's engine roaring at full throttle, it was catching up with them.

Let's see how you handle this...

Chase flipped the Spitfire nose-over-tail, tumbling into an upside-down dive. The wyvern futilely snatched at them as they shot underneath it with inches to spare, its wicked claws snapping shut on empty air.

"Chase!" Connie's furious voice blasted through the headset. "I'm giving you three seconds to straighten out or I swear to God I am taking back control of this plane!"

"If you hit that switch, we'll both be dead!" Chase yelled back.

He pulled the Spitfire out of the dive, praying that they'd gained enough distance from the wyvern to be able to risk a straight dash back toward land. At the moment, they were too far from Brighton for Chase to be able to psychically contact the rest of his fire team. Commander Ash in his

Phoenix form could drive away the wyvern, if Chase could just get close enough to the city to reach him…

DANGER!

Chase instinctively jerked the steering column in response to his stallion's shriek, spinning the Spitfire on its axis. He was almost too late. The wyvern's acid cloud of breath clipped one wingtip, eating dozens of small holes into its metal skin.

"*Chase!*" Connie must have seen the acrid vapor steaming off the acid-etched metal, but of course she had no idea the real source of the damage. "That's it, I'm taking back control. Three!"

"Connie, no!" Chase shouted frantically. "Please! *Trust me!*"

The wyvern's sleek light, sleek body and disproportionally large wings made it lethally fast, much faster than any dragon he'd ever seen. It took all of Chase's flying skill just to stay ahead of it. It matched him turn for turn, no matter what evasive maneuvers he tried.

"Two!" Connie continued relentlessly, as the sea and sky spun madly around them.

She was going to do it. She was going to take back control. And the instant she leveled out the plane, the wyvern would catch them.

"One!"

There was only one thing Chase could do.

He hit the eject button.

CHAPTER 9

"I have control," Connie said, flipping the override switch. "Chase, you are so—"

In front of her, Chase's cockpit abruptly blew open. Chase stood up on his seat, the wind whipping his hair and flight suit. She distinctly saw him drop his unopened parachute back into the cockpit.

Then he launched himself out of the plane.

"What the actual *fuck?*" Connie breathed in disbelief.

Instinctively, she wheeled the Spitfire over on one wingtip, trying to follow his falling figure. She caught the barest glimpse of him as he plummeted toward the distant waves—and then the Spitfire lurched sickeningly.

To Connie's horror, the strange corrosion she seen earlier was spreading further, Swiss-cheese holes appearing in the surface of the Spitfire's left wing. It was as if invisible acid was eating away at the metal. With a *clunk*, the left flap pinwheeled away, the control lever going dead in her hand.

The plane yawed, tipping to the left. Connie fought to steady it, desperately trying to keep the plane level with only half the controls operational.

Out of nowhere, rain pattered across the cockpit. Instantly, pits appeared in the glass, obstructing her view. Through the warped cockpit, she saw more holes appearing in the nose of the plane, eating into the engine housing.

The Spitfire's engine coughed, twice, and died.

"*No!*" Connie shouted, as if she could keep the plane in the air through sheer willpower.

She knew this plane inside and out. She'd worked on every part of it with her own two hands. Now she used that encyclopedic knowledge, drawing on every trick she knew as the Spitfire fell like a dying star.

Screaming defiance, Connie leveled out the wings, stopping the plane's sickening spin. But it was still falling like a stone, nose-first, straight down. If the plane hit the sea like that, it would be like slamming into solid rock. The Spitfire would explode into a million pieces.

Connie inched the plane's nose up, fighting gravity tooth and nail. Agonizingly slowly, the plane responded, straightening up.

If I can just straighten it out... skim across the water like a skipping stone...

Even as she wrestled with the controls, she knew it was futile. Even hitting the water belly-first rather than nose-first, the plane would still sink—in one piece, perhaps, but it was still doomed.

The only sensible thing to do was to hit the eject button. To abandon the plane, and save herself.

NO!

The hungry sea rushed up, eager to swallow both her and the Spitfire in one mouthful. Closing her eyes, Connie prepared to die with her plane.

Glass shards cascaded over her as the cockpit exploded. Connie had only the briefest impression of something huge and black lunging at her, before it grabbed her by the collar of her flight suit. With a powerful tug, it yanked her straight out of the cockpit.

Connie's feet swinging sickeningly over empty air. The... *thing* had her by the scruff of the neck. Her flight suit cut into her armpits, constraining her as she tried futilely to see what had grabbed her. She dangled as helpless as a kitten carried by its mother.

Then it dropped her.

Screaming, Connie flailed helplessly as she plummeted toward the sea. She only fell for a moment, though, before landing solidly on a broad, warm back. Sobbing in terror, Connie clutched at the horse's gleaming black neck.

Wait a second.

...A horse?

Connie raised her face, unable to believe the evidence of her senses. Yet she was, undeniably, sitting on a horse. A *winged* horse. It had magnificent, iridescent blue-black feathers, like an enormous raven. Its long mane whipped at her face as it flew steadily onwards.

I've died, Connie thought blankly. *I've crashed and burned and now I'm dead. And a big winged horse is carrying me up to Heaven.*

"Are you an angel?" she asked the horse, her voice quavering uncontrollably.

The horse curved its neck, one intelligent black eye looking back at her. It let out an unmistakably amused snort.

And suddenly, impossibly, Connie knew exactly what it was. Or rather, *who* it was.

"*Chase?*"

The horse nickered, tossing its head in a nod.

It was too much. The inexplicable disaster, the crash, Chase turning into a winged horse... her overloaded brain simply gave up, refusing to try to make sense of any of it.

Connie put her cheek against Chase's warm, black neck, closed her eyes, and let him carry her away from it all.

∼

If Connie had been capable of being surprised anymore, she would have been startled by how fast Chase's broad wings carried them back to Brighton. It took less time to get back than it had taken to fly out in the Spitfire. Soon they were once again soaring over the beach and promenade—but this time, no one squinted upward at them, pointing and waving. Pedestrians carried on about their business without even an upward glance as the winged horse's shadow swept over them.

Connie was beyond wondering about everyone's curious incuriosity to the impossibility soaring over their heads. Her mind and body had both gone numb. Only one thought repeated in her head, over and over, inescapably.

I lost my mother's plane.

I lost my mother's plane.

Chase descended in a tight spiral, centered on a tall, elegant apartment block. The building's large, flat roof was beautifully planted with lush rosebushes around a vibrant green lawn. Chase landed so gently, Connie barely felt his hooves touch down on the grass.

The pegasus went down on one knee, stretching out one wing like a ramp. When she didn't move, he bent his neck to look back at her again, the dark eye warm and concerned. He nickered, very softly. His velvet-soft nose nudged her limp foot.

Connie slid gracelessly off his back. Her knees couldn't support her. She would have collapsed in a heap, but suddenly Chase's strong arms were around her.

"It's okay, Connie," he said softly. "I've got you. It's going to be okay."

"It is *not*." Abruptly, irrationally furious, Connie shoved futilely at his hard chest. "It's not okay, Chase! Nothing is ever going to be okay, ever again! I crashed, and I lost my plane, and, and, and you're a fucking horse!"

"Pegasus," Chase corrected.

"Do not *dare* argue zoology with me! Or, or mythology, or whatever fucking field of study is fucking relevant here!" Connie pounded her fist against his shoulder. He didn't flinch. "You should have told me, Chase! I crashed and, and all this time you're some sort of shapeshifter, and you should have told me!"

"I know," Chase said quietly. He kept holding her, no matter how she scratched at him. "I'm sorry."

"You should have told me," she snarled at him. Hot tears burned her eyes. "You lied. You're a fucking liar and I hate you and I never want to see you again."

Then she collapsed against Chase's chest, burying her face in his flight suit as she cried.

He let her sob, just gently cradling her as her tears soaked his chest. She could feel the rapid beat of his heart, strong and reassuring.

When she'd cried herself out, he put a finger under her chin, tipping her face up. His steady black eyes met hers.

"It's not lost, Connie," he said, with utter certainty. "We are going to get your plane back. Trust me."

Connie shook her head. "It's gone. I lost my mother's plane, Chase. The only thing I had left of her, and I destroyed it."

"You *saved* it." Chase took hold of her shoulders, making her face him square on. "I saw it sinking as I carried you away. It went down in one piece. We *will* get it back."

"How?" Connie's mind shied away from estimating the

cost of any recovery mission. "It's at the bottom of the sea. It'll be impossible to recover."

One corner of Chase's mouth quirked. "Connie, you just saw me turn into a pegasus. Are you seriously going to argue with me about what's possible?"

She had to admit, he had a point.

She sniffed, swiping the back of her hand across her dripping nose. "Why didn't you tell me? About the pegasus thing, I mean."

Chase let out his breath in a long sigh. "I wasn't allowed to. The rule in my family is that we're only allowed to reveal what we truly are to our mate after marriage."

"So *that's* why you kept proposing. There really was a secret you weren't allowed to tell me." Connie paused, blinking. "Wait. Your family? Are you all… whatever you are?"

"Shifters. We're called shifters. And no, not my whole family. My mom's side of the family are all ordinary humans. But me, my cousin Killian, and my dad are all pegasi. My uncle was too, but he died when I was little."

"So there's three of you." Connie's mind reeled at the thought of there being other people who could do what Chase did. "Three shifters."

"Um. You should probably be sitting down for this bit." Gently, Chase sank down on the grass, drawing her down with him. "There are a lot more shifters than that. There's a whole hidden society of us."

Connie stared at him. "A whole *society* of people who turn into pegasus…es?"

"Pegasi. And no, of course not." Just as Connie started to relax, he added, "The vast majority of shifters are just ordinary animals—bears, wolves, lions, that sort of thing. Pegasi are very rare. Even rarer than dragons."

"Dragons," Connie echoed faintly.

"Ah, well, yes." Chase raked a hand through his hair,

frowning. "I should probably tell you about those sooner rather than later, seeing as how one was responsible for crashing your plane. Well, I think technically it was a wyvern, but you said you didn't want to get into comparative mythical zoology, so let's just call it a dragon for now. Particularly since *I* can hardly believe it was really a wyvern. I thought they were just a story. Like leprechauns or unicorns."

"Oh, good," Connie said, unable to control the hysterical edge to her voice. "Everything is back to normal. You've gone back to talking a mile a minute without making the slightest bit of sense."

"I'm still trying to make sense of it myself." Chase fell silent for a moment, his eyebrows drawing together in thought. "Connie, do your hands feel cold?"

Connie blinked at the apparent non sequitur, then realized that she was shivering. "All of me feels cold."

Chase swore under his breath. "I'm an idiot. You're going into shock. Hold on a second, I need to talk to someone."

She expected him to pull out his phone, but instead he just stared off into the distance, his eyes going unfocused. After a moment, he nodded.

"Right," he said. Before she knew what was happening, he'd scooped her up, without any apparent effort. "Hugh—he's our paramedic—says you need to lie down and warm up. Let's get you inside."

There were so many questions to ask—how he could have a conversation with someone who wasn't even there, how she could have failed to see a dragon attacking her plane, where the hypothetical dragon could have come from in the first place—but abruptly, she was just too tired. She leaned her head against Chase's shoulder, closing her eyes.

"Here we are," she heard him say, and then she was sinking into a deep, soft bed. She didn't resist as he pulled off her shoes and draped a thick down comforter over her. "Feeling any better?"

"Still cold," Connie managed to get out, through her chattering teeth.

The bed dipped as he slid under the cover next to her. He curled around her, fitting his long, lean body against the curves of her back. Pressed against his warm torso, Connie's shivers finally started to ease. She burrowed her head under the covers, like a little kid hiding from monsters in the dark. Just for a moment, all she wanted to do was pretend that none of it had ever happened.

As her own shivers subsided, Connie became aware that *Chase* was shaking, ever so slightly.

"Hey," she said. "Are *you* okay?"

"I thought I'd lost you. I was fighting off the wyvern, and then I saw the plane going down, and I didn't think I was going to get to you in time..." He tightened his grip on her, burying his face in her hair. "Oh God, Connie, I nearly lost you."

She rolled over in his arms, their faces only inches away from each other. She could tell he was trying to control his expression, but his black eyes were raw and vulnerable. For all his strength and uncanny powers, it was clear that the mere thought of losing her struck him to the heart.

"But you didn't lose me." Connie put her hand on the side of his face, feeling how warm he was, how *alive*. "I'm here. We're both here."

Overcome by a sudden, powerful need, she leaned in and kissed him. He crushed her against his strong body, his mouth devouring hers desperately, as if he couldn't bear to ever let her go again.

She had a deep, instinctive desire to reaffirm life in the most basic of ways after her brush with death. Connie fumbled with the zip of his flight suit, jerking it open. The heat of his skin was the only thing that could drive away the ice in her soul.

She slid her palm down his muscled abs, and under the waistband of his boxers. He was hard already, so thick she could barely get her hand around him. Her pussy throbbed, desperate to be filled, as she worked him fast and urgently.

He knew exactly what she wanted. His powerful hands ripped her own flight suit off, the tough material tearing as easily as damp tissue paper. He gathered her breasts in his hands, pinching and teasing her erect nipples through the lace cups of her bra with delicious roughness. His mouth was hard on hers, demanding, taking.

She squeezed her fist around his cock, feeling the contrast of the velvet-soft skin over the iron-hard shaft. He growled low in his throat, his hips jerking involuntarily. Breaking off from the kiss for a moment, he grabbed her buttocks, lifting her up and spreading her wide.

He didn't even bother to tear off her panties. The wide head of his cock shoved the thin silk to one side, pushing deep into her wet folds with a single powerful thrust. His thick shaft impaled her to her core, stretching her with a pleasure so intense it was almost painful.

Unlike last time, he gave her no time to adjust to his overwhelming size. He thrust savagely, uncontrollably into her. Connie arched her back, clenching around his demanding cock with equal passion, overwhelmed by sensation. It was exactly what she needed, to lose herself utterly, even if only for a moment.

"Never again," Chase snarled, his fingers digging into her hips almost hard enough to bruise. "Never losing you. Never. Mine. Mine!"

Yes! Connie's soul sang back, echoing his fierce possessiveness. Every fiber of her being yearned to tell him *yes, yes!*

She was his, and he was hers, and nothing would ever separate them.

Yes.

Yet there was still a bit of her that held back. After a lifetime of having to be the cautious one, there was always a cold-eyed part of her mind that dispassionately evaluated every situation.

That sensible inner voice whispered that it didn't matter how urgent his body was on hers now, how fervently he gasped promises. In a day or two, someone else would catch his eye. It would be someone else's ear he whispered into, someone else's body he strained against.

When Chase gasped "Mine!" she knew he meant it... for now.

But if she replied *yes*, she would mean it forever.

Connie bit down hard on Chase's shoulder, stifling the words that wanted to rise in her throat, even as ecstasy swept her away.

CHAPTER 10

"So," Chase said softly into Connie's ear, some time later. "Constance West, will you marry me?"

Connie raised her head from his shoulder to give him a quizzical look. "I already know you're a shifter. I thought you only needed me to marry you so that you'd be allowed to tell me the truth."

"That was one reason." Chase traced the soft curves of her bare arm, wanting to memorize every inch of her beautiful body. "But mostly, I just really, really want to marry you. So? Will you?"

Connie blew out an exasperated breath. Without answering, she rolled out of the bed, searching the floor for her discarded clothes.

From a flat-out refusal, to a hesitation before refusing, to no answer. Definite progress!

Connie scowled at him. "What are you grinning about?"

Chase attempted to school his face into an appropriately somber expression, without much success. "Nothing. Just admiring the view."

Connie shot him a glare, then held up her ripped flight suit. "This is completely ruined. What am I going to wear?"

Chase slid out of bed himself. "You can borrow something of mine. This way."

"Chase, you're about a foot taller than me, not to mention a completely different shape," Connie said dubiously as he led her into his walk-in closet. "I really don't think that you're going to have anything that will fit me."

"Um." Chase slid hangers of shirts and suits aside, revealing the very back corner of the closet. "Actually, I do."

Connie blinked for a moment at the row of women's clothes. Every one was immaculate and unworn, and every one was exactly her size.

Then she groaned, rolling her eyes. "Of course you have a closet full of dresses. Heaven forbid one of your many one-night stands should have to do the Walk of Shame in last night's outfit."

"No, of course not!" Chase said indignantly. "I bought them for you. Or, well, because they reminded me of you. Sometimes I'd see something, and think *Connie would like that*, or *That could have been made for Connie*. And then I'd have to buy it. Because it was a way of showing myself that I hadn't given up hope. That one day I'd find you again, and give you these clothes, and see you in them."

"I don't know whether that's incredibly sweet or incredibly creepy." Connie sighed, and started to flick through hangers. "But I can't deny that it's convenient. I notice, by the way, that you mainly appear to have been reminded of me by lingerie."

"What can I say?" Chase grinned unrepentantly at her. "I'm an optimist."

"Chase, people who buy lottery tickets are optimists," Connie retorted as she selected a leaf-green, silk summer dress that perfectly matched the shade of her eyes. "People who go around acting as if they've already won the lottery are delusional."

Chase started getting dressed himself. "What about people who've won the lottery, but then drop the ticket, so they end up walking around backward peering at the ground, and everyone thinks they're crazy, but actually they're just taking entirely logical steps to try to recover what they lost?"

"Trust you to run away with a metaphor," Connie muttered from the depths of the dress. "You know, your big secret doesn't actually explain very much. Just because you turn into a big winged horse sometimes doesn't explain why you're so... *you*."

Chase paused in doing up his jeans.

Then he smacked himself on the forehead. "I'm a complete idiot. I forgot to tell you the most important part. The bit that explains everything."

Connie turned to face him, putting her hands on her hips. "Now this, I've got to hear."

Chase briefly wondered whether to suggest that they went up to his rooftop rose garden, for a more romantic setting. His closet had not been the backdrop he'd pictured for the most important conversation of his life.

He settled for going down on one knee instead. "Connie—"

Connie hid both her hands behind her back. "If you propose again, I swear to God I will hit you."

"This isn't another proposal. This is the reason for all the proposals. The reason I've been mad about you ever since I first saw you." Chase took a deep breath, looking earnestly up at her wary face. "All shifters have a mate. Just one single person, in all the world, who's their perfect partner. You're *my* mate, Connie. I knew it the instant we first met. And from that moment on, I've only had eyes for you. You're the only one for me, and you always will be."

Connie looked down at him, her expression completely unreadable, for a long, long moment that seemed to stretch into eternity.

Then, "Do you think I'm a *complete* idiot?" Turning on her heel, she stormed out of the closet.

"Wait!" Chase scrambled to his feet.

That didn't go quite the way I thought it would.

He caught up with her halfway across his bedroom, seizing her arm to stop her in her tracks. "I know it might sound unbelievable to you, but—"

"It *might* sound unbelievable?" Connie whirled on him, her cheeks flushed red and her eyes glittering with barely-restrained tears. "Of course it sounds unbelievable! There's some mystic force which bound you to me the instant you saw me, huh? I'm the one person in all the world for you, am I? Well, that *completely* explains everything. Except for the fact that *you cheated on me!*"

"As I keep trying to explain to you, I *didn't!*" Chase held onto her wrist. She wasn't getting away from him this time. "Connie, I swear, I did not cheat on you. I know what it looked like, but I would *never* cheat on you."

"Liar," Connie snarled.

"I'm telling the truth! I don't remember anything from that night, apart from going to the club and having one drink. I don't know what happened after that."

"Oh, come on. We both know what happened," Connie snapped. "You got blind, stinking drunk, and couldn't resist a pair of pretty girls. You've always been a playboy, and you always will be. I was stupid to think that you'd ever change."

"I'm telling you, you're my mate! It's physically impossible for me to have cheated on you!"

Chase had spent years trying to work out what had actually happened that night, but had drawn a complete blank. The women had sworn that he'd picked them up and had sex with them, but he knew, *knew* that they had to have been lying. There was no way he could have done that, no matter how drunk he'd been.

He fumbled for excuses, knowing that they sounded weak even as he said them. "Maybe they were trying to blackmail me, or, or it was some sort of prank, or—Killian!"

"Your cousin?" Connie blinked. "Are you seriously trying to blame everything on your *cousin*?"

"No, of course not. I mean, he's here!" Chase pulled her toward the door that led to the rooftop garden, his heart rising again. "He said he'd come visit, but I didn't think it would be this soon. This is great!"

If anyone could help fix the mess he'd made, it was his cousin.

∽

Chase took the stairs two at a time, hauling Connie in his wake despite her spluttered protests. His pegasus's special ability to sense people told him that Killian was spiraling in toward the landing area. Chase burst out onto the rooftop garden just in time to see his cousin's hooves settling onto the grass.

"Killian!" Chase waved frantically with his free arm. "Excellent timing! Tell Connie I'm not lying about being fated mates!"

Connie stared at him as if he'd gone mad. So did Killian.

"Chase," Connie said, not even glancing at the enormous winged horse occupying a large part of the lawn. "There's no one here."

Of course, she can't see him.

Killian was still in pegasus form, his stormcloud-gray

wings half-open as if he was wondering whether to take off again. *I'm sorry,* he psychically sent to Chase. *Have I arrived at a bad time?*

"No, this is perfect," Chase replied out loud, so as not to exclude Connie from the conversation. "Go ahead and shift. It's okay, Connie knows everything now. I had to shift to save her life. That's allowed by the law, right?"

Killian let out a snort that morphed into a deep groan as he shifted back into human form. "Trust you to find a loophole."

Connie yelped, jumping backward as—from her perspective—Killian materialized out of thin air.

"Connie." Killian held out his hand to her, flashing a quick smile. "It's nice to see you again. I am very sorry to have to interrupt you on what I understand has been a very traumatic day, but I needed to check that my fool cousin was all right after the crash."

Chase cocked his head to one side. "How did you know about that so fast?"

"You know I always keep a close eye on you. It's why you're still flying around despite years of flinging yourself enthusiastically into every disaster you can find." Despite his dry words, Killian's gray eyes were concerned as he looked Chase up and down. "*Are* you in one piece? Not many shifters go wingtip-to-wingtip with a wyvern and live to tell the tale."

Connie, who had been looking back and forth between them like a spectator at a very mysterious tennis game, flinched at his words. "So it really was a wyvern that attacked my plane?"

Killian nodded gravely. "I haven't had much time to look into the matter, but in the past I've heard rumors that there's a wyvern shifter who works for criminal organizations.

From what I know of your situation, I strongly suspect Sammy Smiles was behind the attack."

"How would Sammy Smiles know a wyvern?" Connie asked, sounding lost.

"I didn't have time to tell you before, but Sammy Smiles is a shifter too," Chase told Connie. He hated to drop all this on her at once, but he knew she was tough. "He's a shark. The Parliament of Shifters—that's a sort of government for our kind— has a tough time controlling sea-based shifters. Sammy's got a whole criminal gang made up of sharks and the like."

"Oh," Connie said. He could practically see her mind racing as she digested this new information. "My plane... it's in the sea. If he can turn into a shark, that means he'll be able to find it, right?"

"Yes, but we're going to get there first," Chase said confidently. "I contacted a friend while I was carrying you back to land. He's already on his way to your plane, and he'll keep it safe. No shark will get past him."

Killian shot him a curious look, but didn't ask for details. "I haven't been able to locate Sammy Smiles yet, I'm afraid. I've never met him, nor met anyone who has, so my pegasus can't track him."

"Mine can." Chase bared his teeth in a feral smile. "And I'm going to pay him a little visit."

Killian sighed. "I was afraid you were going to say that. I suppose there's absolutely nothing I can say to dissuade you."

"Nothing whatsoever," Chase agreed cheerfully.

Killian sighed again. "Then I'll stand guard over your mate while you do so. I'm assuming even you aren't daft enough to take her with you on a trip down a shark's gullet."

"I'm *not* his mate," Connie said sharply.

"Ah." Killian's eyes flicked from her to Chase and back again. "Connie, my idiot cousin has a remarkable ability to stuff all four hooves down his own throat when he's trying to explain himself. Perhaps I could be of assistance? I would be happy to answer any questions you have about shifters in general. Or, indeed, Chase in particular."

You are only going to tell her good things about me, right? Chase sent anxiously to him.

Do you want the conversation to last more than thirty seconds? Killian sent back acerbically.

Connie considered Killian, her expression warming a little. "Yes. Thank you, I would like that."

Killian turned back to Chase. "Connie and I will be fine here. I'll sense if the wyvern approaches again, and get her to safety. Are you ready to go see Sammy now?"

"Not yet." Chase clapped his hands together decisively. "First, we all have to go to the pub."

CHAPTER 11

Connie stared up at the full moon painted on the dusty sign outside the old, whitewashed building. "When he said we were going to the pub," she muttered to Killian, "I thought he was joking."

"So did I." Chase's cousin let out a long-suffering sigh as he held the oak door open for her. "I really should know better by now."

They followed Chase into the pub. Connie was startled by how cozy and clean it was inside, a stark contrast to the grimy, forbidding exterior. Even though it was only early evening, the pub was well-populated by a mixed crowd, lounging at the polished bar or relaxing in mismatched antique chairs.

A general cry of "Chase!" went up as soon as he showed his face. Chase dispensed cheery waves and a few words of greeting as they cut through the crowd.

"I take it you're a regular," Connie said to him.

Privately, she was a little surprised. She would have thought Chase would favor the sort of sleazy gambling dens that her father liked to frequent. But this pub was clearly intended for socializing, rather than hardcore drinking and shady deals.

"The Full Moon is the local shifter hangout," Chase said. "At least, it's the respectable shifter hangout. Rose makes sure everyone behaves themselves. Right, Rose?"

"That's right," the curvy, kind-eyed woman behind the bar agreed amiably.

Personally, Connie had never seen anyone less intimidating in her life. But for all she knew, Rose could turn into a bear or a tiger or who-knew-what. She still could barely believe that there was an entire society of shifters that she'd never even suspected existed.

"Connie, Killian, this is Rose Swanmay," Chase introduced them. "She runs this place. Rose, this is my cousin Killian, down from London. And this is Connie. You don't need me to tell you who *she* is."

Rose smiled at Killian, then did a double-take at Connie. "Your mate!"

Chase shot Connie a *See? I told you so* sort of smirk. She rolled her eyes at him.

"It's lovely to meet you, Connie." Rose looked thoughtful for a moment. "Just to check... you do know he's a shifter, don't you?"

"Yes," Connie replied. "And just to clarify, I am *not* his mate."

"Well, actually, I'm afraid you are," Rose said, her soft lips quirking. "Congratulations, and condolences. I'll always have a free drink and a sympathetic ear ready for you."

"Hey!" Chase protested. "I'm not that bad."

"Yes, you are," Killian muttered.

"The boys are upstairs waiting for you," Rose said to Chase. "Not that you need me to tell you that. Shall I get you the usual?"

Chase shook his head. "I'm just dropping by. Thanks, Rose."

"Why *are* we here, Chase?" Killian asked, as they followed Chase to the back of the pub.

"Because I need to meet with some people," he replied, leading them up a narrow flight of stairs. "And I wanted you to meet them, too."

Chase opened a door, revealing a small private room. Four people were seated around a small circular table. Connie recognized Commander Ash, but she didn't know the other three.

"Connie, Killian, this is my fire crew," Chase said, beaming. Then he frowned. "Or at least, some of my fire crew. Commander, where's Griff?"

"I am afraid he is indisposed," said Commander Ash, rising to his feet. "The usual problem. He sends his apologies. Ms. West, I am pleased to meet you again in, ah, better circumstances."

"Likewise," Connie muttered, unable to help blushing as she remembered their first meeting.

At least I'm wearing clothes this time.

At Ash's gesture, she seated herself gingerly on a free chair. Besides Ash, there were two other men and one woman present. Connie lifted her chin, forcing down a wave of self-consciousness as she met their stares.

Commander Ash was as coolly unreadable as the last time Connie had met him, but a muscular, red-headed man was openly curious. The curvy black woman snuggled under the red-head's arm caught Connie's eye and gave her a conspiratorial wink. In contrast, a young, handsome man with bleached white hair and pale blue eyes was scowling at Connie as if she'd personally offended him somehow.

"Griff's sick again?" Chase frowned as he plopped down

onto a chair next to her. "Damn. I could really use his talent. Hugh, can't you do anything to help him?"

"If I could, don't you think I would have already?" the white-haired man snapped. He rubbed his forehead as if he had a migraine. "I can't heal everything."

Commander Ash raised one hand. "Before we go any further, there is something I must clarify first. Ms. West, are you aware that Chase is a shifter?"

"Yes, of course," Connie replied, frowning. "Why do people keep asking me that?"

"Truly, it is a mystery." Chase looked across at the red-haired man, clearly struggling to keep a straight face. "Any ideas, Dai?"

Dai's ears turned nearly as red as his hair. He appeared to find something intensely interesting about the ceiling.

The woman next to him laughed. "It's one of those annoying in-jokes," she explained to Connie. Her accent marked her as a fellow American, making Connie feel a little less out of place. "When *I* met the crew, there were… a few misunderstandings." She held out her hand. "Virginia Drake. I'm Dai's mate."

"See!" Chase exclaimed triumphantly, as Connie shook Virginia's hand. "Independent evidence, right before your eyes! Mates *do* exist!"

"And apparently Chase is managing to make even more of a mess of things than I did," Dai murmured. He had a pleasant, deep voice with a lilting Welsh accent. "I'm not sure whether to be comforted or alarmed."

"Personally, I'm past alarmed, and well into terrified," Killian said dryly.

Ash leaned forward a little, the slight movement instantly silencing the banter. "Secondly. Are you aware that we are all —Virginia excepted—shifters as well?"

Connie shook her head, but she wasn't actually surprised.

Even though the three men didn't look anything like each other—Dai huge and muscular, Hugh lean and elegant, Ash contained and controlled—there was something similar about them. On some deep, instinctive level, she could sense the power that they possessed.

She cast a sideways look at Chase, realizing that he too had that indefinable feral aura. Killian did as well, though to a lesser extent.

"Let me introduce you both to everyone." Chase waved a hand at Ash. "For those who haven't met him yet, I present Fire Commander Ash. He's the Phoenix, and yes, that's 'the', not 'a'. There's only ever one. "

Killian looked at Ash with awe, and a touch of wariness. "It's an honor, sir."

"He's kind of a big deal in the shifter community," Chase informed Connie, as though this wasn't obvious. "Oh, also, he can burn anything, and I mean *anything*. A slightly odd trait for a firefighter, if you ask me, but it's surprisingly handy."

Moving on, Chase pointed in the direction of the handsome white-haired man in the corner. "Hugh here is our paramedic, and a puzzle wrapped in a mystery wrapped in an enigma wrapped in an incredibly cranky attitude. Please question him repeatedly and persistently about what sort of shifter he is, because he says if *I* ask him one more time, he'll never heal me again."

Hugh leaned away from Chase's finger, his pained scowl deepening. "I am really looking forward to the next time you crash and break a bone."

Chase ignored this. He waved his hand at the huge redheaded man. "And this is Daifydd Drake, but everyone calls him Dai because Welsh names are ridiculous, and I say that even as an Irishman. He's a red dragon—don't worry, he's a nice dragon, not like the one who attacked your plane,

Connie. He's fireproof, which is a very useful thing for a firefighter to be, obviously. And next to him is Virginia, his lovely mate who isn't a firefighter or a shifter but who *is* extremely perceptive and clever and who incidentally I hope is only going to tell you good things about me."

There was a moment of silence.

"And if you were able to follow all of *that*," Dai said ruefully to Connie, "then you really must be his mate."

Frighteningly, Connie had. Navigating through a conversation with Chase was like flying through a storm—there was no point trying to impose your own course. You just had to ride it out and see where you ended up.

"Everyone, this is my cousin Killian, who is a pegasus and Chief Financial Officer of Tiernach Enterprises," Chase said, jerking his thumb casually at Killian. "Don't ask him about his job unless you're suffering from insomnia. Really, don't."

Killian lifted a hand in a brief, embarrassed wave. "Please let me reassure you all that I am nothing like my cousin."

"And, saving the best for last, this is Connie West." Chase made a sweeping gesture at Connie like a sculptor unveiling his masterpiece. "She is the most amazing and beautiful and brave woman in the entire world, and I'm going to marry her just as soon as she stops yelling at me whenever I propose."

Connie jabbed him sharply in the arm with her elbow.

"Ow," Chase said, cheerfully. "As you can see, I've got some way to go with that. Which is why I need all of your help. Oh, and also with the wyvern and the race and all, of course."

"So I take it Chase has already told you about what happened with my plane?" Connie said, looking round at the group.

Commander Ash inclined his head. "Yes. Mythic shifters —those, like ourselves, who turn into creatures out of legend rather than ordinary animals—are able to communicate telepathically with each other. Chase has already briefed us on your situation. If there is anything we can do to assist, we are at your service."

"Thank you. I appreciate that, truly." She shot Chase a sidelong look. "Though I'm not sure how you *can* help. I don't know what Chase is thinking."

"Who ever does?" murmured Killian. "Do you actually have a plan, Chase, or are you making it up as you go along as usual?"

"I have a plan," Chase said indignantly. He hesitated. "Or... I did. Without Griff, I'm going to have to improvise a bit."

Hugh rolled his eyes. "Oh, joy."

"Who's this Griff?" Connie asked.

"Another member of our team," Chase said. "Or, well, technically he *was* a member. He's a dispatcher now, since he had to retire from firefighting. I wanted him to come with me to talk to Sammy Smiles. He can tell if people are lying, you see."

"So he's a shifter too?" Connie said.

All four firefighters exchanged glances. "Yes and no," Ash said. "But that's for Griff to explain, if he wishes."

"Chase, were you going to introduce her to John, too?" asked Dai. "Is he on his way?"

"No, he's tied up at the moment." Chase turned to Connie. "John's the friend that I mentioned earlier, the one who I asked to watch over your Spitfire. He'll stand guard over it until we can get it out of the water. He's a sea dragon shifter, so he can stay underwater indefinitely."

Commander Ash cleared his throat. "Unfortunately, that is not precisely true. John has duties on dry land, as do the rest of the crew. Ms. West, while we can help you in our free time, I am afraid that I cannot allow your predicament to compromise the safety of this city. Our responsibilities must come first."

"But I need John to help with the plane," Chase objected. "And that wyvern is still on the loose. I'll need Dai tomorrow to guard the race."

Ash shook his head. "Alpha Fire Team is scheduled to be on duty tomorrow, and the crew must be at their stations."

"But—"

"No." Ash didn't raise his voice, but his tone was utterly final.

Dai gave Chase a sympathetic glance and a slight shrug. It was clear he wasn't going to go against his Commander's orders.

Chase crossed his arms, slouching back in his chair. "Well, *I'm* not going to be on call," he snapped at Ash. "I'll be busy with the race. You'll have to find someone else to drive the truck."

"Chase," Killian hissed. "Do you *want* to get yourself fired?"

The Commander made a slight, gracious motion with one hand, brushing aside Chase's rudeness. "Given the circumstances, I can extend Chase some leeway. But I too have superiors, and they are starting to ask questions about my driver. Chase, I have managed to keep you off the duty roster during the air race, citing extraordinary personal circumstances, but you *must* be available immediately afterwards. I cannot cover for your absences any further than that."

Chase drummed his fingers on the tabletop. "You won't have to," he said abruptly. "Because I'm quitting."

"*What?*" Hugh and Dai exclaimed together.

Ash's neutral expression didn't change, but he went very still. "Chase, please do not make a decision in haste."

Chase shook his head, his jaw set stubbornly. "You say

that our responsibilities to the city have to come first. Not for me. My mate has to come first, every time."

"Of course everyone here understands that, Chase," Virginia said, touching his hand lightly. "But you can't just quit. The team needs you. And besides, you *love* being a firefighter."

"After all, where else can you get paid for driving like a lunatic?" Dai added, his tone light but his green eyes deeply concerned.

"Ah, who cares about all that?" Chase waved a hand airily. "It's not like I need the job. All I have to do is call my dad, and I'm CEO-in-training of Tiernach Enterprises. Right, Killian?"

"Your father will be thrilled," Killian said, though he himself looked extremely un-thrilled at the prospect of working for his cousin. "He's always hoped that you'd grow out of your reckless phase and take your rightful place in the family business."

"Right. Can't play with cars and planes forever." Chase straightened up, copying Killian's formal, business-like pose. "And I've got to think about providing for my mate, after all. Financial services pays a lot better than merely saving lives."

Despite his flippant words, Connie could tell how much his resignation had actually cost him. His shoulders were set in a tight, unhappy line.

"You don't have to do this for me," she said to him quietly.

He met her eyes levelly, his own utterly serious. "Yes, I do. I'm not losing you again. Whatever happens, wherever you go, I'm going too."

Connie bristled. "Don't I get a say in that?"

His mouth quirked. "Well, you get to decide whether I'm in your bed or pining after you from a distance, but other than that… no, not really."

"I'm afraid that really is how shifters are, when it comes

to our mates," Dai said, with a quick, tender glance at Virginia. "Once you've met her, that's it. There'll never be anyone else for you, ever."

Connie folded her arms. "That's not my experience."

Chase flinched. "That's why I brought you here. I want you to talk to Dai and Virginia about being mated, while I'm busy with Sammy. Please? It was difficult for them at first too."

"I know how strange it is to us ordinary humans." Virginia smiled sympathetically at Connie. "So I think I might be able to explain things better than Chase can."

"A *parrot* can explain things better than Chase can," Hugh muttered.

"Hugh, on the other hand, can't stand being touched and hates all of humanity. This does not make him a good source of relationship advice," Chase told Connie as he stood up. "But he will protect you, along with Dai. And Killian, too. You'll be safe here."

Dai's eyes flashed fiery gold for a second. "No mere wyvern will get past me. I can promise you that."

Chase clapped him on the shoulder, then looked back at Ash. "I was going to ask for your help with Sammy Smiles. But given the circumstances..."

"Even if I will no longer be your Commander," the Phoenix said, rising, "I will always be your friend. How can I assist?"

Chase grinned, though his usual bright sparkle was subdued. "You can eat dinner."

CHAPTER 12

Chase found Sammy Smiles enjoying a lobster dinner at an upmarket waterside restaurant overlooking the Brighton Marina.

Or rather, he *was* enjoying his dinner, until Chase walked in and punched him right in the face.

The maître d'hôtel squawked in outrage, while half a dozen shark shifters scattered through the restaurant shot to their feet. Two tiger sharks seized Chase's arms in crushing grips.

"Well, that sure makes my life easier," Sammy said, dabbing at his bleeding nose with a napkin. "Thanks, son. You're going to be watching the air race from a jail cell. *If* you're lucky."

From the doorway, Commander Ash cleared his throat softly.

The two shifters holding Chase's arms abruptly let go. Another shark shifter hastily blew out the lit candle decorating the dining table.

"Commander Ash." Sammy's eyes narrowed. "What an unexpected pleasure. Can't see any fires here, though."

The Commander gave him a courteous nod, then turned to the flustered maître d'. "Table for one, please."

The maître d' dithered, looking from Ash to Sammy. "Er... shall I call the police, sir?"

"No need. Just a little misunderstanding," Sammy told him. He stared hard at Chase. "Pull up a chair, son. You've got my attention."

I believe that I should remind you that I am forbidden from burning them, even if they become violent. Commander Ash sent telepathically to Chase, so that the sharks couldn't hear. *Under the terms of my asylum, as granted by the Parliament of Shifters, I may only use my powers against other shifters if they commit arson.*

I know that, Chase sent back as he seated himself at Sammy's table. *And I'm pretty sure Sammy knows that, too.*

Commander Ash appeared to be completely focused on his menu. *Then I fail to see how my presence can act as a deterrent.*

Chase grinned, watching the shark shifters. They were all eyeing the Commander as though he was a ticking time bomb. The Phoenix was such a stickler for following the rules, it never even occurred to him that other people could worry that he *might* break them.

I know you don't, he sent to Ash. *Trust me. Try the shrimp, it's excellent.*

"So, son." Sammy leaned back in his chair, his eyes suspicious above his gleaming smile. "What's this about?"

"You know very well." Chase's own smile sharpened, showing his teeth. "You tried to kill my mate."

Sammy spread his stubby hands. "Pretty certain I haven't tried to kill anyone, let alone your mate. I don't even know who the lucky lady is."

"Oh, but you do." Chase's rage burned in his blood. His pegasus was desperate to trample Sammy into a bloody pulp.

"Shane West's daughter, Constance. She was flying his Spitfire when your hired assassin attacked. It's only thanks to me that she isn't at the bottom of the sea along with the plane."

The front legs of Sammy's chair crashed down. "My Spitfire is *where?*"

"Don't play the innocent with me," Chase snarled. "Bad news, Sammy. It takes a lot more than a wyvern to knock me out of the sky."

The Great White shark shifter stared at him, to all appearances genuinely baffled. "Son, I haven't the faintest idea what you're rattling on about."

This is why I really needed Griff...

If Griff had been here, they would have been able to get Sammy arrested—the shifter police force knew Griff well enough to act on his testimony without hesitation. But without the half-eagle shifter's special ability, Chase had no way of proving that Sammy was lying.

Just got to keep charging ahead. Keep Sammy off-balance, in the hopes he'll trip up.

"I know it was you," Chase said. "You're the only one with a motive. And I have iron-clad proof that you hired that wyvern."

"You'll regret it if you try to catch me with fake evidence, son. My lawyer is a real shark." Sammy rubbed his chin, his expression unreadable. "Wyvern, you say? Boys, do any of you know a wyvern shifter?"

A general murmur of "No, boss" ran around the table, as Sammy's goons shook their heads.

"Pity." Sammy snapped a claw off his lobster. "I'm suddenly real eager to make one's acquaintance."

A couple of Sammy's goons quietly got up, abandoning their half-eaten dinners. With the speed of sharks following a blood-trail, they headed out the door.

Gone to find the wyvern... to warn it?

Chase knew that the wyvern wasn't in Brighton at the moment—his pegasus senses covered the entire city, and there was no hint of the wyvern's distinctive scent. But Sammy knew of his ability. No doubt he'd told his hired assassin to stay out of Chase's range.

He was tempted to follow the shifters immediately, in the hopes that they would lead him to the wyvern. But he wasn't finished with Sammy yet.

Yes, his stallion told him. *Fight this one, kill him, now! He threatened our mate!*

Sammy appeared not to have noticed his henchmen's departure. "You say this wyvern knocked the Spitfire down into the drink, son?"

"That's right," Chase said, trying to ignore his stallion's bloodlust. "And if you try to steal it, you'll get a big surprise."

"I remember your sea dragon friend. So he's guarding my plane. That's real neighborly of him." Sammy waved the lobster claw at one of his remaining thugs. "Send the nice dragon a fruit basket from me, will you?"

"It's not *your* plane," Chase snapped. "And it's not going to be."

"Well now." Sammy leaned back again. "Seems to me that it is. The bet's that West's Spitfire will win the Rydon Cup. Even a hotshot pegasus is going to have a mite of trouble winning a race with a plane that's underwater."

Gotcha!

"Thank you, Sammy." Chase stood up. "That's *exactly* what I needed to hear you say. West's Spitfire will win the Rydon Cup, I can promise you that. And I can promise you one other thing."

"And what might that be, son?" Sammy's eyebrows rose.

Chase leaned on the table, staring Sammy straight in the eye. "If you ever, *ever* try to harm my mate again, in any way, no matter how indirectly, I will find you. I will hunt you down wherever you try to hide, and then I will personally kick your teeth out through your asshole."

The shark shifters to either side of Chase bristled, then hesitated. They glanced over at Commander Ash, who was peacefully buttering a bread roll.

"No need, boys." Sammy waved his shifters back down again. "It's understandable that our pegasus friend here is mite het up, seeing as how some pond scum has been threatening his mate. I'm willing to cut him a little slack."

Casually, Sammy popped the lobster claw into his mouth. The thick shell splintered as the shark shifter bit down.

"A *little* slack," Sammy said, pulling the cracked claw out of his mouth. He idly started picking out bits of lobster meat. "I'm as pained as you are, son, I really am. To think of that beautiful plane all tangled up in seaweed... it breaks my heart. I sure would like to have words with the kind of monster that would ruin a noble warbird like that. You let me know if you find this wyvern shifter, you hear?"

"Oh, don't worry," Chase said. "I will."

CHAPTER 13

"And that's how we met," Virginia concluded. She exchanged a long, warm look with Dai, their intertwined hands resting on the top of the table.

Connie felt a little embarrassed to be watching them, like she was intruding on their privacy. There was a deep, unspoken intimacy between the pair that made her feel like a spare wheel. From the way Killian had apparently become fascinated by something at the other end of the bar, he felt just as awkward.

"If you're going to stare at each other like that, for God's sake, get a room," Hugh snapped. He had his back pressed to the wall, as far from Dai and Virginia as he could get without being on the other side of it. "You've already spoken quite long enough about the joys of being mated. No need to provide us with a physical demonstration as well."

Connie couldn't help but notice that the paramedic was keeping a marked distance from her, too. When they'd left the private room to head to the more comfortable main bar area, she'd accidentally brushed against Hugh going down the stairs. He'd jerked away from her touch as if she was radioactive. At least he seemed to have the same distaste for Dai and Virginia as well. The only person he didn't seem to mind being near was Killian, oddly.

Virginia just smiled, clearly well used to ignoring Hugh's surly attitude. "So, any questions?" she asked Connie.

Connie had a hunch that there was a lot more to the story than Virginia had revealed. "I don't mean to pry, but… did you ever doubt your feelings for each other?"

One corner of Virginia's mouth curved upward. "Well, I did flee from him in terror one time."

"Believe me, my mate is very kindly painting me in a much better light than I deserve," Dai said wryly. "I was so cautious when it came to telling her the truth about myself, I very nearly lost everything. I'm glad Chase hasn't made *that* mistake, at least."

"Not talking enough," Killian muttered, "has never been one of Chase's problems."

"But *you* never doubted your feelings for Virginia," Connie said to Dai.

"Never," the dragon shifter said, with utter conviction. "Once you meet your mate, that's it. You just know, bone-deep, that there's no one else for you."

"And that's the way that Chase feels about you," Virginia added, smiling at Connie.

Connie scowled down into her drink. "That's how he *says* he feels."

Killian shot her a sidelong glance. "Could I ask you something?" he said to Dai. "Does Chase have a… reputation?"

"Chase has a *lot* of reputations," Dai said, his tone dry. "Were you thinking of anything in particular?"

Killian sighed. "A reputation when it comes to women."

Of course. He knows why I left Chase.

Killian had been the one who'd called Connie on that horrible morning, three years ago, to ask if she knew where his cousin was. He'd always had to look out for Chase, the same way she'd always had to rescue her dad from *his* drunken mishaps.

Killian had begged her to go make sure that Chase had gotten home safely, so sincerely that Connie had swallowed her hurt pride at being stood up and done so. And so she'd walked in on Chase in the aftermath of one of his infamous one-night-stands... the ones that he'd sworn he'd given up.

And if she really was his mate, he *should* have given them up, without hesitation or a second thought.

"Sorry, Connie," Killian added, throwing her an apologetic look. "But Virginia's story has made it clear that it's best if everyone knows the truth."

"No, that's all right. I want to know too." She turned back to Dai. "You can be honest."

From the conflicted expression on the dragon shifter's face, he really, *really* didn't want to be honest.

"If you know Chase at all, you know that he does everything at top speed and with excessive enthusiasm," Virginia said. She shrugged. "As far as I'm aware, that includes his love life. But does it matter what he's done in the past? *You're* his future."

"That's right," Dai said, shooting his mate a grateful look for rescuing him. "As a shifter, I can promise you that Chase will be true to you. You're his mate. He'll never look at another woman again, now that he's met you."

Killian's mouth tightened. "Chase met Connie three years ago."

Connie avoided Dai and Virginia's shocked stares. Hot humiliation rose in her cheeks. She stared down at the table, unable to speak past the tight pain closing her throat.

"That's not possible," Dai said blankly.

"My cousin is the most impossible person in the world," Killian said, sounding resigned. "But I didn't think that even he could break something as sacred as the mate-bond. Connie, I'm so, so sorry. You're a good person, and you deserve better. It's not your fault."

Maybe it is.

I'm too cautious, I could never bring myself to trust him fully. Maybe we would *have had a beautiful, perfect bond, just like Dai and Virginia, if only I hadn't held back.*

Maybe it is *all my fault.*

Connie angrily scrubbed her knuckles across her eyes, dashing away the tears before they could spill. "It's nothing to me," she said defiantly. "*I'm* not a shifter, after all. *I* don't have some amazing instant connection that means he's the only man for me. Chase can sleep around as much as he wants, for all I care."

"Chase doesn't sleep around," Hugh said. For the first time, he didn't sound even slightly sarcastic. "He hasn't for as long as I've known him."

"It's good of you to try to defend your friend," Killian said to him. "But please, don't lie to Connie. She's been hurt enough already."

Hugh rubbed at his forehead as if he had a headache. "I can't believe I'm doing this," he muttered, apparently to himself. "One mated pair around here is bad enough…"

He dropped his hand again with a sigh, looking at Connie. "If you're going to refuse Chase, do it for something he's actually done, not something he hasn't. Take my word on it, he's not slept with anyone for at least three years. He hasn't even lusted after anyone."

Dai was looking at the paramedic in fascination, as though he'd never heard him talk like this before. "But Chase is *always* flirting with women."

"No, he's just being himself. The same way he is with everyone, male or female." Hugh shrugged. "He's charming and charismatic, and women mistake that for interest and throw themselves at him. But he never takes them up on it."

"How can you be so sure?" Connie asked him, suspiciously.

"Healing is my useful talent." Hugh sipped his drink, hiding his expression. "Not my only one."

"You know, this *would* explain why no one ever asks Chase to walk them home twice," Virginia said thoughtfully. "And why the women always look terribly disappointed afterwards. I just assumed he was an awful lover."

"Evidently not," Hugh muttered, flashing a sidelong glance at Connie.

Connie couldn't stop the blush from rising up her face again... or the hope from rising up in her heart.

Maybe it is true. Maybe Chase really hasn't played around since he met me. Maybe he can't. Maybe I really am his—

She realized that Killian was studying her. He touched her arm. "Can I talk to you for a moment?"

Connie let Killian draw her a little to one side, out of earshot of the others. "Do *you* think it's true?" she asked him.

"I can't say that I do." He blew out his breath, shaking his head. "I want to think the best of my cousin, I really do, but... I know him. He's never been able to keep it in his pants for three days, let alone three years."

Connie's heart plummeted like her plane. "But, what if Hugh really can tell whether someone's been chaste?"

"I've never heard of any sort of shifter who can do that. I think Hugh is just trying to protect his friend. Connie, you're the one who caught Chase cheating on you. You saw it with your own eyes." Killian spread his hands, palm up. "Do you *really* think nothing happened? It just doesn't sound very believable to me."

Chase said nothing happened...
But he would say that, wouldn't he?

"You're right," she said dully.

"Of course he's right," said a cheerful voice. "Killian is always right. You should definitely listen to him."

Connie spun around to see Chase grinning at them. He was a little out of breath, as if he'd been flying hard and had only just walked in.

"As long as he's only been saying nice things about me, of course." Chase's smile faltered as he looked at her face. "Connie? What's wrong?"

"Nothing." Connie shook him off as he tried to take her hand. "Just been talking to your friends. I hope your conversation with Sammy was more productive."

"I got what I needed, though not everything I'd hoped for." Chase reached out to her again, but she stepped away. "Connie, what—?"

"I don't want to talk about it." Connie hugged herself, glaring at him. "I've wasted enough time already. What about my plane, Chase? That's all that matters. How am I going to save my plane from Sammy?"

"But—" Chase started.

"For once in your life, *drop it*," Killian told him. "Seriously. What's your plan?"

Chase looked rebellious, but allowed the change of topic. "The same as before, of course. We're going to win the race in Connie's Spitfire."

"My Spitfire is underwater, Chase," Connie snapped. "Even if your sea dragon friend can get it out, there is no way it's flying anytime soon."

Chase's grin reappeared. "Sammy just said *West's Spitfire* had to win the race. He didn't specify which one."

Connie stared at him. "Are you seriously suggesting that we go out and buy another Spitfire?"

"Oh no." Killian held up his hands, palm out and fingers

spread. "Chase, I can't liquidate assets on a moment's notice. I don't have the ready cash for this sort of purchase."

"Even if you did, it wouldn't do any good," Connie told him. "You can't just buy a Spitfire off eBay. They only come up for sale once in a blue moon!"

"I know that. In fact, I know that better than you do." Chase stuck his hands in his pockets, gazing contemplatively up at the ceiling. "Killian, you remember that money you lent me a little while ago?"

"Strangely, I do indeed remember advancing you several million pounds," Killian said dryly. "It's the sort of thing that sticks in my memory. Why?"

Chase looked insufferably smug. "I think it's time to show you what I bought."

CHAPTER 14

Now this was definitely *worth two and a half million dollars*, Chase thought, delighted by the matching dumbfounded expressions on Killian and Connie's faces as they stared at his plane.

The single-seater Mark IX Spitfire dominated the small private hanger he'd rented. Chase was glad of all the hours he'd spent lovingly polishing the plane's sleek curves. It shone like a vast precious gem, light sparkling from the immaculate paintwork. If they'd been in private, he would have been tempted to try proposing to Connie with it.

"When did you buy a Spitfire?" Connie said at last, weakly. "More to the point, *why* did you buy a Spitfire?"

"I told you." Chase raised an eyebrow at her, unable to control his wide smirk. "Whenever I saw something that reminded me of you, I had to get it."

Killian shook his head, his expression half-amused, half-despairing. "And I thought you needed the money to pay off gambling debts. Well, I suppose that there are worse investments. At least you should be able to resell it in future at a profit."

"Sorry, coz, but no." Chase pulled the Spitfire's registration papers out of his jacket, casually handing them to Connie. "Because it's not my plane anymore."

Connie looked down at the paperwork, then back up at him in disbelief. "You cannot be serious."

"The bet is on West's Spitfire winning the race. Sammy said so himself." Chase pointed first at Connie, then at the plane. "You're West, and now this is your Spitfire. So you can still win the bet."

"*How* much did you say this plane was worth?" Killian's voice had gone high and strangled.

"Two and a half million dollars, give or take a bit." Chase patted him on the shoulder. "Relax, Killian. It's only money."

"I promise, I won't keep it," Connie said to Killian. "As soon as the race is over, I'll give it straight back."

Killian pulled at his dark hair, his gray eyes rather wild. "Do neither of you understand capital gains? This is a very tax-inefficient plan! And what happens if you don't win the race? Does Sammy get to keep both Spitfires?"

Chase shrugged carelessly. "I suppose so. I hadn't really thought about it. We're not going to lose the race, after all."

Connie walked around the plane, scrutinizing every inch with an expert eye. "Well, she certainly looks to be in good repair. I can give her a last-minute tune-up to make sure she's at peak performance. But Chase, are you really sure you can do this?"

"What do you mean?" he asked.

"She's a standard single-seater fighter." Connie pointed up at the cockpit. "Not a two-seater trainer plane like mine. I won't be able to navigate for you. Are you really going to be able to learn the route by tomorrow? Well enough to fly it unaided?"

"Not a chance," Chase said, honestly. "But I'm not going to be piloting. You are."

Connie went white. "I'm *what?*"

"Good-bye, two and a half million dollars," Killian muttered.

Chase kicked the side of his cousin's foot. "Don't underestimate my mate. She knows the course so well, she could fly it in her sleep. She can do this."

"No, I really can't!" Connie yelped. "Chase, you have to fly. You're the one with magic powers!"

"Which means I have to be outside the plane, ready to protect you from the wyvern," Chase said firmly. "I'm certain it's going to come back. I can't fly in the race and evade it at the same time. But I *can* fight it in pegasus form. I can hold it off long enough for you to win."

Connie looked desperately at Killian. "Couldn't you guard Chase while he races?"

"Me?" Killian took a sharp step back, looking dismayed. "I'm not as crazy as my cousin. I'd have to be suicidal to try to take on a wyvern single-handed. Though I'm not going to let *him* take one on by himself, either. I'll back you up, Chase."

"I knew I didn't even have to ask." Chase bumped him affectionately, shoulder to shoulder. "And don't run yourself down. Even if you spend most of your time behind a desk, you're still a pegasus, and a Tiernach. You're tougher than you realize. Just like Connie."

"I'm not." Connie swung her head from side to side in vigorous denial. "I can't, Chase. I can't do it. I'm not as good a pilot as you."

"No. You're not." He caught her chin in his hand, holding her still and forcing her to look at him. "You're a *better* pilot than me. I couldn't have pulled your Spitfire out of that death-spiral, but you did. The only thing that's ever held you back is your sense of caution. You just have to be willing to take a few risks."

"I'll lose, I'll lose my plane, and it will be all my fault,"

Connie said, her voice rising. She reminded him of a cornered animal, lashing out in fear. "It'll be *your* fault for making me do this. I'll never be able to look at you again."

"You aren't going to lose." With all his heart, Chase wished that they were truly mated, so that she could feel his bone-deep confidence in her. "Please, Connie. Trust—"

"Don't you dare tell me to trust you," Connie snarled at him. "Not again. Not *ever* again."

"That's not what I was going to say," Chase said, with perfect truth. He stared deep into her frightened eyes, willing her to believe him, just this once. "Connie. Trust *yourself*."

CHAPTER 15

I can't do this.

Connie felt physically sick with nerves, her stomach clenching around the small breakfast Chase had forced her to eat. An excited crowd was gathering around the edges of the airfield, eagerly waiting for the race to start. Connie tried to concentrate on her plane, but it was hard to ignore the way people kept pointing at her and the Spitfire. The back of her neck burned under the heat of hundreds of curious stares.

"That's everything on the pre-flight checklist," Chase said, ducking under the nose of the plane to rejoin her. "As soon as we get the signal, you'll be cleared for take off. Are you ready?"

"No." Connie's hands were shaking so badly, she couldn't even do up her flight jacket. "Chase, I can't do this."

"Here." Chase carefully fastened her zip for her. "There you go. All set."

"I mean, I can't fly this race!"

"I know what you meant." Chase brushed a stray strand of her hair out of her face, tucking it behind her ear. "And you can. Your practice run earlier was perfect. You comfortably beat everyone else's time."

"That was just the practice run, with a clear sky. It'll be different with the other planes up there too. What if I can't get past the leaders? What if I make a mistake? What if—"

"Connie. You can do this. Just—" Chase cut himself off, his back stiffening. "What is he doing here?"

Connie followed the direction of his gaze, and her heart leapt with anxiety. "Oh God, this is really happening. It's the race marshal. He must be coming to give us permission to take off."

"Not him," Chase said grimly. He was staring hard at an enormous man in a brilliant white suit who was sauntering alongside the approaching marshal. "*Him*. That's Sammy Smiles."

Even if Connie hadn't known Sammy was a shifter, she would have thought there was something odd about his bizarrely top-heavy physique and impossibly wide, toothy mouth. Knowing what he truly was, she recognized them as the unmistakable traits of his other form. He looked more like a shark stuffed into a suit than a human being.

He also looked very, very pleased with himself.

"Ms. West?" the marshal said, consulting his clipboard as he came up to them. "Are your pre-flight checks complete?"

Chase thrust the paperwork at the marshal without looking, never breaking eye contact with Sammy. "You're not welcome here, Sammy. Get back behind the line with the other spectators."

The marshal coughed disapprovingly. "Mr. Smiles, as our *very* generous sponsor, is personally wishing all the pilots the best of luck before take off."

A minute ago, Connie wouldn't have thought that she could possibly feel any *more* sick. "You sponsor the Rydon Cup?"

"Why, didn't I mention that before?" Sammy drawled in a thick Texan accent. He beamed at her, showing double rows of sharp teeth. "And you must be West's daughter. Aren't you just a sweet little thing. Why, who'd have thought such soft, pretty hands could possibly manage to fly a big ol' plane like this?"

No doubt he'd been intending to psych her out... but his underhanded insult had the opposite effect. She was used to patronizing older men trying to tell her how to look after a plane, as if she hadn't cut her teeth on a torque wrench. The butterflies in her stomach turned into angry bees.

"I flew my first Spitfire when I was seven," she spat, clenching her fists. "Sitting on my mom's lap. You'll find that I know what I'm doing."

Chase's chest swelled with pride, his eyes shining with fierce delight as he glanced at her. "Oh, Sammy. You're about to find out that you've jumped out of the frying pan and into the inferno. By the end of today, you are really, really going to regret that you prevented *me* from piloting."

A wounded expression spread across Sammy's broad face. "Now, now. I haven't prevented anyone from doing anything. And if you keep making these accusations, son, I'm going to have to insist you speak to my lawyer. But let's not be unfriendly. We all need to put any little differences aside and be good sports. We want a nice, clean race, don't we?"

Connie noticed that Sammy looked hard at Chase as he said this last bit. She realized that the shark shifter was worried that Chase, in pegasus form, might take it upon himself to interfere with the other planes.

"Cheaters always think that everyone else cheats too." Chase matched Sammy's smile, baring his teeth. "But we're not like you, Sammy. Connie is going to win this race fair and square."

Sammy gazed up at the plane. "Speaking of a fair race…" he trailed off, glancing at the race marshal meaningfully.

"Ah, yes." The marshal, who had been looking rather confused by the hostile undertones to the conversation, straightened up. "Ms. West, due to the unfortunate malfunction on your other Spitfire, we've accepted this rather unconventional last-minute substitution. But, after careful consideration, we have decided that we must adjust your handicap."

Connie had been expecting something like this. As a handicap race, all the planes in the Rydon Cup started at different times, so that it became a test of pilot skill rather than just the plane's raw capabilities. Previously, Connie had been set to start in sixth position, out of a field of twelve.

But Chase's Spitfire—she still couldn't think of it as *hers*—was a fair bit lighter than hers, thanks to only carrying a single person rather than two. It would be fractionally faster in the sky as a result, and therefore needed a bigger handicap.

"Now, wait a second—" Chase began.

Connie stopped him with an upraised hand. "No, it's only fair. So I'm starting in seventh place now, marshal?"

"Er, after impartial review and consideration of some new evidence…" The marshal's eyes flicked briefly to Sammy. "You will be starting in twelfth position."

Connie stared at him in utter horror. *"Dead last?"*

Chase towered over the smaller man, his muscular shoulders bunching ominously. "Let me guess. Did this 'new evidence' come in the form of a fat check, by any chance?"

The marshal held his clipboard in front of him like a shield, visibly paling. "The—the decision of the committee is final," he gabbled. "Please prepare for take off, and await your starting signal."

"This is a real nice plane." Sammy patted the Spitfire

affectionately. "I sure am looking forward to spending more time with her in the future. Nice to meet you, Constance West. Oh, and tell your dad that if he needs a little loan to tide you over after this… he knows where to find me."

"That's it," Connie said, as Sammy sauntered off, whistling. "It's over."

Chase looked as if he could quite happily have murdered the loan shark on the spot. "It is *not* over," he said fiercely. "You said it yourself—you've been flying these planes all your life. You can do this, Connie. Don't think about what you've got to lose. Focus on what you're going to *win*. Think how much you want to rub Sammy's smile in the dirt. Think how satisfying it's going to be to see his face when you come in first."

Connie groped for her earlier flare of rage, but her common sense smothered it. "I'm a good pilot, but I'm not a daredevil like my dad. Overtaking other planes is risky, and I'll have to do it eleven times!"

"Then take those risks." Chase seized her hands, squeezing them in a crushing grip. "Let yourself go, fly like you were born in the sky. This plane has survived me flinging it around, after all. It's not going to come apart around you. And I'm going to be right there at your wingtip. I won't let anything happen to you."

"But—" Connie started.

He leaned down and kissed her, fiercely, deeply, stifling any further protests. Heat ran through Connie's blood. She felt as if his wild energy was spilling from him into her, rekindling the fire in her belly. She pressed against him, as if she could draw his reckless courage into herself, storing it up for the race ahead.

Chase drew back a little, leaning his forehead against hers. "You can do this," he repeated. "I'll see you in the sky, and I'll make sure you can see me too."

Connie clung onto his hands, afraid that once he let go, all her courage would leak away like a deflating balloon. "If you can drive off the wyvern, will you come and fly the race with me? Please?"

"I'll be right by your side, I swear." He gave her one last brief, tantalizing kiss. "Now go. It's time."

CHAPTER 16

Chase could sense the wyvern approaching. He'd barely slept last night, waiting for the shifter to return to the city, but it had only appeared at the edge of his perception as the planes took off for the race. It was still too high and distant to be seen, but it was closing in fast.

Incoming, he telepathically sent to Killian. He accompanied the thought with a mental image of the wyvern's green form, so that Killian's pegasus would be able to get its scent and track it too. *You ready?*

To fight a wyvern? Not even remotely. Despite his words, Killian's wide gray wings beat steadily, his flight smooth and strong as he circled over the racing planes. *I can sense it now, too. Looks like it's planning to intercept over the sea, during the later stage of the race.*

I agree. Chase increased his wingbeats, quickening his pace. *I'm going to see if I can catch it before it gets a chance to interfere with the race. You keep back here with Connie, just in case.*

He couldn't resist glancing down at the race as he powered through the sky. Thanks to Sammy's fiddling with the handicaps, five of the eleven planes that had started ahead of Connie were technically faster than the vintage Spitfire. But that didn't mean that they were faster in practice. A plane was only as good as its pilot.

Connie had already overtaken the plane that had started eleventh, when its pilot had run into some crosswinds at takeoff. Now she was closing rapidly on the next one, the Spitfire's engine roaring at full throttle. She'd taken advantage of the Spitfire's superior climbing ability to get above the light acrobatic plane. The modern plane might be faster in level flight, but not in a dive. All she needed was an opening.

The other aircraft took the turn a little sloppily, wavering from the ideal racing line... just a little.

Now, Connie, now! Be bold!

As if she'd heard his silent exhortation, the Spitfire flashed downward. Its wings sliced through the air like a knife through butter as Connie wheeled it neatly through the turn, cutting ahead of the other plane.

Yes! Two down!

Only nine more to go...

He desperately wanted to fly wingtip-to-wingtip with Connie through the race, sharing in her triumph, but he had a job to do. The racing planes became just distant glints as he flew out to sea at full speed.

Do you have a plan, by the way? Killian sent to him, his mental voice a little faint with distance.

Yes, Chase replied, the wind whistling past his flattened ears. **I'm going to find the bastard who tried to kill my mate, and I'm going to kick his fucking head in.**

There was no further time for talking. He could see the wyvern now. It was a little lower down than him, flying close to the sea. Its long, jagged wings beat steadily, propelling it at incredible speed.

Kill! His pegasus filled his mind with a single-minded need to smash the wyvern out of the sky. *No one attacks our mate! Kill!*

Shrieking in challenge, Chase folded his wings and stooped. The wyvern's wedge-shape head whipped round, its large, acid-yellow eyes widening in alarm as it spotted him. Its narrow chest swelled. It spat out a cloud of acid.

Chase flicked a pinion, swooping around the deadly mist. He lashed out at the wyvern with his razor-sharp front hooves. It twisted its sinuous body, evading his kick. He didn't give it a chance to recover, striking out at it with both teeth and hooves.

If I stay close, it can't use its acid. Just got to watch out for the tail.

The wyvern's deadly, scorpion-like tail curved over its back, the needle sharp tip swinging to target him. Chase was so busy keeping an eye on it that he nearly forgot that the front half of the wyvern was just as dangerous. Its head darted at him, fangs gleaming with poison.

Chase backwinged hard, nearly stalling out as the wyvern's teeth snapped shut on empty air. Off balance, he couldn't avoid the wyvern's tail as it whipped round. It didn't manage to sting him, but the powerful blow still sent him tumbling across the sky.

The wyvern didn't press its advantage. Instead, it increased its wingbeats, shooting away from him like a bullet out of a gun. Although the wyvern's deadly acid and poisonous tail made it more than a match for a pegasus, it didn't seem to be interested in a fight. Chase guessed that Sammy had ordered it to evade him and head straight for the race, to make sure Connie didn't win.

Recovering himself, Chase shot after the wyvern. It twisted its neck, breathing out a couple more blasts of acid to cover its retreat. Chase banked round the drifting clouds in tight, swooping arcs, locked onto the wyvern like a heat-seeking missile, but every evasive maneuver cost him precious time.

The wyvern's long wings boomed with every stroke, propelling it away from him at a phenomenal pace. Chase's powerful flight muscles burned as he tried to keep up. Even at the very limits of his speed, the wyvern was creeping away from him.

The planes are heading out to sea. Killian's anxious mental voice burst into his head. *They'll be nearing you soon. Connie's worked her way up to sixth position. Are you okay? Do you need help?*

Stay with the race! Chase flung back, his psychic voice as out-of-breath as his physical body. He needed Killian there as a last-ditch defense, if worst came to worst.

Chase bared his teeth in a frustrated snarl as the wyvern inched yet farther away. No matter how he pushed himself, he couldn't catch up. He had more strength and endurance, but the wyvern was simply faster in level flight than he was. It only needed to maintain its speed for a few more minutes before it would be in the midst of the air race.

What would Connie do...?

He altered the angle of his wings, striving to gain height rather than speed. The wyvern dropped away beneath him, pulling ahead. Its wedge-shaped head swiveled on its long, sinuous neck as it tried to work out where he'd gone. Borrowing a trick from WWII fighter pilots, Chase headed straight for the sun, hiding in the dazzling rays as he climbed even higher.

He could see the racing planes now, and hear the air-shaking thunder of their combined engines. Connie's Spitfire was immediately apparent, a predatory hawk-shape amidst the smaller light aircraft. A group of RV-7s scattered in disarray as she roared straight through their midst.

The wyvern's head swung, locking onto the Spitfire. It soared up on an intercept course.

He's attacking our mate! His pegasus was frantic. *Protect! Strike! Kill!*

Chase fought for control, struggling to resist the pegasus's overwhelming instinct to immediately dive after the wyvern. He was usually so in tune with his stallion that it felt unnatural to go against its desires.

But for once, he had to keep a cool head. Rushing in too quickly would result in disaster.

Wait, he told the stallion. *Wait! We're only going to get one shot at this!*

The wyvern was too fast and agile for him. He knew that his only chance was to dive at terminal velocity, falling so fast that even the wyvern's hair-trigger reflexes wouldn't be able to evade him. But to do that, he had to get higher.

Now, Killian! he sent to his cousin, as he clawed his way upward. *Delay it!*

Killian swooped at the wyvern. The wyvern shook him off, easily dodging the attacks. It had reached the race corridor now. It avoided a couple of planes, allowing them to pass unhindered, then hovered, waiting. Killian darted at its head like a crow mobbing a bird of prey, but the wyvern just blasted acid at him, forcing him to veer away.

I can't get close! Killian sent to him in dismay. *It's right in Connie's path, and I can't get it to budge.*

Just distract it as much as you can, Chase sent back.

Air burned like fire in his nostrils, his great lungs heaving with exertion as he struggled through the dead air. There was no updraft, no thermal to carry him upward. It was like trying to climb a sheer cliff with his bare hands.

You can't dive from that high! Killian's mental voice was horrified. *You'll break your neck!*

He ignored his cousin's warning, heaving himself up even

further. He was so high now that the planes beneath him looked as small as children's toys. Killian was just a gray speck, whirling round the stationary, bright green dot of the wyvern.

Chase! It's too—I can't—! Killian's psychic message broke apart into a wordless impression of pain.

Chase's laboring heart missed a beat as he saw his cousin's distant form tumble down toward the waves. To his relief, Killian pulled up before he hit the water, but from his wavering, unsteady course, it was clear he was out of the fight.

Connie neatly cut off another plane, flying the twists and turns of the race route with cool, considered efficiency. She was in third place now, but she had a huge distance to make up in order to catch the two race leaders. The Spitfire surged forward as Connie gave it full throttle.

Heading straight toward the waiting wyvern.

Connie had no way of knowing the beast was there. Secure in its invisibility, the wyvern hovered directly in her path. All of its attention was focused on the approaching plane.

NOW!

Chase swept his wings back, folding them tight to his sides. Flying on just the barest tips of his pinions, he flashed downward. His tail streamed out behind him like a banner as he picked up speed, falling faster and faster until he felt like his wings were going to be torn off.

The howling wind lashed his face so hard that it was impossible to draw breath. Black spots danced in his vision as his lungs burned for air. He twisted his wings, swinging round as he fell, hooves ready to strike.

At the very last instant, the wyvern suddenly threw itself to one side, as if someone had shouted a warning at it. But it was too late. Chase was diving so fast that even the wyvern's supernaturally fast reflexes couldn't save it.

All four of his hooves hit the wyvern's flank, the bone-jarring impact nearly making him black out. If he'd hit the wyvern's head, he would have instantly broken its neck. As it was, the beast bowled head-over-tail, spinning uncontrollably down toward the water.

Still dizzy from the dive, Chase was nearly knocked out of the air himself as Connie's Spitfire shot past him with barely a foot to spare. He was tossed helplessly in the wind from the plane's wake, bobbing like a cork on a stormy sea.

By the time he'd righted himself, the wyvern was half-way back to Brighton, abandoning the fight. It flew low to the sea, its wing-beats erratic and labored as it fled.

Follow it! His pegasus pawed the air, eager to finish off the beast. *Catch it, kill it, stomp it flat!*

Chase shook his head to dispel his stallion's instinctive bloodlust. *No*, he told his pegasus. *We have to help our mate. We promised to be there at her wingtip. And we will* never *again break a promise to her, ever.*

He forced his aching wings to beat faster, catching up with the Spitfire. Despite his burning muscles, he fell into formation with the plane.

I'm here, Connie. And now, it's all up to you.

CHAPTER 17

I'm going to lose.

Connie forced her hands to stay steady on the controls. She didn't have the luxury of shaking now. Her eyes stayed locked onto the two race leaders.

They were both modified Mudry CAP 230 aircraft, a high-speed acrobatics plane favored by serious racing pilots. Her own Spitfire was faster and more powerful... but the two Mudrys were far ahead of her.

It's too far. I won't be able to catch them.

Connie pushed the Spitfire as hard as she dared, but she knew it wasn't going to be enough. Her instinctive, finely-honed ability to judge distances and speeds told her that it was hopeless.

Unless they both make a mistake on the final corner...

Unfortunately, that didn't look likely. Both planes were piloted by expert racers. One of the planes, a bright canary yellow with white trim, she recognized as belonging to the winner of last year's Rydon Cup. So far he'd flown a careful, flawless course. The other plane, a cerulean blue, was unfamiliar to her, but its pilot clearly had a lot of experience and absolutely no fear. Connie had come perilously close to slamming straight into him earlier, halfway through the race. Her reflexes had saved them both from a mid-air collision, but she'd lost a lot of time straightening out and getting back under control.

Now she could only watch helplessly as the other two planes jostled with each other for first position. The blue daredevil kept trying to cut into the yellow plane's airspace, trying to force it to drop back. Unlike Connie, the pilot of the yellow plane held his nerve, refusing to cede the racing line to the maniac.

They were approaching the final turn point—the infamous hairpin, a true test of a pilot's ability and daring. Connie was certain that the yellow plane would choose to circle wide, taking the turn slowly but safely. She was equally sure the blue plane would attempt the faster but much more dangerous hairpin maneuver, taking the turn as tightly as possible.

If the pilot of the blue plane pulled it off, he'd win the race. If he stalled out, the victory would go to the yellow plane.

Either way, Connie had lost.

I've lost.

I've lost my mother's plane.

I've lost everything.

An alarming, high-pitched whistle shrieked in warning over the deeper snarl of the Spitfire's overheated engine. Her heart like lead in her chest, Connie eased the throttle back a little. There was no sense destroying Chase's plane, even if it was shortly to become Sammy's plane.

A flicker caught her eye, off her left wingtip. Connie craned her neck, hoping against hope that it was Chase. She'd only seen the midnight-black pegasus once, when suddenly he'd shot down past her like the wrath of God, presumably chasing the wyvern.

All through the race, she'd been half-sick with fear for him. She'd clung to the thought that as long as she was still flying without interference from the wyvern, he *had* to be all right, but it was small comfort. If the wyvern wasn't attacking her, it was only because it was attacking *him*.

Now, however, that impossibly winged, glorious equine shape settled into formation with her. The pegasus was clearly exhausted, but he still kept pace with the plane.

"Chase," Connie breathed, relief filling her.

She couldn't see any wounds on him, though from the stiff way he moved she suspected he was bruised and battered from the fight. She could only assume that the wyvern was worse off, though. Chase must have either killed it or driven it away.

Catching her eye, the pegasus flicked an ear at her. Then he stretched his neck out, his labored wingbeats speeding up so that he inched a little ahead of her. He glanced back at her, tail held high and challenging.

She could read his body language as clearly as if he was speaking directly into her ear: *Well? What are you waiting for?*

Connie set her jaw in determination. If she was going to lose, then she was at least going to go down fighting. She could only pray that she wouldn't *literally* be going down fighting as she gave the plane full throttle once again.

She could feel the stress on the engine in every judder and jerk of the plane underneath her, but this time she held her nerve. The Spitfire howled in fury as it shot across the sky after the two leaders, eating up the distance.

Out of the corner of her eye, she could see Chase struggling gamely to keep up, but she didn't have any attention to spare for him now. All her focus was on holding the plane together, and keeping it true on course. At this speed, the tiniest error could send her tumbling out of control, and out of the race.

Ahead, the two Mudrys had reached the final turn point, the yellow plane still a little ahead of the blue. As she'd suspected, the more experienced pilot in the yellow plane began to bank right, describing a wide, looping circle. The more daring blue plane took the opportunity to dash past it. It banked left, so hard that its wings were nearly vertical, trying to complete the turn ahead of the yellow plane.

Even before the blue plane started its turn, Connie knew in her gut that the pilot had come in too hard, too fast. The blue plane stalled, spiraling out of the air. To her relief, he managed to pull back up safely, but he'd plummeted well past the race boundaries. He was out.

The yellow plane had nearly completed the turn. Connie was almost at the turn point herself, but she still had to complete her own loop. By the time she was even facing the finish line, the yellow plane would already have crossed it.

Unless... I attempt the hairpin.

Connie bit her lip hard enough to draw blood. She had only a few heartbeats in which to make the decision.

I can't. It's too dangerous. If it goes wrong, it'll tear the plane apart.

Time seemed to stretch like taffy, seconds slowing to a crawl. She glanced back at Chase, still grimly struggling in her slipstream. Her eyes locked with his, despite the growing distance between them. In that moment, she could *feel* his perfect trust in her, his encouragement and support.

If it goes wrong...

She knew, down to her very bones, that he would catch her.

Connie slammed the control column over.

The Spitfire heeled over on one wingtip, the other pointing up to the sky, metal shrieking with the stress.

Connie sucked in her stomach, her visioning threatening to go black as the incredible g-forces squashed her into the pilot's seat. She braced herself with her feet, every muscle in her body straining as she fought to keep control of the plane.

The Spitfire whipped round the hairpin like a comet. The yellow plane's wings see-sawed, buffeted by her wake as Connie's plane screamed past mere feet in front of its nose.

The home stretch lay open before Connie, the clear blue sky wide and welcoming.

She couldn't have slowed the Spitfire down even if she'd wanted to. In mere moments, she was back over land, hurtling toward the airfield. The other plane was just a yellow dot in the distance. Even Chase had fallen away behind her. The crowds below were just a blur of color as she shot over their heads.

Across the finish line.

CHAPTER 18

"We won," Connie said yet again, gazing in disbelief at the Rydon Cup. She hadn't put the massive silver trophy down once since Sammy had been forced to grudgingly present it to her. "We *won*."

"You won," Chase corrected, as he rummaged around in her fridge. He couldn't stop grinning. "You're the one who did the hard work. We just made sure the wyvern didn't get in the way. Right, Killian?"

"Hm?" Killian glanced up from his phone. He'd been rather distracted all the way through the awards ceremony. "Oh. Yes. Definitely."

"Come on, put that thing away. You can't have accumulated that many pressing business emails in a single afternoon." Chase pulled out a magnum of champagne, brandishing it at them both. "We have some serious celebrating to do!"

Connie blinked at the enormous bottle. "When did you sneak that in here? Come to that, how did you even fit it into my fridge?"

"If there's one thing I'm good at," Chase said as he

unpeeled the foil, "it's getting oversized things into tight places. As you know."

He was rewarded by the faint flush that crept up Connie's cheeks. "No, if there's one thing you're good at it's jumping the gun. What would you have done with that thing if we hadn't won?"

Chase hefted the magnum, swinging it experimentally. "Well, I suppose I could have clubbed Sammy to death with the empty bottle, after we'd drowned our sorrows. I hadn't really thought about it. I knew you'd win."

Connie rolled her eyes at him, though a smile pulled at her full lips. "You are *impossible*. Don't shake it up like that, you idiot, or you won't be able to pour it."

"Oh, this one's not for pouring," Chase said cheerfully.

Aiming the bottle at her, he popped the cork. Connie shrieked, holding the Rydon Cup up in defense as he gleefully sprayed her with champagne. For good measure, he blasted Killian too. His cousin swore, hastily shielding his cellphone.

"*Chase!*" Laughing, Connie flicked her dripping hair out of her face. Her eyes sparkled, finally free of all worry and fear. Privately, Chase vowed to shower her in champagne *every* day, if it made her smile like that. "What a waste of good booze."

Holding the still-foaming bottle out to one side, Chase slipped his other arm around her. "I didn't say I was going to let it go to waste."

Regardless of the Rydon Cup digging into his abdomen, he drew her close. He dropped his head to delicately lick a drop of champagne from her neck. Connie's breath hitched as he followed the crisp, fragrant trail up her neck.

The silver trophy trapped between the two of them warmed, absorbing the heat of their bodies. He flicked his tongue teasingly against her soft lips. They parted willingly

FIREFIGHTER PEGASUS

for him, allowing him to explore her warm mouth. The sweetness of her kiss was more intoxicating than the champagne.

Killian cleared his throat uncomfortably. "Did you say there was another bottle of that?"

Chase could have happily murdered his cousin as Connie jerked away from him, blushing. "Uh, sorry. Um. Yes, we should all celebrate. Together." She looked down at her wet flight suit, which was clinging to her erect nipples, and her blush deepened. "I'm just going to go shower and put on some dry things."

Don't you have some spreadsheets to fill in or something? Chase telepathically snapped at his cousin, as Connie disappeared into the bedroom.

Killian spread his hands apologetically. *Sorry, but I don't think it's a good idea to leave you alone right now. Sammy is probably in a blood-frenzy of rage tonight, and the wyvern is still out there. I want to watch your back until we know everything's blown over.*

Chase knew his cousin was only acting out of concern for his safety. His pegasus still itched to kick Killian over the horizon. *Killian, in the nicest possible way... fuck off. I'll be fine, trust—*

A loud ringing sound made them both jump. Killian stared in confusion at his silent phone for a moment, then shrugged. "Not mine. You?"

Chase had forgotten he was carrying his work cellphone. He was so accustomed to having to be on call, he'd absentmindedly picked it up that morning even though he'd resigned from being a firefighter. Now he rummaged in his pocket, pulling it out. "Griff? What's up?"

"We're at an incident up in Falmer." Griff's thickened Scottish burr betrayed his concern. "An abandoned apartment block, right at the edge of the city. We think squatters must have accidentally set fire to the place. The caller said she was trapped inside, but Ash and Dai have been in there for ten minutes now and they still haven't found her. It's a real mess in there."

"Shit." In the background, Chase could hear the familiar sing-song shriek of the fire engine. "Hang on, what are you doing on site instead of in the control room?"

"Pretending to be you," Griff said, a touch acidly. "I know you said you were quitting, but Commander Ash hasn't put the paperwork in yet, hoping that you'll change your mind. I volunteered to cover your shift."

"You're on active duty again?" Chase had missed Griff's solid, reliable presence on the team. It had never been quite the same without him.

"Not officially. It's just one of my better days. I can drive a truck, at least. But I can't find people, not like you can. Chase, we really need you."

Chase's first instinct was to leap out the window, to shift and head for the scene at full speed. Nonetheless, he hesitated, glancing at Connie's closed bedroom door. He could hear the shower running in the bathroom.

Go, Killian sent to him, obviously having overheard the conversation thanks to his sharp shifter senses. *You're needed. Don't worry about Connie. I'll tell her where you've gone. And if there's any sign of danger, I'll get her to safety.*

Chase made up his mind. Though it tore at him to leave, there was a life at risk. Connie would understand.

"I'm on my way," he said into the phone.

CHAPTER 19

"Where's Chase?" Connie asked as she came back into the living room.

Killian was on his phone again, thumbing in a text message. "He said he had to dash off," he said, slipping it back into his pocket. "He just jumped out the window and flew away."

"Oh." Connie opened the fridge to look for the second bottle of champagne, hiding her expression.

He probably got some ridiculous idea and had to act on it immediately, she told herself, trying to overcome the sinking feeling of disappointment in her stomach. *He's so impulsive. No doubt he couldn't wait for even a minute.*

...Not even to tell me why he was leaving?

"Did he say when he'd be back?" Connie said, trying to keep her voice light.

"No." Killian touched her arm, making her jump. She hadn't heard him coming up behind her. "Connie, can I ask you something?"

"Sure." She handed him the champagne, and started

hunting for wine glasses. "What's on your mind? You've been kind of quiet ever since the race."

Killian turned the bottle in his strong, long-fingered hands, so similar to Chase's. It was strange how two people so physically alike could be so different. "Are you intending to stay with my cousin?"

Connie paused in opening a cupboard.

The race is over. My plane is safe.

I could go anywhere.

"I mean, you won the bet," Killian said, when she didn't say anything. "You don't need him anymore. I love him dearly, but even I have to admit that he's a challenging person to handle. He's reckless, and ridiculous, and just generally..." Killian trailed off, apparently searching for the right adjective.

"Infuriating?" Connie suggested.

"Right." Killian shot her a wry grimace of shared pain. "And God knows, he's hurt you enough in the past. Any sensible person would never want anything to do with him, ever again."

"Yes," Connie said slowly, leaning back against the work surface next to him. She couldn't deny the truth in anything Killian had said. "I guess a sensible person wouldn't."

Killian gestured at her with the wine bottle. "I think you're the most sensible person I've ever met, Connie. You're basically his complete opposite. To be frank, I still can't believe you two are actually meant to be mates. So are you going to stay with him? Despite everything?"

Am I?

Connie searched the clear-eyed, wary, innermost heart of her soul... and knew the answer.

"You know," she said softly. "Ever since my mother died, I've always *had* to be the sensible one. I had to learn to be cautious, to balance my dad. He could afford to be wild and bold, because I would always be there to fix things if it all went wrong. But if *I* was reckless, and it didn't work out... there would be no one to catch *me*."

"But you were reckless today," Killian said.

"Because I knew I could trust Chase to be there if I fell." A slow smile spread across her face. "And I think I'm finally ready to take another risk."

Killian looked at her, his expression unreadable. "So you'll stay with him."

"Yes." Connie patted his tense arm. "Don't worry, Killian. You won't be picking up the pieces of his broken heart this time."

Killian let out his breath in a long sigh. "That's what I was afraid of."

"What?" Connie stared at him, surprised. "I thought you liked me!"

"I do like you," Killian said. There was a strangely regretful expression on his handsome face. "I truly do. You're smart and responsible and much too good for my fool cousin. I wish you would reconsider staying with him. Are you sure I can't persuade you to just disappear? I can give you money, enough to go wherever you want. All you have to do is promise never to let Chase find you, ever again."

"I don't understand," Connie said blankly. "Why do you want me to leave Chase?"

"Because you're a good influence on him." Killian put down the champagne bottle, straightening as if he'd come to a decision. "Too good. I love Chase, I truly do... but I need him to be his worst self. Wild and irresponsible and completely uninterested in the business."

"This is about your *job?*" Connie still couldn't believe what was happening.

"I've worked too hard for too long to lose my place to

Chase now." Killian's gray eyes hardened like ice. "*I* am going to be the next CEO of Tiernach Enterprises. Not him."

I'm in danger.

The thought finally percolated through her stunned mind. Heart hammering, Connie tried to make a dash for the door, but Killian was too fast for her. He caught her wrist with inhuman strength, easily restraining her.

"I truly am sorry about this," Killian said, sounding genuinely regretful. "I wish I could have just put you off him again, like I did three years ago. I want you to know, Chase never did cheat on you. I drugged him unconscious, and hired strippers to pretend that he'd slept with him. I staged the whole scene to give you the worst possible impression when you walked in on him. I had to do whatever it took to make you go away. And now, I'm afraid, I have to make sure you go away again. For good, this time."

Someone hammered on the door.

"Help!" Connie yelled, praying that it was Chase.

It wasn't.

"Well now," drawled Sammy, ducking through the doorway. There was nothing either friendly or human about his wide, white smile. "Mighty nice to see you again, Ms. West."

CHAPTER 20

Chase's wings were still sore from fighting the wyvern. It took him an embarrassingly long time to reach the site of the fire. He hardly needed to use his pegasus senses to guide him to his fire team; the orange glow of the fire lit up the horizon, clearly visible for miles.

A thick column of smoke billowed from a derelict apartment block, orange flames roaring out of its shattered windows. Hot air rising from the inferno ruffled his feathers as he spiraled down.

Griff was standing by the fire engine, well back from the blaze. The dispatcher's rugged face was lined with barely-controlled pain, but his fists still clenched as he stared at the fire with helpless frustration. He glanced up as Chase landed, clicking off his radio.

"Am I glad to see you," he said. "Can you sense anyone?"

Quickly shifting back to human form, Chase concentrated. He immediately sensed Commander Ash and Dai, searching through the first floor of the building. He questing out further, searching for any other people inside.

Ignore that. There's no one in there. His pegasus tugged at his attention, trying to drag him toward a nearby alley. *Quick! Kill, strike, hurry!*

Confused by his stallion's agitation, Chase turned his attention in that direction... and stiffened.

There wasn't any in the building, but there *was* someone nearby, watching them all.

Someone he recognized.

"Chase?" Griff said in confusion, but he was already running, leaving the dispatcher behind. With no time to shift, he sprinted for the alleyway as fast as mere human legs could carry him.

DAI! ASH! Chase roared psychically at his colleagues. *Get out here! It's the wyvern!*

He caught sight of a dim silhouette lurking in the shadows at the mouth of the alleyway. The small figure hesitated as he ran towards it, then broke and fled—but too late.

With a last burst of speed, Chase hurled himself at the retreating figure. His shoulder connected hard with a soft, yielding form, and the wyvern shifter let out a high-pitched yelp of pain. The impact knocked both of them off their feet. Before the other shifter could recover, Chase threw himself down on top of—her?

"Get off me!" The woman writhed underneath him, her short, plump body no match for his much heavier bulk. "Get off!"

He expected her to shift into her wyvern form, but instead she just grabbed at his wrists with her bare hands. Instantly, a burning pain shot through his skin. Chase swore, involuntarily jerking away from her acidic touch.

The wyvern shifter took advantage of his instinctive recoil to wriggle away from him, rolling to her feet. She turned to flee—

And was stopped dead by a crimson wall of scaled muscle

blocking her path. The red dragon growled at her in warning, his enormous bulk filling the alley.

"Thanks, Dai." Chase got to his own feet. He glared at the wyvern shifter. "Don't even think about shifting. You aren't going anywhere."

The woman lifted her chin, matching his glare defiantly. She was dressed in an eclectic mix of ripped black leather and PVC, and had an asymmetric haircut with a thick green stripe dyed into the front. "Bite me, pony-boy," she spat at him. "We both know I can outfly you any day of the week. If I didn't want to be here, I'd already be gone."

His pegasus raged, demanding to trample the wyvern shifter, but he reined his stallion back. Despite her aggressive attitude, there was something vulnerable about her yellow-green eyes and soft, round face. She wore her punkish outfit as if it was a carefully-constructed suit of armor, a way to protect herself from the world rather than an expression of her true self.

Nonetheless, Chase stayed poised on the balls of his feet, ready to grab her if she made any sudden moves. "What *are* you doing here? Did you start this fire?"

"My employer ordered me to." The wyvern shifter folded her tattooed arms, setting her jaw. "But he doesn't know I'm still here. I stayed because I want to talk to your boss."

"If that is so, you have found him," said Ash's calm, cool voice. "I am the Phoenix."

Dai moved back a little to allow the Fire Commander past. Ash looked as composed as ever, but his feet left black, scorched footprints in his wake. Griff followed him, his sharp golden eyes narrowing as they fixed on the wyvern.

Commander Ash stopped in front of the wyvern shifter, his hands clasped behind his back. "What is your name?"

"Ivy," the wyvern shifter said, flinching a little as she met the Commander's calm gaze. "Ivy Viverna."

"Ms. Viverna, you have already committed crimes that call for judgment before the Parliament of Shifters," Ash said. Even from several feet away, Chase could feel the heat radiating from the Commander's motionless form. "But if you have truly committed arson, then you are under my jurisdiction, and subject to *my* judgment. Do you understand?"

"Some shark shifters tried to scare me into surrendering to them, by telling me that it would be much worse if *you* caught me." Ivy hugged herself, her body language an odd combination of fear and determination. "They said you can burn anything. Even a shifter's inner animal."

Commander Ash inclined his head in silent confirmation.

Ivy's lower lip started to tremble. "Can—can you burn away my wyvern?"

Ash considered her for a long moment. "I could. But why would you wish that?"

"I can't touch anyone." Ivy held up her bare hands. Chase's own wrists still burned an angry red where she'd briefly grabbed him. "I'm poisonous, all the time, even in human form. I just want to be normal."

"If I burned your wyvern, you would be an ordinary human," Ash said dispassionately. "But you would not be the same person."

"I don't care." Tears welled up in Ivy's eyes. "I'd rather be anyone else but me. I can't have a regular job. I sell my poisons on the black market, but sometimes even that isn't enough. Then I have to take dirty money for dirty work, or else my little sister doesn't eat, and, and I've never even held her hand! I don't want to live like this any more."

"She's telling the truth," Griff said softly, his golden eyes compassionate.

"Wait," Chase said suddenly, something about what she'd said earlier nagging at him. "What do you mean, some shark shifters came after you?"

"They said their boss was pissed because I damaged his plane." Ivy swiped her sleeve across her eyes. The PVC hissed where her tears touched, acid eating pits into the shiny black material. "I don't know anything about that. My employer just told me to make sure I killed the pilot. He didn't care about the plane."

"*Connie.*" Red rage misted Chase's vision. He would have gone for the wyvern shifter, but Ash flung out an arm to block him. "You tried to kill *my mate*."

"I'm not an assassin," Ivy flared up, her own fists clenching. "I took the money, but I only ever meant to make the plane crash. I tried to do it slowly enough that the pilot would be able to bail out safely, once they realized what was happening. I didn't want to hurt anyone!"

Chase glanced at Griff, who shrugged. "Still telling the truth."

Chase stared hard at Ivy. "So if you're not working for Sammy Smiles, who *are* you working for?"

Ivy shook her head. "I don't know. I've worked for him for years—selling poisons for him to use against his rivals, mainly. Not to kill them! Just, just little doses, enough to take them out of action for a while, when he needed them out of the way." She didn't meet any of their eyes, shame clear in her young face. "Anyway, he's always been very, very careful not to let me find out who he is."

"Who else would want your mate dead?" Griff asked Chase.

"I don't know, but when I find out *they'll* be dead," Chase growled. "Ivy, if you want to have any *chance* of not spending the rest of your life behind bars, you'd better tell me everything you know about this employer of yours. *Now*."

Ivy flinched a little, her back pressing against the wall of the alley. "I—I don't know much. He normally texts me with what he wants, but occasionally he mindspeaks to me, so I know he's got to be some sort of mythic shifter. Um. I know he's rich. Oh, and he's got a thing about pegasus shifters."

"You mean he hates us?" Chase tried to think if anyone could want *him* dead. The list was, he had to admit, potentially quite long.

"No, the opposite. He was very clear on this job that I mustn't harm any pegasus shifters." Ivy glared at him, rubbing her side absently. "Clearly you didn't know that, though. You should thank me, Rainbow Dash. It's pretty hard to hold back when someone's trying to kick your ribs in."

Chase furrowed his brow, trying to make the pieces fit together. He had a nagging sense that it should be obvious, that he just wasn't seeing something…

"Ivy," he said slowly. "Did you say that your employer told you to start this fire?"

CHAPTER 21

Connie fought with all her strength, but Killian easily restrained her as Sammy strolled into the room. The shark shifter was followed by a lean, cold-eyed man, clearly one of his thugs.

Connie filled her lungs and screamed as loud as she could, desperately hoping to attract the attention of someone in the neighboring apartments. She only got off one yell, though, before Sammy's henchman slapped a calloused hand over her mouth.

"I'm afraid there's no one nearby to hear you," Killian told her, stepping back as Sammy's man took over the job of restraining her. The pegasus shifter turned to Sammy, frowning. "I thought you were just going to send someone. If anyone asks me if you were here—"

"Now, why would they have any reason to do that?" Sammy replied. He kept his hands in his suit pockets, being careful not to touch anything. "Just wanted to make sure the job was done properly."

Killian jerked his chin at the henchman. "You're positive no one will be able to recognize him?"

"See, that's the nice thing about working with undersea types." Sammy's sharp smile flashed. "A lot of us hardly ever come up on land. Makes it real easy to find someone for this sort of quiet work."

"Good." Killian looked at the henchman. "Tell me you're a wyvern shifter. Out loud."

"I'm a… wyvern shifter?" the thug said, baffled.

"That'll do." The pegasus shifter took a small, sheathed knife out of his pocket. "I need to be able to say that I thought you were one. We're ready, then."

Killian unsheathed the knife. It was only a small blade, but Killian handled it as gingerly as if it was a loaded gun. The edge of the steel looked corroded, and was coated in some thick, oily fluid.

Killian held the handle in the tips of his fingers, offering it to Sammy's henchman. The man glanced at it, then looked questioningly at Sammy.

The shark shifter rocked a little on the balls of his feet. "Now, I can't tell you what to do, son. But I will just say that the little lady here has been a mighty sharp thorn in my side. Not that I'd ever want anyone to hurt her seriously, mind."

With a shrug, Sammy's henchman took the proffered knife in one hand, still restraining Connie with his other arm. Connie tried to cringe away from the blade, but even one-handed, the thug easily held her motionless.

With a quick, practiced flick, he drew the sharp edge across her cheek.

It happened so fast that Connie didn't even feel any pain. Then she realized that she couldn't feel *anything*. The absolute numbness spread out from the cut and across her face, terrifyingly fast.

"I hope it doesn't hurt," Killian said to her, in genuine concern. "I specifically told my wyvern to make me a poison that wouldn't hurt. I don't want you to suffer, Connie."

"You… won't… get away," Connie forced out around her numb tongue. "Chase…"

"Will never know the truth," Killian finished for her, calmly. He held his arms outspread, cocking his head at Sammy's henchman. "I need to be able to truthfully say that I tried to fight you off. Please, make it look good."

Connie collapsed helplessly to the floor as the man released her. She could only watch, paralysis spreading through every muscle of her body, as Sammy's thug delivered a swift, thorough beating to Killian.

Chase, she thought desperately.

She remembered Ash saying that mythic shifters were telepathic. Chase was her mate. Would he be able to sense her distress?

CHASE! she called out mentally, praying that he could hear her. Praying that he was on his way.

"Enough," Killian gasped after a few brutal minutes. He held up a hand. "That'll do."

The henchman glanced at Sammy, who lifted one finger, scratching his nose. The henchman swiveled on one foot, swinging one last blow straight at Killian's face. The pegasus shifter cried out, hunching over.

"*That* was for sending my plane to the bottom of the sea," Sammy said, his smile cruel and savage. "It's going to cost me a pretty penny to get it fixed up. You sure your cousin isn't going to notice that it's gone?"

"I'll handle that." Killian straightened again, blood streaming from his broken nose. "He'll be too devastated over losing his mate to care about anything else."

"You better see that you do." Sammy glanced at his henchman, his black eyes cold. "Just one last thing to do, then."

"Boss?" His thug looked confused.

He never saw the pegasus's hooves coming.

"There," Killian said, shifting back again. "Now I can say

that the wyvern shifter broke in here and I killed him, but not before he managed to poison Connie. Even if Chase calls in his truth-teller friend, the story will check out. You should go now."

"Not yet." Sammy crouched down on his heels next to Connie, staring intently into her face. "No one crosses me and lives to boast about it. I want to see the light go out of her eyes."

Chase...

Her vision was going dark. The last thing she saw was Sammy's sharp, triumphant smile.

CHAPTER 22

Chase...

Even though they weren't fully bonded, Chase could feel Connie calling his name. Her faint mental voice was growing weaker by the second.

Chase flew as he'd never flown before. All the aches and pains of his battered body fell away, as nothing compared to the overwhelming need to get to Connie. He flashed across the night sky like a shooting star, not even bothering to make himself invisible. His mate needed him now, *now!*

...Chase...

Even as he arrowed down toward her apartment building, her psychic call faded away into silence. Terror filled his heart. There was no time to land, no time to shift. He folded his wings as tightly as he could, aiming straight at her window.

He burst through in a shower of glass and splinters, taking the entire window and a good deal of the wall with him. Even in the chaos of flying debris, he knew with crystal clarity exactly where Connie was. She lay prone on the floor, barely breathing, Sammy Smiles crouched over her like a vulture.

He tucked up his hooves, leaping Connie's limp form as he knocked the shark shifter away from her. Sammy went flying, smashing hard into the far wall. Sammy bared his teeth, his form starting to swell into a monstrous shark-headed shape—but Chase whirled, kicking him hard in the chest with both back hooves. Sammy went down, and this time, he didn't get up again.

"Chase," Killian gasped. His cousin staggered forward, hand outstretched, his face a mask of blood. "Thank God. Sammy brought—"

LIAR! Chase slammed into him. Killian gasped as a thousand pounds of angry equine crushed him into the corner. *You hired the wyvern! You tried to kill my mate! YOU!*

"I—I would never have hurt you." Killian's eyes swiveled, searching for any way to escape, but Chase had him boxed in with no room to shift. "Just calm down and I'll explain. You don't want to hurt me either, not really. I'm your cousin!"

Not kin. Chase's stallion laid its ears flat back against its skull. *Rival!*

Chase reared over his cousin, his iron-hard hooves directly over Killian's head. It would be so easy...

Too easy.

He flicked out one foreleg, clipping Killian neatly on the side of the head. His cousin collapsed, knocked out cold.

Kill! urged his stallion.

No, Chase told his pegasus, turning away. *He hurt our mate. He must lose everything, as he sought to take everything from us. He will never fly again, never run again, never be free again. He will live the rest of his life behind bars, and every day, every minute of his wretched existence, he will know that he* lost.

Chase heard the sing-song wail of an approaching siren.

Griff's friends in the police were on their way. There was no time to wait for them, though. He could feel Connie's faltering pulse as if her heart beat inside his own chest.

Chase seized Connie's collar in his teeth, awkwardly jerking his head round to sling her across his broad back. She hung limp, arms and legs dangling down. As soon as he had her secure, Chase launched himself out the hole in the wall as smoothly as he could, soaring back up into the cool night air.

HUGH! he sent telepathically, his pegasus senses reaching out to find the paramedic. *I need you, NOW!*

I'm at a traffic incident. Hugh's mental voice was as terse and clipped as his physical one. *I'm a little busy—*

I'm bringing Connie to you. He wheeled round, locking onto the paramedic's location. *I think she's been poisoned by wyvern venom.*

Hugh swore, the mental picture bright and profane. *Then you'd better get here fast.*

Chase flew as quickly as he dared. Every slight slip of Connie's body across his back made his heart leap into his mouth. He kept having to twitch one way or the other to keep her from sliding off.

Fortunately, Hugh wasn't far away. In mere minutes, Chase caught sight of the paramedic's distinctive white hair. Hugh was standing some way back from a couple of smoking, smashed cars piled up at the side of the road. John Doe was there, too, wielding a hose to put out the flaming vehicles—and no doubt surreptitiously using his sea dragon ability to control water to assist the process.

"You're in luck," Hugh said as Chase touched down next to him. The paramedic was cleaning blood off his bare hands with an antiseptic wipe. "I just sent off the ambulance with the casualties. Let's see her, then."

Chase shifted, catching Connie in his arms as he did so.

He lowered her to the ground, stepping back to allow Hugh access. The paramedic crouched over her, his face going intent and focused as he ran his long fingers over her skin. His breath hissed out between his teeth.

"Close your eyes," Hugh demanded abruptly.

"What?" Chase stared at him, taken aback. "Why?"

"Because I have to shift to heal her." Hugh shot a quick glance at John Doe, but the sea dragon shifter already had his back to them, fully occupied with the car fire. The paramedic looked back at Chase, scowling fiercely. "If you want me to save your mate, then close your Goddamn eyes!"

Chase would have happily plucked out his own eyes, if it would save Connie. He squeezed them shut as tight as he could, desperately praying as he did so.

Please. Please let this work...

A soft, silvery light shone through his closed eyelids. A faint, elusive fragrance filled the air, like lilacs after rain. Everything seemed to go very still and quiet. All of his aches and bruises faded away, washed clean by that subtle, healing radiance.

What's this? His pegasus pricked up its ears, nostrils flaring as if catching wind of a familiar scent. *Kin?*

Hush. Chase kept his eyes scrunched shut, not daring to risk distracting Hugh from his task. Privately, he swore he would never, ever again tease Hugh for his mysterious ways, if only he could heal Connie now.

The light faded. "There," Hugh said, sounding exhausted but satisfied.

"Connie!" Chase flung himself down next to her. He cradled her as she drew in a deep, hacking breath.

"She's stable now, but she'll still need fluids and rest." Hugh rose, pulling his customary surgical gloves back on. "I'm going to call an ambulance."

Chase stroked Connie's hair back from her white face.

"I'm here, Connie. I've got you. Everything's going to be okay."

Her eyes fluttered open. They fixed on him, widening.

"Chase," she said, joy and love shining from her face. She nestled against his chest, leaning on him with perfect trust. "Yes."

EPILOGUE

One Week Later

"Are you peeking?" Chase demanded.

"I'm not, I promise!" Giggling, Connie clung to his neck, the blindfold over her face tickling her nose with every step Chase took. "But I swear I will, if you don't put me down soon. When you said you had a surprise, I thought you meant close by!"

"Nearly there," Chase promised, which was what he'd said five minutes ago, when he'd swept her up in his arms, and fifteen minutes before *that*, during the car ride from the hospital. Connie was starting to wonder if the next stage of the mysterious journey was going to involve a charter jet. She wouldn't put it past him.

This time, however, it seemed that they really were nearly there. Connie felt him fumble in his pocket, and heard a beep followed by a louder rumbling that sounded like a vast garage door sliding open. After a moment, the noise stopped, and Chase finally set her down on her feet again.

"I couldn't find a 'Glad You've Finally Fully Recovered from Being Poisoned By A Wyvern' card," Chase said as he untied the silk blindfold from around her head. "Hallmark seem to have overlooked that opportunity, strangely. So I got you a present instead."

Connie blinked, briefly dazzled by the bright lights after having had her eyes closed for so long. For a second, she just had a vague impression of a large, gleaming, olive-green blur in front of her...

"Oh," she gasped, as her vision came clear. "*Oh.*"

The Spitfire listed a little, propped up by scaffolding on one side where the left wheel assembly had been torn away. There were great, crumpled gashes in the plane's underbelly, and both cockpits were completely smashed. The propeller was bent and twisted.

But it was hers.

Her Spitfire.

Her mother's plane.

"I know it looks a mess," Chase said anxiously, as she drifted dreamlike toward the Spitfire. "But John spent ages searching the sea floor, and he swears on the honor of his people that he found all the parts. I've dried everything out and cleaned it as best I could, but I don't know how to fix it myself and I didn't trust anyone else to work on it without your approval. I promise, we'll get her restored, no matter what. You can have whatever you need to repair it, or I could hire specialists, or, or... Connie?"

Gently, as if the Spitfire might bolt away like a startled deer if she moved too fast, Connie laid her hand flat on the plane's battered surface.

"Hello again, baby," she whispered.

Chase let out his breath in a long sigh of relief. "So she's okay?"

"She's *perfect*." Connie stroked the plane, blinking back tears at being able to touch it again. "It'll take some time, but I'll make her good as new. It'll be like... it'll be like working with my mother. Fixing the same things that she fixed, all those years ago."

He came up behind her, softly resting his hands on her shoulders. "I think she would have liked that. She'd be very proud of you." A slightly pained note crept into his voice. "I'd say she'd be even prouder than your dad is, but I'm not sure that's humanly possible."

Connie giggled, leaning back against his broad chest. "So I guess he must have subjected you to the story of how I won the Rydon Cup in a borrowed rustbucket, while flying backward and upside-down."

"Twice. I *did* try to remind him that I was actually there, but he kept talking anyway." Chase sounded aggrieved. "I wish I could tell him what really happened. My version of the story is much better."

"Serves you right, having to hold your tongue while someone else prattles on for once." Connie bit her lip. "Um. While we're talking planes... I have a confession to make. About your Spitfire."

"It's your Spitfire," Chase said, without hesitation. "Your other Spitfire. I'm not letting you give it back."

"Good, because I kind of can't." Connie tilted her head to look up at him. "I traded it to my dad. He can race it, display it, sell it, whatever he wants... but it'll be on his own. I'm done bailing him out now. I love him, but I can't go through anything like this again."

"You won't," Chase said fiercely, his arms tightening around her. "I promise. I'm glad you're spreading your own wings at last. Your dad has to learn to fly on his own, too."

"Speaking of dads." Connie raised her eyebrows at him. "Did you talk to yours yet?"

"Yes." She felt all his muscles tense. "With Killian in jail, Tiernach Enterprises is in chaos. My father needs to stabilize things as quickly as possible. He's got some potential replacements lined up, but he'd still prefer it if I took over as CFO."

Connie put her hand over his, squeezing it. "Will you?"

He looked down at her, his eyes dark and unreadable. "Do you want me to?"

"I want you to be happy," she said. Her thumb rubbed soothing circles on the back of his hand. "And somehow I don't think sitting behind a desk all day would do that."

He let out a brief, sharp laugh. "No."

Chase fell silent for a long moment, his face shadowed. "He got me into firefighting, did I ever tell you that? Killian, I mean. After you left, all those years ago. I was determined to just blindly charge around the world searching for you, but he persuaded me to leave that to professional detectives. I needed something to keep me busy, so he told me about this all-shifter fire crew he'd heard about. He thought it might suit me."

"He did know you very well," Connie said, softly.

"And it *does* suit me," Chase admitted. Gradually, the tension eased from his body, though he still looked subdued. "I like doing something real, that demands all my mind and strength and skill. I like being able to use my talents to help people. You don't mind if I stick with it? I mean, it's a dangerous job. I wouldn't want you to be constantly worrying about me."

"Chase, I fly vintage WWII warplanes for a living," Connie said, a touch acerbically. "Exactly which one of us should be worrying about the other, again?"

He laughed again, and Connie was pleased that it was his real laugh this time, warm and unrestrained. "You have a point, there." He cocked his head to one side. "Hey. You said you traded your other Spitfire to your dad, but you didn't say what for. What did you get in return?"

Connie patted her Spitfire again. "The other half of this. When my mom died, her will left me and my dad both half-shares in her plane. I used your Spitfire to buy him out. She's all mine now."

"And no one will ever be able to take her away from you again," Chase finished for her, with great satisfaction.

"Well... that's not strictly true." Connie turned in his arms, stepping back a little so that she could meet his eyes properly. "Because I'm giving half of her to you."

Chase's mouth dropped open. "Connie—"

She put a finger on his lips, silencing him. "I know you don't need the money. But I don't want to start off our lives together in debt to you, either. So I'm going to insist on this. She's half yours, and half mine, and that's that."

His face went very still, his eyes wide and dark as he looked into hers. "Our lives together?"

Connie stretched up on her toes to kiss him in answer. His mouth was light and gentle on hers, as if he hardly dared to breathe.

Then his hands came up to softly frame her face. His long, agile fingers caressed her as he deepened the kiss. The sweetness of it sang through Connie's body, until she felt as if his hands were the only thing stopping her from floating up, up into the sky.

"In that case," Chase murmured into her lips, "I have a question for you."

Even though she should really have been used to it by now, Connie's heart still skipped a beat as he went down on one knee.

"Constance West." He took her hand. "Will you be my mate?"

Connie blinked down at him. "Okay, I have to admit, that's not what I was expecting. I thought I already was your mate?"

"You are. But we aren't *mated*. It's... different." He looked like he was struggling to find words to explain it. "There's a sort of ritual that we do. Afterwards, we'd be true, bonded mates."

"Like Virginia and Dai?" Connie asked. She remembered the deep, powerful connection between the dragon shifter and his mate, so strong it was almost visible.

Chase nodded. "We'd be able to talk telepathically, like I do with other mythic shifters. We'd know what each other is feeling, share our deepest desires and needs. We'd be truly joined. Forever."

Connie's breath caught. "Oh, yes. *Yes*. Let's do it."

She could so clearly see Chase's joy shining in his eyes, it was like their souls were already joined. "Now?"

Connie laughed, feeling wonderfully wild and reckless. "Yes, now! *Can* we? What do we do?"

"There are a couple of steps, to bring us closer together." Chase stood, taking both her hands in his. "First, we fly back to my nest."

"I assume that's not flying in a plane." Connie's pulse sped up at the prospect of riding the pegasus again—partly with excitement, but also with nervousness.

She'd never learned how to ride. As a kid, when most of her friends had been horse-mad, she'd been wallpapering her bedroom with posters of vintage warplanes.

Chase won't let me fall.

"What happens after we get back to your place?" she asked him.

A slow, wicked grin spread across Chase's face, kindling an answering heat low in Connie's belly. "To find *that* out, you'll have to ride me there."

Rising, Chase retreated a few steps. His tall, strong form shimmered. Between one blink and the next, the black pegasus stood before her.

All the breath whooshed out of Connie's lungs. She hadn't had the chance to see him properly like this before. The elegant arch of his strong neck would have put the finest Arabian stallion to shame. But while he had the graceful, lean build of a thoroughbred racehorse, his back was higher than the top of her head. He was the biggest horse she'd ever seen.

Awestruck, she circled him. He stayed still to let her look at him, though his alert ears swiveled to follow her. The lights struck gleaming purple and blue highlights from his folded wings. His sleek black coat held the same iridescence, but subtler. He gleamed as if carved from black opal.

He knelt, stretching out one wing. Heart thudding, Connie scrambled up onto his back. She had to hike up her dress a little to straddle him, his hide warm and soft against her bare thighs. He stayed steady as she tucked her legs under his folded wings.

"Okay," she said, when she felt as secure as she was going to get. Tentatively, she squeezed his sides a little with her legs. "I'm ready."

Chase took a single delicate step forward, and stopped.

"I said I'm ready." She nudged him again, a little harder. "Let's go!"

Chase curved his neck to look back at her, the deep black eye wide and innocent. Then he began to amble toward the door at a pace so sedate, he could have been overtaken by a tortoise.

Connie rolled her own eyes at him. "Don't think I don't know what you're up to. But, if you insist…"

She kicked him hard in the ribs with her heels, like a cowboy in a movie. "Heigh-ho, Silver! Giddy-up!"

Chase snorted with equine laughter. She instinctively

grabbed at his silky mane as his huge muscles bunched under his velvet-soft fur.

Then, he *ran*.

Connie shrieked, flinging herself flat against his neck as he went from a standing start to a flat-out gallop in barely a heartbeat. The instant they were clear of the hanger, his wings spread, each reaching primary feathers as long as Connie's entire arm. He leaped, his wings sweeping down as his back hooves left the ground.

It was nothing like flying in a plane. The wind roared all around her, whipping Chase's long black mane into her face as he soared upward. The ground fell away with dizzying speed. Connie clung to him for dear life, her arms wrapped around his neck so tight she worried she might throttle him.

Yet for all his terrifying speed and the lack of any sort of safety harness, he bore her up as smoothly as her own plane. She could feel the constant movement of his muscles, adjusting to match every tiny shift in her own body.

Gradually, Connie's hammering heart began to slow. She dared to sit up a little, squinting against the wind. Brighton spread out beneath them, sunset turning its old, stately buildings to gold. She'd never been able to look straight down while flying before. The whole world spread out at her feet, intricate and inviting.

She laughed out loud in sheer, surprised joy. Chase pranced on thin air, showing his pleasure in her delight.

Greatly daring, Connie let go of his mane. Chase stayed steady as a rock underneath her. Closing her eyes, she spread her arms wide. The wind streamed through her outstretched fingers.

For the first time in her life, she truly knew what it was to *fly*, like a bird, on her own two wings.

Chase tipped one wing down, banking. Connie shifted her weight, knowing from the subtle movements of his muscles under her bare thighs what he was going to do even before he started to spiral downward. She could see Chase's rooftop garden below them. Tiny, glimmering lights marked its edges, guiding them to the landing lawn.

Chase's hooves delicately touched down. He knelt again to allow her to dismount. She slid off his back, feeling a little regretful to feel ground under her feet again.

Laying her cheek against his gleaming hide, she hugged his neck hard. "That was amazing. Part of me wishes we could stay up in the sky forever."

The pegasus's smooth, glossy fur dissolved under her hands—and became warm, human skin. Chase's arms slid round her. "Then I'd better make it worth your while to come down."

Connie gasped, feeling his massive erection pressing against her soft stomach as he pulled her close. His eyes were dark pools of desire. Despite his clear need, he kissed her lightly. Connie closed her eyes, melting against him as he gently explored and tasted her mouth. His teasing tongue sent pleasure racing through her veins, and a surge of wetness between her thighs.

Hungry for more, she tried to deepen the kiss—but his hands closed over her shoulders, holding her back. "Slowly," he said, hoarsely. "This time, we take things slowly. I want to learn every inch of you."

Connie slid her hands over his chest, feeling the hardness of his muscles under the soft cotton shirt. She let her fingers drift lower, popping open the button of his jeans. "Do I get to do the same to you?"

Chase caught his breath as she lightly traced the bulge of his straining cock. "Yes. Oh, *God* yes." He caught her wrist. "Though maybe you shouldn't start there."

Backing off a little, he pulled his shirt over his head. Connie's breath sighed out of her. The fading sunset highlighted the beautiful planes of his torso, every muscle sharp and defined. Framed by lush rosebushes edging the garden, he looked like some classical statue brought to life.

Taking her hands in his, he lay her palms flat against his shoulders, wordlessly inviting her to explore. She slid her hands over his warm skin, hardly able to believe that this Greek god of a man could really be *hers*.

His chest rose sharply as she brushed over his hard nipples. Somehow, she could sense the shock of pleasure that went through him, as if it was echoed in her own body. She could feel how his skin sang to her every touch, how the light scratch of her nails made his desire rise, hot and urgent.

Wanting to see all of him, she pushed his jeans and underwear down over his lean hips. He clenched his fists, his abs knotting as she knelt to pull the rest of his clothes off. She could feel how hard it was for him to hold back, how badly he wanted to touch her.

His hard cock strained above her, thick and full. Even though she knew he wanted to take things slow, Connie couldn't resist tasting him, just a little. His breath exploded out of him as she ran her tongue up the thick shaft. He yanked her up, so hard and fast she nearly overbalanced.

"My turn now," he said, a feral heat burning in his eyes.

As if unable to restrain himself any longer, his strong hands quickly undid the buttons at the front of her dress. He pushed the silky fabric off her shoulders, and Connie wriggled a little so that the dress fell to pool at her feet.

"So beautiful." Chase's hand trembled as he traced the curves of her shoulder, sliding her bra strap off. "My beautiful mate. Let me see you. Let me worship you."

His touch left trails of fire on her skin as he slid her bra off. His light, teasing fingers skimmed her curves, moving down to hook under her panties. Slowly, still looking up at her, Chase knelt, pulling her panties down as he did so. His touch on her thighs was exquisite torture, leaving her breathless with desire for more.

"Connie," Chase growled, a rough catch in his voice betraying his own desire. He pulled her down, catching her in his arms and laying her back on the soft grass. His hands slid up her legs, spreading them wide so that he could kneel between them. "My mate."

Totally exposed before his hungry gaze, the gentle breeze caressing her bare skin, Connie had never felt more beautiful. He looked at her as if she was a miracle, a goddess, everything he could ever want.

Chase dipped his head, planting a trail of kisses up her sensitive inner thigh. Connie moaned, winding her fingers into his hair, trying to urge him on faster. Yet still he held back, taking his time, making her quiver with frustrated lust as he slowly, so slowly worked his way upward.

When his tongue finally traced her wet folds, Connie's hips jerked upward at the electric shock of it. Spreading her wide with his fingers, he licked her firmly, every touch making her writhe and sob with helpless pleasure. That growing connection between them showed him exactly how to circle her, exactly what she needed to reach her peak. She arched up as orgasm rushed over her.

Please, please, more, now!

"Yes," Chase gasped.

Drawing back, he flipped her over. His strong hands on her hips urged her onto her knees, pulling her up against him. His torso pressed against her back as he effortlessly lifted her to exactly the position he wanted. Anticipation sang through Connie's body as his hard cock rubbed against her eager entrance, her juices slicking the swollen head. She'd never felt so ready, so desperate.

With a single hard thrust, he sank fully into her. It was as if he sank into her mind, her very soul, at the same time. His love for her enfolded her even as her body enfolded his. She cried out, lost to everything, everything except him. She matched him thrust for thrust, spiraling up into ecstasy in perfect union.

My mate!

He bit down on the base of her neck as he thrust one last time. The edge of pain made an exquisite counterpoint to her ecstasy, sweeping her over the edge. His fierce satisfaction at marking her filled her, as much as his hot seed did.

She was his now, as he was hers.

Forever.

They collapsed down onto the grass together, breathing as hard as if they'd just run a marathon. Connie felt deliciously exhausted, undone in every muscle.

She snuggled back into Chase, intertwining her fingers through his. "So... are we mated now?"

Oh yes. His voice sounded not in her ears, but inside her head. Connie twitched in surprise, and Chase laughed. *Very, very thoroughly mated.*

Good, she thought at him, and knew that he'd heard her from the jolt of pleased surprise that he sent back. She wriggled round in his arms to face him. *In that case, I have a question for you.*

Oh? Chase smiled at her, his love enfolding her like strong wings.

She could feel his complete happiness, his awestruck delight that *she* had chosen *him*. She could sense his bone-deep determination to be worthy of her.

Chase Tiernach. Connie looked deep into his warm black eyes. *Will you marry me?*

FIREFIGHTER GRIFFIN

FIRE & RESCUE SHIFTERS 3

CHAPTER 1

GRIFF

"Ma'am, is it your son or your cat who's stuck up the tree?"

The words snagged Griffin MacCormick's attention as he finished handling another grueling emergency call. Pulling his headset off his ears, he cocked an eyebrow at his colleague at the opposite desk. Kevin caught his eye, and rolled his own, mouthing "time waster" as he pointed at his own headset.

"Let me see if I understand you, ma'am," Kevin said to the caller, his tone leaden with jaded weariness. "Your cat, who is like a son to you, is stuck up a tree. And you would like the fire services to send a very expensive emergency vehicle, which is meant for *emergencies*, to attend to your…pussy."

Having just spent an heart-pounding thirty minutes on the phone with a traumatized caller who was pinned under two tons of smashed, burning car, Griff could sympathize with his colleague's irritation with the nuisance call, if not his unprofessionalism in letting sarcasm seep into his tone. The East Sussex Fire and Rescue Service was stretched thin just handling the major crises. The seaside city of Brighton might not be particularly large—especially not compared to London—but it was one of the most vibrant cities in England, attracting millions of visitors with its quirky, alternative culture. And lots of drunk, excited tourists looking for a wild night out meant a *lot* of work for fire dispatchers like Griff.

Especially when quite a few of those drunk, excited tourists were dragons.

Not that Kevin, or indeed any of Griff's other colleagues in the control room, knew *that* little secret about their city.

Kevin raised his eyes to the heavens—or at least, to the control room ceiling—as if praying for the strength to deal with the idiot in his earpiece. "I'm sorry, ma'am, I'm not sure I'm following you. Are you trying to tell me that your son turned *into* a cat and shot up a tree?"

Now *that* got Griff's full attention. Bringing up the office chat utility on his PC, he typed to Kevin, *Want me to take over?*

Kevin shook his head at him across the desk. *Nah,* he typed back, one handed. *Nearly got rid of her.*

"Yes, ma'am, that does sound unbelievable," Kevin said into his headset. "I see. Yes, ma'am, this *was* a bad idea. You do that. In future, please don't call the fire department unless you actually have an emergency. Goodbye." Pushing his headset down around his neck, he stretched with a groan. "Goddamn bored housewives. I swear that one must have been high on her kid's meds or something."

"Sounded like an interesting call," Griff observed mildly.

"Nah, just another time waster." With a push of one foot, Kevin propelled his office chair backwards to the whiteboard in the corner, where the dispatch team kept a highly unofficial tally of handled calls. Picking up the blue pen, he added another tick to his row with a sarcastic flourish. "At this rate, I may beat even your record for prank callers this week. I swear you're some sort of magnet for the weirdos."

Griff smiled, privately amused. *You have no idea.*

"Hey, what was your call just now? Another crazy?" Kevin waved the blue pen. "Or a real one?"

"Big traffic pile-up," Griff said. "I sent Alpha Team to sort it out. They've got it under control."

"Alpha Team's the one you used to work with, right?" Kevin said idly, swapping the blue pen for a red one in order to put a tick next to Griff's name. "Back when you were a firefighter, I mean."

All Griff's muscles tensed, sending a jolt of pain through his bad leg.

"Yes," he said, in a flat tone that he hoped made it clear he didn't want to discuss his previous profession.

Unfortunately, Kevin's career as a dispatcher had given him the sensitivity of a rhinoceros. "Must have been interesting. Is Alpha Team really as good as people say they are?"

"No." The corner of Griff's mouth twisted wryly. "They're better."

A little pang went through his chest as he thought of how Alpha Team would be working together right now, saving lives with their unique combination of shifter skills. Fire Commander Ash calmly controlling the flames while John Doe called down the rain to quench them...Chase sensing where victims were trapped, fireproof Dai charging headlong into the blaze to pull people out to where Hugh would be waiting to heal them...

Griff shook his head, forcibly dispelling the memories. *I did my part*, he tried to tell himself. *I took the call. I got them there, told them what to expect. I'm still part of the team.*

His inner eagle stretched its wings proudly. *We watch and guide. We fly high, scouting out the way. Our role is essential.*

His lion snarled in bitter denial, baring its fangs at the eagle. *We cower in the den when we should be defending our pride! And it is all* your *fault!*

Griff mentally thrust his two inner animals apart before they could start fighting yet again. He could still feel the eagle's fury and the lion's rage as he wrestled them down to the back of his mind. The effort of keeping the two beasts separated and subdued gave him a splitting headache...but that was better than the alternative.

He became aware that Kevin was giving him an odd look. "I'm sorry, what were you saying?"

"Just that you must have some good tales to tell." Kevin eyed him for a second. "You know, you really should see a doctor about the way you keep spacing out, Griff. What if it happens on a call?"

"It won't." Griff said firmly. "And actually, I am."

For all the good it does me.

"I'm just saying, you have to be fit for the job," Kevin blundered on, displaying his usual tact and compassion. "We dispatchers may not need muscles like the front line meatheads, but that doesn't mean we have room for cripples. If your condition interferes-"

"I *said*, it won't." Holding Kevin's stare, Griff let him see just a hint of the lion behind his own golden eyes.

Kevin flinched back in his chair, and Griff immediately felt ashamed of himself for letting his temper get the better of him. Unleashing his dominance on a regular human—not to mention a colleague—was not only rude, but unsporting. Even another shifter would have a hard time standing up to an alpha lion's commanding nature.

He called his lion back, allowing his eagle to rise again. His vision sharpened, letting him see Kevin's slight nervous sweat and increased pulse rate.

"I can do my job," Griff said, more gently. "You have my word on that. Speaking of the job...did that caller just now really say that her son had turned into a cat?"

"Uh, yeah." Kevin scooted his chair back to the desk,

though Griff noticed he stayed a few inches further away from him than previously. "That was a new one on me. You'd think she'd pick something more plausible, if she was hoping to score a hot firefighter booty call."

Before Griff could quiz him further, a light on Kevin's phone started to flash. "Damn it, I was just about to grab a fresh coffee…" Kevin let out a heart-felt, long-suffering sigh, pulling his headset back into place and jabbing a button. "East Sussex Fire and Rescue Service. Where is your emergency?"

Griff took a sip of his own stone-cold coffee, thinking. With a swift glance around to make sure no one else in the control room was watching, he pulled up the record for the call Kevin had just handled. He wasn't technically supposed to be able to do that, but there was no hiding passwords from his shifter senses. When his eagle was ascendent, he could tell what someone was typing from ten feet away, just from the sound of their fingers hitting the keys.

Kevin might have the compassion of a rock when it came to callers who he thought were time wasters, but he did at least follow proper procedures. He'd dutifully logged the woman's name and address, before starting to ask questions about the nature of her "emergency."

Griff logged out of Kevin's account and sat back, frowning at the screen. A few more clicks showed him that Alpha Team was still fully occupied with the car crash he'd sent them to. Just as well, really. He could just picture Fire Commander Ash's expression if Griff tried to send him—the one and only Phoenix, and quite possibly the most powerful shifter in Europe—to go rescue a cat from a tree.

Even if the cat is really just a scared little boy…

Problem was, all the shifters in the East Sussex Fire and Rescue Service were in Alpha Team. And while Griff knew a lot of the other shifters in Brighton, it would be a gross breach of confidentiality to share a caller's address with someone not in the service.

We must go, his eagle said, unexpectedly. *She called. We must answer.*

The bird is right, his lion rumbled. *Go, now, quickly!*

Griff blinked. He could count on the fingers of one hand the number of times in his life that his two inner beasts had ever been in agreement on *anything*.

"And another 'dumb kids setting fire to leaves in the park' for me," Kevin grumbled, flipping up his headset's microphone. "Only six more bloody hours to go. Griff, not that I'm complaining about the amount of unpaid overtime you put in, but you do realize your shift ended over an hour ago, right? Isn't it time you went home?"

Letting out his breath, Griff pushed himself to his feet. "Apparently not," he murmured.

CHAPTER 2

HAYLEY

As a single mom, Hayley Parker was used to having to handle every parenting challenge on her own. With no one else to back her up, she'd always tried to make sure she was prepared for anything. She'd borrowed and read every child development book in the library. She'd scoured the internet for tips on raising a son without a father figure present. She'd even spent uncounted hours plowing through her old college textbooks, making sure she was up-to-date on Early Years literacy and numeracy educational strategies.

None of these, however, had given her any hint on what to do when your five-year-old unexpectedly turns into a lion cub and shoots up a tree.

"Okay, Danny," she said, fighting to keep her voice calm and steady. It was important to always give the appearance of being in control, she knew, so that your child could feel safe and secure. No doubt that was doubly important if your child happened to be a lion. Animals could smell weakness, couldn't they?

Oh God, this can't be happening.

"The fire trucks are a little busy right now," she continued, clasping her hands together so that he wouldn't be able to see how they were shaking. "So we're just gonna get you down ourselves, okay? Now, do you think you could scoot back a little? Just move one foot...um, one paw at a time. Nice and slow."

She could just make out Danny's round, fuzzy face, peering down at her through the leaves. He let out another tiny, desperate mew, and her heart broke. She knew, just *knew*, that he was calling for her. Calling for Mommy to rescue him.

"Don't worry, baby," she forced out past the tightness in her throat. Her heart hammered at every slight sway of the branch. "You just keep your, your nice sharp claws locked tight in that tree, okay? That's my big, brave boy."

Hayley fought down a hysterical giggle. *Big brave lion.*

My boy turned into a lion.

Please, I'd really like to wake up now.

She looked wildly around their small backyard, hoping against hope that some inspiration would strike. Her gaze snagged on her discarded cellphone, and she flinched. Her ears still burned from the blistering sarcasm of the emergency call handler.

How was I supposed to know that the fire services in England don't deal with cats stuck in trees?

To be fair, Hayley wasn't sure they did back home in California, either, but with her baby thirty feet off the ground and squalling in panic, her first reflex had been to dial emergency. Thank Heaven the dispatcher *hadn't* believed her. Halfway through the call, she'd had a sudden horrific vision of what could happen if firefighters turned up and discovered that she really did have a lion cub in her backyard. Her little boy could have ended up in the local pound. Or the zoo.

Or some secret government lab, being sliced apart to discover how he transforms...

Hayley jammed a fist in her mouth, stifling the whimper that wanted to rise in her throat. She hadn't had the luxury of weakness since Danny's father had left, in the early days of her pregnancy. She definitely couldn't afford to fall apart now.

Taking a deep breath, she straightened her spine. *Just another unexpected crisis,* she told herself firmly. *Pull it together, Hayley. Danny needs you. It's not like anyone else is going to come to the rescue.*

"Hello?" called a strange male voice, and Hayley nearly leapt out of her skin. Someone knocked on the side gate, which led from the backyard to the narrow alleyway that ran alongside her house. "Ms. Parker? Sorry, didn't mean to scare you, but you weren't answering the doorbell."

Of all the times for a door-to-door salesman or charity collector to come round!

"Th-this isn't a good time!" Hayley yelled over her shoulder.

"I know it isn't," the unseen man said. His warm, rolling Scottish accent wrapped round her like a comforter on a cold night. "That's why I'm here. My name's Griffin MacCormick, and I work for the East Sussex Fire and Rescue Service. May I come in?"

Oh no, they sent a firefighter after all!

Visions of secret labs and gleaming scalpels flashed through Hayley's mind. "No! I…it was just a prank call. I'm really sorry. I swear I'll never do it again."

Danny had gone very still and quiet up in the tree, his small round ears pricked toward the sound of the man's voice. She prayed he wouldn't meow again.

"It wasn't a prank call," the man said, his voice a deep, reassuring rumble. "Your son turned into a lion cub, and now he's up a tree and can't get down."

He knows Danny's a lion? But he can't see the tree from the alleyway. And I said 'cat' to the fire dispatcher.

"How...?" Hayley whispered to herself.

"I can smell him," the man added, as if he'd heard her.

...He can smell him?

"Please let me help you," the man said gently. "I know what's happening. I promise you, everything will be fine."

Biting her lip, Hayley sidled over to the gate. She hesitated a moment with her hand on the latch, but somehow she had an instinctive, gut feeling that she could trust this stranger. Before she could have second thoughts, she opened the gate.

"That's it," he said as the gate swung open. "Now-"

The man stopped dead as his eyes met hers.

"Oh," he breathed, very softly. "*Oh.*"

Hayley found herself equally stunned, mesmerized by his astonishing eyes. They were gold—not just a pale hazel or light brown, but a deep, rich, true gold. They glowed like fall sunlight through yellow maple leaves. Caught by those eyes, she felt as if she'd turned to glass, as if that penetrating gaze could see straight through to the secret, innermost center of her heart.

The man blinked, breaking the moment. "Well now," he said, his voice a little rougher than before, as if he too had been shaken to the core. "That explains a few things. But I think we ought to see to the wee lad first, aye?"

Hayley pulled herself together, worry swamping the odd moment of recognition. "He's- he's up in the chestnut tree. This way, Mr...MacCormick, was it?"

"Call me Griff." The man brushed past her, and Hayley's pulse thudded at the momentary touch of his arm against hers. "Ah, I see him, the poor brave lad. We'll have him down in a tick, just you see."

Okay, maybe I am *still dreaming. Even firefighters don't look like* that. *At least, not outside of Vegas shows.*

Griff must have stood at least six foot two, and gave the impression of being at least that wide across the shoulders as well. His stocky, muscular build made Hayley feel dwarfed in comparison, even though she was hardly tiny herself. He moved with the easy confidence of a powerful man comfortable in his own skin, but there was the slightest hint of a limp to his stride as he headed for the chestnut tree. Hayley couldn't help staring at his broad back as she followed, hypnotized by the sheer strength he exuded. She wondered if she would even be able to span his chest with her arms...

How can I even be noticing his chest at a time like this? Danny's in danger! Hayley mentally slapped herself. *I'm a mom, I shouldn't be thinking of anything other than my baby!*

Stopping under the tree, Griff tilted his head up, his thick mane of blond hair brushing his broad shoulders. "Well, you've certainly got yourself good and stuck there, hey laddie?"

Danny had cowered low to the branch, leaving only a dangling, tufted tail visible. A faint, scared mew drifted down.

Griff put his hands in his pockets, looking completely unperturbed by the situation. "Funny thing," he said conversationally to Hayley. "My littlest sister did exactly the same, first time *she* shifted."

"Your...*sister?*" Hayley echoed faintly. A pair of wide yellow eyes appeared over the edge of the branch, thirty feet up.

"Aye." Griff chuckled fondly. "Near panicked the rest of us, see, 'cause Da had told us all to take good care of the baby while he was out. My other sisters shifted in reflex to climb up after her, and then *they* got stuck too. So there they were, four little lions in a tree, all too scared to shift back. And only me left with human hands and wits, trying to figure out how to get them all down before our da came home." Laughter lines creased around his amber eyes as he smiled at her. "At least there's only one cub to rescue this time."

His sisters...can turn into lions too? It's not just Danny?

The thought echoed around Hayley's stunned mind as Griff pulled off his shoes and socks. Planting his bare feet in the grass, he looked consideringly up at the overhanging tree branches for a second. Then, he leapt.

Hayley gasped as Griff caught hold of a branch at least twelve feet above the ground. His biceps strained against his shirt sleeves as he pulled himself up.

He can't be a regular human being, she thought, watching in amazement as Griff climbed the tree, using his arms more than his legs. *Does* he *turn into a lion too?*

"Ah, and that's as high as I can go," Griff said, edging out along a branch that dipped and creaked under his weight. Danny was still out of reach, on a thinner branch higher up. "So the next bit has to be up to you, laddie. What's your name?"

"He's-" Hayley started, but Griff waved her to silence. He kept his head cocked, his eyes fixed calmly on Danny's.

Hayley didn't hear Danny make even the faintest meow, but Griff nodded in satisfaction. "Pleased to meet you, Danny," he said. "Now, I'm going to use human words to talk to you, but you can talk back just like that, aye?"

A pause, then Griff laughed. "I suppose I do talk funny to you. 'Aye' means 'yes,' or 'okay,' where I come from." He laughed again. "No, not Africa. We have lions in Scotland too, believe it or no. Now, Danny, I can't come to you, so you're going to have to come to me. Your claws can't grip so well going backwards, so I need you to turn yourself around."

Hayley's heart leapt into her mouth as the leaves rustled. "Be *careful*, Danny!" she called out.

"No, don't look at your ma down there, Danny. You keep your eyes on me," Griff said, a hint of steel entering his warm voice. "Hayley, we're doing just fine up here. Could do without any distractions, please."

Hayley bit her knuckles, in agony as Danny gingerly edged around until he was facing Griff. Under Griff's patient coaching, he inched along the swaying branch toward the firefighter. Bits of bark pattered around Hayley like fine rain, dislodged by Danny's scrabbling claws.

Danny stopped directly above Griff, but even from the ground Hayley could tell that he was still a couple of feet out of the firefighter's reach. She wanted to call up to ask what Griff was going to do, but didn't dare distract them again.

"That's good, Danny," Griff said. Carefully, he drew himself up to a crouching position on the branch. His bare toes gripped the bark.

He can't possibly be considering standing up *on that twig?*

If he had been, he thought better of it. With a grimace, Griff dropped back down to straddle the branch again, rubbing absently at his left knee. "Danny," he said, very calmly. "In a moment, I'm going to ask you to do one more thing. But you're going to have to trust me."

Danny made a small, suspicious noise, half-mew and half-growl.

"No, I'm not going to tell you yet. When I do, I need you to let your lion instincts take over, without your human mind getting in the way. I promise you, I won't ask anything you can't do. But for this to work, you need to trust me as your alpha. Your lion will understand what that means."

"What are you doing?" Hayley called, unable to help herself. She couldn't control the tremble in her voice.

Griff made a short, quelling gesture at her with one hand, never taking his eyes off Danny's. "In return, I'll give you this promise. I will keep you safe. I will protect you. I will never,

ever let anything harm you, not while I have breath in my lungs and blood in my body. That's what an alpha lion does for his pride, and that's my promise to you. So. Will you trust me?"

Danny had gone absolutely motionless, not even the tip of his tail twitching. Hayley couldn't move herself, every muscle frozen rigid by a combination of terror and Griff's magnetic, compelling charisma.

"Good," Griff said softly. He locked his legs around the tree branch, freeing his hands. "Then as your alpha, I tell you...*jump.*"

Hayley shrieked, her hands flying to her mouth—but Danny was already in mid-air. Without a second of hesitation, he leaped straight into Griff's outstretched arms.

"There now!" Griff hugged the cub close, rubbing his cheek against the side of Danny's muzzle in an oddly feline gesture. "Well done, laddie, well done."

Hayley rushed forward, hands stretching futilely upward. "Danny!"

"Let's get you down to your ma," Griff said to Danny, tucking him under one arm. The little cub snuggled against him, leaning trustingly against Griff's broad chest.

Hayley hopped impatiently on tiptoe as Griff descended, a little more awkwardly than he'd gone up. Danny leaped for her before Griff had even reached the ground, claws tearing the firefighter's shirt in his desperate haste to get to her. Hayley staggered as he barreled into her, nearly knocked off-balance by his surprising weight. She clung to him, tears finally spilling down her face at the feel of his little heartbeat hammering against her chest.

"Steady now, lass." Griff's strong hands grabbed her shoulders, supporting her as her knees threatened to give way. "It's all right. Everything's fine now."

"No, it's not! My baby's a lion!" Hayley's relief gave way to a familiar sense of parental outrage at her offspring for having made her worry in the first place. She thrust Danny out at arm's length, glaring at him sternly. "Daniel Jamie Parker, you turn back human right this instant!"

Danny scrunched up his face, his little lion nose wrinkling. He let out a plaintive, distressed squeak.

Behind her, Griff chuckled ruefully. "It'll be easier if you aren't shaking him like a wee rag doll, Hayley." Gently but firmly, he pushed down on her shoulders, guiding her to sit on the grass. "Let's all just catch our breaths for a moment, hey?"

Hayley cuddled Danny on her lap, stroking his soft, spotted fur. "He *will* go back to normal, won't he?" she asked anxiously.

"Oh, aye," Griff said, and the tightness in Hayley's chest eased at the utter certainty in his tone. "Just needs a little prompting, that's all." He knelt down next to her, the slightest hint of a wince flickering across his rugged face as he bent his left knee.

"Are you okay?" Hayley asked. She'd noticed him favoring that leg earlier.

"Ah, just been a while since I climbed a tree," Griff said lightly, though she was oddly certain that he was in a lot more pain than he was letting on. "What about you? How are you feeling?"

"Me?" Hayley said blankly. It had been so long since anyone had been concerned about how *she* was doing, she almost couldn't process the question. "That doesn't matter. What-"

"Yes, it does," Griff interrupted, with a hint of that strange, commanding tone he'd used on Danny. "You've had quite a shock. I have a friend who's a paramedic. Would you like me to call him? Don't worry, he's a shifter too."

"Shifter?" Hayley latched onto the strange word. "Is that

what…" She gestured helplessly at both him and Danny.

"Yes, we're called shifters. There are quite a few of us, all different kinds, even just here in Brighton. And you still haven't answered my question."

Hayley shook her head, trying to grasp the idea of a whole secret world of people who turned into animals. "What question?"

"How. Are. *You?*" Griff spaced out each word clearly, poking her shoulder lightly in emphasis.

His touch burned on her skin even through two layers of clothing. She was abruptly, acutely aware of how close he was. His intense eyes were focused on her with absolute attention. She could lose herself in those molten, golden depths…

He's concerned about me because it's his job. *And here I am staring at him slack-jawed like some hormonal teenager.*

"Fine. I'm fine," she stammered, her cheeks heating with embarrassment. Under the pretext of moving Danny to a more comfortable position in her lap, she scooted a little further away from Griff. "I don't need any help. Thank you."

Fortunately, the firefighter hadn't seemed to notice her inappropriate reaction to his proximity. Then again, looking the way he did, he was probably used to women losing their train of thought in his presence. "You just let me know if you change your mind about that, all right? In the meantime, let's see about getting Danny back into his usual shape. Come here, laddie."

Danny was normally very shy with everyone except Hayley, but he climbed down from her lap without hesitation. He stumbled a little over his outsized paws as he padded over to Griff, his big yellow eyes fixed trustingly on the firefighter's deep gold ones.

The corner of Griff's mouth quirked upward in amusement. "Still a wee bit stuck, hey?"

Plopping his fuzzy hindquarters down on the grass, Danny let out a woeful yowl of agreement.

Griff cocked his head to one side, looking down at Danny thoughtfully for a moment. "You must be hungry after your adventure. My sisters always told me that shifting takes a lot of energy, usually while stealing food off my plate. Bet you could do with a snack."

Danny's ears perked up. He let out a hopeful whine.

"That sounds perfect," Griff agreed. He turned to Hayley. "Danny seems to think there might be a few chocolate chip cookies lurking in your kitchen. Mind if we have some?"

"How do you do that?" Hayley asked as she got to her feet. "Know what he's saying, I mean."

"Most shifters of the same general type can talk to each other telepathically," Griff said, following her into the house. Danny bounced along at his heels. "Wolves to wolves, bears to bears, cats to cats, mythic to mythic...you get the idea. Makes it easier to communicate."

So he is *a lion shifter.*

And there are wolves, and bears, and...what did he say?

"Mythic?" she repeated, frowning. "What on earth is a mythic?"

"Oh, you know, uncanny beasties," Griff said casually, as if there was anything *normal* about people turning into lions and bears and whatnot. "Dragons, pegasi, wyverns, that sort of thing."

Hayley stopped dead in the doorway of the kitchen, turning to stare at him. *"Dragons?!"*

"Don't worry. They aren't like the fiery monsters from stories." Griff hesitated for a fraction of a second. "Mostly. But two of my best friends are dragon shifters, and they're some of the kindest, bravest, most honorable men I've ever known. I'll introduce you to them, and you'll soon see that there's nothing to be afraid of."

Danny let out an impressed squeak, staring up at Griff in wide-eyed amazement.

"Aye, real dragons just like in Mike the Knight," Griff said with a laugh. "One of them *is* a knight, actually. A proper one, on a quest and all. I'm sure he'd love to tell you all about it."

Hayley wasn't sure *she* was quite so excited at the prospect of meeting an honest-to-God dragon, but her heart did give an odd little skip at Griff's casual assumption that she'd be meeting his friends.

Don't read too much into it, she told herself sternly as she stretched on tiptoe to fetch the cookie jar down from its hiding place on top of the fridge. *He probably just wants us to meet other shifters so that Danny can learn to control his powers from them. Griff can't possibly want to spend his free time tutoring a stranger's kid.*

"Mm, these do smell good," Griff said, taking a cookie from the jar. "Homemade, too. My favorite." He took a big, appreciative bite.

Danny jumped up, dancing on his hind legs as he pawed at the cookie jar.

Griff shot him a stern look that made the cub instantly sink back against the floor. "Time for a lesson in lion manners. Alpha always tastes first, then mothers, then other grown-ups, and finally cubs. That's how you show respect for other members of the pride. You want one, Hayley?"

Hayley was dying to ask him what he was up to, but held her tongue, trusting that he knew what he was doing. She shook her head.

Danny whined, his rump wiggling in barely-restrained anticipation.

"Good lad. Yes, it's your turn." Griff flipped a cookie to him.

Danny leaped to catch it, his jaws closing with a *crunch*. Then he froze, a comical look of dismay spreading across his face. He went cross-eyed as if trying to see into his own muzzle.

"Eh? No, don't think so." Griff ate the rest of his cookie with every sign of enjoyment. "Tastes fine to me."

Danny's jaws worked a few times. He spat out the soggy cookie, glaring at it with an air of wounded betrayal.

"Of course, lion tongues do work a bit different to human ones," Griff added casually, as though this thought had only just occurred to him. "Can't taste sweet things. Now, real lions don't know what they're missing out on. But you know how that cookie *should* taste…"

Griff trailed off, a broad grin spreading across his face as the air around Danny shimmered.

"*Danny!*" Hayley snatched her son up, overcome with joy. She anxiously patted him, searching for any remaining hint of whiskers or fur, but he was entirely back to normal.

And also, stark naked.

He wriggled impatiently out of her embrace. "Can I have a cookie now, Mommy?"

"You can have a cookie." Nearly faint with relief, Hayley shoved the whole jar into his hands. "You can have *all* the cookies." Leaving Danny to his feast, she threw her arms around Griff. "Oh, thank you, thank you, *thank you!*"

She felt his hard chest rise with a sharp intake of breath. His strong heartbeat thudded against her cheek, his pulse as fast as if he was running a marathon, though he was absolutely motionless under her hands.

"Oh!" Hayley jerked back as if he was literally rather than just metaphorically hot. She was certain she was blushing from throat to forehead. "I-I'm so sorry, I just-"

"My pleasure," he interrupted her, his voice a deep, rough rumble. He cleared his throat, glancing down at Danny. "Lad, where'd you leave your clothes?"

"Out in the yard," Danny mumbled, spraying crumbs.

"Are you clever enough to get dressed all by yourself?" Danny nodded in response. "Off you go then, before you have any more of those. I need to have a word with your ma here."

Griff waited until Danny's bare backside had scampered out of sight before he spoke again. "Dad not around, I take it?" he murmured, very quietly.

Hayley couldn't help flinching a little at the old wound. "No," she said, trying to sound casual. "He left before Danny was born. He...wasn't ready for kids. Why?"

"Shifting is hereditary. You get the occasional surprise quirk of genetics, but as a rule, shifter kids have at least one shifter parent." He cocked an eyebrow at her in unspoken query.

"Well, he certainly didn't get it from my side of the family! But Reiner never said anything..." Hayley gasped, one hand creeping up to cover her mouth. "Oh. *Ljonsson*."

"Dad's last name, I take it?" Griff grimaced. "I'd say that's pretty conclusive, then. Reiner Ljonsson. Hmm. He never told you what he really was? Not even after you became pregnant?"

Hayley shook her head. "He didn't want anything to do with it."

A low, savage growl ripped from Griff's throat, making Hayley jump. "Sorry," he said, looking a little embarrassed. "Lion got the better of me. We're rather big on family. Or at least, we're *supposed* to be. Do you have a way of getting in contact with him?"

"I can try," Hayley said dubiously. "But I don't think-"

"Mr. Griff, Mr. Griff!" Hayley cut herself off as Danny ran back into the room, his face aglow with triumph. He had his T-shirt on inside-out and his pants back-to-front, but he proudly presented himself for Griff's inspection. "I did it all on my own!"

Griff's eyes gleamed with suppressed laughter, but his face was solemn as he looked the boy up and down. "So you did, Danny. Well done."

"Mr. Griff?" Danny sidled closer, his expression turning a little shy as he peered up at the towering firefighter. "Can... can I see *your* lion?"

Something flashed across Griff's face, too quickly for Hayley to read. "I'm afraid not, lad," he said, ruffling Danny's blond hair. "I have to go, unfortunately. No doubt it's nearly your teatime, and I'm expected back home for my supper too."

Danny's hopeful face fell. Hayley felt just as disappointed, which was completely silly of her. She couldn't help glancing at Griff's left hand. He wasn't wearing a wedding band, but lots of men didn't.

Of course a man like him would already have a partner. It's no business of mine, anyway. Why should it make any difference to me whether or not Griff has someone waiting for him at home?

The corner of Griff's mouth twitched up. "Just a friend who needed a place to stay," he said, as if her entire embarrassing train of thought had been printed on her forehead. "He's still a bit new to the entire concept of cooking, so it's best if I'm home before he can get into too much trouble. It's unfortunate for a firefighter to set his own kitchen alight, after all. But I'd like to come and see you both again soon, if that's all right with you?"

"O-of course," Hayley stuttered, trying not to let her expression betray the ridiculous leap of her heart at the prospect. "I'd love that. I, I mean, I have a lot of questions I'd love to ask you."

"Here's my number," Griff said, handing her a card. "If Danny shifts again, or you're worried about anything— anything *at all*—give me a call. I promise I'll come straight away."

"Can you come back tomorrow?" Danny asked eagerly, bouncing along in their wake as she led Griff toward the front door. "Mommy, can he? *Pleeeeeease?* Can he stay for dinner? Can we-"

"Danny!" Hayley covered his mouth before he could propose that 'Mr. Griff' stayed for a sleepover. "I'm sure Mr. Griff is very busy."

"Actually, I'd love to come round tomorrow," Griff said, crooking a smile at her that made her go weak at the knees. "If it wouldn't be too much of an imposition."

"Oh, no!" Hayley bit her lip. "I mean, after everything you've done, the least I can do is cook you dinner. We didn't have any plans for tomorrow, anyway."

"In that case, why don't I come by around four?" Griff winked at Danny. "That gives us plenty of time to play before supper, eh lad?" He looked back at Hayley, his expression turning more serious. "And maybe after Danny's in bed, you and me could have a wee chat about…a few things."

Was she imagining the heat burning in the depths of those golden eyes?

Don't be a fool. Of course you are. You're a tired, stressed single mom wearing no makeup and a sweater with spaghetti sauce stains. No man—especially not one like him—*is going to look at you* that *way.*

Hayley tore herself away from Griff's charismatic gaze, feeling the blush creep up her cheeks again. "Yes," she said faintly. "I'd…like that."

"Bye Mr. Griff!" Danny waved vigorously after the firefighter's retreating back. "See you tomorrow!" He heaved a great, heartfelt sigh. "Mommy, I wish he could stay *now.*"

Hayley smoothed his hair. "I know, baby. I know."

So do I.

CHAPTER 3

GRIFF

Not even the deep, throbbing pain in Griff's overstrained knee could dim his elation as he drove home.

My mate! I've found my mate!

He'd never dared to hope that he even had one true mate, like a normal shifter. He'd lain awake many nights, worrying that his two inner animals would mean that he had two separate mates—one for the lion, and one for the eagle. What would happen if his lion fiercely pulled him towards one woman, while his eagle equally fiercely pulled him away…?

In his darkest moments, he'd even hoped that he didn't have a mate at all. A lifetime alone would be better than having his mind torn apart by his bitterly jealous beasts.

But as it turned out, his fears had been groundless. For once, his lion and his eagle were in perfect agreement. Hayley was their mate.

Hayley was *his* mate.

And what a mate! Griff sighed in longing at the thought of her sweet round face and glorious curves. With her son in her arms, she'd made a perfect picture of lush, fertile womanhood, the sort that stirred a man's deepest, most primal urges to claim and protect. Soft yet strong, tender yet fierce...so fearless in defense of her child, yet so sweetly shy when it came to herself.

Griff had tried his best to stay professional, but a man would have to be deaf, blind, and dead not to react to her plump hips and full breasts. Yet she'd blushed and looked away when she'd noticed his appreciation of her stunning body. Not in the manner of a woman who didn't want such attention, but in the way of one who didn't believe anyone could possibly look at *her* with desire. She'd reacted like someone who'd become so used to thinking of herself as a mother, she'd forgotten that she was a woman as well.

Griff burned to show Hayley that side of herself again. To trace slow, lingering kisses across her softly rounded shoulders, to cup those bounteous breasts, his thumbs teasing their erect tips, while-

Griff shook his head, forcing such thoughts away as the ache in his groin threatened to rival the pain in his bad leg. He made himself concentrate on the road until his cock grudgingly subsided. Much as he wanted with every fiber of his being to sweep Hayley off her feet and into his bed, he couldn't.

We can, corrected his eagle, impatiently. *She desires us, as much as we desire her. It is obvious from the way she looked at us. Simply clasp her close, and-*

Stupid bird! interrupted his lion. *She is a mother! Her first thought must always be for her cub. We must approach her slowly, carefully, in order to win her trust. We must show her that we mean him no harm.*

His eagle clicked its beak in irritation. *Of course we will treasure her fledgling as our own. She would never even doubt that, were it not for you, accursed cat. She is only wary because she can sense your savage, feline nature-*

ENOUGH! Griff roared inwardly, shoving between his two inner beasts as they went for each other's throats. Searing pain split his skull, the lion's claws and the eagle's talons raking across his soul.

Gritting his teeth, he swerved to the side of the road, ignoring the annoyed honks of the cars behind at the abrupt maneuver. Safely parked, he focused on his breathing, trying to subdue the feral energy racing through his veins. His hands clenched on the steering wheel. His skin felt hot and tight, stretched wrongly over his bones...

Not here! Not now!

In desperation, he focused on the memory of Hayley's shy smile and warm brown eyes. He concentrated on how she made him feel, the things his inner beasts agreed on—the bone-deep need to protect her, the fire she sparked in his blood, the hunger for her touch and the all-consuming longing to be with her.

It worked. Griff scarcely dared to believe it, but his inner beasts subsided, drawn back into disgruntled alignment by the overpowering instincts inspired by their mate. His lion still paced and snarled, and his eagle still mantled its wings and stared at the cat balefully, but at least he was no longer being tugged apart by them.

Griff let out a shaky breath, painfully straightening his cramped fingers. He rolled his shoulders and neck, loosening his knotted muscles before he restarted the car. He pulled back onto the road, relieved and astonished that he'd managed to avoid a full-blown fight between his inner beasts.

If this is the effect Hayley has on them, maybe I should tell her what she means to me. Sooner rather than later.

You won't, though, growled his lion, right at the back of his mind. *You agree with me.*

Griff made a noncommittal noise, unwilling to provoke

his eagle by siding too clearly with his lion. But it was true. Regardless of his own personal situation, he had to think of what was best for Hayley. And what was best for Danny.

From Danny's endearing, heartbreaking eagerness to win his approval, Griff was certain that the little boy had never had any sort of father figure at all. Hayley and Danny had been alone together, just the two of them, for a very long time. But for all their obvious devotion to each other, there was still a secret, hungry hole in Danny's soul. Griff longed to fill that gap, nearly as much as he ached to heal the matching wound in Hayley's heart.

But if he did...he'd just be setting them up for future pain.

Griff set his shoulders, pushing his impossible longings into a small, sealed box in the back of his mind. He refused to let the bleak reality of the future spoil the joy of meeting his mate. He made himself concentrate on what he *could* do for his mate and her son, rather than what he wanted to do.

I can be Hayley's friend. I can be Danny's alpha. I can help them, support them, take care of them...at least for now. That's more than I ever thought I'd have. It'll have to be enough.

His eagle and his lion both bristled in protest, but he overruled their objections. Hayley and Danny had already been abandoned once. He was not going to break both their hearts again.

That would make him no better than Hayley's ex.

If we ever meet this Reiner Ljonsson, his lion and his eagle snarled as one, *we shall make him suffer for what he did to our mate and her son.*

"At least we all agree on something," Griff said under his breath as he pulled into his driveway.

His house was just a small semi-detached—*a duplex, Hayley would call it* he thought with a small smile, remembering her American accent—but it was still *his*. His nest, his den. Both his lion and his eagle relaxed at being back in their own territory again.

He could tell immediately that John was already home, both from the enormous pair of muddy boots neatly lined up on the doormat and the sound of humming emanating from the kitchen. Not that most people would have recognized the peculiar sound as "humming." It sounded more like a couple of bassoons having a relaxed, friendly conversation, with occasional comments from a passing humpback whale.

Griff grinned, recognizing the melody. John was cleaning.

A lot of people hummed as they did chores. With John, you could tell exactly which chores he was doing...though not what *else* he was doing at the same time.

Griff poked his head round the door of the kitchen. Sure enough, John was washing the dishes. This meant that he was standing at the stove, stirring a pan and humming, while six feet behind him a floating sphere of water industriously rinsed off a stack of plates in the sink.

Living with a sea dragon certainly had its moments.

"You know," Griff observed, leaning on the door frame, "we *do* have a dishwasher."

The dishwasher barks. John's deep mental voice echoed in Griff's head. The enormous shifter didn't pause in his humming, maintaining his control over the water washing the plates. **Its tone of voice is too abrupt. I prefer to ask the water politely.**

Griff had never worked out why his two inner animals meant mythic shifters like John could communicate with him telepathically, but it came in handy. Of course, it would be even handier if he could actually talk back that way, but he couldn't even send to fellow lions or eagles. If he tried, his own mental voice just came out as a doubled, incoherent jumble, rather like two people screaming in an echoing cavern.

"Well, I guess I should be grateful you at least approve of the shower's manners," he said out loud. "Not to mention the toilet. Sorry I'm late, I got delayed. Everything under control?"

I believe I have correctly burned the fish this time. John's telepathic tone radiated pleased accomplishment. *It is now black on the outside, but the machine in the ceiling has not yet screeched at me. This is the way humans like it, yes?*

"Smells done to me." Well past done, actually, but at least John hadn't set off the smoke detector. By John's standards, that counted as a culinary triumph. Griff clapped him on the shoulder, having to reach up to do so. "Good job. It all looks delicious."

This was a *slight* exaggeration, but Griff liked to be encouraging. And John *had* come on amazingly, considering he'd only a year ago he'd been new to the entire idea of "cooking." Or indeed, "fire." Most of John's people spent their entire life in sea dragon form, at the bottom of the ocean. Much of life on land was utterly foreign to them.

Like the difference between "fruit" and "vegetables," Griff thought to himself, eying a simmering pot of what smelled suspiciously like a mixture of diced carrot and apple. *Oh well, at least it has to be more edible than that banana-tuna casserole last week.*

"Did you have a good day?" he asked John, starting to set the table. "What happened with that car crash I sent you all to?"

The water churning in the sink fell still as John stopped humming. His broad forehead creased thoughtfully. "I had an argument with a cloud," he said out loud in his deep, oddly-accented voice. "The water had travelled unusually far, and wished to continue its journey. But I managed to persuade it to taste English soil in the end."

Griff suppressed a wry chuckle. Even though John had

lived with him for almost a year now, the sea dragon's unique perspective could still surprise him. "I meant, what happened with the trapped people," he said patiently.

"Oh." John shook his head, the golden charms braided into his long, indigo hair chiming against each other with the motion. "Yes, we saved them all. There were no serious injuries. We vanquished the flames easily, without great challenge to our skills."

John sounded mildly disappointed. Then again, he'd once told Griff that the literal translation of "have a nice day" in his own language was "may you be sorely tested by worthy opponents," which said an awful lot about sea dragons.

"And you?" John asked, a little hesitantly. "Did you too have a…productive day?"

John's stoic, controlled face was hard to read for most people, but to Griff's eagle eyes the sea dragon was an open book. John was worrying about making him feel inferior. After all, John's job involved charging into infernos and saving lives. Griff, on the other hand, got to answer telephones.

Griff appreciated John's tact, but for once it wasn't a sore point to compare their respective days. "Fairly good," Griff said casually. "Handled calls. Dispatched fire teams. Found my mate."

John's spatula clattered to the ground as the sea dragon spun round to stare at him.

"Funny story, actually." Griff dropped his pretend-casual tone, unable to contain his broad grin. "She called the fire department, and-"

That was as far as he got, before all the air whooshed out of his lungs as John seized him in a bone-cracking hug. An excited torrent of sound like an entire woodwind section having a party burst from the sea dragon shifter's mouth.

"Language, John!" Griff managed to gasp out. He was

hardly a small man himself, but John had still managed to lift him clean off the ground. "I don't speak sea dragon, remember?"

John reluctantly switched back to English, though he still half-sang his words with excitement. "But this is wonderful news, oath-brother! Where is she? Why have you not brought her back with you? Oh!" He abruptly set Griff back on his feet, a slight shadow crossing his overjoyed expression. "Of course, I understand. I will pack my hoard immediately."

"Whoa!" Griff caught John's arm as the sea dragon turned for the door. "Hang on, what do you mean, pack? You don't have to go anywhere."

John cocked his head to one side. "Surely you wish privacy for you and your mate?"

Griff's blood heated at the thought of Hayley in his house. In his *bed*. "Oh, you have no idea how much I *do* wish that." He couldn't help letting out a wistful sigh. "Unfortunately, it's not likely to be necessary."

John blinked at him. "But...she is your mate. Will she not be moving into your territory immediately?"

"I'm flattered that you think I work that fast. But no, of course not. I only met her this afternoon, John!"

"But she is your mate," John repeated, sounding utterly baffled. "You have met each other. How can you not have mated already?"

It was Griff's turn to blink. "Is that how it works for your people? You meet your mate and immediately, ah, mate?"

"Of course," John said, looking just as dumbfounded as Griff felt. "This is *not* how it works for you land shifters?"

"Alas, no. Though I have to admit, your way sounds rather appealing." Griff shook his head, a little envious of John. It must be nice, living in a culture where everyone knew about shifters and their mates, and understood the overwhelming power of that instant bond. "It's more complicated for us."

John shook his head too. "Humans. I shall never understand you. Are you certain you are not over-thinking this, my oath-brother? As I recall, Dai and Chase consummated their respective unions with appropriate speed when they met *their* mates."

Griff shot him a level look. "Are you seriously suggesting I take *Chase* as a role model in matters of romance? Or even Dai?" The two other firefighters were still the subject of much good-natured teasing down at the pub for the ridiculous problems they had caused themselves in the course of pursuing their mates.

The corner of John's mouth curled up. "Hmm. Perhaps not. But still-"

"There are complications," Griff interrupted him. His overworked knee was threatening to give way at last. He sat down in one of the kitchen chairs, stretching his bad leg out with a wince. "Not all of them on my side, too. She has a wee son, you see."

"So she is fertile," John said approvingly as he turned to retrieve the forgotten plates of food. Sliding one in front of Griff, he sat down too, having some difficulty fitting his seven-foot tall bulk behind the table. "Why would that be a complication? Unless—*oh.*" His expression changed abruptly to understanding sorrow. "Oh, oath-brother. The father still lives? She is still joined?"

"Married, you mean? No, he's not in the picture." Griff suppressed a growl at the thought of Danny's worthless so-called father. *If I ever get my hands on him...*

John was back to looking lost again. "Then…is she still in mourning for her former partner? A noble sentiment, of course, but surely joining with her one true mate would ease that grief?"

Griff leaned his elbows on the table, contemplating the sea dragon shifter across it. "This is one of those times when we're having two entirely separate conversations, isn't it?"

John let out a rich, rueful laugh. "It would indeed appear we have swum into a cultural misunderstanding." He picked up his fork. "Perhaps you should explain how human women can apparently have children without fathers."

"Do you really not have absent fathers, among your people?" At John's blank look, Griff clarified, "When a man doesn't want to take responsibility for his child, so refuses to have anything to do with them."

John spat out a brief, low phrase in his own language, a rippling arpeggio of shock and disgust. "No," he said, switching back to English. "We do not have that."

"Huh. Wish I could breathe underwater. Your people sound increasingly appealing the more I learn about them. In any case, that's what's happened to Hayley. The bastard got her pregnant and then abandoned her. He was a shifter, too. So's the boy, as it turns out."

John shook his head, slowly. "I begin to see what you mean by complications. So your mate is now wary of men, having been cruelly betrayed by this, this…" He made a noise somewhat like an angry tuba, apparently not finding an insult strong enough in English. "Well. Do not be disheartened, oath-brother. I shall compose a great ballad of your noble deeds! When she hears it, her heart will swim straight into your hands."

Good God, he's actually serious. "Ah, that's a…very generous offer. But unnecessary. I'm not going to mate with her. Not now. Not ever."

John stared at him as if he'd announced his intention to give up breathing. "You cannot possibly mean that, oath-brother. You will rip your soul into pieces if you try to deny your mate."

"Better me than her." He gestured at his leg. "Think about it, John. What have I got to offer?"

John's blue eyes darkened as he took Griff's meaning. "I think that you can offer her the same that any man can offer his mate," he said forcefully, each word ringing out like the clarion call of a hunting horn. "All of you, unstintingly, for as long as your heart still beats."

"You great soft numpty," Griff said affectionately. "No wonder you can charm the very rain down out of the sky. But I'm not a cloud, and you can't sway me with pretty words. I'm not going to mate her." He held up a hand as John opened his mouth, forestalling him. "And that's final."

We shall see, whispered his eagle…and Griff shivered at the cold threat in its voice.

CHAPTER 4

HAYLEY

To: reiner.ljonsson@nordindustri.dk
From: lionmom192@gmail.com
Subject: Hereditary medical condition

Reiner,
I've just discovered that Danny has a rare condition which I think he must have got from you. I don't want to say too much in an email, but let's just say it's a big shift in our lives. If you know what I'm talking about, then please get in touch.
I promise, I don't want money or anything. I just want information.

Hayley paused with her fingers on the keyboard of her laptop, uncertain how to sign off. "Regards" seemed rather impersonal, considering that Reiner was the father of her child. On the other hand, "Best wishes" would be a flat-out lie. She couldn't wish him well, not when Danny always stared wistfully at other kids playing with their dads in the park.

With a sigh, she just typed "Hayley," and hit Send. The message whooshed cheerfully off into the ether, leaving her staring at her empty inbox. She'd thought it best to create a throwaway account, just in case he had her regular email address blocked.

He'll probably just delete it as soon as he realizes who it's from, anyway.

When Danny had been a newborn, she'd bombarded every phone number and email address she had for Reiner with cute baby photos. She couldn't understand how anyone —let alone his own father—could look at those big brown eyes and adorable chubby cheeks and remain stone-hearted. But Reiner had never responded, not even to demand that she stop bothering him.

She still sent Reiner a photo and update every month, but it was more out of habit than any real hope that he would finally get in contact. Hayley had a sinking feeling that this time wouldn't be any different.

At least Danny has Griff to help him.

Hayley bit her lip, glancing across the living room to where Danny was sprawled belly-down on the carpet, hypnotized by the TV. It was the first time all day he stopped chattering about "Mr. Griff," asking if it was four o'clock yet and whether they could go to the playground and if they could be lions together for Halloween. He was clearly completely star-struck by the firefighter.

Not that Hayley could blame him...

I can't let him get too attached. Griff seems nice, but he won't be around forever. I have to make sure Danny understands that. Better a little disappointment now than heartbreak later.

She knew *that* from experience.

"Mommy?" Danny said thoughtfully, his bare feet kicking

in the air. On the TV screen, Mike the Knight and his dragon friends were puzzling over how to clear a giant tree trunk that had fallen across a path. "How big do you think Mr. Griff's lion is?"

"I don't know, honey." She had a sudden mortifying image of Danny innocently asking Griff how big he was, and she hastily added, "It probably wouldn't be polite to ask."

"I bet he's *real* big," Danny said in deep satisfaction. "I bet he could just knock that tree trunk away with his paw, bam! I bet he's big enough to beat anything. Even Darth Vader. Mommy, do you think Mr. Griff could beat the Hulk?"

Oh dear. "Baby, turn off the TV and come here a second, okay?"

Danny made a *what-have-I-done-now* face, but dutifully climbed onto her lap. Hayley hugged him tight, still treasuring the feel of his human-shaped little body. "I know you like Mr. Griff a lot, and I'm sure he likes you too, but you need to remember that he's a big, grown-up man. He won't want you clinging to him and following him everywhere. He needs to spend time with his own grown-up friends."

Danny squirmed a little in her arms. "But I'm going to play with his dragon friends too. Mr. Griff said so."

"Yes, but…sometimes people make promises that it turns out they can't keep. You mustn't be disappointed if it doesn't work out."

"Mr. Griff won't break a promise to me," Danny said matter-of-factly, with perfect confidence. "Never ever. He's my alpha."

Where on earth had he learned *that*? Now that she thought back, she remembered Griff using the same word. She knew that wolf packs had alphas, but lions? "What do you mean, honey? What's an alpha?"

"Mr. Griff is," Danny said, with the serene circular logic of a five-year-old. "When will he be here, Mommy?"

All thoughts of mysterious alphas fled from Hayley's mind as she glanced at the time. "Oh, fudge! In ten minutes!"

Danny yelped with excitement, bouncing off her lap as she hastily stood. "Is that now?"

"It might as well be now!" Hayley cursed herself for spending too long agonizing over the email to Reiner. She'd meant to have a shower, she'd meant to change-! "Honey, can you be a good boy and sit quietly watching TV while Mommy tries to make herself pretty?"

"Silly Mommy." Danny rolled his eyes at her as plopped down in front of the TV again. "You're always pretty."

Hayley wasted precious seconds scooping him up for another hug—he squawked in protest, wriggling to keep the screen in sight—before dashing upstairs to her bedroom. She struggled out of the torn jeans and old, comfy sweatshirt she'd been wearing, flinging them carelessly across the bed. She'd worked hard all day to try to get the rest of the house cleaner than its usual state of child-induced chaos, but at least this was one room she didn't have to worry about keeping tidy. It wasn't like Griff was going to be seeing it.

More's the pity.

Squashing the stray, ridiculous thought, she rifled through her clothes in the vain hope of finding something that was both respectable and attractive. Unfortunately, the only things she owned that weren't stained and tired were her work clothes, and as an elementary school teacher she didn't exactly dress to impress.

I'm being silly, Hayley told herself firmly as she grabbed a pair of black leggings that weren't too badly bobbled. *It's not a date. Griff isn't going to care what I'm wearing. He's coming to see Danny, not me.*

Nonetheless, she pulled on a low-cut floral tunic that she normally wore over a vest. She hesitated for a second, trying to decide whether it was *too* revealing, but it was too late to

FIREFIGHTER GRIFFIN

change her mind. She barely had enough time to drag a brush through her limp, mousy-brown hair and dab a bit of concealer on the dark circles under her eyes before—on the stroke of four o'clock—the doorbell rang.

"Mommymommymommymommy!" Danny shrieked at the top of his lungs. So much for not getting too attached. His feet thundered toward the front door. "He's here, Mr. Griff is here!"

Hayley charged for the stairs. "Danny, don't open the-!"

Too late. She got to the landing just in time to see an overenthusiastic lion cub hit Griff squarely in the chest.

"Whoa!" Griff hastily stepped inside, making sure his broad bulk shielded Danny from view of the road. He kicked the front door shut behind him. "Good thing I wasn't the mailman. Oof! I hope you haven't been pouncing on your ma like this."

"Danny!" Mortified, Hayley ran down the stairs. "Get down off Mr. Griff this second!"

"Ah, it's fine." Still hugging Danny in one powerful arm, Griff handed her a stunning bouquet of soft pink roses, smiling. "Just glad I didn't drop these."

Hayley stared at the bouquet in her hands, momentarily speechless. No one had *ever* given her flowers before. Not even Reiner. "What- why-?"

It's just a hostess present. British people are very strict on good manners, remember?

"I mean, th-thank you!" Hayley stuttered, certain that her cheeks were as pink as the roses. How had he known that exact shade was her favorite color? Just co-incidence? "Please, come in. Um, come in more, that is. Danny, get *down!* And, and human!"

Danny reluctantly dropped to the ground, but seemed a bit lost as to how to obey the latter command. He shuffled his paws, then mewed plaintively at Griff.

The firefighter shook his head. "You got yourself into that shape, you can get yourself out of it, laddie. Think about it." He looked back at Hayley. "This the first time he's shifted since yesterday?"

Hayley nodded. "Thankfully. How often is he likely to do this?"

"Let's just say you may want to keep the lad in big old T-shirts and the like for a while," Griff said ruefully, tilting his head to indicate the abandoned, shredded remnants of Danny's best—and only—dress shirt and pants. As I recall, most of my sisters spent the best part of a year running around in the cheapest, baggiest shifts my da and ma could find."

"He's going to shift every time he gets too excited?" Hayley gasped, her hand flying to her mouth as a horrible thought struck her. "Oh God, he's got kindergarten tomorrow. And I'm a teacher, I can't just phone in sick and keep him at home."

"Ah now, don't fret." Griff put one hand on her shoulder, his golden eyes warm and understanding. His strong fingers squeezed lightly, reassuringly, before letting go again. "That's one of the reasons I'm here. I can make sure he doesn't go lion in public." He hesitated, his expression turning more serious. "I need to ask your permission, though. I should really have done so earlier, up in the tree, but things were…a mite hectic."

She could still feel the brief touch of Griff's hand, a heat that raced through her blood. It ignited a long-forgotten fire deep in her belly, so distracting that she very nearly lost track of what he was saying. "Um…what?"

The man must think I'm an absolute idiot. *Pull it together, Hayley!*

Griff absently flexed his hand, and Hayley had the sudden mad thought that maybe the brief contact had made *his* skin tingle too. "I'm an alpha lion, ye ken." His accent had thickened, the Scottish brogue becoming more pronounced. He cleared his throat. "That means I can influence Danny's lion. With your permission."

"Oh." She scrabbled to try to appear like a competent, functioning adult and not a hormone-addled woman who hadn't had sex for five years. "So...an alpha's like an authority figure? You can set a rule he has to follow?"

Danny put his ears back. He hissed.

"Only with *your* permission too, lad," Griff told him. His tone turned deadly serious, with an odd undertone of compelling power that made chills run down Hayley's spine. "A true alpha never forces anyone. You remember that, always."

Danny seemed a little overcome by Griff's sudden intensity. He hunkered down a little, his body language reminding Hayley of a worried dog, and whined.

"Baby, this is real important," Hayley said, crouching down so she could look Danny straight in the eyes. "If someone saw you turn into a lion, they might get scared and want to lock you up in a zoo. You wouldn't like that, would you?"

Danny's eyes widened. He cuddled up against her, pressing his broad fuzzy head against her side as if trying to hide.

"I'd never let anyone take you away," Hayley said hastily, worried that she'd scared him *too* much. "But it would be best if no one finds out what you are. Like...like you're a superhero, okay? And you have to protect your secret identity."

He peeped out from under her arm, and Griff chuckled as if at something Danny had just said. "Aye, just like Spiderman. Danny, all I want to do is to make sure your lion has to check with you before taking over. You'll still be able to shift when you want. I'll just make sure you don't shift when you *don't* want. That sound okay to you and your lion?"

Danny's ears flicked back and forth a few times, as if he was considering it. Then he padded trustingly over to Griff and bumped his forehead against the firefighter's legs.

Griff's golden eyes went very soft as he looked down at the cub. "Aye," he said, a catch in his voice. "And I'll try to be worthy of that." A little stiffly, he knelt. "Now, we're going to do some practicing today to improve your control, and I'm going to get my lion to give yours a little nudge sometimes to help. But first, I want to see if you can shift back all by yourself. You remember how we did it yesterday?"

"I made more cookies," Hayley volunteered. Unable to sleep, she'd spent hours last night baking after Danny was in bed. "Just in case."

"That was good thinking," Griff said, and she felt ridiculously pleased at having won his approval. "But let's see if he can do it without one actually in front of him first. Danny? Just focus on the memory of the cookie."

The lion cub's nose wrinkled up in concentration…and a moment later, a stark naked Danny leaped into Griff's arms again. "I did it Mr. Griff! I did it all by myself!"

"*Danny!*" Hayley could have died of embarrassment. She seized Danny round the waist, whirling around to try to hide him from sight. "Get your clothes back on right this second!"

Behind her, Griff burst out laughing. "Ah, don't fash yourself, Hayley. We shifters are pretty relaxed when it comes to nudity."

Nonetheless, he politely looked away as Hayley wrestled the protesting Danny back into underwear. "But *Mommy*, I don't wanna get dressed! I wanna be lions with Mr. Griff!"

"He does have a point," Griff said to Hayley, apologetically. "Some types of shifter can include their clothes in their transformations, but lions can't. And I do need to work on his shifting with him. If you want, I could wear a blindfold?"

"No, no!" Griff didn't set off any of Hayley's finely-honed protective mama bear instincts. "I don't think you're a pervert or anything like that. I mean, you've already done more in one day to help than-"

Hayley cut herself off. She never, ever disparaged Reiner in front of Danny. Even though Danny had never met him, he was still his father. "Anyway. If you're fine with the, um, lack of clothes thing, then so am I."

If Griff was going to teach Danny about shifting, would *he* have to...? Hayley blushed furiously, unable to suppress a tantalizing mental image of the firefighter stripping off.

Griff cast her a rather amused look, a sly gleam in his golden eyes. "Don't worry. I'll keep my clothes on."

Hayley wanted to sink through the floor. Was she *that* easy to read?

"But Mr. Griff!" Danny tugged on Griff's hand, looking worried. "If you keep your clothes on, you'll rip them up and then *your* mommy will be mad."

An oddly wistful half-smile tugged at Griff's mouth. "Quite the reverse, actually." He raked his hand through his blond hair as if he was debating something with himself, then sighed. "Might as well get this out of the way. Hayley, do you mind if we all go out into the garden?"

"Um, okay." Hayley's heartbeat sped up a little, with a mixture of curiosity and apprehension. It was one thing having Danny turn into a cute little cub, but Griff would be a full-size male lion...

She led the way through the house and out the back. One of the reasons Hayley had picked this house in the first place was because it was right at the end of the street, with a secure backyard that wasn't overlooked by any of the neighbors. One thing she still hadn't gotten used to about England compared to California was how *small* everything was. Brits might have mastered the art of pretending they couldn't see straight into each other's properties, but Hayley preferred actual privacy.

Not that she'd ever imagined she'd be using it for *this*.

Griff cast a swift, appraising look around at the high fences, nodding in approval. "This is good. We're safe to practice here. But…Danny, I'm afraid I can't show you my lion."

Danny's bottom lip stuck out. "Why not?"

"Danny," Hayley said warningly, though she too couldn't help feeling a bit disappointed. "It's not polite to pry. I'm sure Mr. Griff has his reasons."

"I do." Griff sat down on the grass, his left leg stretched out awkwardly. "And the reason is that I can't." He tapped the center of his chest. "My lion's stuck in here, Danny. He can't get out, not the way that yours can."

"But I thought you were a shifter," Hayley blurted out.

Griff's eyes flashed a brilliant, animal yellow. "I *am* a shifter," he said, and the hairs on the back of Hayley's neck rose at the deep, primal growl in his voice. "I am more of a shifter than most. I am descended from generations of shifters, on both sides of my family. I have inner beasts, I can touch minds with the beasts of others, I have a m—" He paused fractionally, as if thinking better of whatever he'd been about to say. "I have all the instincts of a shifter. In every way that matters, *I am a shifter.*"

"I know you're a shifter," Danny said, sounding more puzzled than alarmed by Griff's sudden outburst. "Who says you aren't? They're mean. And stupid."

The barely-leashed savagery vanished from Griff's eyes. "Ah, you're a kind wee soul," he said gruffly. "Kinder than most." He glanced up at Hayley, looking a little ashamed of himself. "Sorry. Sore spot. I'm sure you can imagine what other shifters think of one of their own who can't actually shift."

Her heart went out to him—even if it *was* still beating hard at the shock of the sudden reveal of the raw, feral strength hidden behind Griff's amiable exterior. "I'm so sorry. I didn't know. That must be…very hard."

"But *why* can't you shift?" Danny demanded, with a little kid's unabashed rudeness. "You've got a lion, just like me. I know you have."

Griff beckoned to him. "Come here, lad. Let's see if I can show you." He cupped the back of Danny's neck, drawing him close until their faces were only inches apart.

Danny stared deep into Griff's eyes for a long moment. Then he jerked back, his own widening. "*That's* not a lion."

"No, it isn't." Griff released him, letting out a long breath. "That's my eagle. My father's a lion shifter. But my mother's an eagle shifter. That's why they named me Griffin—that's a pretend beastie that's half-lion, half-eagle, ye ken." His mouth quirked wryly. "My ma and da don't have a lot in common, but they do share the same *terrible* sense of humor."

"So if your father's a lion and your mother's an eagle, that makes you…both?" Hayley asked.

"And neither." Griff grimaced. "My eagle and my lion don't get along. Shifters aren't supposed to have two animals. Neither one of mine will let the other one fully take control. If I try to shift, I end up tugged back and forth between lion and eagle."

That sounds awful. And painful. From the way both Griff and Danny talked, Hayley had the impression that a shifter's animal was like some sort of alter-ego in their minds. The idea of having *two* of them, at odds with each other…it was amazing Griff wasn't completely schizophrenic.

"But you said your sisters are lions," Danny said, his forehead wrinkling. "How come they only got one animal, but you got two?"

"Because…ah, just unlucky, I suppose," Griff said. Hayley wondered what he'd decided not to say. "Four of my sisters are lions, and three are eagles, and I'm neither fish nor fowl nor good red herring."

Danny frowned. "If you can't shift, how're you gonna teach me?"

"Lad, I've studied more theory than most shifters even know exists. I taught all seven of my sisters how to control their animals." Griff poked Danny playfully in the ribs, making him giggle. "And *they* taught me how to wrestle a lion. Come on. Shift back, and I'll show you."

CHAPTER 5

GRIFF

Griff hummed to himself as he put the last few plates in Hayley's dishwasher. He smiled a little, thinking of John as he started the machine. He hoped the sea dragon shifter was having a good time at the pub right now.

On a Sunday evening, they always went down to the Full Moon together to meet up with the other firefighters on Alpha Team. It was usually both the high point of Griff's week, and a kick in the teeth. Alpha Team were his closest friends...but also a reminder of everything he'd lost.

The afternoon with Danny and Hayley had been similarly bittersweet. Romping with the cub should have been pure joy, but even as they chased and wrestled and pounced, Griff had kept being stabbed by pangs of wistful longing. Much as he tried to just enjoy the moment and be content with what he could have, he couldn't help wanting more. He couldn't help wanting to *be* more.

Danny should be *his* cub.

He is our cub, his lion said matter-of-factly. *He is the son of our mate. That makes him ours.*

Griff shook his head, muzzling the lion again. No matter

what his inner beasts whispered, he had to remember that he had no claim to Danny.

Or to Hayley.

He heard her close Danny's bedroom door upstairs, and the soft tread of her feet down the stairs. Realizing she was heading toward the front room, he quietly called out, "I'm in here, Hayley."

She retraced her steps, coming into the kitchen. "Oh!" she exclaimed, her jaw dropping as she took in the tidy work surfaces and sparkling floor. "You cleaned?"

"I could hardly sit on my backside while you were busy putting the bairn to bed, now could I?" Griff dried his hands on a tea towel, smiling at her.

He was simultaneously pleased by her evident astonishment…and infuriated. Not at Hayley, but at the previous men in her life. If they'd treated her right, she wouldn't have looked so flabbergasted that a man might do a few chores.

Reiner Ljonsson, you have a lot *to answer for.*

He nodded at the two glasses he'd placed on the kitchen table, an inch of deep amber liquid from his hip flask at the bottom of each. "Do you drink whisky? It's from my clan's distillery. I'll warn you now, though, my ma's spirits aren't for the faint-hearted. It's a bit like swallowing the sun."

"I could do with that," Hayley said ruefully, seating herself and picking up one of the glasses. "I don't think I've been warm since we came to this country." She took an incautious sip. "Hey, this is act-"

She stopped mid-word. Her eyes went very wide.

Griff laughed out loud as she struggled valiantly not to cough. "I did warn you. It's bloody freezing in the Highlands. Especially at fifteen thousand feet. Eagle shifters need a bit of fire in their bellies."

He took the other glass, and sat down as well, surreptitiously stretching out his aching leg. "So how does a warm-blooded Californian lass end up in this cold, wet land, anyway?"

"Work," Hayley replied succinctly, taking a second, rather more respectful sip of her whisky. "I'm from SoCal. School funding there is slashed to the bone. I happened across an article about teacher shortages in England, and, well, it seemed like a good idea."

Griff took a tiny sip of his own whisky, savoring the sweet burn. It was a taste of home—and one he couldn't indulge in very much any more. Alcohol didn't interact well with his pain meds. "Long way to come for a job."

She went a little pink. "Well…this is going to sound stupid, but I thought coming to Europe might help with Reiner. I hoped that if Danny was closer, easier to visit, he might finally get in touch."

Griff's lion snarled, and his eagle's wings spread. *Not now*, he told them, not letting his beasts' anger show on his face. "He lives over here?"

"Yes. Well, not England. Denmark, or rather a little island near it. He was always kind of evasive about exactly where."

"Hmm." Griff furrowed his brow. *An island near Denmark…?* "Was it Valtyra, by any chance?"

Hayley's eyebrows rose. "I think so. You know it?"

"It's actually a shifter country. There are a couple of them in Europe. Tiny wee places, out of the way, keeping themselves to themselves. Hard to get into, generally."

"Oh. I was hoping to at least take Danny to see his dad's homeland someday, but it sounds like that's going to be harder than I thought." Hayley pursed her lips a little. Griff firmly repressed a fantasy of how that full, enticing mouth would feel under his. "Griff, if there are entire shifter countries…does the government know about you, then?"

"Aye. Well, some of the government. Our existence is a state secret, but we're quietly interwoven through most of society here in the UK. Our own Parliament, our own courts, our own additional laws."

Hayley sighed with relief. "So does that mean I don't have to worry about Danny being dragged off to some Black Ops secret lab?"

"Not in this country." He flashed a grin at her. "The Queen looks out for our interests. The entire British royal family have been dragon shifters ever since the War of the Roses."

"Wow," Hayley breathed. He loved the way her face lit up with delighted curiosity. "Now I *really* want to read a shifter-written history book. What about America? Is there a, a secret shifter President or something?"

"Ah, no. Shifters in America have to be more careful. There are rumors...well, let's just say that shifters who go to ERs over there don't tend to come out again. If you're thinking of going back..." His heart lurched at the thought. He realized his knuckles were going white, and made himself relax his hand before he broke the glass. "Talk to me first. I can put you in contact with some good people, who can watch out for you and Danny. Shifters in the States have to stick together."

Hayley had gone a little pale. "Okay. Though I don't actually have plans to return. There's nothing for me in California."

Thank God. "No family?"

Hayley's shoulders tensed fractionally, betraying an old, deep pain. "No. My mom died when I was at college, and I never knew my dad." She attempted a smile. "You have no idea how envious I am of your family. Seven sisters! I would have killed to have grown up in a big pack like that."

Griff turned his glass absently, watching the amber liquid catch the light. "Ah, well, it wasn't quite such a horde as you're imagining. We were never all in the same place at once. Technically they're my half-sisters, you see."

"Oh." Griff could see Hayley's mind working as she put two and two together. "*Oh.* So that's why you're the only one who's both a lion and an eagle."

"Aye. I've got the same da as my lion sisters, and the same ma as my eagle sisters." Griff grimaced a little. "I'm not ashamed of it or anything, but…I wasn't sure how much you'd want me to tell Danny. It's a bit complicated to explain to a wee bairn, especially one who doesn't know about shifter customs."

He read a hint of sudden wariness in the way she eyed him. "Um, is it usual for shifters to be…" She appeared to be groping for a word. "That is, to have kids by lots of different partners?"

Griff choked on his whisky. "Good God! No!" That was one misapprehension he *really* didn't want her to have. "Quite the opposite, in fact."

Hayley looked rather relieved, but also confused. "What do you mean?"

Oh, we're flying into dangerous winds now…

Griff hesitated, wondering whether it was safest to just deflect her line of questioning. But clan loyalty meant he was reluctant to leave her with an erroneous bad impression of his kinfolk. Or, indeed, shifters in general.

"My ma and da met in their late twenties," he said slowly, picking his words with care. "They both knew that they weren't the love of each other's lives. But they got on well enough, and they both wanted the same sorts of things, especially when it came to kids. So they settled."

Hayley looked down at her hands. "A lot of people do."

"Aye. Shifters are just like regular people in that respect. So they got married, and had me, and were happy enough." Griff tapped his chest. "This was before it became obvious there was something wrong with me, ye ken. For a few years, everything was fine."

Hayley's round, pretty face was filled with compassion. "And then?"

"Then my da *did* meet the love of his life," Griff said, simply. "So he left."

Hayley's mouth dropped open. "Just like that? Abandoning his wife?" She was suddenly as fierce as a lioness, outrage flooding her features. "Abandoning his *child*?"

"No, no, it wasnae like that! He didnae shirk his duty to me or my ma." He took a deep breath, getting his emotions back under control. "Not like Reiner and you and poor wee Danny. My da would have stayed with my ma, if she hadn't released him. But she knew that he would have been miserable. So she let him go. Though…she was sad, for a while. Very sad."

Griff tossed back the rest of his whisky. He welcomed its searing fire, a distraction from the painful memories of that black time. Hayley said nothing, watching him.

"Anyway, a year or two later my ma met *her* mate," Griff said thickly, when he could speak again. "So it all worked out for the best in the end. For everyone."

"Except you," Hayley said, very softly.

"Ah, well, I did all right. Got a passel of sisters and two loving homes out of it. Not many are so lucky." Griff was painfully aware that his light-hearted tone was not fooling Hayley in the slightest.

She frowned, putting her empty glass down on the table. "So your mother let your father go just because of shifter custom? I'm sorry, I don't mean to offend you, but that sounds…kind of awful. I get that your dad fell in love elsewhere, but I'm afraid I don't think much of a married guy who lets his eye wander like that."

"He didn't," Griff said, struggling to keep his voice even. It took all of his control to pretend that all of this was just of academic interest. "That's where we *are* different from regular humans. Every shifter has one true mate. Many are never lucky enough to meet them. But those who do…well, that's it. My da didn't want to leave my ma. But he *had* to. He'd met his mate, and from that moment on, there was no one else he could want, no one else he could be with, ever again."

"But how did he know?" Hayley pressed.

I shouldn't be doing this.

Griff dropped his gaze, afraid that she would see the truth in his face. "He just did," he said roughly. "From the moment he saw his mate, he knew. From her scent, from her glance, from the fire of her barest touch. He just *knew*."

Even without looking at her, he could tell that Hayley had gone very still. He kept his eyes fixed on his empty glass. Her hand rested on the table a little way from his own.

Slowly, tentatively, Hayley moved her hand, until the very tip of her little finger just brushed his knuckle. So quietly that even his shifter senses could barely catch her words, she breathed, "Like this?"

He closed his eyes, fighting to control the surge of his blood at even that tiny contact. He should move away, he should draw back, he should stop this before it went too far…

Without his own volition, his hand turned, capturing her small soft fingers under his broad calloused ones. "Aye," he said, still with his eyes closed. "Just like that."

Yes! roared his lion, and *yes!* called his eagle. His two animals were in such accord, it almost sounded like they spoke with one voice. They beat against the bars of his mind, fighting to break the iron chains of his control. *YES!*

He could feel her fast pulse thrilling through her fingertips, hear the tiny catch of her breath. "Griff-"

"Wait," he interrupted. Steeling himself, he opened his eyes, although he didn't release her hand. "There's something you need to know, before you decide if you want to take this any further."

"*If* I want to take this any further?" Hayley's face was flushed with disbelief and astonishment and slowly rising joy. She let out a short, giddy laugh. "Why on earth wouldn't I?"

He forced himself to meet her shining eyes. "Because I'm dying."

CHAPTER 6

HAYLEY

For a moment, Hayley was convinced that she had to have heard him wrong.

Griff, dying?

That can't be right. Just look at him!

Surely sick people couldn't possibly radiate strength and power like Griff did. He could have appeared on the cover of GQ, or in an ad for protein supplements. How could he be dying?

Sure, she'd noticed he limped a little, but she'd thought he must have just sprained his knee or something. Nobody died of a bad leg, after all.

Unless...

Hayley couldn't help flinching a little, horrible images of her mother's final weeks slicing through her mind. She knew that he'd noticed her reaction from the way he instantly released her, drawing his hand back.

"Aye, well." Griff's voice was rough, betraying the depth of feeling walled off behind his suddenly closed, impassive expression. He looked away from her. "So now you know."

"No, I don't! I don't understand—I mean, you can't be-"

The words burst out of her of their own accord, tearing themselves free from the depths of her heart. She drew in a deep, shaky breath. "I'm sorry, it's just that this is a lot to take in. And you need to know, if, if what you've got is bone cancer…that's what my mom had. It wasn't treatable for her, either."

Griff winced, his face softening back into its usual open, compassionate lines. "I'm sorry for bringing up bad memories. If it helps at all, I don't have cancer." He shook his head, looking rather rueful. "Is it terrible if I say that sometimes I wish I did? At least doctors believe in cancer."

"But not in shifters, I'm guessing." The pieces were falling into place in Hayley's head. "What's wrong with you…it's to do with your two animals, isn't it? You're-" The word *dying* stuck on her tongue. Saying it would make it too real. She substituted, "sick because you can't shift."

"Exactly. We shifters are *supposed* to shift. We have to. If we don't do it of our own volition, eventually our animal takes over and forces the issue." Griff's mouth tightened. "I'm better than most at controlling my inner animals. But I can't keep them chained all the time. And when they get free… well. It isn't pretty. So you see, I'm in no position to think about a mate. I don't have anything to offer you. I don't have a future."

Something about his resigned tone made her irrationally angry. "But you said that you've never been able to shift," she said, as if she could somehow *argue* him better. "And you've survived this long, haven't you? Who's to say you can't survive just as long again? I mean, you seem fit, healthy…you climbed that tree as if you were just strolling down the sidewalk. For Heaven's sake, you're a *firefighter!*"

His head jerked upward, surprise flashing across his expression. Then he let out a brief bark of humorless laughter. "It really is my day for disappointing people, it seems. I *was* a firefighter, Hayley." He gestured at his left leg. "Not anymore. About a year ago, I had one of my seizures, a bad one. I came back to human eventually, but not quite in the same shape I started. It ended my career."

Hayley blinked at him, taken aback. "But I thought you said you worked for the fire service."

"I do. As a dispatcher. That's how I knew to come to you. I overheard your call." He fell silent for a moment, head bowing. "Hayley, my condition…the episodes are getting more frequent. And worse. At some point, it's going to be more than just a leg that goes wrong. Probably sooner rather than later."

The weary slump to the set of his shoulders stabbed her to the heart. Hayley desperately wanted to touch him again, but he'd retreated back out of her reach. The few feet of space between them seemed like an impassable chasm, impossible to bridge.

Griff let out a long, slow sigh. "Maybe it would have been better for you if I'd sent someone else. If we'd never met. You've already been through this kind of thing once, with your mother. I can't ask you to do that again. I *won't*. But…"

He raised his head, meeting her gaze at last. Hayley's breath caught. His eyes had gone that intense, feral yellow again…but this time they burned with something other than anger.

"I'm not sorry," he growled, low and forceful. "I don't regret coming myself. No matter what happens, I won't ever regret meeting you."

The naked desire in his gaze ignited an answering heat in her core. Hayley found that she was leaning forward, every part of her drawn towards him like a moth to a flame. If he touched her, if he moved toward her, even just a little…

But he didn't.

Griff closed his eyes for a moment, and when he reopened them they'd gone back to their usual deep, warm gold. "It's enough," he said, very softly. "Enough just to have known you. Thank you."

It's not enough for me!

But her rational mind overruled her yearning body. She pressed her thighs together, trying to cool the throbbing need between her legs with cold logic.

He's right. This can't go further. What about Danny? How can I let Griff into our lives, knowing that we're going to lose him? How can I expose Danny to that sort of pain? What kind of a mother would I be? Think of Danny!

Grief filled her chest, heavy and leaden. It was more than just mourning for what-might-have-been. The thought of Griff's kind, generous soul being snuffed out, lost to the world forever…it was intolerable.

Desperate for any glimmer of hope, she asked, "Is there really no treatment? Nothing that might help you?"

He hesitated, and her heart leapt into her mouth—but then he said, firmly, "No. Nothing."

And she knew, *knew*, that he was lying.

"There is!" She jumped to her feet, crossing the distance between them in a single stride. "There is something, and you don't want to tell me what it is. Why? What are you trying to hide?"

Griff was shaking his head with increasing vehemence. "No. No!" It sounded more like he was shouting at himself than at her. He knotted his fists, his face contorting in sudden pain. "I. Will. Not! *No!*"

"Griff!" Frightened, Hayley grabbed his head between her palms, forcing him to look at her. "Is it your beasts? Is it one of your episodes? What am I supposed to do?"

His breath hissed between his clenched teeth. With a jolt, Hayley noticed that they'd visibly sharpened, the canines extending down into leonine fangs. His skin prickled under her palms, as if fur or feathers were trying to break through. "My eagle wants—me to tell you—*no.*"

"Whatever it is, just tell me!" Hayley yelled at him, terrified he was about to start shifting uncontrollably right there in her kitchen. "Do what it wants! *Please*, Griff!"

Griff grabbed hold of her hands, clinging onto them as if he was lost in a howling storm. His blazing golden eyes locked onto hers. Hayley couldn't move, couldn't even breathe, as he focused on her as if she was the only thing in existence, the only thing in the entire world.

Griff drew in a deep, shuddering breath—and relaxed. The spasms shaking his muscles slowed, stopped. "All right," he said hoarsely. He let go of her hands, scrubbing his palms across his face. "I didn't want to tell you this. I didn't want it to influence…bloody hell, this is going to sound like the worst line ever. But there *is* something that helps."

"Well, why didn't you *say* so?" Overcome with a mixture of relief and anger, Hayley jabbed him in the shoulder, glaring. "Spit it out! What is it?"

He dropped his hands, tilting his head up to meet her eyes. "You," he said, simply.

Caught off-guard, Hayley gaped at him.

"You…bring me and my beasts into harmony," Griff continued reluctantly, every word sounding like it was being forced out of him. "It's like you're the missing part of us. Just now…you stopped me from starting to shift. And yesterday, I was on the brink of a seizure, but the memory of you brought me back. I've never been able to do that before."

If just the memory of me did that…what else could I do?

"This doesn't put any sort of obligation on you," he said forcefully, before she could speak. His expression was fierce, determined. "You mustn't feel that this means you have to—that is, just the thought of you helps. That's enough. More than enough. You don't-"

Hayley gently put a finger on his lips, silencing him. "Does it help more when I'm close to you?"

Griff held very still, as if her touch had frozen him in place. "Aye," he whispered, his lips barely moving against her hand.

"And this?" Hayley traced a path over his chin and up the strong line of his jaw. The slight, rough drag of stubble caught at her fingertips. She laid her whole palm flat against the side of his face. "Does this help even more?"

Very slightly, never taking his eyes off hers, he nodded.

Hayley leaned in closer, closer, until those golden eyes filled her world, until his warm breath caressed her parted, eager lips. "What about this?"

Fire raced through her blood at the first touch of his mouth against hers. The kiss stayed soft and gentle for barely a moment before Griff's strong hands seized her upper arms. Hayley gasped against his mouth as he yanked her down to straddle him, her wet, eager core pressing tantalizingly against the hard bulge in his jeans. She rubbed shamelessly against him, unable to help herself, every touch sparking lightning bolts of pleasure through her body.

Once they'd started, there was no question of stopping. Desire swept them both up, as all-consuming as an inferno. His tongue plundered hers, seeking and claiming. His hands roved up over her shoulders, pulling down the soft fabric of her top and exposing her breasts. His mouth still hard on hers, Griff growled deep in his throat, the vibration thrilling through Hayley's bones. He broke the kiss, ducking his head down, licking and nipping.

Hayley arched against him, her fingers twining through his hair as his mouth found her taut nipple. Even through the fabric of her bra, the sensation was almost more than she could bear. A hot, powerful ache built between her legs. She writhed against him, desperate for release, tormented by the layers of clothing separating them. "Griff—please, I need—"

His mouth captured hers again, silencing her plea. His large hands scooped under her butt, effortlessly lifting her. With one powerful motion, he flipped her up onto the kitchen table, carelessly knocking the empty glasses aside. Before she even knew what was happening, he'd stripped away her leggings and panties.

He spread her legs wide, kneeling down between them. Hayley had a brief, fleeting moment of concern for his bad knee—and then his mouth closed over her, and she was lost to everything except him.

"Griff!" she cried out, as powerful waves of pleasure shook her. He didn't stop, his tongue still circling and teasing as her thighs shuddered and her breath came in helpless gasps. He entered her with two strong fingers, and she clenched around him, throwing back her head. *"Griff!"*

He straightened at last, bracing himself against the tabletop, one hand on each side of her hips. His own breath came in ragged pants, but a devilish, satisfied smile curved his lips. He kissed her again, long and slow and lingering.

"You were right," he said, pulling back a little. "That *does* help."

Hayley hooked her fingers through his belt loops as he started to push away. "Don't you dare. You haven't taken all of your medicine yet."

Even despite the lingering flutters of pleasure, she was still wet and eager, needing more. She fumbled with his fly, releasing his cock. She caught her breath at the sight—so thick and full, the broad, glistening head straining toward her.

Griff groaned as she ran her fingers over him, thrusting forward a little with his hips in an involuntary, jerking motion. "Hayley…are you sure?"

"Yes. *God*, yes." She needed him inside her, *now*—

She stopped abruptly. "*Fudge*." Long habit made her substitute the swearword, even at a moment like this. "I don't have condoms."

Griff shot her a sideways, gleaming look. "Will you think terribly of me if I happen to pull one out of my wallet?"

In answer, she grabbed his head, drawing him down for a deep, devouring kiss. Releasing him again, she leaned back on her elbows, waiting impatiently as he efficiently sheathed himself.

"Ah…" Despite his rock-hard, eager cock and the animal hunger in his eyes, Griff hesitated. He sheepishly gestured at his left leg, then at a chair. "Do you mind if we…?"

"Any way you want," Hayley gasped, wiggling off the table. "Seated. Backwards. Upside down. Just *now*, Griff!"

Griff laughed, a deep, delighted growl at her eagerness. Seizing her hips, he guided her down with him as he sat, once more pulling her onto his lap…but this time, there were no clothes between them.

Hayley arched her back as at last, *at last* he slid into her. His thick girth stretched her deliciously wide. Her inner walls clenched, the friction of his cock along her most sensitive areas nearly pushing her over the edge with his first thrust.

He snarled, arching up against her for a moment as though fighting for control—then his fingers dug into her hips as he surrendered himself to her, pounding into her with unrestrained need.

Hayley wrapped her legs around his torso, grinding to match every thrust. His powerful arms flexed, lifting her so that she slid intoxicatingly against his full length with every stroke. A last intense wave built within her, as unstoppable as a tsunami.

She covered his mouth with hers as he arched up into her

one final time, muffling both their cries of ecstasy as they came together. For a timeless moment, he filled her utterly, body and soul. Together, they were complete.

Hayley collapsed against Griff's shoulder. For a long moment, all she could do was lie there, languid and wrung-out. His chest heaved below her, gradually slowing.

It had been so long since she'd last had sex, her memory was a little hazy...but she was pretty certain it had never, ever been like *that* before.

"Well, I don't know about you," she mumbled into his neck. "But *I* certainly feel better." She felt as relaxed and glowing as if she'd just spent a week on a beach in the Bahamas.

Griff's soft, low chuckle rumbled in her ear like a cat purring. He traced a lingering, gentle caress down her spine. "I've never felt so well in my entire life."

"Good." Reluctantly, Hayley pushed herself up off him, sitting upright. Suddenly a little self-conscious about how disheveled she must appear, she tugged her tunic back up to cover her overspilling breasts.

Harsh kitchen lighting, and I'm not even wearing my good bra! What I must look like-

"Hayley." Griff caught her wrist, bringing it up to his lips. He inhaled deeply, his eyes half-closing in rapture, then pressed a gentle kiss to the delicate skin. His other hand skimmed the curves of her waist and hips, lightly, reverently. "You look beautiful. God, you're so beautiful."

The simple sincerity in his tone chased away her insecurity. "How do you do that?" Hayley asked as she scooted off his lap so he could deal with the condom. Away from his intoxicating heat, gooseflesh rose on her bare legs. She retrieved her panties and leggings. "Always know the right thing to say. It's like you know what I'm thinking."

"I do, somewhat," Griff said absently as he zipped himself

back up. "I'm good at reading people, thanks to my eagle." He dropped the condom into the garbage. "My mother's clan are white-tailed sea eagles, renowned for our uncanny perception. *Olar sùil na grèine*, we're called in Gaelic."

Hayley's toes curled at the rolling, beautiful words. She'd always been a sucker for a gorgeous accent. "What does that mean?"

"'Eagle of the sun's eye.'" He pointed at his own bright eyes, winking at her. "When you can spot a fish swimming underwater from ten thousand feet up in the sky, noticing tiny tells in the body language of someone within arm's reach isn't hard. I can spot when people are lying, or trying to hide something. And now you're getting nervous about that. But you're also reassuring yourself that you don't have anything to hide anyway, so it doesn't matter that I can read you like this. And *now* you're starting to get just a wee bit annoyed with me-"

"Griff!" Hayley took a mock-swing at him, which he avoided easily, laughing. "Stop that!"

Her heart skipped a beat as she noticed that he'd casually put his full weight on his left leg, without a hint of a wince. There was something looser, easier about his movements. She hadn't realized before just how constantly he'd been in pain.

Until now, when that pain had finally ceased.

Did I do that? Hope rose in her soul, sparkling light and effervescent as champagne bubbles. *Is it permanent, or will it wear off? Not that I mind if we have to keep doing this...*

Griff's gaze heated, roving over her body hungrily. "Me neither."

"Okay, that really *is* unfair." Hayley pouted at him, crossing her arms. "I wish I could tell what *you're* thinking." Of course, from the growing bulge in his pants—*seriously, already?*—she actually had a pretty good idea at the moment, but still.

"Well..." Griff hesitated, the playfulness in his expression turning more serious. He shot her a sidelong, strangely shy glance. "You could, actually. If...you wanted to. Eventually. One day. You see, if we were fully mated-"

And then he collapsed.

CHAPTER 7

GRIFF

There was no warning. One moment his inner beasts were sprawled happily in separate corners of his soul, smug and satiated—and the next, they were lunging at each other, screaming in rage.

Relaxed by pleasure, he was caught completely off guard. The eagle's claws and the lion's teeth tore into his unprepared mind as if it was the soft, unprotected underbelly of a rabbit. Griff doubled over, every nerve in his body abruptly aflame with agony.

Our mate! his lion roared at his eagle, mane bristling and teeth bared. *Ours!*

No! Our mate! His eagle folded its wings and stooped on the lion, talons outstretched and deadly. *We will kill you!*

"Griff! *Griff!*" Hayley's voice sounded as if it was coming from very far away, drowned out by the storm of snarling and shrieking in his head. Dimly, he was aware of her hands on his shoulders, shaking him. "What is it? What's happening?"

"I—don't—know!" he managed to gasp out. His bones twisted sickeningly under his skin as his body instinctively tried to shift in response to the sudden assault. The kitchen floor hit his knees, cold and hard. "They just-!"

WHY? he shouted futilely at his raging animals. *Nothing's wrong! No one's threatening our mate! WHY ARE YOU DOING THIS?*

"Look at me!" Hayley's face swam before him, through the red haze of pain. She pressed her forehead against his, her hands on each side of his skull as if trying to forcibly hold his dissolving mind together. "I'm right here. I'm here, Griff!"

Desperately, he tried to focus on her, to anchor himself in her steadfast presence. But this time, the sight of her just seemed to enrage his beasts further. They were each still filled with the drive to protect her, to worship and cherish her...but added to that was a new, fiercely burning possessiveness that could only be satisfied by the utter destruction of any rival.

Including each other.

Our mate! Not yours! His lion sank its teeth into the eagle's powerful wing. Griff convulsed, phantom fangs plunging into his shoulder. *Ours to claim!*

You will not have her! His eagle's talons gouged great gashes in the lion's tawny hide, each one slashing across Griff's own back. *We will claim her, we alone! She is ours! Die!*

"Oh God, why isn't it working?" Hayley sounded frantic. She released him, jumping to her feet. "Griff, I'm calling an ambulance."

"No!" He grabbed at her ankle, stopping her. She cried out in surprised pain, and with horror he realized that his fingernails had already sharpened into claws.

That had only ever happened once before, at the very height of his worst uncontrolled shift. *That* episode had cost him his leg. If the claws were coming *now*, right at the start of the seizure...

STOP! he roared at his animals. *Or we're all going to die!*

It was no use. They ignored him utterly, and he didn't have the strength left to separate them forcibly. His eagle and lion tugged on his body like two dogs fighting over the same bone. If he didn't do something, they'd tear him limb from limb.

There was only one thing he could do. The last, desperate resort that he'd hoped never to have to use.

"Hayley." Griff fought to keep his throat and tongue human enough to speak. His voice came out somewhere between a lion's snarl and an eagle's shriek, monstrous and distorted. "My coat. Hallway. Now!"

Thankfully, she seemed to understand his slurred words. She dashed off, her bare feet slipping on the tiled floor in her haste. Griff locked his jaw, curling into a tight ball as another wave of pain wracked his muscles. Only the thought of waking Danny up kept him from screaming.

Let him stay asleep, he prayed desperately. *Don't let him see me like this...*

"I've got it, Griff!" Hayley flung herself back down next to him, his heavy leather jacket in her arms. "What am I looking for?"

"Inside pocket," he gasped. "Box. Hurry!"

"Where—oh! Is this it?" Hayley's eyes widened as she freed the small, slim case from his jacket. Stark yellow biohazard and poison warning stickers covered the black steel. "It's locked. Griff, what's *in* this?"

"Medicine," he lied. "Key." He scrabbled at the thin chain around his neck, his own claws cutting his skin. Breaking the chain, he dropped the small key into Hayley's waiting hand. "Open. *Carefully.*"

"Okay." Gingerly, Hayley extracted a syringe, holding it in the tips of her fingers. "You want me to inject you?"

"Yes." He screwed his eyes shut, trying to concentrate, struggling to keep his human mind intact in the maelstrom of animal instincts. There was something else she had to do first, something critically important…"No! Wait!"

Too late.

He didn't even feel the tiny pinprick of the needle through the storm of torment—but then the wyvern venom hit his veins.

The pain of uncontrolled shifting was as *nothing* compared to that.

Black ice raced through his blood, shattering every cell in his body in its wake. His lion and eagle screamed together, once, as the terrible void swallowed them all.

"Call Ash!" he said, or tried to say, with his last breath. *"Call-"*

Everything stopped.

CHAPTER 8

HAYLEY

"Ash?" Hayley shook Griff's shoulder. "Griff! Who's Ash?"

His whole body rocked under her touch, rigid as a statue and just as unresponsive. His limbs were still twisted into impossible configurations, but at least he didn't seem to be transforming any further. Between one breath and the next, the vicious spasms ravaging his muscles had completely stopped.

That has to be a good thing...right?

Hayley had a horrible certainty that it wasn't. Something was wrong. Very, very wrong.

"Who's Ash?" she repeated futilely. It had to be important, from the way he'd suddenly yelled the name...

Struck by sudden inspiration, she pawed through Griff's jacket again. Her hand closed on the thin hard rectangle of a cellphone.

It was locked, protected by a fingerprint scanner—she glanced at Griff's twisted, half-animal hands and immediately dismissed *that* possibility—but a small button at the bottom of the screen read *Emergency Contact.* Praying, Hayley touched it.

Dialing Ash, read the screen, and Hayley's breath whooshed out of her in an explosive gust. "Please pick up, please pick up," she pleaded as the phone rang in her ear. "Oh, please-"

"Griffin?" said a calm, cool male voice.

Hayley could hear laughter and clinking glasses in the background, as if the speaker was in a restaurant or pub. "Are you Ash?"

"I am Fire Commander Ash, yes." The man seemed perfectly unperturbed to be called by a complete stranger using his friend's phone. "Who is this?"

"Griff said to call you," Hayley blurted out, too panicked to even tell him her name. "Oh please, you have to come, he's collapsed and I gave him the medicine but I don't think it's working!"

"Medicine?" Ash sounded nonplussed—and then his tone abruptly sharpened. "You gave him the syringe? The one with the warning stickers on it?"

"Yes, he-" Hayley found herself talking to a dead line.

He hung up? But I didn't even tell him where to find us!

She frantically jabbed *Redial*, but the phone just blinked *Caller Unavailable* at her. "You can't be unavailable!" she yelled at the phone. "You're supposed to be his emergency contact! Griff, what do I do now?"

He didn't respond. He was motionless.

Completely motionless.

He wasn't breathing.

Hurling the useless phone aside, Hayley flung herself to her knees next to his rigid body. She pressed her fingertips to his neck, feeling for a pulse. His skin was freezing cold. He was as stiff under her hands as if he'd been dead for hours.

Chest compressions, she thought, suddenly icy calm. Griff

needed her, *now*, and there was no time for any emotion but the single-minded need to save him. The CPR procedure sprang into her mind with crystal clarity, as if the textbook was open in front of her.

She pumped his chest, hard, counting the rhythm under her breath. At the right moment, she paused to give him mouth-to-mouth, not caring that his protruding fangs cut into her lips. It didn't matter that he was twisted and stretched, half-beast. This was *Griff*, her Griff, her mate. She knew that he was still there, a spark of life hidden deep inside that still, barely human form. And she would *not* let that life slip away.

Compressions, ventilations. Compressions, ventilations. Focus, Hayley. Keep the rhythm.

Hayley cursed herself for throwing Griff's cellphone away, out of reach. She knew she needed to call an ambulance, but she didn't dare leave his side yet. He needed her to be his heart, to be the air that he breathed...

Fiery light flooded suddenly through the window. Acting on pure instinct, Hayley flung herself across Griff's body, trying to protect him as the glass imploded inward.

An eye-searingly bright shape hurtled into the kitchen, white-hot flames streaming behind it like the tail of a comet. For a split second, the vast, bird-like form spread fiery wings over them both, its eyes as fierce and lethal as the heart of the sun.

The bird-shape vanished, leaving a man standing where it had been. He looked to be in his mid-forties, but he was still muscular and broad-shouldered, military training clear in his straight-backed stance. Wisps of smoke rose from the scorched floor around his feet.

Hayley gaped at him. "Who—what-?"

"I am Ash." He was already kneeling, his calm gaze

sweeping over Griff's motionless form in assessment. "When did you give him the venom?"

"Venom?" Hayley said blankly.

He glanced up at her, briefly, and she rocked back on her heels as the power behind those dark eyes struck her like a blow. "The wyvern venom. In the syringe. When?"

"I—I don't know," Hayley stammered. *Poison? He said it was medicine!* "Not more than ten minutes ago."

Ash's expression stayed completely unreadable, but his breath hissed through his teeth. He looked at the window, as if he was waiting for someone.

Or possibly, some*thing*. Hayley stared in disbelief as a horse stuck its long, black head through her kitchen window. A...*winged* horse?

The pegasus retreated a little, folding its wings. Someone scrambled off its back and through the window—another man, much younger than Ash even though his short hair was a pure, brilliant silver. He didn't spare Hayley even the most cursory of glances as he shoved her aside to get to Griff. From the unerring, expert way his long fingers swiftly assessed Griff's vital signs, Hayley guessed the newcomer had to be some sort of medic.

"You fool," the white-haired man snarled savagely, apparently to his unconscious patient. "I warned you this was an idiotic idea. If I ever get my hands on that *bloody* wyvern-!"

"Is he going to be okay?" interrupted an anxious Irish voice. Yet *another* man climbed in through the window, this one lean and agile with a shock of wild, curly black hair. "Hugh, can you heal him?"

"Who *are* all you people?" Hayley demanded.

"Get her out of here, Chase," the white-haired man snapped without looking up. "I have to work fast if I'm going to have any chance of saving this moron."

"What? No!" Hayley tried to twist away, but the Irish man

FIREFIGHTER GRIFFIN

—Chase, she assumed—was inhumanly fast. He seized her wrists, bundling her out of the kitchen despite her kicks and protests. "Let me go! I have to stay with Griff!"

"I'm sorry, but you can't." Chase elbowed the door shut behind them, still effortlessly restraining her. He was a *lot* stronger than his lean physique suggested. "Hugh won't shift if you're watching, and right now he's Griff's only hope."

"He's a shifter?" Hayley stared at Chase's windswept hair, suddenly making the connection. "You're *all* shifters. You were the pegasus."

"Yep." He flashed her a brief, strained grin, though the rest of his face was still set in grim, worried lines. "Chase Tiernach-West, at your service. The two back in there are Hugh Argent and Fire Commander Ash." He cocked his head to one side, as if suddenly hearing someone call his name. "And…just landing outside are the last two members of our team. We'd better let them in, or else John will kick your door down. Or possibly your wall."

"Team?" Hayley said, towed helplessly in his wake as he headed down the hallway. "Landing? What?"

"We're firefighters. Alpha Team. And Griff's still one of us." Chase opened the front door. "He'll *always* be one of us. And we look out for our own."

Hayley's breath froze in her throat.

There was a dragon in the road.

It looked exactly like an illustration from a fairytale book —horned, winged, with a long, sinuous tail and glittering crimson scales. There was a man astride its broad neck, and *he* could have stepped straight out of a fantasy novel too. His long, braided blue hair and fierce, rough-hewn features made him look like some barbarian warrior.

"They're in plain sight!" Hayley exclaimed. British people might be good at politely ignoring each other, but surely none of her neighbors were going to overlook a huge red dragon in the street. She looked wildly around at the surrounding houses, but no one's curtains had so much as twitched. "Why isn't anyone noticing?"

"It's a mythic shifter thing," Chase said. He waved at the dragon and its rider. "We have a kind of mind-trick we can do, which stops ordinary people from seeing us in our animal forms. Comes in handy."

The man jumped down from the dragon's back. The instant he was clear, the dragon's bulk shimmered, condensing into a red-headed man. Even though the dragon had been the size of a bus, in human form he barely came up to the long-haired man's shoulder. The two men strode toward the house.

That's weird, Hayley thought inanely, still half-numb with shock. *Who'd have thought a dragon shifter would be…so…little…*

Oh.

The dragon shifter wasn't little. In fact, he was even taller than Griff.

It was just that the man next to him was *motherfudging enormous.*

"Where is he?" the giant rumbled as he squeezed himself through her front door. He couldn't even stand up straight inside. Despite his bulk, there was an intelligent, noble look to his chiseled face that meant Hayley couldn't feel afraid of him.

"With Hugh and Ash. We're to stay out of the way," Chase said, shutting the door. Turning to Hayley, he pointed at the red-headed dragon shifter. "This is Daifydd Drake—but you can call him Dai, he accepts that the rest of us find Welsh names unpronounceable." His finger swung to the giant. "And *this* is John Doe, whose real name is *literally* unpronounceable if you're breathing air, so don't worry about that. Dai, John, this is…" Chase hesitated, looking down at Hayley. "Actually, I haven't the foggiest idea who you are. Sorry."

"I do," said John Doe. His voice had an odd, musical quality, and she couldn't place his accent at all. He sank gracefully to one knee in front of her, bowing his head. "My lady. I am the Walker-Above-Wave, Knight-Poet of the Order of the First Water, Guardian of the Pearl Throne, Seeker of the Emperor-in-Absence, Firefighter of the East Sussex Fire and Rescue Service, and Griffin's sworn oath-brother. If by my life or my death I can serve you, I will."

Hayley blinked at him, completely lost for words. From the startled looks on both Chase and Dai's faces, she wasn't the only one.

"Uh, John?" The red-headed dragon shifter—Dai—tapped John's massive shoulder. "Care to explain what's going on?"

John got to his feet again, keeping his head tilted to avoid hitting it on the light fitting. "She is my oath-brother's mate, kin-cousin. As he would defend me, so will I defend her."

"She's Griff's *what* now?" Chase exclaimed, staring at Hayley in astonishment.

"Mommy?" To Hayley's horror, Danny stood at the top of the stairs, rubbing sleepy eyes. "I heard noises."

"Holy sh-" Chase started. Dai elbowed him hard in the ribs, silencing him.

Danny flinched back, hiding behind the banister. "Who're they? Mommy, where's Mr. Griff?"

"It's okay, baby." Hayley twisted out of Chase's suddenly slack grip. She hurried up the stairs. "These are—these are some of Griff's friends."

Danny peeked round her at the three huge men. "Mr. Griff's dragon friends?"

"That's right." Hayley tried to block his view of the hallway, terrified that at any moment the kitchen door might open. "Mr. Griff's dragon friends. We're just talking. You go back to bed now."

"Hey," Chase protested. "*I'm* not a dr-"

This time both Dai *and* John elbowed him. He wheezed, shutting up.

"Why're they here?" Danny dragged his feet, resisting as she tried to hustle him back toward his bedroom. "Why're you all funny-looking, Mommy? Are you crying?"

"No, of course not." It was the hardest thing she'd ever done in her life, but she managed to paste a convincing smile onto her face. "Everything's fine. Come on, you've got school tomorrow and you need your sleep."

By the time she'd gotten Danny resettled in bed—which involved a trip to the bathroom, a glass of water, two lullabies and finally making him pinky-promise to *really, really* go back to sleep now—and returned downstairs, the firefighters had moved Griff from the kitchen to the couch. Her small front room seemed completely filled with broad shoulders and beefy arms, barely able to hold so many big men.

Hayley only had eyes for Griff's limp body. Although he was still deeply unconscious, he'd finally relaxed from that tormented, curled position. His chest rose and fell with his shallow breathing. All the breath rushed out of Hayley's own lungs with relief.

"Oh, thank God." She pushed her way through the wall of muscle to his side. "Is he stable? Is he going to be okay?"

"I've neutralized the poison. That was the hard part. Now I'm healing the carnage it did to his heart." Hugh was resting his bare hands on Griff's exposed chest with a look of intense concentration. He glanced up at her, his handsome, finely-drawn face pale and exhausted. "At least you did the right thing, starting CPR right away. It stopped him from getting permanent brain damage." He scowled back down at his patient. "Not that any of us would have been able to tell the difference. *Idiot.*"

"The poison did do what he hoped it would," Dai pointed

out. "It paralyzed his body and knocked out his animals. It stopped him from shifting further."

"Yeah, because it practically *killed* him," Chase retorted. His fists clenched. "That psychopathic wyvern shifter is a fucking menace. We should have flung her into prison and thrown away the key when we had the chance. I am going to kick her scaly little-"

Ash cast Chase a quelling look, and the pegasus shifter subsided. "Thank you for calling us," the Fire Commander said to Hayley. His tone was still perfectly level, his face betraying no sign of the tension in the other men's expressions. "I apologize for the inconvenience, but we cannot take him away yet."

"I don't want you to take him away!" Hayley anxiously studied Griff's distorted face. His ears were still sharply pointed, his mouth almost a muzzle. "If you're healing him, why isn't he going back to human form?" she asked Hugh.

"I can only fix what's damaged." Hugh adjusted the positions of his fingertips, his jaw clenching briefly as though he was somehow drawing pain out of Griff and into himself. "Not what doesn't know it's broken. His body thinks that this is the way it's supposed to be. He has to make it shift back on his own."

Dai hissed what sounded awfully like a swear word in Welsh. "You know he can't, Hugh. There has to be something you can do."

"I'm a paramedic, not a bloody miracle worker," Hugh snapped, which seemed a bit strange coming from a man who was currently healing a damaged heart with his bare hands. "If Griff wants to be human, he's going to have to take care of it himself."

"Not entirely," John rumbled. He looked at Hayley. "Call him back to us, my lady. You are his mate. He will always come to your call, across fire, across water, across death itself. Call him back."

Hayley hesitantly started to put her hand flat against the side of Griff's face—and then snatched it back, remembering what had happened last time. "I can't. I tried to help before, when his seizure started, and I only made it worse. I don't dare touch him."

Dai and Chase exchanged uneasy glances. "Maybe she'd better not, John," Dai said. "He's alive and stable now. It doesn't matter what he looks like."

"You think his face is messed up, you should see his pancreas," Hugh muttered. "I'm with John. The worst she can do is kill him again."

Hayley put her hands behind her back. "I'm not risking that!"

"You are his *mate*," John insisted stubbornly. "You cannot harm him, no more than he could ever harm you. You must try. You are the only one who can."

All four firefighters glanced at Ash, and Hayley found that she too had turned in his direction. The Fire Commander had such an air of quiet authority, it seemed only natural to look to him for a decision.

Ash met her eyes calmly. "Try."

Feeling self-conscious under the weight of all their stares, Hayley put her hand against Griff's cheek. She cringed a little as her palm brushed his skin, half-expecting him to cry out again in agony—but he just made a small sigh, turning fractionally into her touch.

Encouraged, Hayley bent to put her lips to his ear. "Griff?" she whispered. "It's okay now. I'm here. Your friends are here. We won't let anything happen to you. It's okay to come back now."

The drawn tightness around Griff's closed eyes eased a

little. Slowly, so slowly, his face softened back into more human features.

Chase made a strangled yelp, as though he'd started to whoop with joy and then remembered that Danny was sleeping upstairs. He snatched Hayley up, spinning her round in a brief, dizzying hug. "You did it! You did it! I could kiss you!"

"You do, and Griff will punch your lights out when he wakes up." Grinning, Dai rescued her from Chase's arms, depositing her back on the ground. "But thank you. From all of us." He hesitated. "Ah, I don't think we even know your name."

"Hayley Parker," she said dazedly. "And thank *you*. All of you. How did you even know where we were?"

Chase bowed extravagantly. "Just one of my many talents. We pegasus shifters have a knack for finding people."

"I can still barely believe that there's even such a thing as pegasus shifters. Or dragons." She glanced up at John Doe. "You're a dragon too, right? Griff mentioned you. He said he had a friend who was a dragon knight."

John smiled, inclining his head in assent. "Sea dragon, and Knight-Poet, to be completely precise."

"And..." Hayley looked at Ash in awe, remembering the fiery bird that had swooped into her kitchen. "You're a phoenix, aren't you?"

"*The* Phoenix," said Ash, mildly. "Since we are being precise."

There's only one? Just like in the old myths?

Hayley felt like her entire worldview had been turned upside-down and shaken. She turned to Hugh, wondering what sort of walking legend *he* would turn out to be. "And you're...?"

"Bloody exhausted." Hugh took his hands off Griff's chest at last, flexing his fingers as if he had pins-and-needles.

"There's nothing more I can do now. I want to leave him here, with you, if that's all right. He's not fully back to human yet. Maybe you can get him the rest of the way."

"I'll try." Hayley sank cross-legged to the carpet, taking Griff's hand. His fingers were still curled into claws, but they relaxed a little at her touch. "I won't leave him alone."

"And we won't leave you alone." Dai looked around at the other men. "So, who's taking first watch?"

CHAPTER 9

GRIFF

*G*riff woke up with every part of his body aching with a bone-deep, throbbing pain.

That was a pleasant surprise. He hadn't been expecting to wake up at all.

Wincing, he very cautiously pushed himself upright on the couch. All the vertebrae in his back ground against each other like granite rocks, but at least he wasn't hunched over on all fours like a beast.

His knuckles popped as he flexed his fingers, testing their movement. All his fingernails had gone back to human, but three of the fingers on his right hand were now crooked, curled into hooked claw-shapes. Grimacing, Griff tried to straighten them. The joints were locked solid.

Guess I'll be learning to write left-handed, then.

He couldn't believe he'd gotten off so lightly. Even with the wyvern venom instantly halting his uncontrolled shift, he'd expected to come back to a body that was more animal than man...if he'd come back at all.

What happened?

His eagle was still catatonic at the very back of his mind,

leaving him with only human levels of perception. Griff looked around, blinking to clear his dry, strained eyes. Everything seemed dim and foggy, as if he was looking through smoked glass. He was so unused to the limitations of human sight that it took him a moment to recognize Hayley's living room.

Hayley herself was curled up on the floor next to the couch, within arm's reach of him. She was still wearing the same floral top and black leggings she'd worn yesterday. From the dark circles under her closed eyes, Griff guessed that she had to have been awake most of the night.

His eagle and lion both stirred at the sight of their mate, yearning toward her even in their poisoned, weakened state. Griff's jaw tightened. He brutally chained his beasts back down again, binding them so tightly he could barely feel them in the depths of his soul.

Got to keep a tight leash on them. This can't happen again.

Which meant other things couldn't happen again.

Griff forced himself to look away from Hayley. Moving very slowly so as not to wake her up, he levered himself to his feet. His left knee screamed in protest as he tried to put his weight on it. He remembered that it hadn't hurt, for those few magical minutes last night after he and Hayley had succumbed to the pull of the mate-bond…but it was definitely back to its normal state of wrongness now. His knee joint felt as though someone had been hammering rusty nails through it.

Oh well. It's not like I'm not used to it.

Leaning on the wall for support, he managed to limp his way to the kitchen. He halted in the doorway, startled by the shards of glass scattered across the tiled floor and the scorch marks on the walls.

"What in God's name happened here?" Griff muttered to himself. His dry voice rasped like sandpaper in his throat.

I am afraid that I did, Ash's calm, quiet telepathic voice said in his mind. *I was in something of a hurry.*

Squinting out the broken window, Griff caught sight of Ash perched at the very top of the tree outside. The Phoenix's fire was dimmed and controlled, but he still burned brighter than the sun rising behind him.

"Thank you," Griff said out loud, wishing that he could communicate back telepathically, to show Ash the deep and sincere gratitude in his mind. "So Hayley did manage to contact you?"

Just in time. The Phoenix swooped down to perch on the windowsill, his sweeping tail feathers brushing the ground outside. Griff could feel the heat radiating from the massive, eagle-like form even from six feet away. *Hugh said that a minute later, and there would have been nothing he could do.*

Griff picked his way across the broken glass to the sink. He splashed cold water on his face, then drank from his cupped hand, too parched to waste time finding a cup.

"I owe Hugh an apology," he said, when he emerged again. Catching sight of his cellphone lying discarded in a corner, he bent to pocket it. "That can't have been pleasant for him, having to touch me right after Hayley and I had…ah, well, you know. Must have given him a splitting headache."

Hugh was remarkably tight-lipped about the nature of his shifter animal…but there was no hiding such things from Griff's eagle. He'd long ago worked out exactly what Hugh was, though he respected Hugh's desire to keep it a secret even from the rest of Alpha Team. Griff couldn't blame him for it. Hugh's species was meant to be extinct, every last one hunted down and slaughtered way back in the Middle Ages.

If I was the main ingredient in a potion that's meant to grant eternal youth, I'd be pretty damn secretive about my existence too.

Ash's foot-long talons shifted on the windowsill, leaving scorch marks in the wood. Griff knew that the Fire

Commander knew that *he* knew about Hugh, but Ash's cast-iron sense of honor meant he would never openly confirm the paramedic's true nature. *He is tired, but he will recover. Will you?*

Griff shrugged, gesturing with his crooked hand at his bad knee. "Ah, well, I doubt it. But I'll live a while yet, thanks to you all. You can go back home and get some rest now. I'll be fine."

Ash spread his wings...then paused. He turned his head, considering Griff for a long moment with one blazing eye.

I am sorry, Ash said at last. *I understand what it is to taste something, only to have it snatched away. I share your pain. It is possible to live with it....but you will have to be strong. For your mate's sake.*

Before Griff could respond, he was gone. A trail of sparks swirled in his wake, quickly winking out.

He's right. I have to be stronger in future. This was all my fault.

If he hadn't succumbed to temptation and indulged his base, carnal desires, he would never have provoked his inner beasts' jealous rage. He'd selfishly taken advantage of Hayley, and as a result, had nearly left her with a monstrous corpse cooling on her kitchen floor. How would she have explained *that* to Danny?

I can't ever touch her again.

The thought was as cold and bleak as the grey dawn light filtering through the broken window. But it was the truth. He couldn't put Hayley through this again. He *wouldn't*.

I have to leave. Now. Before she wakes up.

Nonetheless, he delayed long enough to sweep up the floor. It wasn't safe to leave broken glass lying around, not when little bare feet would be charging downstairs at any moment.

His heart clenched at the thought of Danny bouncing into

the kitchen, how his eyes would shine in delight if he found Griff still there...

No. I have to disappear, completely. It's better for them both.

At the back of his mind, his lion roared, flinging itself futilely against its cage. Griff ignored it. Slipping on his coat and shoes, he limped down the hallway. He didn't dare let himself take one last look at Hayley, for fear his animals would break loose and undo all his good intentions. Very quietly, for the last time, he eased open the front door-

And found himself unexpectedly confronting a man on the doorstep.

The man had obviously just been reaching for the doorknocker. He dropped his outstretched hand, taking a sharp step back in surprise. Griff had never seen him before in his life, yet there was something eerily familiar about his features.

The man's nostrils flared. A low, deep growl ripped through his throat, possessive outrage flaring in his amber eyes.

The stranger's scent hit Griff like a brick. He suddenly knew *exactly* who the man was.

"Who the hell are you?" demanded Danny's father.

CHAPTER 10

HAYLEY

Hayley jolted awake to the sound of snarling. Her body flooded with adrenaline in instinctive reaction, her deepest monkey brain screaming at her that there was a dangerous predator nearby.

Oh my God! He's shifting again!

Heart pounding, she scrambled to her feet. "Griff!" Following the snarls, she raced into the hallway—and stopped dead.

Griff was still human, although the sounds ripping from his throat were pure lion. He had his back to her, his hands braced on each side of the doorframe as he squared off against a man outside.

The other man was a little taller than Griff, but much leaner. Nonetheless, he matched Griff snarl for snarl, forcibly trying to push his way into the house. His angular, handsome face was contorted with feral rage.

Even though Hayley hadn't seen that face for five years, she instantly recognized him.

"*Reiner?*" she gasped.

The sound of her voice broke the two men's stand-off.

Griff lurched as he turned, his bad knee buckling. Reiner took advantage of the firefighter's momentary weakness to shove past.

"Where is he?" he demanded in the clipped Danish accent she'd once found so sexy. "Where is my son?"

"He's—what—how-" She felt as unsteady as Griff, her legs threatening to give way with sheer shock. "Reiner, what are you *doing* here?"

"I was in London on business. I came as soon as I got your email." Reiner took a step toward her, his fists clenching. Hayley couldn't help shrinking back from the raw, animal power emanating from him. "Now, *where is my son?*"

"Don't. Move." Griff caught Reiner's arm, jerking the other lion shifter back. Even though Griff could barely stand upright, his golden eyes still blazed with primal fury. "You aren't going anywhere near him until Hayley says you can."

"He is *my* son!" Reiner knocked Griff's hand away. "Stand in my way again and I'll rip out your throat."

"No!" Hayley thrust herself between the two men as they started to snarl at each other again. "Reiner, it's okay, he's my…he's a friend."

Reiner's nostrils flared. His withering amber gaze flicked down her body. "It would seem he's rather more than that. Unless you routinely fuck your friends."

Hayley's cheeks heated in humiliation. "That is *none* of your business, Reiner!"

"He's under the same roof as my son. That makes it my business." His muscled chest pressed hard against her shoulder as he leaned forward, glaring across her at Griff. "This is *my* territory. Get out!"

"Mommy?" said a small, sleepy voice from the stairs. "Are Mr. Griff's dragon friends still here?"

All three of them froze.

Danny caught sight of Reiner, and his light brown eyes

widened. Hayley had never realized it before, but they were the exact same shade as his father's.

"Oh," Danny said, in a very small voice.

All of the aggression in Reiner's stance instantly vanished, replaced by awestruck wonder. He took three swift steps to the bottom of the stairs. Hayley let him go, unable to stand in the way of such obvious pure, simple joy.

"My son," Reiner said, his voice shaking. He held out his arms. "*My son.*"

"Daddy." Danny practically fell down the stairs into Reiner's embrace. He clung to him with every limb, burying his face in Reiner's chest. His little shoulders shook in wracking sobs. "Daddy. Daddy. Daddy."

Tears sprang into Hayley's eyes. An unbearable, unnamable swirl of emotions choked her throat. She had to turn away before she broke down entirely—and found herself facing Griff. Sheer, overwhelming jealousy was written in every line of his face as he watched Reiner and Danny.

He caught her looking at him, and his expression instantly went blank. "I should go," he said gruffly.

"Wait!" Hayley caught his sleeve as he turned for the door. "You're in no state to go anywhere." She lowered her voice, casting a quick glance over her shoulder at the still-oblivious Reiner. "You nearly died last night, Griff! Stay, let me take care of you. I don't care how much Reiner growls about it-"

"I *have* to go," he interrupted, not looking at her. His shoulders hunched. "I can't stay here. Especially not now."

Anger and upset churned in her stomach as she realized that he already had his jacket and shoes on. "You were just going to leave, weren't you? If Reiner hadn't arrived, you'd have been gone before I even woke up."

"It would have been for the best," he said, very quietly. He met her eyes at last, and the broken agony in his own shattered her heart. "Hayley. Last night...we can't let that happen again. Not ever."

Memories of his contorted, half-animal form flashed through her mind, red-hot and searing.

He nearly died because of me. How can I ask him to risk that again?

She made herself open her fingers, letting his wrist fall from her grip. Even though she knew it was the right thing to do, it felt wrong, deeply wrong, to let him go.

"Will you at least come back to see Danny?" she asked hopelessly, as he limped away.

"No." Griff didn't look back. "He doesn't need me any more."

CHAPTER 11

DANNY

*D*anny scowled ferociously down at his drawing. It was so unfair! His daddy had finally, *finally* come to see him, and yet he'd still had to go to school. Danny didn't see why *he* couldn't have stayed home with Daddy, even if Mommy did have to go out to work. Maybe Mommy just didn't want him and Daddy having fun together without her.

We could pretend to go to the bathroom, Simba suggested. Mommy used to call Simba his "imaginary friend," but Danny had always known that he was real. The lion cub bounced with eagerness in his mind, urging him to shift. *We could jump out the window and run away.*

Danny shook his head. Just like Mr. Griff had taught him, he held Simba back, not letting the lion take control of their body. The effort made him feel itchy all over. He took out his frustrations on his drawing, scrubbing so hard with the chunky yellow crayon that he nearly went through the paper.

Simba's ears pricked up. *The woman is talking about us,* he informed Danny.

Danny cocked his own head, concentrating. Simba helped him to hear better, picking out his teacher's voice from the low chatter of the rest of the classroom. Miss Hunter was over at the door, talking to someone Danny couldn't see. He couldn't make out everything she was saying, but he definitely heard his own name.

Are we in trouble? Simba asked anxiously.

"I don't know," Danny whispered as quietly as he could. He tried not to talk to Simba too much at school. He didn't like the way it made the other kids stare and giggle behind his back.

"Danny?" his teacher called. She beckoned him over to her. "Someone's here to see you."

Worried, Danny slid off his chair. Halfway to the door, he caught wind of a familiar scent. "Daddy!" he yelled in joy, leaping up into his arms.

Daddy rumbled, bumping his forehead against Danny's. That was lion for "hello" and "happy to see you." No one had ever had to tell Danny that—he just *knew*, way down deep inside where Simba lived.

"You see?" Daddy said to Miss Hunter. He sounded a little mad, but it wasn't with Danny so it didn't matter. "I told you, this is my son. I have a right to take him."

"You came to get me?" Danny wriggled with excitement. "But Mommy said-"

Hush, Daddy said in his head.

Danny fell silent obediently. It was different from when Mommy told him to be quiet—he could argue with Mommy, but Simba *really* didn't like it if he tried to argue with Daddy. Or Mr. Griff.

Miss Hunter hesitated, fidgeting uncertainly with her long, curly hair. "I'm sorry, but you're not on the list of people authorized to pick Danny up. I'm going to have to call Ms. Parker."

"She's at work, and cannot be interrupted." Daddy glared down at Miss Hunter, his lion looming behind his narrowed eyes. He looked like he was thinking of eating the teacher in one big mouthful—*owp!*—just like the Tiger Who Came To Tea. "You will hand my son over to me. *Now.*"

Miss Hunter flinched, her face going white and funny-looking. "I-I- I suppose we can make an exception. Just this once. Danny, go get your things."

Danny hopped down out of Daddy's arms, racing to collect his bag and coat before his teacher could change her mind. He grabbed his picture too, being careful not to crumple it.

"I made this for you," he said, a little shyly, as they walked out of the school. "It's a present."

Daddy's fierce eyes softened as he took the paper. "This is very good. This is you, here, isn't it? And here's your mother, and here's…" His eyebrows drew together. "Wait. Why have you drawn me with long hair?"

"That's not you. *That's* you." Danny helpfully pointed out the big lion he'd drawn. "That's Mr. Griff, holding Mommy's hand."

We've been bad, Simba whimpered, as Daddy's mouth tightened into a hard, thin line.

"No we haven't," Danny whispered to his lion…though he wasn't entirely sure about that himself. Daddy looked awful mad about something.

"And why," Daddy said, a hint of a snarl in his voice, "is 'Mr. Griff' in this picture?"

"Because it's a picture of our family," Danny said, puzzled. "Mr. Griff's my alpha." He brightened as something occurred to him. "Does that mean he's your alpha too, Daddy?"

He jumped as Daddy ripped the paper in half, crumpling up the piece with Mr. Griff and dropping it on the ground. "He is not your alpha. *I* am your alpha. Now, come on."

He isn't our alpha. Simba's ears flattened. *Why is he saying he is? Has he beaten our alpha?*

"Daddy, you didn't fight Mr. Griff, did you?" Danny asked nervously, having to trot to keep up with Daddy's much longer legs.

"Not yet," Daddy growled. He glanced down at Danny sharply, suddenly looking a little wary. "Why? Do you think he's stronger than me?"

Yes, Simba said, with complete certainty.

"Um…" Somehow, Danny didn't think Daddy would be happy to hear that. "Mommy says it's not nice to fight people, anyway."

Daddy snorted. "'Mommy' isn't a lion." He pointed at a car—a *real* nice car, sleek and low and so shiny Danny could see his own face in the bright red paint. "Here we are."

Danny's eyes widened. "Wow! Is this really yours, Daddy? It's like a real-life racing car!"

"It *is* a real-life racing car." Daddy looked happier, his tight shoulders easing down. "Bet your so-called alpha doesn't have one like it. In you get. We're going for a ride."

Thrilled, Danny climbed into the leather passenger seat—then hesitated. "Daddy, there's no booster seat."

"So?" Daddy slid behind the wheel. "There's a seat belt."

Danny squirmed, torn between his desire to ride in the amazing car and dutiful obedience to Mommy's repeated safety warnings. "I'm not allowed to ride without a booster seat. It's against the law."

"Human law." Daddy snorted again. "We're *lions*. We make our own laws. Now buckle up."

Simba nudged him, wordlessly urging him to obey the bigger lion. Danny didn't need much persuasion. He happily clicked his seat belt shut. "Where are we going, Daddy?"

The car roared like an animal as Daddy started the engine. "It's a surprise."

CHAPTER 12

GRIFF

"You have been pining all day," John announced without preamble, barging into Griff's room without knocking first. "You need to eat."

"I'm not pining," Griff said, without looking round. He lay on his back on the bed, staring up at the ceiling. "I'm resting."

"'Resting' involves taking care of your body, oath-brother. *You* are pining." John thumped a tray down onto Griff's bedside table. "I have made you nourishing soup. By boiling things."

From the smell that hit Griff's nostrils, John had made soup by boiling *all* the things. "Thanks. But I'm not hungry."

John hummed, ominously. Griff rolled over to see the sea dragon glaring at him with narrowed eyes, the mysterious soup rising up out of the bowl like a cobra.

You will feed yourself, John said telepathically, as tendrils of soup wove around his outstretched hand. *Or I will feed you.*

Faced with the prospect of having terrible soup magically forced into his bodily orifices, Griff sat up quickly. "Ah...on second thought, I'm starving. Need more than soup. Would you be offended if I made myself a sandwich?"

I would be delighted if you made yourself a sandwich. John didn't stop humming as he followed Griff to the kitchen, the soup coiling around his wrist like a monstrous snake. *I will keep the soup ready, though. Just in case you lose your appetite.*

Griff shot him a level look as he started slicing bread. "John. Did you make terrible soup on purpose?"

I do not follow your meaning, John sent, his blue eyes as wide and tranquil as a tropical lagoon. *I am just a simple sea dragon who does not understand your strange land ways. Eat your sandwich.*

Griff shook his head ruefully, but complied. John waited until he'd swallowed the last bite before letting the reeking soup slide off his hand and down the drain.

"There," the sea dragon shifter said, sounding pleased. "Now you have fortified yourself. Restored in body, you are prepared to steel your soul and face your destiny."

"What destiny?" Griff said suspiciously.

John slid Griff's cellphone across the kitchen table.

Griff looked at it. "My destiny involves the phone."

"Your *destiny* involves your mate." John pointed at the phone. "Call her."

Griff groaned, rubbing his palms over his face. "John…"

"More terrible soup," John rumbled, "could be made."

"I don't care if you force feed me cream-of-pickled-herring-and-peanut-butter," Griff snapped, crossing his arms over his chest and glaring at the sea dragon. "I am *not* calling Hayley. For a start, I don't even know her number."

His forbidding expression never changing, John handed him a scrap of paper. "Now you do."

Griff's lion and eagle stirred, hackles rising with suspicious jealousy. He thrust them back down again. "Why do *you* have Hayley's number?"

"Because I asked her for it, last night." John shrugged one massive shoulder, his stern face softening a little. "I know you, my oath-brother. I knew that you would choose to tear out your heart rather than risk causing your mate future pain. But there is some pain that can only be embraced. Your sacrifice is noble, but misguided. You are being too honorable."

Griff let out a short, ironic huff of breath. "Says the literal *Knight*?"

"Honor is not a shield to hide behind." John nudged the phone closer to him. "It is a sword, to give you the strength to face your demons. You must face what frightens you, oath-brother. You must not flee from it."

Griff slammed his fist down onto the table, making his empty plate jump. "For God's sake, I'm not *frightened* of Reiner! It's just that he's Danny's father. He's the one that Danny wants, the one he needs. Not me. I can't get in the way."

"I did not mean Reiner. I meant what *truly* frightens you." John met his eyes, his own deep and dark. "Living."

Griff was saved from having to try to unravel *that* one by his phone ringing. He caught it as it vibrated off the table. *Unknown Caller*, read the display, followed by a number. He glanced from the screen to the note. It was the same number.

Hayley's number.

"Your mate cries out for you," John said, as Griff's thumb hesitated over the *End Call* button. "Will you truly ignore her plea?"

His eagle and lion both leaned against his mind, from opposite directions, until Griff felt like he would be crushed flat between them. A warning, prickling energy ran over his skin. Griff clenched his jaw, but had no choice but to submit to his animals' desires. He didn't have the strength to resist another uncontrolled shift.

He put the phone to his ear, silently cursing his own weakness. "Hayley?"

"Griff!" Adrenaline surged through Griff's blood at the sheer panic in his mate's voice. "Reiner took Danny. They're gone."

CHAPTER 13

HAYLEY

Hayley clung to Chase's long black mane, the wind whipping her own hair across her face. At any other time, soaring through the sky on the back of a pegasus would have been a magical experience. But right now, she was too sick with dread to think of anything other than her missing son.

"Reiner hasn't taken him to the airport, at least," Griff shouted into her ear. His powerful body pressed reassuringly against her back, his strong arms holding her steady. "He can't be more than a few miles away. Chase says that he can sense Danny clearly."

At least that means he's alive. Hayley held onto that thought as tightly as she gripped the pegasus. It was cold comfort. Alive wasn't the same as unharmed.

"Hayley." Griff's arm tightened around her waist. "I'm Danny's alpha. I'd sense if he was in trouble."

Please let that be true, Hayley prayed.

Chase curved his neck, looking back at Griff with one black, intelligent eye. Hayley felt Griff nod as if in response to something the pegasus shifter had said. "Chase says they're down there, in those woods up ahead. Hang on."

Despite the warning, Hayley still lurched as Chase banked hard. Only Griff's grip kept her from sliding off the pegasus's slick back as they spiraled down.

Griff leaned over, his intent eyes scanning the trees below. "There, Chase! I saw them. Put us down in that clearing over there."

Chase obligingly swooped down to the clearing, beating his wings hard to settle gracefully to the ground. Griff slid off his back first, with a brief grimace as he landed on his bad leg. Nonetheless, he lifted Hayley down easily, setting her on her feet.

"They saw us landing," he said, pointing into the woods. "They're coming to meet us."

"Danny!" Hayley cried out, unable to keep the shrill note of panic out of her voice. She stumbled across the clearing, tufts of dry brown grass catching at her feet. "*Danny!*"

An excited *mrrrr-row!* answered her. Hayley fell to her knees, sobbing in relief as Danny bounded out from between the trees. He was in lion form, his spotted, tawny coat perfectly blending with the autumn leaves. There was something more confident, bolder, about his movements as he bounced toward her. He no longer tripped over his own paws, or let his tail trail forgotten behind him. He had the fluid, beautiful grace of an animal. A *real* animal.

He's not a little boy dressed up as a lion, Hayley realized, properly, for the first time. *He is a lion.*

She was knocked flat on her back by the power of his pounce. He bumped his forehead enthusiastically against her own, clearly delighted with himself—and then paused. He sniffed her, an anxious-sounding *mrrr?* rumbling in his throat.

"Your ma was worried sick about you," Griff told him.

He didn't raise his voice or look at all angry—just stern, and serious. "We all were. We didn't know where you'd gone."

"It's all right now," Hayley said quickly, feeling Danny cringe under Griff's obvious disapproval. She hugged him tight, rubbing her face against his soft fur. "Everything's okay, baby. I'm just glad you're safe."

Danny's rough pink tongue licked gently at her tear-streaked cheek. He whimpered, looking up at Griff.

"You weren't to know," Griff said. His gaze moved to the tree line, and his jaw set in a hard, tight line. "But he *didn't* tell us."

Hayley's pulse leaped as she caught sight of an enormous, golden form slinking through the undergrowth. Every instinct in her body screamed at her to grab her child and run, *run*, away from the dangerous predator.

It's only Reiner, she tried to tell herself...but there was no "only" about it.

She'd only ever seen lions lazing around in zoos before, safely behind bars. She'd never realized before just how *big* they were. Reiner's massive jaws could have comfortably engulfed her entire head. His paws were bigger than dinner plates. She couldn't move, couldn't take her eyes off that powerful, terrifying form as he stalked toward her.

Griff's hand fell on her shoulder, protective and comforting. There was more than a hint of snarl in his voice as he addressed Reiner. "That's enough. Stop trying to intimidate her."

Reiner halted, though his lip wrinkled back a little, exposing a fang. He sank to his hindquarters, curling his tail over his front paws. His entire attitude was insouciant, just daring them to object to his behavior.

Maybe it was Griff's solid presence at her back, or maybe just anger sparked by Reiner's arrogant, entitled air, but

Hayley found her courage at last. Danny jumped off her as she surged to her feet.

Striding up to Reiner, she poked him right in his big pink nose. "You do *not* take Danny anywhere without telling me first! *Ever!*"

Reiner glared right back at her. His tawny form shimmered, turning back into a man. "I am his father," he said haughtily, apparently completely unselfconscious about being stark naked. "I have the right to be with my son."

Reiner might be entirely unabashed by his lack of clothing, but Hayley wasn't. She jerked her eyes back upward, her cheeks heating. He was just as athletically muscular as she remembered. She didn't find him at all sexually attractive anymore, but she had to admit he was still, objectively speaking, a beautiful man.

Once, that sculpted, powerful body had completely addled her mind, blinding her to the flaws hidden under the attractive surface. She didn't regret the relationship—she'd gotten Danny out of it, after all—but she couldn't believe she'd been so stupid.

From Reiner's sudden smirk, he'd caught the involuntary drift of her attention. "Thinking of old times, Hayley?" He flexed a little, his abs tightening. "If you're feeling a pang of regret, I might be persuaded to give you a second chance."

"*You* left *me*, Reiner!" Hayley jabbed him again with her finger, this time in the middle of his hard chest. "You do not get to just waltz in here and claim full parental rights. You haven't even *acknowledged* Danny before now!"

"Hayley," Griff said warningly. He turned to Danny. "Lad, me and your ma and da need to have one of those boring grown-up conversations now. Why don't you go play with my friend Chase over there? Practice your pouncing."

Chase stomped one back hoof, shooting Griff a look that was clearly the equine equivalent of *I will get you for this.*

Nonetheless, he pranced away, swishing his long black tail invitingly at Danny. The lion cub didn't need any further encouragement. With the enthusiasm of a kitten spotting a laser pointer, he bounded after the pegasus.

"I thought this was something you'd probably prefer he didn't hear," Griff murmured to Hayley apologetically. His voice hardened as he turned to Reiner. "You only became interested in Danny once you learned he was a shifter, didn't you?"

"Of course," Reiner said, as if this was not only understandable but admirable. "What on earth would I want with a human child? I kept track of him, naturally, just in case it turned out the shifter genes bred true."

"If he'd never shifted, you would never have gotten in touch?" Hayley said, unable to comprehend how anyone could be so cold. "He's your son, Reiner, regardless of whether he turns into a lion or not!"

"If he was not a shifter, he would be no son of mine." Reiner looked across the clearing at Danny, who had managed to leap onto Chase's back. Reiner's expression softened as he watched Danny cling onto the pegasus with all four paws, his milk-teeth nipping playfully at Chase's neck. "But he is. And he is a son to be proud of. Look at him! So bold and fearless. He will be a true alpha one day."

Hayley couldn't deny that there was genuine affection in Reiner's voice. "Well…I'm glad you've at least decided to take an interest now. But Reiner, you have to see things from my perspective. I know you're trying to make up for lost time, but I nearly died of terror when I went to pick Danny up from school and discovered that he wasn't there. You *can't* do that again."

Reiner glared back at her, his customary arrogance sliding back in place like a mask. "I will do what is best for my son. He needs to learn shifter ways, not to be locked up in some useless human school. Why did you worry? You knew he was with me."

"Yes, but I don't *know* you, Reiner! You wanted me to kill Danny before he was even born!" Angry tears sprang into Hayley's eyes as she remembered his horrible parting words, years ago. "How was I supposed to know you didn't just come back to finish the job?"

Reiner's muscles bunched with outrage. "How *dare* you imply that I would ever harm my son!"

"Both of you, that's enough." Griff spoke quietly, but his voice rang with that odd, iron-hard note of utter command. "He'll hear you if you start shouting at each other."

Hayley had indeed been about to yell at Reiner, but she found that her mouth had snapped shut of its own accord. Reiner too subsided, though he didn't look at all happy about it.

"*I* am Danny's alpha," Griff said to Reiner, that ominous, forceful growl still edging his words. "He is a member of my pride, and I am bound to protect him. I can tell that you would indeed never hurt him, but that does not mean I trust your judgment. Until I am satisfied that he is safe in your care, you *will not* take him anywhere without my permission."

Reiner held Griff's stare. His lips pulled back from his teeth, like a lion baring its fangs. "I could challenge you for him."

Griff's eyes flared yellow, as bright and fierce as the heart of the sun. "Try. It."

Reiner flinched back a little. He scowled down at the ground, breaking eye contact. "What if Danny *wants* me as his alpha?" he muttered.

"Then I would release him to you," Griff said coolly. "If you can win his heart and trust, I'll not stand in your way. But until then, I am his alpha, and you will respect my decisions for him. *Is that clear?*"

Reiner's eyes blazed with frustrated resentment, but he grudgingly nodded.

I'm his mother! Hayley wanted to scream at both of them. *Don't I get a say?*

But she didn't dare interrupt. Whatever was going on was clearly a shifter thing. She couldn't risk destabilizing the fragile peace agreement that Griff seemed to have negotiated with Reiner.

She knew that Griff could tell what she was thinking from the swift, apologetic glance he shot her. "Hayley, do you want Reiner to take you and Danny back home? Or would you rather that Chase take you and Danny, and I'll go with Reiner?"

From the look Reiner was giving Griff, if the firefighter got into a car with him, only one of them would be coming out again. "We'll go with Reiner," Hayley said hastily. She hesitated, eying the glowering lion shifter.

He always hated not getting his own way. I have to be the bigger person, give him a way to save face. If he is going to be a real father to Danny, I'm going to have to learn how to compromise with him.

"We don't have to go straight away, Reiner," she said to him, forcing herself to speak respectfully. "If you want more time with Danny, that is."

Any hope that he'd accept this peace offering died in the withering glare he gave her. "Thank you so much for offering me a few paltry hours with the son I haven't seen in *five years*," he said sarcastically. "It's *so* generous of you."

"I'll just go say goodbye to Danny, then Chase and I will be on our way." Griff took Hayley's arm—to all appearances casually, but she could feel the tension in his strong grip. "Quick word, Hayley?"

"What is it?" she asked under her breath, as he led her away from Reiner.

He shook his head at her, very slightly. He didn't speak again until they were at the other end of the clearing, where Chase and Danny were playing tag. Danny broke off his pursuit of Chase, bouncing happily up to Griff. The firefighter ruffled the cub's fur, then looked at Chase.

"If you want to go say hello to Reiner," Griff said to the pegasus, very quietly, "now would be a very good time."

Chase's ears flicked back and forth in apparent confusion. Then he snorted, tossing his head. He trotted toward the lion shifter.

Halfway across the clearing, he shimmered, turning human. Hayley was relieved to see that *he* at least kept his clothes on when he transformed.

"That should keep Reiner occupied for a few minutes," Griff said, as Chase loudly hailed a somewhat bemused-looking Reiner. "No one can pay attention to anything else when they're being subjected to Chase in full flow."

"What's going on?" Hayley was starting to feel very nervous by the level of secrecy. "What don't you want him to overhear?"

"This." Griff went down on one knee, so he could look Danny straight in the eyes. "Danny, this is very, very important. You must not tell your da that I can't shift."

Danny tilted his head quizzically. He must have said something telepathically, because Griff shook his head.

"No, he doesn't." Glancing up at Hayley, he added, "And we're *bloody* lucky that's true. He'd have challenged me in a heartbeat, otherwise."

Hayley went cold as she realized the implication. "A challenge is a physical fight? He'd attack you in lion form?"

Danny's tail lashed back and forth. He let out an indignant hiss.

"Shifter law isn't always fair," Griff said grimly. "Danny, if your da challenges me and wins, he'd become your alpha.

And then he'd be able to order you never to see me again. He doesn't like me."

Danny's eyes widened in distress. He made a plaintive mewling sound, which even Hayley could tell was the lion equivalent of *why?*

"Because he loves *you* so much. He wants to have you all to himself. He doesn't want to share, not with me, not with your-" Griff stopped, abruptly, but Hayley knew what he'd nearly said.

Not with your mother.

"Griff," Hayley whispered, her mouth dry with fear. "Reiner's going to find out eventually."

"I know," Griff said grimly. "We're on borrowed time. Let's hope it's long enough."

"To do what?" she asked him, hoping against hope that he had a plan.

Griff straightened, his expression hard as stone. "To get you a really, really good lawyer."

CHAPTER 14

GRIFF

"What do you mean, we can't take Reiner to court?" Unable to keep still, Griff paced across the lawyer's office. Frustration and anger boiled under the surface of his skin. "You're a bloody fae hound, Michael! Since when do the Wild Hunt sit on their arses and let wrongdoers go unpunished?"

Michael's professionally neutral expression didn't alter, but his dark eyes flashed blood red for second. "We don't," the shifter lawyer said coolly. "But in the eyes of the law, Reiner Ljonsson isn't a wrongdoer. Much as I'd like to pull him down for you, I can't. And as your lawyer, I have to warn you that if you take Reiner to court over custody of Danny now…you're going to lose."

"But I'm Danny's mother," Hayley protested. Her brown eyes were huge in her frightened face. "Children always stay with their mother, don't they?"

Michael shook his close-shaven, elegant head. "Not shifter children. That's why we have our own court, to handle these cases. Our laws are designed to protect our children from being kept away from their birthright. Except in very, *very* exceptional circumstances, the shifter parent always gets custody."

Hayley swallowed. "But...Reiner lives in Valtyra. Surely the law can't really force Danny and me to move to a country where we don't even speak the language."

"Not both of you," Michael said grimly, and Hayley went stark white. "Just Danny. I've looked into Valtyran law. As a non-shifter, you can't even enter the country without a Valtyran sponsor. And from what you tell me of Reiner, he's not exactly likely to be willing to do that. Griff, if you're going to punch something, use that wall over there, please."

Griff, who had indeed just been about to smash his fist into the nearest wall, caught himself. The one the lawyer was pointing at was covered in dents and scratches, some of them alarmingly deep.

His lion eyed the marks warily, its rage abruptly dimming. *Territorial marks? They are very large. Very, very large. Are we trespassing?*

"What in God's name did that?" Griff asked, staring up at a particularly impressive crater near the ceiling.

"Wooly mammoth," the lawyer said. He shrugged one shoulder. "Very touchy people, mammoths."

Stupid cat, Griff's eagle taunted his lion. *Frightened of marks on a wall. And you think* you *can protect our fledgling?*

Griff pressed his fist to his forehead, pain splitting his skull like an axe as his two beasts went for each other. He clenched his teeth. *I don't have time for this!*

Deliberately, he thought of Reiner. His lion checked itself in mid-spring, while his eagle aborted its plunging dive, both diverted by the mental image of their common enemy. Griff took advantage of his beasts' distraction to grab them both by the scruffs of their necks, forcing them back into their separate areas of his mind.

"Griff?" Hayley touched his hand, hesitantly. "Are you okay?"

Griff's headache faded, washed away by the exquisite fire sparked by the lightest brush of her skin against his. His lion and eagle leaned forward in unison, yearning for more.

All her problems...and she's still worried about me. I'm just another burden on her.

He took a step back, thrusting his hand into the pocket of his jacket. "I'm fine now. Michael, tell me there's something you can do. Or the next time you see me, you'll be prosecuting me on murder charges."

"I'm a fae hound of the Wild Hunt, Griff." Michael's eyes flashed red again. "Don't even joke about that sort of thing in front of me."

Griff matched his stare, not backing down. "Who said I was joking?"

"Griff, you can't," Hayley said. She rubbed her hands over her face, emerging looking wan but determined. "Reiner's rich, but even he hasn't got the funds to search all of America. I'll take Danny and disappear, if I have to."

Michael glanced up at the ceiling, a wince crossing his handsome face. "As someone who has to uphold child welfare even before client confidentiality, I did not just hear that." He sighed, looking back across at them both. "Look, neither of you do anything rash. I said you would lose if you took Reiner to court *now*. I didn't say ever."

Hope rose in Hayley's face. "You mean, there's something we can do to help win a favorable judgment?"

"Possibly." Michael steepled his long fingers, leaning his elbows on his polished desk. "It depends how far you're willing to go. For example, if you were to marry a shifter-"

Hayley didn't even wait for him to finish. "Griff, will you marry me?"

YES! Griff's lion and eagle roared as one.

"No," he said, roughly. He had to look away from the shocked hurt in her eyes. "That won't work. Tell her, Michael."

"Legally, he's not a shifter," Michael said to Hayley, apologetically. "By definition, a shifter has to be able to shift. Otherwise any human criminal could claim to be one of us, and demand to be judged according to our laws. It doesn't matter how you, or me, or anyone may personally view Griff…according to the law, he's just a regular human being."

Hayley stared at the lawyer. "Are you seriously advising me to marry any old random shifter? What do you expect me to do, get one out of a mail-order catalogue?"

Griff let out a brief, humorless bark of laughter. "No need for that. John Doe owes me a life-debt." He pinched the bridge of his nose, fighting down a migraine as his animals howled with rage at the merest *idea* of giving their mate away to someone else. "Bet he never expected me to call it in like this."

"I am *not* marrying John!" Hayley said hotly. "Not even for pretend!"

Michael coughed, looking a little embarrassed. "Ah, it would have to be for real. The court would see through a fake marriage."

"Well, there you go." Hayley folded her arms, glaring at the lawyer. "Do you have any *practical* suggestions?"

Michael spread his hands. "If this comes to court, your only chance of winning custody is to demonstrate that you can provide Danny with a supportive shifter role model. If you can't do that through your mate, the next best thing is to have multiple close shifter friends. You need to get yourself—and him—integrated into the local shifter community. As quickly as possible. Fortunately, you shouldn't have any problems there. Griff's very well-connected."

Hayley bit her lip, glancing up at Griff. He could read her

expression as clearly as if her thoughts were printed above her head in glowing neon letters: *But that means we'll have to spend a lot of time together...*

His eagle keened a high, piercing cry of loneliness. *She fears we will plummet out of the sky, leaving her alone in the storm. She does not want us at her wingtip. She knows she cannot rely on us.*

"It'll be all right," Griff told Hayley, forcing the words past the ache in his chest. "I just have to make the initial introductions for you. You'll be able to take it from there by yourself."

She looked down at her hands, her hair swinging forward to shadow her face. "Okay," she said, very quietly.

Michael cleared his throat, breaking the uncomfortable silence. "The longer you can keep Reiner in the dark, the better. I have to reiterate, it's best if you can keep this out of court entirely. If he does find out, I strongly recommend that you settle with him privately, if you can. Persuade him that it's in Danny's best interests to stay with his mother."

"That would require Reiner to become an actual alpha, rather than an insecure beta spoiling for a fight," Griff said darkly. "We've probably got a better chance of *me* learning to shift."

"What a good idea. Please do that." Michael shuffled through papers on his desk. "It would make my life immeasurably easier. Now, about the other matter-"

Griff held up his hand, forestalling him. "Hayley, would you mind waiting in the car? I've got some…private business I need to discuss. This will only take a moment."

Hurt flashed across Hayley's face, but she left without argument. Griff waited until he'd heard the office door swing shut behind her downstairs before turning back to Michael. "You have it ready for me to sign?"

"All in order." Michael slid the paper across the desk, along with a pen. "I can witness it now, if you like."

"Good." Griff flipped through the pages, quickly checking that everything was as he'd specified. "I appreciate the rush job. How much do I owe you?"

"Oh, call it a few bottles of your mother's best Scotch. It doesn't take long to draw up a will when there's only one beneficiary." Michael cocked a curious eyebrow at Griff. "Why don't you want her to know?"

"Because she'd probably argue." Griff scrawled an awkward, left-handed signature. "It's easier this way."

Michael's gaze flicked to Griff's crooked, frozen right hand. "That's new," he observed, quietly.

Griff made a noncommittal noise. He pushed the will back to Michael. "Thanks for this. It's a weight off my mind to know that at least Hayley will be taken care of financially when something happens to me."

Michael cast him a level look as he countersigned the document. "You mean *if* something happens to you."

"No," Griff said simply. "I don't."

CHAPTER 15

DANNY

Grown-ups, Danny had decided, were just plain *weird*.

He couldn't understand it. Everything was wonderful, yet Mommy, Daddy, and Mr. Griff seemed determined not to be happy. They all pretended that they were, but Danny could tell the difference.

Daddy came round nearly every day to take him out into the woods to be lions together. When Mommy hugged Danny goodbye, it was always a little too hard and long, as if she was still worried about Daddy picking him up. Danny couldn't work out why. Daddy had gotten a booster seat for the amazing car, after all.

Danny loved being lions. Daddy was always much happier on four paws than he was when he was a person. When he was a person, he talked too much about how Mommy and Mr. Griff were doing things wrong and how much better everything would be if *he* was Danny's alpha.

It made Danny feel strange and nervous when Daddy talked like that. It was better when they were just being lions. Everything was simpler as lions.

Mr. Griff was around a lot, but somehow it felt like he wasn't. It was like whenever he played with Danny, his lion was a very long way away, keeping a wary distance. And he never, ever touched Mommy. That was wrong, Danny knew, though he wasn't quite sure why. It was something to do with needing to have both a mommy alpha *and* a daddy alpha in a pride, otherwise there wouldn't be any new little lions. Simba worried about it a lot, anyway.

Mommy worried a lot too. Danny could hear her crying sometimes, late at night, when she thought he was asleep. She didn't know that Simba let him hear her. Sometimes he really, really wanted to climb out of his bed and into hers, to give her a big hug and tell her everything was going to be okay.

But he didn't dare. Mommy always thought that she had to fix things all by herself. If she knew Danny's big plan, she might ruin the whole thing.

The problem, Danny had decided after careful thought and a lot of discussion with Simba, was that Mommy and Daddy hadn't properly understood their places in the pride. Mommy was supposed to be Mr. Griff's mate—which was like being married, but more so, according to Simba—but for some reason she didn't seem to want to be. And Daddy was supposed to be beta, helping defend the territory and raise the cubs, but for some reason *he* didn't want to be.

It was all very strange. Why didn't Mommy and Daddy want to be in Mr. Griff's pride? Couldn't they *see* that Mr. Griff was the biggest, bestest alpha ever?

Danny had tried to explain all this to Daddy, but he just got all grumbly and snarly and wouldn't listen. It was like he was jealous of Mr. Griff, which was silly because being an alpha or not wasn't something anyone could help. It didn't make Mr. Griff *better* than Daddy, any more than Daddy having a nice car meant he was better than Mr. Griff. It just meant that they had different jobs.

Danny had learned a lot about alphas and being a shifter from Mr. Griff and his friends. Mr. Griff had *amazing* friends.

That was what had given Danny his idea. Mr. Griff had introduced him and Mommy to some of his friends who were mated, and that had made it clear to Danny that Mommy and Mr. Griff just weren't doing it right. They needed someone to help them out.

Danny and Simba had a plan. They were going to make sure that Mommy and Mr. Griff became a proper alpha pair. They were going to make sure that Daddy *realized* that Mommy and Mr. Griff were a proper, mated alpha pair. Then everyone would be in the right place, and everyone would be happy.

And they had the perfect opportunity to carry out their plan, because soon it was going to be a very special day. A day when nobody, not even Daddy or Mommy or Mr. Griff, could possibly be sad. The very best time of year, apart from Christmas! Danny could hardly wait.

At Halloween, he was going to fix *everything*.

CHAPTER 16

HAYLEY

"It's Halloween!" Danny shrieked at the top of his lungs, the cape of his Mike the Knight costume flying behind him as he ran in excited circles around Hayley. "It's finally Halloween! Hurry, Mommy, hurry!"

He hasn't even eaten any of his candy yet, Hayley thought in amused dismay. *What's he going to be like* after *the sugar hits?*

"Okay you, calm down," she said, trying to keep him in the beam of her flashlight as they walked down the street. "Mr. Griff isn't going to want to take us to the party if you're screeching like a crazed monkey."

Danny instantly took her hand, his brown eyes wide with concern. "I'm being good. I really am. Promise, promise, *promise* we can go, Mommy?"

Hayley couldn't help laughing at his over-the-top look of cherubic innocence. "I promise. I know how much this means to you."

He's so excited about this party. I guess he just can't get enough of being around other shifters.

The thought gave her a pang in her chest. Over the past few weeks, she'd seen Danny blossom as he explored this new, secret world. She'd come to realize just how cruel it would be to keep him apart from his birthright. And Reiner was part of that. No matter how uncomfortable Hayley found it, Danny *needed* his father. He had to have someone who fully understood what it meant to be a shifter.

Griff isn't enough, whispered a small, traitorous voice in her mind. *Maybe even Griff's friends aren't enough. Maybe the law is right. Maybe I can't ever give Danny what he truly needs.*

Hayley banished the sickening thought. She wasn't going to let any of her worries taint Danny's enjoyment of this special night. Resolutely, she straightened her rabbit-ear headband, trying to get into the Halloween spirit.

How many chances do you get to go to a Halloween party with real, actual shapeshifters? This'll be fun. Halloween is meant to be a break from reality, a chance to pretend to be someone else. I could do with being someone else, for a bit.

I certainly look *like someone else, at least.*

The costume shop hadn't had a lot of options for larger ladies. She'd been going to go as a ghost, but Danny had pitched a fit at the prospect. In the end she'd had to relent and allow *him* to pick out her costume…though she'd drawn the line at donning the fuzzy bikini. After a bit of a battle, Danny had grudgingly allowed her to wear the ears and fluffy tail paired with a soft but figure-hugging knitted black dress. The overall effect, she feared, was still rather closer to Playboy bunny than was entirely appropriate.

I shouldn't have let Danny talk me into this outfit. It's not fair to Griff.

Or me, for that matter.

Hayley's breath sighed out. Ever since *that* night, Griff had treated her with meticulous, painful courtesy, as if he just saw her as Danny's mother and not a woman at all. In return, she did her very best to pretend that *he* was just some odd kind of sports coach for Danny.

But she couldn't forget the fire of his touch, or the heat of his mouth between her legs. When he was playing with Danny, she couldn't stop herself from avidly watching the flex of his biceps or the powerful curve of his back. And, just a few times, she'd caught Griff looking at her too, with a feral, exciting intensity that made her core clench in longing.

But then…he'd look away, taking a deep breath, and when he met her eyes again the burning desire in his own would be tamped down again, fiercely repressed. She knew that he didn't dare risk another uncontrolled shift. She knew that they couldn't ever touch again.

That would be Hayley's cue to find some excuse to leave the room, hiding away until she too could contain the feelings threatening to overspill in her heart. Though sometimes her body yearned for his so badly that she physically shook with longing, she would *not* give in to her selfish desires.

If he could suppress his deep, animal instincts, then so could she. She'd sworn she wouldn't make it any harder on him than it already was.

Hayley looked down at her costume. *Why, why,* why *didn't I just drape a sheet over my head?*

"There's Mr. Griff's house!" Danny yelled, forgetting in his excitement that he was being good. "Come on, Mommy!"

Shaking her head to dispel her gloomy thoughts, Hayley let him tow her up Griff's driveway. Small, hand-carved pumpkin lanterns lit the way. Hayley was privately pleased by the subdued, minimal decorations. She knew some people liked to go all-out with spooky graveyards and bloody zombie hands nailed to the door, but she personally didn't think they were suitable for little kids.

This is nice. Tasteful. Nothing scary at-

The door opened. Danny shrieked in terror, cowering behind Hayley as a towering apparition in demonic spiked armor loomed ominously over them both.

"Why do small children keep doing that?" said John Doe's deep voice from behind the draconic helmet, sounding bewildered.

Heart still hammering, Hayley blinked at his outfit. Curving, oddly organic-looking plates of some opalescent material armored John's massive shoulders and arms, leaving most of his impressive torso bare. Thick, scaled leggings protected his legs. He had a sword longer than Hayley was tall strapped to his back, a fist-sized pearl gleaming on the pommel.

"That...is quite some costume, John," Hayley said weakly.

"I am not wearing a costume," John said, flipping up his visor. "This is the formal armor of the Order of the First Water, sworn defenders of the Pearl Throne."

Danny peeked round Hayley's legs. "You mean that's *real* knight armor, Sir John?"

"Yes. I do not get many opportunities to wear it, these days." The sea dragon shifter let out a deep, heartfelt sigh. "I am beginning to regret my decision to do so tonight. By my count, I have now made thirty-seven small children cry."

"Yes, but you've also inspired at least that many teenage crushes," Griff's amused voice floated around John's shoulder. "I swear there's one group of girls who keep swapping costumes and coming back. Hello, Danny."

"Mr. Griff!" Danny frowned, looking Griff up and down. "Why are you wearing a skirt?"

"It's a kilt, lad," Griff said, spreading his arms to display his plaid. He let out a rich chuckle. "I'm cheating too. This is just the way my clan traditionally dresses on formal occasions. But you Sassenachs find it exotic, so I thought it would do for a costume. Do you like it?"

"I told you to wear something awesome. Like a Batman suit. Not a *skirt*." Danny turned to Hayley, looking doubtfully up at her. "Mommy, do you like Mr. Griff's costume?"

"Guh," Hayley managed to say.

And I was worried about my *costume being too sexy.*

She tore her eyes away from Griff's muscular calves, moistening her dry lips. "Y-yes," she said weakly. "I think it's very…nice."

"Mph." Danny did not sound convinced. He pushed Hayley forward, his tone brightening. "Mr. Griff, look at Mommy's costume!"

Griff's golden eyes heated, and she knew that he could see her arousal. His hungry gaze swept down her own figure-hugging outfit.

Oh, I really, really, really *should have come as a ghost.*

"He picked it," she said hastily, cheeks hot with mortification. "Um, I mean, I'm meant be a bunny. Like, a *real* bunny."

"That's right," Danny said happily. "Because lions and eagles *both* like bunnies."

Oh dear Lord, was that *his logic?*

"Aye. We do," Griff said, his voice a deep growl. He cleared his throat, looking back down at Danny. "Well, lad, ready to get going?"

"Yes!" Danny shouted, seizing Griff's hand. "Are you coming too, Sir John?"

"I must stay and guard the door." John flipped his visor shut again. "Though I must admit, I am not accustomed to stopping assailants by offering them lollipops."

"All right if we stop off at a couple of my friends' places along the way?" Griff asked Danny as they started up the road. "They're two you haven't met yet, but I think you'd like them."

Danny looked a little worried. "We won't be late for the party, will we?"

"I promise, we'll get there in plenty of time." Griff looked over Danny's head at Hayley, smiling. The sight made her heart leap—he hadn't smiled properly like that since, well,

Reiner. "I've never known a boy to be so excited about a party. I only hope it lives up to his expectations."

"I'm sure it will," Hayley said, smiling back. *Just friends,* she reminded herself sternly. *Friends on a nice fun night out. As friends.* "He's been obsessed ever since you mentioned it. So, who are you taking us to visit?"

"Hugh, for one." Griff turned off the main street. "He won't come to the party—too many people—but he secretly loves getting trick-or-treaters. Most people don't realize it, but he's got a hidden soft spot for children, our Hugh. But first, I wanted to drop by on someone else. I want to have one last try at convincing her to join us."

The street got narrow, and darker, as Griff led them deeper into the maze of alleyways. There weren't many pumpkins in *this* neighborhood. Hayley wouldn't have felt safe on her own, but she trusted Griff to know what he was doing.

"Here we go," Griff said, stopping outside a dented door with peeling paint. Someone had carefully cut *Happy Halloween!* out of newspaper print, sticking the letters to the inside of the window. "You want to knock, Danny?"

Danny gave Griff a slightly dubious look, but dutifully knocked. The door opened instantly, as if someone had been waiting right on the other side.

"Trick or treat!" announced a beaming teenage girl in a home-made fairy princess costume and a wheelchair. Pink glittering ribbons were woven through the spokes.

Danny frowned. "That's what *I'm* supposed to say!"

"Sorry," the girl said cheerfully. "I just like saying it too. I never get to go out myself. Hi, Big G! And you're Hayley, right? I'm Hope."

"Nice to meet you," Hayley said, carefully shaking the offered hand. Hope's bones were as delicate as a bird's, her fingers barely able to grip Hayley's. "Are you a…?"

"Shifter?" Hope wheeled her chair back a little, letting them into the narrow hallway. "Nope, that's my sister. Unfortunately. You're wasting your time, G. She won't come. She won't even let *me* come."

"Hmm." Griff's mouth tightened. "Well, let me see what I can do."

"Good luck." Hope did not sound hopeful. Her thin shoulders heaved in a tragic sigh. "I cannot *wait* until I'm eighteen, and can finally do what I want."

Griff patted her on the shoulder as he edged round her wheelchair. "She's just trying to look out for you, you know."

"Yeah, well, I wish she wouldn't." Hope turned her attention back to Danny, brightening again. "Hey, I hope you like candy, because I've got a *ton*. Turns out most kids around here prefer throwing eggs to getting treats."

Hayley left Danny rummaging enthusiastically in the offered bucket of candy, following Griff down the short, dark hallway. "What sort of shifter is her sister?" she asked in an undertone.

Griff shot her a swift, strangely guarded glance. "Wyvern."

Wyvern? Where have I heard that before...?

Hayley grabbed Griff's wrist as he raised his hand to knock on a closed door. It was the first time she'd touched him for weeks. She made herself ignore the rush of desire that shot through her blood.

"Wyvern as in wyvern venom?" she hissed. "As in the poison you made me inject you with? The poison that nearly *killed* you?"

"That wasn't her fault." Shaking her off, Griff firmly knocked on the door. "Ivy? I know you're in there. You can't hide from me."

The door opened a crack, revealing one green eye and a

sliver of sulky expression. "You should listen to your friend, G. Just go away."

"I can't do that, Ivy." Griff put his shoulder to the door, shoving it open. "Please come out."

Hayley wasn't entirely sure what she'd expected a wyvern shifter to look like, but she had to admit Ivy wasn't it. The young woman was soft and curvy, with a round, pretty face despite her ferocious scowl. She was dressed head-to-toe in layers of leather and denim, every inch of her skin below the chin covered.

She folded her gloved hands under her armpits, glaring at Griff. "You come back for some more poison? One heart attack wasn't enough for you?"

"Ivy, I told you, I don't blame you for anything," Griff said patiently. "It was entirely my own idea, and you tried to talk me out of it, and in any event, you probably saved my life. Now, are you going to stop hiding yourself away and come out to meet everyone?"

"Yeah, because all your friends would just *love* to hang out with me." Ivy snorted. "I'm sure ponyboy will even buy me a drink."

"I'll handle Chase," Griff coaxed. "Come on, Ivy. For Hope's sake, if not your own."

Ivy's green eyes narrowed. "Tell you what, G. I *will* come. If you just let me do one thing first." She stepped toward Hayley, stretching out her hand. "After all, if you want me to go to a big, crowded party, then you must be okay with me doing *this*…"

Hayley, who'd automatically started to take Ivy's offered hand, yelped as Griff knocked her own arm aside. His broad form was abruptly between her and the wyvern shifter, every muscle tense.

Ivy's lip curled. "Yeah. Didn't think so."

Griff sighed, raking his fingers through his hair. "I'm

sorry, Ivy. I didn't mean to do that. Just instincts. You know how it is."

"Yeah, well." Ivy stepped back, closing the door again. "If you really want to help me, G…you know what you can do."

"What was that all about?" Hayley asked Griff, after they'd collected Danny and said goodbye to Hope.

"Ivy's touch is poisonous," he said quietly, so that Danny —running excitedly on ahead waving a glow stick—didn't overhear. "Even in human form. She's fairly safe when she's wearing gloves, but…well, 'fairly safe' isn't good enough for my inner beasts."

"Poor kid." Ivy's wary defensiveness took on a whole new meaning. Having seen how much a community of fellow shifters meant to Danny, Hayley felt sorry for the isolated wyvern shifter. "What did she mean, you could help her?"

"Not me, really." Griff let out his breath in a long sigh. "Ash could, but he won't. Ivy wants me to try to persuade him-"

"Griff?" Hayley found that she was walking by herself. She turned to see that he'd frozen in mid-step. "What is it?"

All the blood had drained from his face. "Distract me."

"Huh? Danny!" Hayley shouted over her shoulder as she hurried back to Griff. Her blood ran cold as she realized that he was fighting his inner beasts. "Griff! What set them off?"

"I thought of—something." His left fist clenched, shaking. Sweat beaded on his forehead. "But I can't—let them know —*distract me!*"

She could only think of one thing to do. Stretching up on tip-toe, she kissed him.

She'd meant it to be short, just to shock his animals out of their anger. But once she'd started, she couldn't stop. She laced her fingers round the back of his neck, pulling him down further, his mouth as hungry and demanding as hers. He made a low, desperate sound deep in his throat, crushing her against his strong body. It was like they were two magnets, drawn together by some unstoppable, cosmic force.

"Mommy? Mr. Griff?"

They leaped apart guiltily.

Brow furrowed, Danny looked between them, first at Hayley, then up at Griff. His small shoulders heaved in a huge, relieved sigh.

"*Finally,*" he said in satisfaction.

CHAPTER 17

GRIFF

Griff very carefully concentrated on the feel of Hayley's fingers wound through his. He focused on the exquisite softness of her skin, the intoxicating heat of her body next to his. He let his overwhelming desire for her surge...covering up the idea that Ivy had sparked in his mind.

He could feel his eagle's stare boring into the inside of his skull, trying to see what he was concealing from it. His lion was less suspicious. It rolled in delight, luxuriating in their mate's presence like a kitten in a bed of catnip.

Hayley stole a sidelong glimpse of his profile as they passed under a streetlamp. "Have they settled down again?" she asked.

"Aye. All's well. For the moment, at least." *Which means that I should really let go now...*

As if reading his mind, Hayley's fingers tightened on his hand. "You know," she said softly, "I was thinking earlier about how Halloween lets you pretend to be someone else, just for one night. I was thinking how much fun that would be."

"That does sound like a grand time." He looked down into her upturned face. "Who would you like to be?"

"Just a woman." Tentatively, as if doubting her welcome, she leaned into his side. "Just a woman, out with her son. And her man."

Griff drew in a short, sharp breath, longing piercing his heart like an arrow. He was fiercely aware of every point of contact between her body and his.

I shouldn't. It'll only make it harder to stop.

"Aye," he said, his voice as soft as hers had been, as if reality couldn't notice them as long as they were whispering. "I'd like to pretend that too. Just for one night."

He felt Hayley's tense muscles relax. She leaned her head against his shoulder. "Just for one night."

"Why are you slowing down, Mr. Griff? Hurry!" Danny pulled at Griff's other hand, straining ahead like an eager puppy on a leash. "I can hear music! We're nearly at the party!"

A couple of betas from the local wolf pack were hanging casually around the entrance to an alleyway, ready to politely —or not so politely—turn back any too-curious mundanes. Recognizing Griff, they waved the three of them through without challenge.

Griff hadn't taken Hayley and Danny to the Full Moon before. Normally, the shifter-only pub was also an adult-only establishment. Not that it was a rowdy drinking den—Rose Swanmay, the proprietor, made sure of that. But it *was* a place for shifters of all types to relax and enjoy the company of their own kind, which meant it sometimes got a little boisterous. Children were not exactly banned, but they were usually discouraged.

But not tonight. Tonight, strings of tiny orange lights crisscrossed the narrow alleyway, turning it into a magical, glittering tunnel. The outside of the old, whitewashed pub had been transformed into a witch's cottage from a fairytale, with fake cobwebs under the eaves and a mysterious, glowing cauldron bubbling next to the door. Jack o' lanterns grinned cheerfully, candles flickering in the dark.

"*Wow*," breathed Danny and Hayley together.

Griff smiled, enjoying the astonishment and delight shining from both their faces. "Halloween's a bit of a special time for shifters," he said as he led them toward the pub. "Traditionally, it used to be the night we let our animal sides run wild. Most of us don't go out looking for some poor soul to chase down anymore, but we do still like to let our hair down a bit."

"There's Chase!" Danny waved excitedly at the pegasus shifter, who was standing near the door of the pub with a giggling pack of children gathered around him. "Hello, Mr. Chase!"

"Danny! Excellent, another child!" Chase hurried over, his entourage of kids following him like a line of ducklings. "Listen, I have a big favor to ask you. Also, completely coincidentally, I just so happen to have a great deal of chocolate."

Griff blinked at Chase as light from the open pub door illuminated the pegasus shifter's face. "*What* have you done to yourself?"

Chase spread his arms wide, beaming. "I, my friend, have *outdone* myself."

Chase's previously black hair was now almost every color of the rainbow, dyed in thick stripes from red to violet—every color, that is, except blue. *That* seemed to have been reserved for the rest of him.

His flight suit was blue. His boots were blue. His hands, face, and every single inch of exposed skin: Blue.

Griff shook his head. "I haven't the faintest idea how you did that. Or, more importantly, why. What are you meant to be, a Smurf?"

"Your cultural references are sadly outdated," Chase informed him haughtily. "If you were as down with the kids as *I* am, you would instantly recognize who I am."

"Oh my." Hayley giggled. "You haven't. You're actually…?"

Chase shimmered. Kids screamed in joy as the powder-blue pegasus pranced on the spot, his rainbow-striped mane and tail rippling.

"RAINBOW DASH!" Danny collapsed with laughter.

"What on earth is a Rainbow Dash?" Griff said, bewildered.

"Don't ask," said Chase's mate Connie, coming up beside him. She rolled her eyes at her mate, who was now shamelessly posing for his delighted audience. "If you'd told me this time last year that I'd be spending the night before Halloween painting a horse blue, I'd have laughed in your face."

"I didn't even know you *could* paint horses." Griff's sharp eyes noticed that none of the dye was coming off on the hands of the small girls enthusiastically stroking Chase's fur. "Ah…that stuff isn't permanent, is it?"

"It wasn't meant to be. I think Chase may have accidentally embedded it into his skin and hair, though, when he shifted back to human." Connie smirked. "You should see where the rainbow stripes on his tail ended up."

Hayley came back from admiring Chase, wiping away tears of laughter. "Hi Connie." She gave Chase's mate a brief, warm hug. The two had become fast friends since Griff had introduced them. "So, you weren't tempted to go for a matching outfit? You'd make a *wonderful* Twilight Sparkle."

Connie shot her a mock-glare. She was dressed as a WWII fighter pilot—though Griff strongly suspected that it was a real vintage uniform, not a costume. She did own a genuine, original Spitfire, after all. "Maybe next year." She gave Hayley a long, speculative look. "That's quite some costume you've got on yourself."

Hayley blushed a little. "Danny picked it," she mumbled. "He just thought it was a bunny costume, and I couldn't really explain to him...well, you know."

"Hmm." Connie's gaze flicked from Hayley to Griff and back again. She wound her arm firmly through Hayley's. "Can I steal you for a little while? Girl talk, Griff. Would bore you silly."

Hayley raised an eyebrow at him, and he shrugged back. He was no more able than she was to guess what was on Connie's mind. "Have fun. You want me to look after Danny while you're chatting?"

"No need," Chase said grandly, shifting back into human form. "*I* shall watch him. I am watching *all* the children tonight. I am the official designated babysitter, so that all the hard-working parents can enjoy themselves safe in the knowledge that their precious darlings are in safe hands. Or hooves."

"Chase," Griff said suspiciously. "Did you kidnap these kids?"

"Why do people keep asking me that?" Chase looked wounded. "Is it so hard to believe that parents would voluntarily hand over the fruits of their loins to me? I *am* extraordinarily good with children, after all."

Griff stared at him. "Since when?"

Chase shot him a glare. "Since always."

"Since his biological clock started ticking," Connie corrected, dryly. "Even though I've told him he doesn't have one."

"*We* have one. We only have so many fertile years available to us," Chase said to her earnestly. "If we don't get started soon, we'll have difficulty fitting in all fourteen children."

Connie jabbed him in the stomach. "*You* can have fourteen children. Just as soon as you work out how to become a seahorse shifter and gestate them yourself. *I'm* drawing the line at three."

Chase beamed round at Griff and Hayley. "Last week she was drawing the line at two. I'm winning."

Connie threw Hayley a pleading look. "You see why I need to talk to you?" She dragged her off toward the pub. "Please, please, *please* tell me many horrible stories about spending months throwing up constantly and waddling around like an elephant with a thyroid problem. Bring me back to my senses."

Griff chuckled as they disappeared inside. "Fourteen kids?" he said to Chase. "Really?"

"I'm actually going for four," Chase confessed. "Always start negotiations high." He elbowed Griff in the side, giving him a sly grin. "So, you and Hayley were looking awfully cozy. Walking hand-in-hand, I noticed."

"No comment. Did you happen to notice whether Ash is here, or were you too busy stealing children?"

"I am not *stealing* children. I plan to give them back." Chase shrugged. "And he's inside. Though you'd better catch him quick, you know he only ever puts in a token appearance at this sort of thing."

"Good point." Griff cocked an eyebrow at Danny. "Well, lad? You want to play out here with Chase for a while, or stay with me?"

No matter how much Griff might enjoy pulling Chase's leg, he didn't actually have any hesitation in leaving Danny in the pegasus shifter's care. He knew that Chase's playful exuberance concealed a protective streak a mile wide. Danny would be safe with him.

"I want to hang out with Chase," Danny said promptly. His decision may have been slightly influenced by the fistful of candy bars Chase had just produced out of one of his many pockets. "Can I come and find you later, though?"

Griff ruffled his hair. "Anytime. Just ask Chase when you want me. He can find anyone, you know."

Leaving Chase organizing the kids into teams for some sort of game, he ducked into the pub. The main room was packed with shifters of all sorts, laughing and talking. Behind the long wooden bar, Rose was handing out drinks and smiles. She wore an extravagant feathered carnival mask, the glossy blue-black plumes perfectly complimenting her flawless ebony skin.

Griff caught a glimpse of Hayley and Connie perched on stools at one end of the bar, along with Virginia, Dai's mate. Hayley seemed to be in the middle of explaining something that required a great deal of hand gestures. From the somewhat horrified yet fascinated expressions on the other two women's faces, Griff strongly suspected that the conversation had turned rather gynecological in nature.

Definitely not going to interrupt that.

He picked his way through the crowd, exchanging brief nods and greetings as he went. It was so crowded and busy, even his eagle wasn't immediately able to spot Ash. He did see Dai, half a head taller than anyone else and wearing a glittering gold helmet and flowing red cape, but it was too noisy for Griff to catch his attention. Griff cursed his own inability to mindspeak to his teammates. *That* would have made finding Ash much easier.

The back of the pub had been cleared for dancing, with a tiny stage erected for a local all-shifter ceilidh band. The lead fiddle player struck an eerie, keening note across his strings, like an alpha wolf calling to his pack. The other members joined in, flute and guitar and accordion howling back in answer. The drum pounded like a heartbeat, and the band launched into a wild, racing tune. Shifters cheered, surging onto the dance floor.

With the crowd thinning, Griff finally managed to spot Ash, alone in a quiet, shadowed corner booth. Griff was amused to note that, once again, Ash had come as a firefighter.

"You know, Halloween is meant to be for dressing up," Griff teased, sliding into the seat opposite the Fire Commander. "Pretending to be someone else."

"I am dressed up," Ash said, mildly. He made a small, brief gesture, indicating his dark blue suit with its gold rank insignia. "This is a dress uniform. In any event, you are also just wearing formal attire, I note."

"Ah, well, you have me there." Griff straightened the plaid draped over his shoulder, smiling. "Though…my outfit choice *may* have something to do with the fact that I happened to notice that Hayley has a complete collection of Outlander novels. In hardback."

The Fire Commander tilted his head a degree, acknowledging the point. "You are in a good mood tonight."

Griff's smile twisted, just a little. "I'm pretending to be someone else."

"Ah." Ash's dark eyes studied him for a long moment. Even to Griff's eagle-sharp senses, the Fire Commander was a completely unreadable book—not just closed, but bound in chains and locked away in a deep vault. "So the situation is unchanged. I am sorry to hear that."

Griff leaned his elbows on the table, folding his arms. "I went to see Ivy this evening."

Ash didn't so much as blink at the apparent topic jump. "And is her situation also unchanged?"

"Aye. She still wants you to burn away her wyvern."

"No," Ash said flatly, without even a second of hesitation.

Griff let out his breath. "She just wants to be able to touch people, Ash. Even if that means becoming a mundane human instead of a shifter."

Ash was respected in the shifter community for who he was…but he was feared for *what* he was. It was widely known that the Phoenix could burn anything. Not just physical materials like stone and steel, but metaphysical things as well.

Memories. Personality traits. Even a shifter's inner animal. Griff knew that he'd only done it a handful of times, in situations of dire need, but it was the reason most shifters kept as far away from the Fire Commander as they could.

Ash shook his head. "She does not know what she is asking. If the Parliament of Shifters had not demanded that I use my power to punish arsonists, I would not do it to any shifter under any circumstances. Not even to my worst enemy."

Griff looked out at the cheerful crowd without speaking for a long, long moment. "How about to a friend?"

"I will not burn away Ivy's wyvern. Not even for you."

"To a friend, Ash," Griff said, very quietly. "Not for a friend."

Out of the corner of his eye, he saw Ash go very, very still.

"Is this a conversation which it is safe to have?" Ash said at last, just as softly. "I would have thought your beasts would…object."

Griff's eagle was motionless, staring intently into his soul as though his thoughts were prey scurrying through long grass. His lion stirred a little, disturbed by the eagle's focus but unable itself to understand what had caused it.

"If we speak elliptically, we should be fine." Neither of his animals were good at abstract thought, or following a metaphor. Nonetheless, Griff kept a tight rein on his emotions, erecting a firm mental wall between himself and them. "I'll let you know if there's a problem."

Ash nodded in understanding. "Do you remember Bertram Russell?"

Well, I did *tell him to speak elliptically.* Griff had no idea where this was going. "The dragon shifter who attacked Dai and Virginia?"

Griff had never met him in person, but all of Alpha Team had been involved in helping Dai protect his mate from the arrogant, ruthless dragon shifter. Ash, however, had been the one to finally stop Bertram. The Phoenix had burned away his dragon, permanently removing his ability to shift.

Ash toyed with his glass of water. "Do you know what happened to him, afterwards?"

Griff shook his head. "No idea. Didn't really care, as long as he didn't bother us again."

"He is a tour guide at a small Roman heritage site," Ash said quietly. "He helps visiting schoolchildren dress up in costumes and color in pictures of the mosaics. He answers their questions, as much as he can. By all accounts, he is happy."

Ice ran down Griff's spine. Bertram had been fiercely competitive, a brilliant academic with an ego the size of his dragon.

And now he's content in some little backwater local museum...

"Our animals are woven through our souls," Ash said, when Griff didn't speak. "Even I cannot tell where the fire will race, once I light the spark. I took a dragon, and ended up also taking a man's pride, his ambition. I once had to take a man's wolf, and it left him unable to work in a team ever again. What else could I end up inadvertently destroying? A man's courage? His astuteness?" He looked straight at Griff. "Everything that made him who he was?"

Griff moistened his dry lips. "A man might be willing to destroy anything, in order to protect his mate."

Something flared behind Ash's eyes, a black fire like a

dying sun. "I understand that well." The crack in his calm lasted barely a heartbeat, sealed over so quickly that Griff almost doubted he'd ever seen that brief moment of anguish at all. "It is…possible, that I could burn away just enough, and no more. It is possible that I could take one thing, and leave another. But I do not know for certain."

"I understand that. And I appreciate that you'd rather not be having this conversation at all. But…it might be the only way. If Hayley married a shifter, Reiner wouldn't be able to claim Danny. And she has, ah, very firm opinions on which shifters she might be willing to marry."

"I imagine that it is a very short list." It was the closest Griff had every heard Ash come to making an actual joke. The Phoenix *was* rattled, underneath that rigidly controlled exterior. "Griffin, I must tell you something. To my…perception, you are indeed different to other shifters. I can sense the divide in your soul. But I cannot tell which half is which."

"That's all right. In a way, I'm glad." Griff smiled with black humor. "You know the old moral dilemma about only having one space in a lifeboat, and having to choose which family member to save? Better not to have to make that choice. Better to leave it to random chance."

Ash took a sip of his water. "Best not to be at sea at all."

"That ship sailed a long time ago, alas." Griff leaned back with a sigh. "Ash, I promise, I won't rush into anything. I won't ask this of you unless there is no other choice. But…it is good to know that I *do* have at least one choice. If it comes to it."

Whatever Ash said in response was drowned out by Chase's agitated mental voice abruptly crashing into Griff's head. *Griff, we've got a problem. Reiner's here.*

CHAPTER 18

HAYLEY

"Let me get this straight." Connie held up her hands, counting items off on her fingers. "Bloating. Vomiting. Swollen ankles. Heartburn. Mood swings. Weird food cravings."

"You forgot hemorrhoids," Hayley said helpfully.

"I'm *trying* to forget the hemorrhoids." Connie shuddered. "And on top of this, you spend the last few months unable to so much as get out of a chair without a fork lift truck. And, just to cap it all off, you then get to experience absolutely the worst pain of your entire life."

Hayley sipped her cocktail, hiding her grin. "That's about the size of it."

Connie threw up her hands in despair. "Why would anyone *do* this voluntarily?"

"I'm beginning to wonder that myself," Virginia murmured.

Hayley had only met Virginia once before, and she was still a little in awe of her. She *was* a world-famous archaeologist, after all. As if that wasn't bad enough, she was also drop-dead gorgeous. Hayley had caught more than a few men wistfully eying Virginia's stunning curves, accentuated by the skin-tight shorts and cropped vest of her Lara Croft costume. She was the perfect match to her mate Dai, as beautiful and strong as his dragon, and intimidatingly self-possessed.

Now, however, there was the tiniest crack in Virginia's confident air. One of her hands had crept to rest on her rounded belly. Hayley put two and two together.

"Oh my God!" she gasped, her hands flying to her mouth. "Virginia, are you…?"

A hint of a blush darkened Virginia's warm ochre cheeks. "We weren't going to tell anyone yet, because it's still so early. But yes."

"I can't believe it!" Connie threw her arms around the taller woman, hugging her. "Congratulations! When are you due?"

"Around May." Virginia's full lips curved in a wry smile. "From what Hayley's been telling us, I'm now really glad I'm not going to be heavily pregnant in mid-summer, and wallowing in my own sweat like a hippo."

"I wouldn't have said all those things if I'd known!" Hayley exclaimed, feeling mortified. "I was exaggerating. Honest. It's really not so bad."

Virginia raised one eyebrow at her.

"Okay, it kind of is," Hayley confessed. "But seriously, all the discomfort and everything…it's worth it. You forget it all, the instant you have your baby in your arms."

"Truly?" Virginia didn't sound her usual polished, self-confident self. Her brown eyes begged for reassurance. "You aren't just saying that?"

Hayley put her hand over Virginia's, squeezing a little. "Let's put it this way. When I had Danny, I was on my own, flat broke, having to take any temp work I could get just to keep a roof over our heads. I had no sleep, no money, no partner, and no support at all. And if I could go back in time…I would do it all again. In a *heartbeat*."

Virginia squeezed back, the calm strength returning to her face. "Thank you," she said sincerely.

"Now I feel like a complete wuss." Connie folded her arms, glaring down into her drink. "I wish I was as brave you two."

As brave as you two? Hayley couldn't imagine being thought of in the same category as brilliant, bold Virginia. "Hey, you fly vintage fighter planes for a living. I teach little kids. Which one of us is the brave one again?"

"You," Connie said promptly. "I'd rather face a tornado than a class of thirty children. I'm terrified of having to cope with even one kid. Let alone the whole herd that Chase wants."

"Well, fourteen does sound a little excessive." Hayley grinned at her.

"Oh, he really wants four. It's just more fun to pretend that I don't know that. He can be very inventive when he's trying to get his own way." Connie bit her lip. "I do want kids, I think. It's just…my mom passed away when I was little, and my dad isn't exactly the best parental role model. I'm so scared that I might turn out to be a terrible mother."

"*I'm* still terrified that I'm a terrible mother," Hayley said ruefully. "You aren't alone in that. And I think you'd be a great mom. Chase will make a great dad, too. Danny likes both of you a lot."

"He's such a sweet kid." Connie sighed. "If I could be certain that mine would turn out half as well, I wouldn't be nearly so worried. Rose," she turned to the woman tending the bar, who was cleaning glasses nearby, "what do *you* think?"

Hayley was a little startled by this unexpected appeal to the pub owner…but then Rose glanced up, and she understood. Even half-concealed behind the feathery carnival mask, Rose had the kindest, wisest face she'd ever seen. She could only have been in her mid-forties, but she possessed a sort of deep, unhurried calm that made her seem ageless. In a strange way, she reminded Hayley of Ash—the same sense of hidden power, tightly leashed.

"I think that you should never let fear stand in the way of your heart's desire," Rose said to Connie...but her eyes flicked briefly to Hayley. She had an odd sense that Rose was aiming the statement at *her*, just as much as Connie.

"That's the problem, I don't know if it *is* my heart's desire." Connie looked hopefully across the bar at Rose. "Can you tell for me, Rose? I mean, you can see mate bonds, after all. Can you see other sorts of things in people's hearts too? Like, how maternal someone is?"

Rose laughed. "I can see some things, true, but not that. But I don't need special powers to know that you're going to make a fine mother. You have enough love in your heart to nurture an entire brood of children." She dropped her voice a little. "Your own mother made sure of that."

Connie blinked rapidly, as if having to fight to hold back sudden tears. "Thanks, Rose," she whispered. "That...that means a lot."

"You can see mate bonds?" Hayley said to Rose, partly to give Connie a chance to recover her composure, but mainly just out of interest. "Really?"

Rose nodded in assent, her hands still busy cleaning glasses. "It's one of the reasons shifters come here. I can instantly tell if I've met someone's mate before, even if *they've* never met. I've matched up more than a few of my customers by now."

"I wish you'd find your mate, Rose," Virginia said. "It doesn't seem fair that you're still alone, when you've helped so many of us."

"Ah, well. Just fate, I suppose." Rose smiled, a little sadly. "I travelled the world when I was younger, searching, but never found him. Maybe he'll walk through my door one of these days."

Hayley bit back the question on the tip of her tongue, unsure whether it would be rude to ask what Rose's animal was. She didn't yet know enough about shifter ways to have a firm grasp on their unspoken rules of etiquette.

She *had* learned enough, though, to know that a shifter's power came from their inner beast. Griff's perceptiveness came from his eagle, while his innate ability to command came from his lion. But what on earth could give Rose the sort of power that she had?

Rose glanced at her sidelong, a teasing smile tugging at her lips. "I can feel your curiosity from here. Go on. Guess."

From Virginia and Connie's grins, they already knew. Hayley narrowed her eyes, scrutinizing the bartender. Rose might look soft and round, but the elegance in the way she held herself would have made a prima ballerina green with envy. Even just polishing glasses, there was a breathtaking grace to every movement of her delicate hands.

Something strong, but not dangerous. Not a predator. Something calm and graceful. And...something that symbolizes devotion? Something that mates for life, and pines away if that love is lost...

The graceful curve of Rose's neck and the long, shimmering black feathers on her mask gave her away. *"You're a swan!"*

"Not many get that right. You've got good eyes." Rose tilted her head a little, her expression enigmatic behind her mask. "Sharp eyes are a good match to an eagle. But you need courage if you're going to match a lion. Especially when his own courage falters."

"Griff, falter?" Hayley wasn't sure whether to laugh or

take offence at the idea. "I don't think Griff's ever been afraid of anything in his entire life."

"Up until recently, I'd have agreed with you." Rose looked at something over Hayley's shoulder. "But not anymore. You might want to ask him about that."

"Hayley." She spun round at Griff's voice, right behind her. He was looking grim. "We've got a potential problem. Reiner's here."

"Reiner? *Here?*" Hayley couldn't imagine Reiner voluntarily coming to a Halloween party. He'd always looked down his nose at the holiday, calling it a 'vulgar American perversion of ancient traditions.' "Why?"

"I don't know, but we have to try to head him off." Griff took her hand, helping her down from the bar stool. "There are too many people who know me here."

She gasped as she realized the danger. "Someone could let your secret slip."

Connie cocked her head to one side, lips moving soundlessly for a moment. "Chase is improvising a very, very long joke outside," she said, and Hayley realized that she'd been communicating telepathically with her mate. "But he says to hurry, because Reiner doesn't look like he's going to wait for the punchline."

Virginia's expression went a little unfocussed as well. A moment later, Dai's tall form cut through the crowd toward them.

"Virginia says you might need some backup," the dragon shifter said to Griff. In his Anglo-Saxon warrior costume, he looked more than ready to step onto a battlefield.

"No fighting on my premises, boys," Rose said warningly. "All shifters are welcome, as long as they behave themselves. I won't have anyone acting like this is their personal territory. Not even Alpha Team."

"I'm sorry, Rose, but I can't just let Reiner come in here

and start chatting," Griff growled. "You don't understand. I *can't* let him find out what I really am."

"You're trying to wear too many masks. It might do you good for some of them to slip." Rose gave him a level look. "I mean it, Griff. My house, my rules. You do *not* have the right to decide who enters here."

"You will respect Ms. Swanmay," said Ash, making Hayley jump. She hadn't even noticed him standing quietly behind Griff. For such a powerful shifter, the Phoenix had a remarkable ability to make himself blend into the background.

Frustrated growls rumbled in both Griff and Dai's chests, but they didn't try to argue with their Commander. "Let's see if we can *peacefully* persuade Reiner to go somewhere else, then," Griff said, not sounding optimistic. "Otherwise we're going to have to somehow ride herd on him all night."

"Or just get Chase to annoy him so much that *he* throws the first punch," Dai murmured. He briefly touched Virginia's bare arm, love and worry clear even in just that small gesture. "Stay here. Just in case."

With a quick, apologetic wave of farewell to Virginia and Connie, Hayley followed the two men out of the pub. Gooseflesh pimpled on her arms as she stepped out into the night. It felt much colder after the warmth inside.

Reiner was looking both bewildered and besieged, with Danny clinging onto one of his hands and Chase onto his other sleeve. The trio were encircled by the pack of shifter kids, all apparently hanging onto Chase's every word as he rattled nonsense at top speed.

"So then the actress says to the Bishop-" Chase broke off as Griff and Dai strode up. He let go of Reiner with a relieved sigh. "Oh, thank God. I really wasn't sure how I was going to finish that in a way suitable for young, eavesdropping ears. Come on kids, who wants to go get something to drink?"

Griff set his feet, facing the lion shifter head on as Chase herded the kids safely into the pub. Dai took up position at his shoulder, green eyes narrowed behind his helmet.

"What are you doing here, Reiner?" Griff said bluntly. His fists were bunched, muscles tense and ready despite Rose's warning. "I'm not having you spoil Danny's Halloween. If you're looking to start trouble, do it some other time."

Reiner's hand tightened on Danny's. "I'm here because *my son* wants me here."

"I told Daddy to come," Danny piped up cheerfully. Hayley was relieved that he didn't seem to have picked up on the hostile undercurrents. "I want him to share Halloween too."

Hayley's heart broke at his innocence, even as she wanted to throttle him for setting this up without running it past her first. "That's very sweet of you, honey, but, um…I don't think Daddy likes dancing and dressing up and all that kind of thing."

Reiner bristled. "If my son wants me to dance, then I will dance," he announced grimly. He looked like he'd have much preferred it if Danny had asked him to eat a nice heaping plate of worms.

"It's okay, Daddy. I know you don't like dancing." Danny beamed up at Reiner. "I don't, either. But Mommy does, so I thought maybe she and Mr. Griff could do that while you and me could go be lions instead. Because you said that *your* Daddy always took you out hunting at Halloween, so I want to do that with you too. Would that be okay, Mr. Griff?"

Griff blinked at him, looking as taken aback by this speech as Hayley was. "Ah…I think you'd better ask your ma."

"Um…" Hayley remembered something that Griff had mentioned about traditional shifter Halloween customs. "Exactly what kind of hunting, Reiner?"

Reiner's shoulders stiffened in offense. "I'm not going to take him hunting humans, if that's what you're asking. Deer or rabbits will have to do." His gaze slid down her costume. "*Real* rabbits."

Hayley wasn't desperately thrilled by the prospect of her gentle boy sinking his teeth into some poor little bunny, but there was no denying that Danny *was*. He hopped up and down with eagerness, his face alight with anticipation.

"Please, Mommy?" he begged. "Pleeeeeease? I promise I'll eat it all up, every last bit."

Is that supposed to help? Shuddering with revulsion, Hayley shot a pleading look at Griff. He shrugged apologetically.

"We *are* lions, at heart," he murmured into her ear. "Let him go. It will mean a lot to both of them, and I think we can trust Reiner this much, at least. In any case, I'll know through the pride-bond if Danny gets upset for any reason, and Chase can always take us straight to them."

Hayley sighed, giving in. "All right," she said reluctantly. "You can go."

"Yaaaaay!" Danny flung his arms around her. "You're the best mommy ever!"

Hayley hugged him back, wishing that she never had to let him go. "Just make sure you stay away from roads and, and people and everything, okay?"

Reiner put a possessive hand on Danny's shoulder. "*I* will make sure *my son* stays safe."

"See that you do," growled Griff, with a flex of alpha power in his voice. Reiner gave him a resentful glare, but jerked his chin in a nod.

"Mommy," Danny said thoughtfully, letting go of her and taking Reiner's hand instead. "We're probably going to be up *real* late. Maybe I should sleep over at Daddy's. Is that okay?"

Absolutely not! Hayley wanted to yell. But Reiner was staring down at Danny with such a thunderstruck look, like a man who'd just been given a present he hadn't even known he'd wanted, that the words died on her tongue.

"Well…but you haven't got pajamas or a toothbrush or anything."

"Lions don't *need* pajamas or toothbrushes," Danny said confidently. "Do they, Daddy?"

"They do if they want to keep their fangs, lad," Griff rumbled before Reiner could speak. "Real lions don't eat chocolate, but from the look of your face the same isn't true of you."

"I know an all-night store near my place," Reiner said to Griff. For once, he didn't sound arrogant. His expression was more vulnerable than she'd ever seen before, still half-dazed with wonder. "I could pick up the basics, just for tonight. And I'll drop him back off by nine tomorrow morning. I swear on my family name."

Hayley would have preferred it if Reiner had acted as though *she* had the final say, rather than Griff, but maybe that would have been one miracle too many. She nodded at Griff, very slightly.

"Very well." He gave Reiner a stern—but not aggressive—look. "Don't make me regret this."

"Oh, Mr. Griff," Danny said, turning back as Reiner started to lead him away. His brown eyes were wide and guileless. "Make sure Mommy isn't lonely, okay? She's never had to sleep without me there. She might get scared of the dark without a lion around."

Hayley's mouth hung open. So did Griff's.

"And to think you told me *I* was incompetent in matters of romance," Dai murmured as Danny skipped off. The dragon shifter clapped a hand on Griff's shoulder, a broad smirk spreading across his face. "Congratulations, my friend. You've just been set up by a five-year-old."

CHAPTER 19

GRIFF

"Are you really sure Danny's still all right?" Hayley asked anxiously as they turned into her driveway.

"Aye, truly," Griff replied, for the tenth time on the long, otherwise silent walk back to her house. He could feel the cub's excitement through the pride-bond, like a small sparkling firework at the back of his mind. "He's having a grand time. Probably the best Halloween of his entire life."

Bitter jealousy gnawed at his bones. *He* was Danny's alpha. *He* should be taking Danny on his first hunt. Griff would have given his right arm to be able to do that for him.

But would you give up your eagle? whispered a tiny, private thought, so deep even his animals couldn't hear. *For just the chance of being able to be a true alpha lion for Danny? Would you truly burn away half your heritage?*

He still didn't know if, at the bitter end, he'd be able to force himself to do it. If it was just the choice between that or death, he wouldn't even have considered it. But if it was the choice between Ash's fire, or Reiner taking Danny…

"I'm so sorry for spoiling your Halloween, Griff." Hayley fumbled in her purse for her house keys. "I just wasn't in the mood to stay at the party. I'll be okay now, if you want to head back to rejoin your friends."

"To tell the truth, I'm not really in the mood for a party myself." Griff tried to muster a casual smile. "I think I'll just head home too."

No, rumbled his lion. Its eyes gleamed in his mind, hot and predatory. *The pride is happy on the hunt, occupied elsewhere. Now it is time to stalk and claim* our *prize.*

The moon is full and the winds are wild, his eagle murmured. *It is not a night to be alone in the nest.*

Griff clenched his jaw, trying to ignore his beasts' whispers. He noticed that Hayley had hesitated at the open door, biting her lip as she stared into the dark corridor. "Something wrong?"

"The house is just so…quiet," she said, softly. "So empty."

Before Griff could respond, she squared her shoulders. Light blazed as she flicked the switch, turning on the hall lamp. She turned back to him with a wan, forced smile. "Just being silly. I haven't spent a night on my own since Danny was born. It'll, it'll be nice to have some time to myself."

Her bottom lip was trembling, ever so slightly. "Hayley," Griff said gently. "Do you want me to stay?"

"No, no, no!" Her head swung in emphatic arcs of denial, even as every line of her body screamed *yes!* "I wouldn't—that wouldn't be fair to you. I couldn't ask you to do that."

"It's no trouble." Griff forestalled any further argument by stepping in and closing the door behind himself. "This way, if you wake up in the night and are at all worried about Danny, you can just ask me to check the pride-bond for you."

Yes, purred his lion. *We will be right at her back, all night…*

No we won't. Out loud, Griff said, "It's not like I haven't spent a night on your sofa before, after all."

"Oh, you don't have to sleep on the sofa!" He could tell just how relieved Hayley was by the way that she didn't try to talk him out of staying. "You can sleep in my bed, if you want."

Griff cleared his throat, fighting down a surge of lust at the idea. "Ah. Now that *would* be trouble."

Hayley went a delightful shade of pink. "I meant, I can sleep in Danny's! I'd fit into it better than you."

Griff was fairly certain he'd be able to get much more rest wedged into a kid-sized bed than he would trying to sleep surrounded by Hayley's intoxicating scent. "If it's all the same to you, I'd rather take Danny's room." He tried to make a joke of it, smiling at her. "I always *did* want dinosaur wallpaper when I was little."

Hayley giggled, rather more loudly than the feeble jest deserved. "Well, I'll get you some clean sheets, at least."

Hayley started up the stairs, the white puff of the rabbit tail on her rear bobbing enticingly. Without conscious decision, Griff found that he was following her, as intently as a stalking lion. He wrenched his gaze upward, forcing himself to fix on the back of her head instead of the luscious curves of her backside.

Unfortunately, that just meant that when she turned around to say something, he inadvertently locked eyes with her.

"Oh," Hayley gasped.

He quickly looked away, but he knew she'd already seen the hunger burning in his soul. "I'm fine. It's just—I'll be fine. Give me a moment."

"Is it your beasts?" She stepped closer, putting a hand on his arm. Just that simple touch nearly broke his resolve. Only iron control kept him from crushing her up against the nearest wall and taking her there and then. "Are they fighting again?"

He let out his breath, shakily. "My beasts and I all want the same thing right now. That's rather the problem."

A flush crept up her neck. He could see her nipples stiffening through the soft clinging fabric of her dress, and his cock surged in answer. He knew he had to step back, put some distance between them, but he couldn't force himself to move away.

"Rose said something strange to me tonight." Hayley hadn't moved back either. "She said I should ask you what you're afraid of." She hesitated, her eyes searching his face. "Is it...Griff, are you afraid it might happen again?"

He knew she meant his uncontrolled shift, after they'd made love. Her expression was open, vulnerable, demanding that he tell her the truth.

"No," he said, honestly. "That doesn't frighten me. Hayley, even if I knew for absolute certain, without a shadow of a doubt, that I'd die if I touched you again...I would do it, in a heartbeat. I would rather live for a single hour in your arms than another fifty years apart. I'm not afraid of dying."

A tear overspilled, tracking down her cheek, but her eyes were steady, uncompromising. "So what *are* you afraid of?"

"Hurting you," he whispered. He drew in a deep breath, bracing himself. "I can't stand the thought of leaving you alone. It's not only Reiner, and what it would mean for Danny. Even setting aside all those complications...Hayley, when I die, at least I won't be in pain anymore. But I'm frightened that I'll leave *you* in pain. I'm terrified that I'll break your heart."

"Isn't that my risk to take?" Hayley looked fierce as a lioness, even through her tears. "Griff, your life is yours to risk or not, but it's *my* choice what I do with my heart. Rose said I needed to have courage, if I was to be a lion's match. I'm tired of wearing a mask, pretending that there's nothing between us. Whether we ever touch again or not, nothing will change that fact that I love you. I'm not afraid of that. I'm not afraid of what that might mean, in future. I love you *now*. That's all that matters."

He pulled her into his arms, unable to hold back any longer. He kissed her fiercely, his hands coming up to cup her face. His heart swelled with joy and terror, until he felt like it might break in his chest from the sweet pain of it.

He pulled back a little, leaned his forehead against hers. "You have courage enough for both of us," he said, his voice rough. "I'm the one who has to match *you*."

He bent to claim her lips again. She melted into him, her mouth sweet and tender under his. Succumbing to his desire, he pushed her up against the wall, pressing the whole length of his body against her soft curves. His cock was a rigid bar between them. He craved to sink into her warmth, to be utterly enfolded by her.

"Griff," she gasped, as he left her mouth to start kissing his way down her neck. Her hips thrust a little, helplessly, and he very nearly came in his kilt there and then. "Wait. Are you sure this is safe?"

It felt as hard as hauling his animals apart when they fought, but he managed to pull back from her. "You did say my life was mine to risk."

"Yes, but…" Flushed pink with mingled desire and embarrassment, she bit her lip. "I'm going to sound like a complete hypocrite, but *I'm* scared of causing another one of your uncontrolled shifts."

She had a point. He braced his hands against the wall on either side of her head, trying to control his ragged breathing. "Give me a second. I was caught by surprise last time. I'll see if I can take some precautions."

Closing his eyes, he forced himself to take stock of his soul. His lion and eagle were too blind with lust to even notice each other at the moment, but after last time, he knew that could change in an instant. Gritting his teeth, he repressed his beasts, using the discipline of long practice to lock them away. He strengthened their mental cages, building high, thick walls to keep them apart from both each other, and himself.

It was rather like putting on a full-body condom. He had a nagging, uncomfortable sense of a barrier between himself and the world, dimming all sensation. Still, it was better than risking an uncontrolled shift.

"There. That should be safer now." He opened his eyes again, and Hayley made a small, startled sound. "What is it?"

"All the gold's gone." She traced the corner of his eye lightly with her fingertip. "You look…human."

He wished that he could interpret her expression, but with his eagle chained, his perception was a tenth of its usual level. "I hope you're not too disappointed. I *am* just a normal human at the moment, when my beasts are caged like this. But that's the way it has to be."

This is the way it might have to permanently *be…*He shoved the chilling thought back down.

"I'm not disappointed!" As if to prove it, Hayley slid her hands around his chest, drawing him back close again. "It's you I love, not your powers. I'd love you even if you were only human."

A shiver ran down his back at her unwittingly ominous words. He stopped her from saying anything more by kissing her, more slowly this time. It was different without his beasts' urgency snarling through his blood, but she was still Hayley, his Hayley. She was still his mate.

"There *is* one advantage to keeping my beasts chained, you know," he murmured, his lips brushing hers. He straightened, drawing her with him into her bedroom. "It means I can take my time."

Slowly, he eased down the zipper of her dress. Her breath caught as he ran his hands up her exposed back, tracing the gentle dip of her spine. He worked the soft, clinging fabric of the dress down, uncovering first her plump, enticing shoulders, then the delicious swells of her breasts. He couldn't resist nuzzling between them, nipping gently at her creamy skin as he pushed her dress off completely, letting it puddle on the floor around her feet.

"Hayley," he breathed, tasting her, inhaling her, trying to memorize every glorious inch of her body. "Mine."

He wanted to kneel to unpeel her tights from her gorgeous thighs, but pain screamed through his bad leg when he tried to bend it. The long walk back to the house from the pub had made the joint seize up.

Evidently noticing his wince, Hayley stretched up on her toes to kiss him. "I'll do it." Peeking up at him a little shyly through her lowered eyelashes, she slipped the tights off, leaving her standing in only a lacy bra and matching panties.

At the sight of her, all the breath left his lungs, as if he'd been punched in the stomach. His cock strained, desperate for her. "I've changed my mind. I *can't* take my time."

Her lips curved in a naughty smile. "Tough, because now I want to take *my* time." She ran her fingers under the looped fabric of his plaid, tracing the lines of his chest. "I've never seen you naked. And I've always wondered what a Scotsman wears under his kilt…"

Griff couldn't help chuckling as she tried to slide the plaid off his shoulder, only to be baffled by the way it was tied. A traditional great kilt really wasn't something a novice could dismantle. "Ah, you do realize that I'm wearing eighteen feet of fabric?"

She cast him a half-exasperated, half-amused glare, still wrestling with the mysteries of the garment. "Then I guess I'll *really* be taking my time."

"Here." He undid the outer belt, then guided her hands to the thinner, hidden belt that held the kilt pleated. He grinned at her as the heavy folds of fabric fell away. "Fortunately, my ancestors were very impatient men."

"Well *you* can just be patient a bit longer," Hayley retorted tartly. With teasing slowness, she started to undo the buttons of his shirt.

A growl rose in his throat as she worked her way down. Even with his beasts tightly restrained, every slight brush of her fingertips against his bare skin made his cock throb with need.

"Okay, now I am a little disappointed." Hayley had encountered his briefs. "So the rumors aren't true?"

"Actually, they are," he gasped as she knelt to slide them down over his hips. The cool air was almost agonizing on his freed cock. "Don't tell anyone I was bringing shame on my forefathers."

Still on her knees as she stripped him of his last few garments, Hayley's eyes gleamed slyly up at him. "My lips," she murmured, sliding her hands up the backs of his legs, "are sealed."

He groaned as her warm, soft lips enfolded the head of his cock. He wound his fingers into her silky hair, fighting for control as she took him deeper. Her tongue curled around the underside, flicking exquisitely over his most sensitive areas.

"Hayley," he growled, every muscle in his abdomen tight and rigid as he desperately tried to restrain himself. "Stop. I can't—can't wait."

In answer, she closed her mouth tight around him, sucking hard. His hips bucked as she milked him urgently, her fingers digging into his thighs. He couldn't hold himself back any longer. Hands clenching around her head, he yanked her closer, his thrusting cock entirely filling her welcoming mouth.

White-hot sparks burst in his vision as he came hard,

emptying himself into her. She took every drop, her tongue teasing and flicking in encouragement until he was utterly, completely spent.

Shuddering with the aftershocks of pleasure, he relaxed his grip on her head. She came up gasping for air, but with an expression of intense, smug satisfaction. She gave his cock one last parting kiss—it burned like a brand on his oversensitive, still-engorged head—before allowing him to lift her to her feet again.

"I don't have condoms," she admitted. "And I was fairly certain you wouldn't have restocked either."

He kissed her, deep and lingering, tasting the faint traces of his own salt on her tongue. At the back of his mind, his lion and eagle flung themselves against the walls of his control, intensely aroused by that intoxicating mingling of their scents. Walled off from his consciousness, his beasts hadn't partaken of his own release. From the ominous pain gathering inside his skull, he knew he wouldn't be able to hold them much longer.

"Lion or eagle?" he murmured against her lips. "I have to let one of them out now, or risk them both breaking free of their own accord."

Hayley leaned back a little to look at him curiously. "Does it make a difference? Which one you release, I mean."

"Very much so." He trailed his finger over the curve of her breast, savoring her sharp intake of breath. "And since you're right—I *don't* have condoms—it had best be my eagle. My lion can be a bit...dominant."

From the way her pupils went wide and dark, he thought she rather liked the sound of that. His senses sharpened as he allowed his eagle to soar free, and he abruptly knew just how *much* she would like that. He knew other things too—how the nape of her neck begged to be seized in his teeth, how her thighs trembled to feel his caress, exactly where he should be gentle and where he should be rough...

"Oh," she gasped, as he started to put his observations into practice. "I—I think I'm going to like your eagle. The lion will have to wait for another time." She looked up at him with sudden fierceness, her determined expression at odds with the obedience of her body as he pushed her down onto the bed. "Because there *are* going to be other times, Griff. Lots and lots of them. Promise me that."

"Aye," he said softly, before he covered her mouth with his own. "I promise."

And in that moment, he made his decision. He knew that he would do whatever was necessary to keep that promise.

Tonight for the eagle. Griff kept the thought hidden away in the most private depths of his mind, out of sight of his beasts. *And tomorrow, a night for the lion. I can give them both one night with our mate, at least.*

Before I submit us all to Ash's fire...and we see how much survives the inferno.

CHAPTER 20

REINER

"That was the best Halloween ever." Danny bounced on Reiner's guest bed, his borrowed T-shirt flapping around his knees. It was the smallest shirt Reiner owned, but it still drowned the boy. "I liked it best when you pounced right on that deer, Daddy, pow! You knocked him right down flat!"

Reiner caught Danny in mid-jump, making him shriek in delight. "I'll knock *you* down flat if you don't get yourself into bed. I can't believe you're still so full of energy."

Pride swelled in Reiner's chest as Danny wriggled and giggled, trying to free himself. Not even six years old, on his first hunt, and the boy had still managed to achieve a throat-lock on a fully-grown deer. If he'd been just a little older and bigger, Reiner was certain that he'd have throttled the animal all by himself.

Wouldn't that just wipe the smugness off my dear brother's face? When none of his own ever-so-perfect pure-bred offspring have managed to lay paw on so much as a rabbit yet...

"You know, I was only able to pounce on that deer

because you were holding him for me," Reiner said to Danny. "Really, the credit is half yours."

Danny's eyes widened. Reiner still got a little thrill every time he gazed into those amber eyes—so similar to his own that it was like looking at his reflection in a mirror. "Really, Daddy? You mean *I* killed the deer too?"

"Absolutely." Reiner smiled, triumphant. "When we tell everyone back home, that's exactly what we'll say."

Let's see how my dear alpha brother likes that. *I can't wait to see the moment he realizes that his sons are going to be beta to mine.*

His lion flicked its tail in mild irritation. *We have our own place, as our cub will have his. We are no less valuable to the pride than any other. Not even the alpha.*

Reiner's jaw tightened a little at his lion's unquestioning acceptance of the pride hierarchy. Why, why couldn't *he* have had an alpha lion, fiercely proud and ravenous for power? No matter how he fought to win the place and respect he deserved, he'd always been hampered by his inner lion's instinctive submissiveness. It wasn't fair.

But at least life would be better for his son.

No asshole alpha is ever going to push you *around,* Reiner silently promised Danny as he tucked him into bed. *I'll teach you to be so strong and dominant, you'll just have to stare at another lion to have them whimpering and showing you their belly. I'll make sure you can have anything you want. I swear it.*

Danny stretched out like a starfish, his arms and legs not even coming close to reaching the edges of the double bed. "This is the biggest bed ever, Daddy! And the biggest bedroom. Why's your house so huge?"

Reiner blinked at him, taken aback. "This, huge? This is just a hovel, compared to my real house back home."

"What's a hovel?" Danny asked.

Reiner waved dismissively around at the bedroom, with

its sleek, minimalist furniture and views out over the fishing lake. "This is. You just wait until you see the Ljonsson estates back home. Then you'll understand."

When Reiner had learned that Danny was his true son, he'd immediately rented out the best house he could find near Brighton—an old hunting lodge set in fifteen acres of private woodland, half an hour away from the city. Even so, it was barely adequate for a real lion's needs. He couldn't comprehend how any shifter could possibly stand to live in built-up Brighton itself.

My poor son has been utterly deprived if he considers this *to be a huge house.* A prickle of anger ran through his blood. *I trusted Hayley to provide at least a minimum level of care. How can she have failed so badly? It's a good thing I stepped in when I did.*

"Wait until I take you to Valtyra," he said to Danny. "You'll love it. Everyone knows about shifters back home. We'll be able to be lions whenever we want, without having to worry about frightening stupid humans."

Danny looked suitably excited at the prospect. "Are there more deers there? Can we hunt them?"

"There are deer, and boar, and even elk. We'll hunt them all. I promise."

A stab of homesickness twisted his guts. He wished that he could just take Danny back on the next flight.

If only that asshole alpha didn't have his claws in my son!

"I wish we could go there tomorrow," Danny said wistfully, and Reiner's heart melted at the unwitting echo of his own thoughts. "But I've got to go to school and Mommy has to go to work. Maybe we can go during summer vacation." He frowned a little. "We'll have to ask Mr. Griff. Daddy, do firefighters get to take summer vacation?"

Reiner clenched his jaw. *Can I not have* one *conversation with my son without that damned alpha coming up?*

"I don't think they do," he said, trying not to sound too curt. "So your alpha won't come. Anyway, wouldn't you like to take a trip together? Just the two of us?"

"Without Mommy?" Danny pulled the covers up to his chin, as if hiding from a monster in the dark. "But I've never been away without Mommy. Can't she come too?"

"She wouldn't want to come. She and your alpha would jump at the chance to have private time alone together. They were eager enough for you to come with me tonight, weren't they?"

A twinge of jealousy shot through him at the mental image of that arrogant alpha in Hayley's bed. Even if she was a bit fatter and more tired-looking than when he'd known her, she was still an extremely attractive woman. Reiner wouldn't have said no to a second round…but of course there was no chance of that, now that she only had eyes for her oh-so-alpha mate.

Reiner consoled himself with the thought that at least *he'd* had her first. And she'd been younger and riper then, too. If only she'd been a shifter! But there was simply no way he could ever have taken a mundane human home to his family. Not when his perfect older brother had already mated a perfect alpha lioness and started producing perfect pure-bred cubs…

Our cub is perfect, his lion said, its mental voice a soft purr.

So he is. Reiner shook off his dark thoughts, focusing on the shining promise of the better future ahead.

"Your mother and her mate don't want a cub like you getting in the way all the time," he said to Danny. "They'd be happy if you stayed with me for longer. They just don't want to hurt your feelings by telling you so."

"Oh," Danny said quietly. His little face was shadowed in the moonlight. "I didn't think of that."

"Don't worry. *I* always want to have you around." He

stroked Danny's golden hair back from his forehead. "You go to sleep now, my son. I'll be right next door if you need me."

"Okay, Daddy." Danny yawned hugely, his expression relaxing again as he snuggled down. "I did really like hunting tonight. Can we do that again? Here, I mean. Not back at your proper home."

"You'll have to ask your alpha." He couldn't resist adding, "Make sure you tell him you want *me* to take you hunting, not him."

"Oh, Mr. Griff won't mind." Danny's voice had gone soft and sleepy. "He doesn't hunt."

"He doesn't?" Reiner's hand paused. Some traditionalists —Reiner's own grandfather among them—still held that hunting was women's work. Was that bastard Griff laughing at him even now? "Why? Does he think it's something only lionesses should do?"

Danny giggled. "That's silly. Who would think that?"

"Never mind. It's not important." Reiner relaxed a little. At least that asshole alpha wasn't filling his son's head with ridiculous old-fashioned nonsense. "But why doesn't Griff like hunting?"

"I think he'd *like* to," Danny mumbled, his eyes drifting shut. "But he can't. He wouldn't be able to bite the deer, after all. Not with person teeth."

...Person teeth?

"Why would he try to hunt without shifting?" Reiner asked, bewildered.

"Ummm." Danny's eyes popped open. He suddenly looked as guilty as if Reiner had just caught him eating his entire stash of Halloween candy. "Never mind." He rolled over, squeezing his eyes tight shut again. "Night-night, Daddy."

Reiner switched the bedside light back on.

"Hey!" Danny flung his arm over his face. "I was sleeping!"

Reiner ignored the protest, leaning over him intently.

Inside, his lion crouched, every muscle tense, tail lashing. Normally, it was the voice of caution, holding him back...but not this time.

If the alpha cannot even catch a deer, his lion snarled, *he cannot protect the pride. He cannot protect our cub. If the alpha is unfit...*

"Danny." Reiner let his lion rise, let its force show in his voice and eyes, despite the way it made Danny cower. "Tell me *exactly* why Griff can't hunt."

CHAPTER 21

HAYLEY

As soon as I get off work, I'm going straight to the store, Hayley thought as she watched Griff move around the kitchen. *And I'm buying condoms. Lots and* lots *of condoms.*

Lacking other options, Griff had put his Halloween outfit back on again this morning—though the unselfconscious ease with which he'd donned the kilt had made it clear it really wasn't just a costume for him. Hayley wondered how often he wore it. She wondered how often she could *persuade* him to wear it.

"As often as you like," Griff said, without looking up from buttering toast.

Hayley made a face at his broad back. "Okay, clearly we're going to have to lay some ground rules about using your eagle powers."

Griff threw her a teasing glance. "I thought you rather liked my eagle."

"What I like in the bedroom and what I like in the kitchen are two entirely separate things," Hayley informed him grandly.

As one, they looked at the kitchen table, then at each other. They both burst out laughing.

The doorbell chimed. "That'll be Reiner and Danny," Hayley said, trying to bring her giggles under control. She really, really didn't want either of them asking what the joke was. "Right on time, too. You were right, we *could* trust Reiner. Maybe we can make sleepovers at Daddy's a regular event."

Griff caught her for a kiss as she went past. "I certainly hope so."

Still glowing from the brief embrace, Hayley beamed as she opened the front door. "Hi-"

"*Where is he?*" The door slammed back as Reiner thrust his way inside. Hayley gasped as he barged past, knocking her into a wall.

"What on earth-?" Griff appeared in the door of the kitchen, still holding a butter knife. His eyes abruptly blazed gold, and his voice cracked like a whip. "Reiner! Stop!"

Reiner shrugged off Griff's alpha command, never pausing. He had a wild, triumphant expression, his teeth bared. Towing a struggling Danny by one wrist in his wake, he strode right up to the firefighter.

"You have no power over me," he snarled, right into Griff's face. "Griffin MacCormick, *I challenge you!*"

"I'm sorry, Mr. Griff," Danny babbled. His face was stricken with guilt. "I didn't mean to tell. I'm sorry, I'm *sorry!*"

"It's not your fault, lad." Griff kept his eyes locked with Reiner's. He hadn't backed down so much as an inch. "Reiner, let the cub go. Now."

"You have no power over me," Reiner repeated, but he opened his hand. Danny flew straight into Hayley's arms.

"It's all right, baby, it's all right," Hayley whispered futilely to him. His entire body shook as though he had his fingers in an electrical socket.

"Hayley, take Danny upstairs." Griff's voice was very calm, betraying none of the tension in his body. "This isn't something he should watch."

"Go up to your room, baby." She pushed Danny in the direction of the stairs, but didn't follow him herself. "The grown-ups need to talk for a minute. It'll be ok."

When Danny had disappeared into his bedroom, Hayley swung round to confront Reiner. "You. Get out of my house."

Reiner laughed scornfully, glancing at her with a sneer. "*You* have even less power over me than he-"

Without a hint of warning, Griff punched him straight in the face. Reiner staggered, and before he could recover Griff had him up against the wall, one forearm shoved across the lion shifter's throat.

"You will respect my mate's territory," he said, still with that deadly calm. "You can challenge me, but you have *no right* to intrude here."

"Then let's take this outside," Reiner spat. His eyes glittered feverishly. "I challenge you for your pride, alpha. Shift and face me like a lion."

"He can't, Reiner, you know he can't!" Hayley tried to pull Griff away, but she might as well have tried to move a mountain. "Griff, just toss him out. He can't make you fight him."

"Oh yes, I can," Reiner said. "And I am. Fight me, alpha. Defend your pride, or lose it."

Very slowly, Griff released Reiner. "There's a dueling arena at the courthouse. We will do this properly, with witnesses."

"Griff, he'll *kill* you!" Hayley whirled on Reiner. "Reiner, I beg you. Just let him go. *Please.* For Danny's sake, don't hurt him."

Reiner straightened a little, his chest swelling as if he was enjoying her pleading. "I suppose I could accept a formal surrender."

"He surrenders, of course he'll surrender," Hayley babbled, before Griff could say anything. She grabbed Griff's arm, his muscles as hard as iron under her fingers. "Griff, *please*. Do it."

A savage snarl tore from Griff's throat. Hayley could see sweat beading on his brow, could tell how hard he was having to fight to keep his animals under control.

If this continues, Reiner won't even have to touch him. His own beasts will rip him apart first.

"Do it for me," Hayley whispered, begging him with every fiber of her soul to listen to her.

Griff swallowed, hard. Gently, he freed himself from her grip. Never breaking eye contact with Reiner, he lowered himself to his knees, tilting his head up to expose his throat.

Reiner's eyes gleamed. "Down further, beta. Down on your belly."

"Reiner-" Hayley started, but Griff shook his head at her, very slightly.

"It'll be all right," he said quietly. "Don't worry."

Then he prostrated himself fully in front of Reiner, lying on his front with his head turned to one side. Smiling savagely, Reiner put his booted foot on the side of Griff's neck. The firefighter didn't so much as move a muscle.

"I accept your submission," Reiner said triumphantly. "*I* am Danny's alpha now." When Griff didn't respond, Reiner glared at him, pressing down on his throat with his full weight. "I've defeated you! Give him to me!"

Hayley didn't see Griff do anything at all, but a sudden piercing, heart-broken shriek came from Danny's room. Whatever had happened between the two lions, Danny had clearly sensed it.

"All right, it's done, let him up!" Hayley shoved at Reiner, as Danny's door banged open upstairs. "Let him go, before Danny sees!"

Reluctantly, Reiner took his foot off Griff's neck. Hayley wanted to help Griff up, but she didn't know whether that would just be one more humiliation. In an agony of indecision, she hovered over him as he stiffly levered himself to his feet.

"Griff, *Griff!*" Danny hurled himself down the stairs and straight into Griff, nearly knocking him over again. "Where are you? Why aren't you in my head anymore? You said you'd never leave me, you *promised!*"

"I'm sorry, lad." Griff hugged him once, briefly, then let him go. "Just remember what I told you about a true alpha."

"Come here, Danny," Reiner ordered. "*I* am your alpha now."

Danny shook his head in incomprehension. "But Mr. Griff-"

"I said, *come here!*" Reiner's voice snapped with that odd, commanding note that Hayley had only ever heard Griff use before.

Danny jerked away from Griff at Reiner's order, like a dog yanked back by its collar. He stared from Griff to Reiner to Hayley in mute betrayal, as though they'd all suddenly turned into strangers.

"It'll be fine," Griff said, as much to Hayley as to Danny. The bitter, shamed set of his shoulders betrayed his lie. "Don't worry. I'll go now."

"No, *he's* going." Hayley confronted Reiner, wishing with all her heart that *she* could turn into a lion. "Get out before I call the cops. And don't you dare come here again."

"I will be back to collect my son," Reiner retorted. "As and when I choose. Or would you prefer to hear from my lawyer?"

Griff's hand fell on her shoulder, squeezing in warning. "There is no need for that." He addressed Reiner's feet, not raising his head. "You are alpha. You have the right to see your cub."

"And you do not." Reiner's tone took on that eerie undercurrent of alpha command again. "Danny, you will not see this man again. You will not be under the same roof as him. If he comes here, you must leave immediately." His voice rose with a sort of giddy malice, like a child waving around a stolen handgun. "You will not meet him, nor speak to him, under any circumstances. *Do you understand?*"

"Yes, Daddy," Danny whispered, his small face still white with shock. Immediately, he started retreating from Griff, his movements forced and jerky. A panicked whimper rose in his throat as his back hit the wall.

"It's all right, lad." Griff circled round Reiner, never turning his back on him. "I'm going. Hayley, I'll call you later. Don't worry. I promise I'll fix this." With a last indecipherable glance at her, he left.

"You- you-" Hayley's hands curled into impotent fists. "*Get out.*"

Reiner backed away, but paused in the doorway. He smirked at her. "You can have your son. Or you can have your mate. But not both. Let's see which one you love more."

CHAPTER 22

DANNY

He is the alpha, Simba kept insisting. *We have to obey the alpha.*

Danny stared rebelliously at his untouched dinner. He didn't *want* to obey. Not like he'd wanted to obey Mr. Griff.

But Mr. Griff wasn't his alpha anymore. Daddy was.

Daddy's eyebrows drew down. "I *said*, eat your dinner."

Danny could feel Daddy's lion glaring at Simba in his head, just like Daddy was glaring at him across the table. It made Simba flatten against the bottom of Danny's mind, whimpering in submission. No matter how much Danny tried to reassure the cub that it was okay, that Daddy would never, *ever* hurt them, the cub was still scared of the bigger lion.

Just to stop Simba being scared, Danny scooped up a forkful of dinner and put it in his mouth. It was peas. Danny didn't like peas.

He ate them anyway. His alpha wanted him to.

"That's better," Daddy said, back in his normal voice, not the horrible alpha voice that felt like a leash around Danny's neck. "Listen, if you eat up your vegetables, I'll take you out hunting. You'd like that, wouldn't you? Just like last night, remember?"

Danny scowled at him. "I don't wanna go hunting. I want to go back home. I want Mommy."

"Well *I* want you here," Daddy snapped back. "You're going to be staying with me now. And if your mother tries to get you to go anywhere with her, you come and find me and tell me, understand?"

Obey the alpha, Simba whispered. *Alpha is big and we are very small. Obey.*

Daddy's lion made Danny's head jerk down in a nod. But he couldn't make Danny be happy about it. He couldn't even make Danny *pretend* to be happy about it.

An alpha could control every bit of him…but not the bit that made feelings.

Daddy said a very bad word, one that Danny wasn't supposed to know. "Listen, my son." Danny could feel the effort he was making to keep his voice normal, when he really wanted to shout. "I know it's different, but this is the way things are supposed to be. You should be happy! We're a proper pride now. Everything will be better. You'll see."

Danny could feel Daddy's lion pushing at him, like fingers trying to force the corners of his mouth up into a smile. He set his jaw stubbornly.

"This is all *his* fault," Daddy muttered. "You're supposed to follow the strongest lion, without question. Not pine like a dog after some sick cripple. I should have fought him in front of you. Then you'd have seen me defeat him. You'd know I'm the strongest, that I deserve to be alpha."

A very, very tiny growl rumbled in Simba's throat. *He didn't defeat our real alpha. Our real alpha stepped down. We could tell the difference.* The growl shifted up to a whine, Simba's ears flattening in confused misery. *Why did he abandon us? Why didn't he fight for us? Were we bad? Doesn't he want us any more?*

Danny hugged Simba, trying to comfort him. He couldn't explain to his lion that Mr. Griff couldn't fight Daddy, not when he couldn't shift. Simba didn't see Mr. Griff as a person at all—just as the biggest, strongest lion ever.

"It'll be better once we're in Valtyra." Daddy sounded like he was trying to convince himself, as much as Danny. "Living with just humans for so long has you all confused. Once we're back home, you'll soon learn proper ways. I'll teach you. We'll go into the wilderness and live as lions, just the two of us, until we're a true pride."

Just the two of us?

Daddy had said something about going on vacation without Mommy before, but Danny hadn't thought he'd really *meant* it. "What about Mommy?"

Daddy blinked at him, as though he'd almost forgotten Danny was a separate person able to speak for himself. "What?"

"Mommy," Danny repeated. He was starting to get a horrible sick feeling right in the bottom of his stomach. "Mommy has to come too."

"No, she'll stay here. I know this seems hard to you now, but one day you'll realize it was all for your own good. She's just a human. She can't understand you, not like I do."

Simba whimpered, pressing against the inside of Danny's head. The cub wanted him to be quiet, to avoid making the bigger lion angry.

Danny forced words out anyway, through his tightening throat. "I'm not going anywhere without Mommy! Not ever!"

"You will go where I tell you to, when I tell you to!" Daddy's burning eyes filled Danny's whole head, trying to drive out all his own thoughts. "I am your alpha! You will do as I say!"

A true alpha never forces anyone, said Mr. Griff's voice in his memory. *You remember that, always.*

"No." He met Daddy's eyes, and the surprise in them gave him the courage to stand up, clenching his fists. "No! I won't go, and you can't make me!"

Daddy shot to his feet, looming over him. "I am your alpha! You *will* obey me!"

No! Simba was on his feet too, fangs bared at the presence at the back of their mind. *You are not worthy to be alpha! We challenge you!*

Simba leaped, claws bared. Daddy's lion had to retreat in the face of Simba's fearless attack. With a *snap*, the pride-bond went dead.

"I don't want you as my alpha!" Danny yelled, right into Daddy's shocked face. "You hurt Mr. Griff, when it wasn't even fair! I wish *he* was still my alpha! I wish *he* was my daddy! I don't want you! *Go away!*"

Daddy snarled, his hands clenching. Danny's skin prickled as Simba surged forward—but Daddy stopped dead. He stared at his own fists, then down at Danny. His face went white.

"No," Daddy whispered in horror. "I nearly—no!"

Daddy whirled, his own form shimmering. His clothes tore away as he shifted. On four paws, he charged blindly out the door. Danny heard him crashing through the trees. His enraged, agonized roars faded away as he disappeared into the woods.

Simba wanted to run too, all the way home to Mommy, but Danny held his lion back. "It's too far," he said to the cub out loud. "And we don't know the way."

We can't stay here. Simba's tail lashed in agitation. *What if he comes back?*

Danny made himself a deep breath, focusing on staying calm, just like Mr. Griff had taught him. Frowning, he tried to think with his human head instead of his lion's heart. "We need a plan."

The front door was nice and thick. It made a big bang when Danny pushed it shut. He found a big metal key in the lock, and turned it with a reassuring click. Then he went through all the rooms downstairs, checking that all the windows were closed too.

"There," he said to Simba, when he was satisfied that Daddy wouldn't be able to get back in. "Now we just need to call for help."

Simba looked mournfully at the dark, cold place where the pride-bond—the *real* pride-bond, not Daddy's fake one—had been. *How?*

There was a phone in one of the bedrooms upstairs—a funny old-fashioned phone that was plugged in, not like a proper phone that you could put in your pocket. It took Danny a little puzzling how to work it, since it didn't have a screen to touch, but in the end he figured out which buttons to press.

He didn't know Mommy's number, but there was one number he *did* know. It was a different number from the one in America, he remembered. Mommy had made sure that he learned it by heart. She'd told him to call it if he was ever hurt or scared or needed help.

He definitely needed help now.

"999," said a stranger's voice in his ear. "What is the nature of your emergency?"

"Can I talk to the firefighters?" Danny remembered to add, "Please?"

There were a few clicks, then a different man said, "East Sussex Fire and Rescue Service. Where is your emergency?"

Danny thought this was a very strange way of saying hello. "Is Mr. Griff there?"

There was a pause. "What do you think this is, the damn

Yellow Pages? I'm a fire dispatcher, not an operator. Is there a fire near you? Do you need a fire engine?"

"No, thank you," Danny said politely. "I just need Mr. Griff. He's a firefighter, so I know he works here. Could you get him for me? Please?"

"Oh, for the love of-" The man sighed heavily. "Kid, unless you've actually got a fire—a *big* fire—don't call the fire department. Got it?"

"Um…okay," Danny said, dubiously. "But-"

The phone made a funny beeping sound in his ear. The man had hung up.

Now what? Simba wanted to know.

Danny hopped down off the bed. "Now I guess we look for some matches."

CHAPTER 23

GRIFF

Griff had never felt less like going in to work.

He'd spent half the day waiting impatiently for Ash to come off duty. But when Griff had finally managed to accost him at the fire station, the Phoenix had flatly refused to try to burn away one of his shifter animals right away.

"You are not in a fit state of mind to make this decision now," Ash had told him. The Fire Commander hadn't even had a chance to change out of his turnout gear, the scent of smoke still heavy around him. "And in any event, I am not in a fit state physically to attempt it. I must rest, and you must reflect. You must be absolutely certain that this is the only way forward. Think. If you have me do this, it cannot be undone."

The best Griff had been able to do was to force Ash to reluctantly promise to make the attempt tomorrow, if Griff didn't change his mind before then. He knew that he wouldn't. Now that Reiner was Danny's alpha as well as father, he had a double claim to the boy. His legal position was practically unassailable.

Griff knew that Hayley had hidden Danny's passport, but that wouldn't delay Reiner for long. All he had to do was get a Valtyran passport for Danny, and he'd be able to take him out of the country any time he liked. There would be nothing standing in his way.

I have to stop him. I have to be able to shift.

If Ash burned away his eagle, leaving him a lion shifter, then he'd be able to challenge Reiner directly. If his eagle was the one to survive...well, the situation would be less straightforward, but at least he'd legally be a shifter. Hayley would have a strong case for retaining custody of Danny.

If neither of his animals survived...Griff refused to even contemplate that possibility. Which left him with nothing to do except watch the minutes crawl past, agonizingly slowly. If it hadn't been for his bad leg, he would have been pacing like a caged lion.

His own lion *was* pacing, endlessly circling in his mind, its rage and humiliation boiling under his skin. His eagle's accusing eyes tracked the lion's every move. It blamed the lion for losing Danny to Reiner, and it took all of Griff's control to keep its fury leashed. Its talons clenched on his bones, trying to twist them into its own shape. He could feel his body vibrating, ever so slightly, right on the edge of an uncontrolled shift.

Normally, he would have called in sick—he couldn't risk having a seizure in the middle of the control room. But he was scheduled to cover the evening shift, which was always short-handed thanks to the unsociable hours required. If he didn't turn up, he'd be leaving the fire department dangerously short-staffed. He couldn't put the city at risk just for his own personal crisis.

Plus, of course, I'd probably get fired, Griff thought with bleak humor as he rode the elevator up to the control room. *Pun intended.*

He was already on probation, thanks to his frozen hand. Unfortunately, being a fire dispatcher involved a *lot* of typing. Another black mark on his record would cost him his job. And *that* would cost him his life insurance…which would in turn cost Hayley a lot of money.

At least there's one advantage to having a terminal condition that doctors don't believe in. The insurance industry doesn't believe in it either.

At the moment, he was worth a lot more to Hayley dead than alive. He could only pray that after Ash finished with him tomorrow, that would no longer be true.

"You look like hammered shit," Kevin greeted him as he entered the control room.

"Good to see you too," Griff replied, stiffly folding himself into his chair. He looked around at the otherwise deserted office. "Where's Claire? I thought she was on duty tonight with you."

"Guess you weren't the only one spending Halloween getting wasted. She called in sick." Kevin scowled in irritation, pulling his headset off his ears. "You have no idea how glad I am to see you, even if you do look like dog vomit. I have been bursting to piss for bloody hours."

"I'm logged in," Griff said, slipping his own headset on. He cast a quick, practiced glance at the status of the department, noting that all the fire engines were already out attending to incidents. "Busy night, I see."

"Like you wouldn't believe. I've even been having to route calls to our backup control centers to handle." Kevin was already heading for the door. "Hey, got a funny story about a prank call earlier, actually. I'll tell you when I get back."

Griff frowned at his screen as Kevin left. He didn't like how backup control had been allocating resources, keeping nothing in reserve. Every single crew was stacked up already. If a new call came in-

As if on cue, his headset beeped at him. With a practiced flick, he hit the answer button. "East Sussex Fire and Rescue Service. Where is your emergency?"

"Mr. Griff!"

His heart stopped at the familiar voice. *"Danny?"*

"I tried to call earlier but you weren't there. The other man told me not to call again unless there was a big fire." Danny stopped, coughing. "I think the fire's big enough now."

GO! roared his lion. Griff lost valuable seconds to a full-body spasm, the lion's frantic claws ripping across his mind. His eagle was a storm of wings and talons, beating against the inside of his skull. *Our cub is in danger! GO!*

"Danny, where are you?" he managed to gasp out through the pain.

"Daddy's house. Daddy's not here. I, um, yelled at him a lot, then he ran into the woods and I locked him out." Danny coughed again, the sound of it like a saw blade across Griff's own throat. "Mr. Griff, the fire's getting *really* big now."

"I'm sending help to you, Danny." His good hand flew across the keyboard, steady despite the agony wracking his bones. He briefly muted Danny's line, switching instead to the all-crew broadcast. "Code red, code red, all crews respond! I've got a kid trapped in a burning building! I need a team, *now!*"

Without waiting for a verbal response, he switched back to Danny. He kept his voice soft and calm, no matter how his inner beasts screamed at him. "Okay, Danny. I need you to tell me exactly where you are in the house."

"Upstairs in the bedroom, where the phone is."

"That's good," he said encouragingly, though it wasn't. Upstairs was very, very bad indeed. "And where's the fire?"

"Downstairs." Danny's voice went high and wobbly. *"All* downstairs. I'm sorry, Mr. Griff, I didn't mean to!"

"It's okay, Danny." Griff snarled soundlessly at the ETAs popping up on his screen as crews responded to the alert. *Too slow, too slow!* "Is the bedroom door closed?"

"Yes, I closed it to stop the smoke but it's still coming in real fast." Danny gulped down a sob. "I tried to open the window but it's stuck. Please, please, come get me."

Griff had to grab at the desk, bracing himself as a seizure shook his body. His beasts were single-minded with the need to reach their cub. His muscles writhed against each other, trying to twist into wings and paws. Every fiber of his being cried out to run to the boy's aid.

But Danny needed his human mind now, not his animals' instincts.

"Help is coming, Danny." Griff's hand shook on the control board as he frantically re-prioritized tasks, dispatching every fire engine he could to Reiner's house. "Just stay down low, out of the smoke."

His fingers cracked and bent halfway through dialing Ash's emergency contact number. He scrabbled futilely at the keys, his paw-hands unable to press single buttons. His control board flung up a dozen errors as the system tried to process the gibberish commands.

ASH! he tried to send telepathically—but he could feel the mental shout just bounce off the inside of his own skull. He'd never been able to contact other shifters that way.

He just had enough dexterity left to jab the mute button on his headset. "KEVIN!" he roared. "GET IN HERE!"

"Jesus Christ! Can't a guy even take a piss around-" Kevin stopped dead in the doorway.

"Take over!" Griff fell out of his chair, forced to all fours as his spine twisted. "Call Ash!"

Kevin shook his head in mute incomprehension. Face white with shock, he started backing away.

Griff didn't have time to explain, or to cajole. He locked

eyes with the other dispatcher, unleashing his full alpha dominance. "*Stop.*"

Kevin froze like a deer caught in car headlights.

"Go to the control board." Griff fought to keep his throat and tongue human. "Call Fire Commander Ash."

Moving as stiffly as a robot, Kevin did so.

A rush of relief shot through Griff as he heard Ash pick up the call. "Ash, get the team to Danny," Griff ordered, not waiting for Ash to speak. "He's trapped in a fire. *Go!*"

The phone line instantly went dead, Ash not wasting even a second to respond. Nonetheless, Griff could feel the Phoenix's acknowledgement in his mind, a brief, blazing telepathic communication like a rescue beacon flaring in the night.

I can sense him, Chase's mental voice crashed through his head, as swift and unstoppable as the pegasus himself. *We're on our way, Griff.*

I'm already in the air, Dai sent too, a second later. *I'm bringing John and Hugh.*

We will not fail you, oath-brother. John's telepathic tone was fierce and focused. Griff could feel him calling clouds across the sky, shaping them into a torrent strong enough to drown any inferno. *Tell your son that we come!*

Griff let out his breath. He relaxed his alpha hold over the shaking Kevin. "Sorry. Now, I need you to-"

Kevin bolted like a rabbit. Griff didn't have a chance to reestablish his dominance before the other dispatcher had fled out of sight.

Griff snarled, cursing himself, but it was too late to do anything about it now. His erratic heartbeat lurched as he realized he hadn't heard anything from Danny for at least a minute. His headset was still on, askew over his lengthening skull. He managed to get his talons round the microphone, unmuting it again. "Danny? Can you hear me?"

"Please come, Mr. Griff, please!"

The panic in Danny's voice hurt worse than his twisting bones. "My friends are on their way now. I'm going to stay right here with you until they arrive. It won't be long. Chase can find anyone, remember?"

Got to keep him calm. Give him something to focus on. Just a little longer...

"Danny, I've got a very important job for you," Griff managed to get out through gritted fangs. He closed his eyes, focusing on the sound of Danny's scratchy, labored breathing in his ear. "I need you to check the door for me. Crawl over on your belly, like a snake. Don't open the door, just touch it and see if it's hot. Can you do that for me? Now?"

He heard shuffling, then a yelp of pain. "It burned me!"

That meant there was no escape that way—and if Danny opened the door, the fire would be sucked into the room. "Danny, do *not* open the door. Can you see any blankets or pillows?"

Danny went into a long coughing fit. When he finally answered, his voice was hoarse and raspy. "Yes. There's lots."

"I want you to stuff as many as you can under the door. Block it up so the smoke can't get in. Make sure you stay down low, understand?"

"Okay," Danny whispered, sounding very small and scared. "I have to put the phone down. You won't go away, will you?"

"I promise, I'll be here. I'll won't leave you, ever."

Distantly, he was aware of curling into a ball, fur and feathers ripping from his skin, joints snapping and contorting. But as long as he could still speak, everything else was irrelevant. He ignored the pain, ignored his beasts, ignored whatever was happening to his tortured body. Nothing mattered except Danny.

Even though Reiner had broken their pride-bond, he

could still feel an echo of it, like a phantom limb. Griff focused on it fiercely, blocking out everything except that faint, tenuous link. He sent all his own strength, all his pride, all his courage down that slender connection.

We can see the house. Ash's mental voice sounded faintly in his head. *We are nearly there, Griff. Tell him to hold on just a few moments longer.*

"I did it!" Danny's voice came back, much stronger than before. "The smoke's not coming in so fast any more."

"Well done, lad," Griff gasped. "My friends are nearly there. Just hold on."

"Mr. Griff, are you okay? You sound funny."

"Don't worry about me." A primal fire was roaring through his blood, devouring his consciousness. He fought for just a few more seconds of lucidity. "Crawl over to the window. Can you see my friends yet?"

"Umm...no. Just—" Without warning, Danny shrieked.

"Danny?" The line had gone dead. *"Danny!"*

I've got him! Dai's triumphant telepathic roar echoed around Griff's shattering mind. *We've got him, Griff. He's safe.*

That was all Griff needed to hear.

Danny's safe. I can let go now.

His beasts rose up, and devoured him.

CHAPTER 24

DANNY

No one was listening to Danny.

He tried again. "Please, Dr. Hugh. I just want-"

"Don't try to talk yet." Dr. Hugh's white hair kept changing color, red-blue-red-blue, in the whirling lights of the fire engines. His hands felt nice on Danny's neck, a tingly sort of warmth driving away all the soreness. "You've breathed in a lot of smoke. Just hold still while I fix it."

"He needs to get to hospital!" Daddy snarled at Dr. Hugh. "Where's the damn ambulance?"

"How should I know?" Mr. Hugh snapped, glaring right back as if he wasn't scared of Daddy's lion at all. "For the last time, move *away*. You're giving me a migraine, hovering so close. I can't work with you breathing down the back of my neck."

Daddy didn't budge one bit. He'd run out of the woods right as Mr. Dai was putting Danny back down on the ground, and he hadn't let go of Danny's hand ever since. Danny didn't mind, not now that Daddy was back to being just Daddy again. Daddy was much nicer when he wasn't pretending to be an alpha. He didn't even seem mad about Danny burning up his house.

Danny hoped he wouldn't be mad about Mr. Dai knocking down the wall, either. Turned out that dragons were *real* strong.

Danny kicked his feet impatiently, willing Dr. Hugh to hurry so that he could talk. He stared out the back door of the fire engine, watching all the firefighters run around through the smoke and rain. Danny wasn't quite sure why so many of them had decided to turn up, when Mr. Griff's friends had already rescued him.

He also didn't understand why they were all rushing around so excitedly. Mr. Ash and Sir John were doing all the *real* work, after all. They weren't making any fuss about it, either. Well, Sir John was singing, but that was a nice noise, not like all the yelling the other firefighters were doing.

Danny wished they would all quiet down so that he could hear Sir John better. Maybe if he could learn the words, *he'd* be able to make it rain by singing to the clouds too. He'd have to ask Sir John to teach him, some other time.

"*Danny!*"

Danny's stomach flipped over at Mommy's scream. She sounded as scared as if *she* was trapped in a fire.

"Mommy!" He tried to wriggle free of Daddy and Dr. Hugh, but they both held him tight, stopping him from jumping out of the fire engine. "Let me go! *Mommy!*"

"You can't run out there, it's not safe." Dr. Hugh jerked his chin at the flickering red glow of the still-burning house. "Don't worry. Chase is bringing her straight here."

Sure enough, a second later Mommy scrambled up into the back of the fire engine too. At the sight of her, Danny wrenched himself free from Daddy and Dr. Hugh. A *hundred* dragons couldn't have kept him out of Mommy's arms.

"My baby, my baby," she sobbed, squeezing him so tight he couldn't breathe.

Danny didn't care. He buried his face in her neck, smelling her, smelling home. Dr. Hugh's hands might be able to heal, but Mommy's touch was stronger magic. The aching tightness in his chest finally vanished.

"Are you okay?" she said, thrusting him away so that her anxious eyes could inspect every inch of him. "Are you hurt?"

"He's going to be fine," Dr. Hugh answered for him. "Just a little smoke inhalation. I've fixed all the damage."

"He should still go to the hospital," Daddy said stubbornly. "I want him to be checked over properly."

"I don't care what you want! You get no say in anything, ever again!" Mommy clutched at Danny as if she thought Daddy might try to snatch him away. "How could you let this happen? *Where were you?*"

Daddy's eyes slid away from Mommy's accusing ones. "I only went outside for a moment."

Danny stared at him. It was *bad* to tell fibs. "But-"

Daddy's lion flashed behind his eyes, and Danny fell silent. He didn't want to start another fight. It was better when members of the pride weren't mad at each other.

"It was only for a moment," Daddy repeated, as though he could make it true if he said it enough times. "Danny was having a tantrum. I had to give him space to calm down, so I went outside."

"Without any clothes on," Dr. Hugh murmured.

Daddy glared at him, clutching the shiny silver blanket he'd borrowed tighter around his waist. "I was shifted! How was I supposed to know he'd lock me out? Let alone decide to set the place on fire!" He turned his glare on Mommy. "This is all your fault! He could never have come up with such an evil idea on his own. You've been poisoning him against me!"

Mommy bared her teeth at him, just like a lion. "How *dare* you!"

"No fighting!" Danny yelled at the top of his lungs. His voice was still all scratchy from the smoke, but it was loud enough to make all the grown-ups stop and stare at him. "You can't fight now. We have to go find Mr. Griff."

Daddy made a small, disgusted sound at the back of his throat. "Indeed I do. The other half of this scheme. I won't let him surrender to me *this* time. I'm going to-"

"You will be silent." Mr. Ash appeared at the back of the fire engine, outside in the rain. He didn't yell or look mad or anything, but Daddy's mouth still snapped shut.

Nobody talked back to Mr. Ash.

Ask the Alpha-of-Alphas about our *alpha,* Simba urged Danny, as Mr. Ash started telling Mommy and Daddy something too complicated for Danny to follow. *Our alpha belongs to him. He must know where he is. Hurry!*

Despite his lion cub's urgency, Danny hesitated. Mr. Ash wasn't *scary*, exactly, but he made Danny's tongue stick to the roof of his mouth. He wasn't an easy person to talk to at the best of times, and now was definitely not a good time.

Mr. Ash wasn't wearing safety gear like the other firefighters. His regular clothes were covered in little holes where sparks from the burning house had blown on him. He wasn't wet at all, despite Sir John's rain. Danny could hear the faint hiss of raindrops sizzling into nothing just before they hit his skin.

Danny swallowed hard, gathering up his courage. "Mr. Ash?"

Mr. Ash, who had been in the middle of talking about reports and procedures and boring grown-up stuff with Mommy and Daddy, stopped mid-word. Danny flinched a little as that dark, deep gaze fell on him. "Yes, Daniel?"

"Where's Mr. Griff? Is he coming too?"

"I am afraid he cannot. He is needed back in the control room, where he can monitor what is happening and tell us all what needs to be done."

"Can I talk to him? Please?"

"He'll be very busy right now, honey," Mommy said to him. "We'll go see him as soon as we can. You can thank him then." She gave Daddy a hard stare. "We can *all* thank him."

"I need to talk to him *now*," Danny said stubbornly. "Please, Mr. Ash. Can you talk to him in your head? I can't find him and I want to know if he's okay."

"I have been attempting to keep him updated as to what is happening here, but I do not know if he is listening. He is unable to respond to me telepathically." Mr. Ash considered him for a moment, his eyebrows drawing down a little. "Daniel, do you still have a pride-bond to Griffin?"

"Sort of. I think. I could feel him earlier, when he was talking to me on the phone, but he's gone again now." Something about that eerie silence at the back of his head made Danny's stomach churn, like he needed to throw up. "Please, Mr. Ash. Something's wrong."

Mr. Ash leaned back, flagging down a passing firefighter. "Excuse me. I need to talk to the control room, please."

"I'll fetch the radio, but it won't do you any good, sir." The firefighter shook her head, looking annoyed under her helmet. "They've got absolutely no clue what's going on down here. Or up there, for that matter."

Mr. Ash frowned. "Is Griffin MacCormick not still handling this incident?"

"I wish. We can't raise anybody at our control room. We've had to switch to backup control from the next area, and *those* muppets can't tell their arses from their elbows."

Mr. Ash went very still.

"Sir?" The firefighter waved her gloved hand in front of his face. "Do you still want the radio, sir?"

"No," said Mr. Ash, as Dr. Hugh started frantically flinging things back into his doctor's bag. "Thank you. Please ask the second-in-command to take over here. Alpha Team must attend to another emergency."

CHAPTER 25

HAYLEY

*A*ccording to the hospital floorplan, Ward S officially didn't exist. According to the signs above the door to the small annex, it was the Highly Contagious Diseases Research Centre (Access Strictly Restricted).

What it actually was, past the triple-locked doors and hulking security guards, was the shifter ward.

After six hours curled up in an uncomfortable plastic chair in the tiny waiting room, Hayley was desperately hungry and longing for a coffee, but she didn't dare leave to find a vending machine. She was scared that she'd never manage to get back in again. She'd only managed to enter in the first place because she'd been personally escorted by Fire Commander Ash.

The Phoenix had been allowed through to Griff's private room, but Hayley had been firmly stopped at the door. Apparently Griff was still in critical condition. No matter how much she begged passing nurses and doctors for any more information, that was all anyone would tell her.

Why's Ash allowed in, but not me? What's taking them so long? Why won't anyone tell me what's happening?

All Hayley could do was clutch her phone, exchanging comfortingly banal texts with Connie about when Danny was likely to wake up and what he was allowed for breakfast. She and Chase had agreed to stay over at Hayley's house, so that she could head to the hospital to be with Griff. Hayley was deeply grateful to them both. There was no way in *hell* she was letting Reiner take Danny. Not ever again.

I'll flee the country first. I'll disappear. He is never, ever going to have sole responsibility for Danny. Not after this.

"Hayley?" She jumped, her dozing head jerking up at Hugh's voice. The paramedic looked ten times as shattered as Hayley felt, his pale skin ashen in the harsh fluorescent lights. "You're still here?"

"Of course I'm still here." Hayley jumped to her feet. "How is he? Is he going to be okay?"

"He's stable." Hugh swayed on his feet. "For now."

Hayley instinctively reached out to support him, but he recoiled from her hand so violently that his back slammed into the wall. She'd forgotten that the paramedic hated to be touched.

"Sorry," he muttered, staying as far away from her as it was physically possible to get. "Too tired to keep my psychic walls up. Hayley, I've done everything I can for him. He's conscious and lucid, and I don't think he's in immediate danger."

The unspoken *but...* hung in the air between them.

Hayley swallowed. "But?"

Hugh sighed, raking a hand through his disheveled silver hair. "He's half-shifted. His body is a horrendous mismatch of parts, and it's putting extreme stress on his internal organs. His heart and lungs are barely functional, but his digestive system...well. You get the picture. It's a bloody mess."

"He was stuck halfway before." Hayley remembered how

she'd watched Griff's twisted, half-beast form gradually ease back to human, during that long vigil weeks ago. "He came back then. He can come back now, can't he?"

"I don't think he can. I've never seen anything like this before." Hugh scrubbed his hands over his face, rubbing at his bloodshot eyes. "Ash was trying to burn out one of Griff's animals and get him unstuck that way...but Griff and his lion and eagle are too intertwined now. Even Ash can't distinguish between the three of them."

Hayley stared at him. "Ash has been trying to do *what?*"

Hugh shook his head. "The details aren't important now. It didn't work. Ash can't do anything. I can't do anything. Hayley, he's got weeks left at best. Possibly days."

No.

Hayley's knees wanted to buckle. She made herself stand up straight and tall, spine rigid. "I want to see him."

Hugh hesitated. "He's...he doesn't want you to see him. Not like this."

"I don't give a damn. I am his mate and I *will* see him. *Now.*"

Wisely, Hugh didn't try to argue. Without a further word, he escorted her down the corridor, flashing his hospital ID pass as they passed yet another security checkpoint.

Hugh opened a plain, unmarked door, revealing a small private room. A couple of beeping machines lined the foot of a hospital bed, wires trailing off under the covers. Most of the bed was blocked from view by a privacy screen.

"I told you not to let her in here, Hugh," said a low, pained voice. The words were so badly distorted, Hayley could barely understand them. "Ash. Take her away."

Ash emerged from behind the screen. The Phoenix did not look quite so collected as usual. He was still wearing the same clothes he'd been earlier, at the fire. The smell of smoke hung around him, and something else too—a hot, scorching scent like desert winds and burnt metal.

"Ms. Parker," he said, nodding at her.

Hayley braced herself for an argument, but Ash just touched Hugh's elbow, drawing him away. The pair left, and the door clicked softly shut behind them.

"Bastards." A deep growl drifted out from behind the screen. "Hayley, *please*. I don't want you to remember me like this."

Hayley's heart hammered, but her hand was steady. She pushed back the privacy curtain.

"Like what?" She met his mismatched eyes without flinching. "Like the man I love? Like my mate?"

All the breath sighed out of him. His muzzle wrinkled a little, like he was trying to smile. "I love you."

"I love you too." Hayley threaded her fingers through his left paw, careful of the claws. "Don't ever try to keep me away again. I thought we'd agreed you weren't going to do that anymore."

"I won't." The sheets stirred oddly, next to his bent legs. It took Hayley a moment to realize that it was a tail, flicking under the covers. "Where's Danny? I can feel he's sleeping, and that he's safe and happy, but not more than that."

"He's back home, with Chase and Connie. He wanted to come to the hospital too, but I wouldn't let him."

"Good," Griff said, simply. "Don't."

"Griff-"

"*Don't*." His right arm—no, his right *wing*—flexed in agitation, the gleaming feathers unfurling and closing again like a massive golden fan. "Promise me."

"All right, I promise. I won't bring him unless you say it's okay." She tightened her hand on his, feeling the roughness of his thick, feline pads. "But he wants to say thank you. And he'll want to say, to say…"

She couldn't finish the sentence, words jamming up in her tightening throat.

"To say goodbye," Griff finished for her. He leaned his head back against the pillows with another deep sigh, closing his eyes. "I'll think about it. Turns out I'm a lot more vain than I care to admit."

Even under the fur, she could see the pain in the drawn tightness of his distorted face. "You're tired. You should rest."

"I've got all of eternity to rest." He opened his eyes again, though she knew the effort it cost him. "We need to talk about you. And Danny. And Reiner."

"Later. You need to concentrate on regaining your strength." She stroked his feathery mane back from his forehead. "Don't worry about any of that now."

"I *have* to worry about it now," Griff said fiercely. "I'm not going to be able to worry about it later. And I am *not* going to die and leave you at the mercy of that, that-"

One of the machines connected to him let out a shrill whistle.

"Hugh!" Hayley shrieked, as Griff convulsed.

The door banged back. It wasn't Hugh who rushed in, though, but a whole pack of white-coated nurses. They swept Hayley aside, one of them grabbing her arm as the rest converged on Griff's thrashing form. She caught a brief glimpse of two of the nurses struggling to hold down his powerful, mismatched limbs while a third plunged a syringe into the side of his neck, before she was hustled out the door.

"Let me go!" Hayley twisted futilely against the nurse's grip, but he was clearly a shifter. He held her captive with inhuman ease. "I want to stay with him!"

"I don't care what you want," the nurse snapped as he dragged her back along the corridor. "I don't have time to deal with hysterical humans. How did you even get in here in the first place?"

"I have a right to be here." Hayley looked around wildly for Ash or Hugh, but they were nowhere to be seen. "You can't throw me out. I'm his mate!"

"I have no idea what that freak is, but he's certainly no shifter." The nurse dumped her unceremoniously outside the ward doors. "And that means he can't have a mate. You have no rights here. Get out, and stay out."

∼

There was a police car parked outside her house. Hayley stared blankly at it as she paid her taxi driver, her numb mind struggling to process its presence.

Police car. Here.

Why would Connie call the police? Has Reiner been trying to get in?

"Connie? Chase?" she called softly as she let herself into the house. She could tell immediately from the stillness that Danny was still asleep, even though it was nearly ten in the morning.

He must be exhausted after everything last night. We'll both need lots of rest today. I'll have to call school, and work...

Her brain stalled out. She was simply too tired to think of what else needed to be done. At least she could count on Griff's friends—*her* friends—to help out.

"Connie?" she said again, heading for the front room. "Why's there a police car-?"

She stopped dead.

There wasn't just a police car outside.

There were police officers in her house.

"Hayley!" Connie leaped up from a chair, taking her hands. The curvy pilot's face was pale and worried. "I'm so sorry. I couldn't tell you over the phone. I didn't want you to feel like you had to rush back."

"She *should* have rushed back," muttered a man sitting on her sofa. He was wearing a sharp suit and an extremely pissed-off expression. "She's kept us waiting over an hour."

If looks could kill, Chase would have *buried* the man over an hour ago. The pegasus shifter radiated menace as he glared at both the man, and a woman seated next to him. Every muscle in his shoulders and chest was tense and ready.

"I'm sorry too, Hayley," he said. "We couldn't keep them out. But just give me the word, and I swear I will *kick* them out. One way or another."

The two police officers flanking the sofa growled, low in their throats. With a jolt, Hayley realized that they possessed the subtle but unmistakable feral aura of shifters.

"There's no need for that," said the woman, rising. Her pink twinset had clearly been chosen to appear friendly and approachable, but there was a certain firmness to the set of her jaw that meant the overall effect was of a Rottweiler wearing a fuzzy cardigan. "Let's not have any unpleasantness."

"What is this?" Hayley looked around at them all, unable to comprehend why there were so many strangers in her house. "What's going on?"

"Me first," the man on the sofa interrupted as the woman opened her mouth. "I've wasted enough time here today already." He got up, unceremoniously thrusting a folder of papers into Hayley's hand. "Ms. Hayley Dana Parker, on behalf of my client, Mr. Reiner Hans Ljonsson, I am formally notifying you of our intent to sue for full, sole, and immediate custody of Daniel Jamie Parker."

Papers fell out of Hayley's suddenly nerveless hand. "*What?*"

"Due to extreme and urgent concern for his son's safety and welfare, my client has petitioned the court for an extraordinary hearing as per the Juvenile Shifter Protection

Act of 1968, Section three, paragraph eighteen," the lawyer rattled on in a bored monotone, ignoring her interruption entirely. "You may expect a court summons imminently. Until the case has been settled, you are legally required to keep Danny within Brighton city limits. Should you break these conditions, you will be pursued by the Wild Hunt and, should you survive capture, may face penalties of up to fifteen years' imprisonment. You will find all the details required by your defense team in the provided brief. Any questions? Good. See you in court."

Without waiting so much as a second for a response, the lawyer strode out of the room. Hayley stared after his back in shock, then switched her gaze to the woman. "What?" she repeated.

"I'm sorry, Ms. Parker. I know this must all be rather overwhelming." The woman extended a hand with a smile that didn't reach her hard eyes. "I'm from Shifter Social Services. I'm afraid I'm going to need to ask you some questions."

CHAPTER 26

GRIFF

"Are you certain you are strong enough for this, oath-brother?"

"John, if you ask me that one more time, I swear I'm going to get out of this wheelchair and walk the rest of the way on my own three feet," Griff retorted. "Push me faster, damn it. I'm not made of glass. If we don't hurry, we're going to miss the final verdict."

John sang a soft, worried chord, but sped up his pace. Despite what Griff had told the sea dragon shifter, every tiny rattle of the wheels over the courtroom foyer's tiled floor sent agony spiking through his guts. He gritted his teeth—as best he could, given that his jaw didn't close properly anymore—and endured.

We must be there. We must be at our mate's side, in her hour of need.

Griff didn't know whether the all-consuming, driving thought came from his lion, or his eagle, or his own mind. All three of them were so intertwined that even he couldn't tell them apart anymore. His lion's instincts, his eagle's instincts...they were all just *his* instincts now.

And every instinct compelled him to go to his mate.

If Griff had had his own way, he would have been at Hayley's side for the entire three-day hearing. But the hospital doctors had flatly refused to sign him out. When he'd raged at them, they'd just shot him full of sedatives and restrained him. Apparently any display of anger was just another symptom of his unstable, bestial state.

Of course, when Griff had woken up and tried calmly reasoning with the doctors instead, they'd decided that obviously Hayley couldn't *really* be his mate, as he wasn't showing enough emotional agitation at her predicament. Griff had been very tempted to show them exactly how much agitation he could cause, but that would have just got him tied down to the bed again.

Instead, he'd smiled and nodded. And, as soon as the doctors had left, called John.

Shortly thereafter, the hospital had suffered a severe, sudden, and curiously localized flood. The shifter ward staff had been much too busy panicking over the two feet of seawater sloshing around their break room to even *notice* a patient being quietly wheeled away.

"I do appreciate this, you know," Griff said to John. "You can consider this payment of your life-debt."

John grunted as he picked up the entire wheelchair—Griff included—in order to carry it down a flight of stairs. "This, payment of a life-debt? This is a worthy adventure, oath-brother. *I* am indebted to *you* for allowing me to participate in it."

Griff's breath hissed between his fangs as the wheelchair bumped down to the ground again. "You're going to have to allow me to call the debt quits one day, you know."

"Perhaps." A slight smile tugged at John's stern mouth. "But not this day. Through here?"

"Yes." Griff could hear Michael's refined, measured voice

even through the thick closed door. "Quietly. They're making final statements."

We must stay high and hidden. We must scout out the terrain in order to judge how best to join our mate in this hunt. We must stalk softly until we are ready to pounce.

Unfortunately, a seven-foot-tall blue-haired knight pushing a completely shrouded figure in a wheelchair tended to attract people's attention. Especially when someone started shrieking and waving at them the instant they appeared.

"Mr. Griff!" Danny yelled in delight. Only the restraining hand of the social worker seated next to him kept the boy from hurling himself straight at Griff. "You're here, you're *here!*"

Griff grimaced underneath his concealing hood as heads turned all around the large, circular hearing chamber. To Michael's credit, the lawyer barely hesitated a second before smoothly continuing to deliver his closing statements. The judge and court officials also returned to the business at hand, though many of them stared curiously at him for a few moments longer.

"I didn't know you were coming!" Hayley whispered, as John parked his wheelchair next to her seat. Her hand found his, squeezing it in gratitude through the sheets swathing his distorted body. "I didn't even know you were being discharged!"

"Neither did the hospital," Griff murmured back. "Tell you later. How's it going?"

Hayley shook her head. "I thought that Reiner wouldn't have a leg to stand on, not after what happened at his house. But somehow his lawyer twisted all Danny's testimony, made it sound like he's some sort of juvenile delinquent arsonist. Now it all keeps coming back to the question of who can be Danny's alpha. Michael's arguing that it can't be Reiner, since he can't be trusted with Danny's welfare."

The dark circles under her eyes looked like smudges of soot against her ashen skin. Griff knew that the rest of Alpha Team had been looking after her—he'd made sure of *that*—but she still looked like she'd barely eaten or slept for days.

"...Outstanding testimonies from varied, prominent citizens in the local shifter community," Michael was saying. The overhead lights struck blue highlights from the faerie hound's midnight skin as he pointedly held up a thick sheaf of papers. "Not least of which is a personal statement from the Phoenix, known as Ash, testifying that it is his professional opinion that my client holds absolutely no blame for the fire on the evening of November the first. I submit that this utterly refutes and repudiates Mr. Ljonsson's claim that this incident can be used as evidence to deny my client custody. I further counter that as the fire occurred while Mr. Ljonsson had sole responsibility for Daniel Jamie Parker-"

Griff noticed that Reiner's lawyer was staring hard at him. Griff recognized the man—he was a shark shifter of some notoriety, with an excellent track record and a reputation for deviousness. The last time Griff had encountered him had been at an arson trial. Griff had been giving evidence against the shark shifter's client.

On *that* occasion, the lawyer had lost.

The shark touched Reiner's sleeve, leaning over to murmur in his ear. The two fell into an intent, whispered conversation.

Hayley had spotted them too. "What are they up to now?"

"I don't know." To Griff's frustration, he couldn't quite make out the words over Michael's impassioned defense. "But it's something to do with me. And Reiner doesn't look happy about it."

Hayley chewed on her lip. "Let's hope that means it's a

good sign for us."

"Thank you, Mr. Cabell," the judge said, as Michael finished his statement. "Do you or your client have anything further to add?"

Michael flashed a quick, inquiring look at Hayley and Griff. They both shook their heads slightly in answer.

"We have no further evidence to present, Your Honor." Michael sat down on Hayley's other side.

The judge turned to Reiner and his lawyer. "Mr. Paucus, your closing statement, please."

The shark shifter stood. "Before proceeding to my closing statement, I would like to submit one further testimony on behalf of my client, Your Honor."

The judge steepled her fingers, casting Paucus a stern look over the tops of her glasses. Griff didn't recognize her. He'd only been involved in criminal court cases before, not family court matters. He could tell from her body language that she was a wolf shifter…and also that she was eager to close the trial. She didn't look pleased by this last-minute disruption.

"You have had three days to present testimonies on behalf of your client, Mr. Paucus," the judge said to the lawyer. "Is there a reason why this one seems to have slipped your mind until now?"

The shark shifter made a courteous little bow. "This witness was previously unavailable. I apologize for the irregularity, but I strongly believe that this testimony should be heard before you reach your final decision."

The judge blew out her breath. Her eyes flicked to the clock, and back to the lawyer. "You may have five minutes. No more, Mr. Paucus. This is not the only hearing scheduled for today."

"Thank you, Your Honor." The shark looked straight across at Griff. "We call Griffin MacCormick to the stand."

CHAPTER 27

HAYLEY

"What are they up to?" Hayley whispered to Michael.

Her lawyer shook his head, watching his opposite number with narrowed eyes. "I don't know. I'd have said Paucus was planning to cast doubt on Griff as a reliable witness...except that he *isn't* a witness. I didn't include any testimony from him in our defense case, for exactly this reason. His condition means he's too easy to discredit."

Hayley twisted her hands in the hem of her tunic, her palms sweating as Griff stiffly struggled out of his wheelchair. The hospital sheets wrapped around him like a shroud, hiding even his face from view. Waving off John's assistance, he managed to get himself into witness box on his own two feet, though she could tell the effort it cost him to stand upright.

He shouldn't even be here. What if the stress causes him to have another seizure? Is that Reiner's plan? Is he vindictive enough to hound Griff into a heart attack, just because Griff's twice the lion he'll ever be?

Reiner, however, didn't look like this was all part of some

scheme. His jaw was set in a tight, unhappy line, his muscular arms folded across his chest. Paucus said something to him, and Reiner snarled back under his breath, glaring at his lawyer. Hayley was certain that whatever was going on was Paucus's idea, not Reiner's.

That wasn't very comforting. Reiner was petty and arrogant, but not devious. Paucus was another matter.

"Mr. MacCormick, kindly remove your...coverings," the judge said, when the official had finished swearing Griff in. "The court must be able to see your face."

"Mr. McCormick has a severe medical condition," Paucus said smoothly, before Griff could speak. He looked meaningful across the courtroom at Danny. "Some here would find his appearance upsetting. I respectfully beg that the court permit Mr. MacCormick to retain his privacy, Your Honor."

The judge nodded. "Granted. You may proceed with the witness. Five minutes only, Mr. Paucus."

The shark shifter turned to Griff, hands clasped loosely behind his back. "Mr. MacCormick, would you please state your heritage and nature for the benefit of the court?"

"My maternal line are eagle shifters, and my paternal line are lion shifters," Griff said warily. "I possess two inner beasts, both lion and eagle."

"Mr. MacCormick's unusual status is a matter of public record," Paucus said to the room in general, as a small murmur ran round the court. "Mr. MacCormick, you possess the renowned perceptive abilities of the Scottish Highland white-tailed sea eagles, do you not?"

"I do." Even with the sheet hiding his face from view, Hayley could tell from the way he leaned forward that he was focusing those very powers on the lawyer right now, alert for any hint of trickery.

"In layperson's terms, Mr. MacCormick, is it accurate to

say that you are able to detect when other people are lying or concealing the truth?"

"Yes." Griff's growl made the word a threat.

"And you have previously been called to use those powers when testifying in criminal court cases, haven't you?"

"Yes," Griff repeated, starting to sound slightly perplexed by the line of questioning.

Hayley was too. She had no idea where Paucus was going with this, and the uncertainty made her heart hammer in her throat.

It's like Paucus is trying to build up *his credibility, not knock it down...*

Paucus addressed the judge. "I have personally been present at trials where Mr. MacCormick's testimony was accepted as proof as to the veracity of other witnesses. I can provide references on request. For now, Your Honor, are you willing to accept that Mr. MacCormick can indeed do what he claims?"

"I am," the judge said, glancing at the clock again. "Time is running out, Mr. Paucus. Is there a point to this?"

"Just a few more questions, Your Honor. Mr. MacCormick, you are romantically involved with Ms. Hayley Parker, and were previously alpha to her son, Daniel Jamie Parker, correct?"

"Yes," Griff said shortly.

"Is it true to say that these facts naturally lead you to be antagonistic toward my client, Mr. Reiner Ljonsson?"

"I don't like him, if that's what you're asking," Griff said dryly. "Though I would dislike him just as intensely if Hayley was *not* my mate. He-"

"Apologies for interrupting," Paucus said, in a tone that was anything but apologetic. "As time is short, please restrict yourself to answering only the questions I ask. In the past, have you physically confronted Mr. Ljonsson?"

"Yes. Several times. He started them all."

"Just the direct question, please, Mr. MacCormick. You also lost a dominance challenge to him, and were forced to relinquish alpha rights over Daniel Parker?"

Griff's assent was more of a snarl than a word. Reiner smirked across the courtroom at him.

"But he-" Danny started. His social worker whispered urgently in his ear, making him quieten down again.

"In summary, Mr. MacCormick, is it fair to state that you violently dislike my client, and personally wish him to lose this case? You have no reason to come to his defense?"

"You're the one who hauled me up here," Griff growled. "Yes. All of those statements are true."

"Thank you. Just one last question. Please answer based on both your eagle powers of observation, and your personal knowledge of my client." The shark shifter bared all his teeth in a cold, predatory smile. "Would Mr. Ljonsson ever knowingly endanger his son?"

Click. Hayley could practically hear the trap springing shut. Her breath froze in her throat.

From Griff's absolute stillness, he'd stopped breathing too. He didn't say anything.

"Your answer, please, Mr. MacCormick," Paucus pressed. "I remind you that you are under oath."

"I…" Griff hesitated. "Reiner's judgment is-"

"It's a simple question, Mr. MacCormick! Would my client ever *knowingly* endanger his son? Yes or no?"

"Objection, Your Honor!" Michael leaped to his feet. "Mr. Paucus is badgering this witness!"

"Overruled." The judge was gazing thoughtfully at Griff, her brow furrowed. "Please answer the question, Mr. MacCormick."

Griff's shrouded head bowed. "No," he said, very softly.

Paucus turned his back on him, smiling sweetly up at the judge. "No further questions, Your Honor."

Michael's eyes were burning red with anger. "Your Honor, I would also like to question this witness."

"You have already made your closing remarks, Mr. Cabell. You had plentiful previous opportunity to gather a statement from Mr. MacCormick if you so wished." The judge checked the time again. "I will take a moment before rendering my verdict. Mr. MacCormick, you may step down."

Hayley jumped up, running to the witness box so quickly she even beat John. Griff's paw clutched at her arm as she helped him back into the wheelchair.

"I'm sorry," he said into her ear, his distorted voice filled with bitter agony. "I shouldn't have come. You should never have met me. I just make everything worse for you."

"Don't say that." Hayley grabbed his shoulder through the sheet, shaking him a little to break him out of his spiral of self-recrimination. "Don't *ever* say that. It wasn't your fault. And it probably won't have made any difference anyway. The judge must have already made up her mind by now, surely."

Griff's concealed face turned in the direction of the judge. She was bent over her notes, her pen tapping thoughtfully on the paper. Hayley couldn't read anything in her professionally blank expression...but Griff made a low, agonized sound deep in his throat.

"She *had* made up her mind," he said. "And now she's changing it."

All Hayley could do was grip his shoulder, trying to comfort him even as she took comfort just from his presence. Minutes crawled by like hours. Across the courtroom, Reiner and his lawyer exchanged triumphant glances.

The judge sat back at last, taking off her glasses. "I am

prepared to render my judgment. Ms. Parker, Mr. Ljonsson, please approach with your councils."

Hayley didn't want to leave Griff behind, but she had no choice. Michael took her elbow, escorting her up to the front of the courtroom. The judge's box seemed as high and intimidating as a mountain. Hayley had never felt so scared or so helpless.

"Ms. Parker, Mr. Ljonsson." The judge folded her glasses, placing them neatly before her. "Based on what I have heard, it is clear that it is in Daniel's best interests to have contact with both of you."

Hayley's heart started beating again.

"However," the judge continued, and Hayley's pulse thudded, "this presents logistical difficulties, given Mr. Ljonsson's stated intention to continue to reside in Valtyra. It is clear that we will have to find a way to divide Daniel's time between your two countries."

Reiner scowled. "But-"

The judge gave him a quelling look. "I have not finished, Mr. Ljonsson. It is *also* clear to me that Daniel is in urgent need of a pride. His recent willful and reckless behavior stems from the lack of a true alpha lion to curb his instincts. This situation cannot be allowed to continue. Although it is not ideal to remove Daniel from his school mid-term, I believe that his shifter education must come first. Mr. Ljonsson, for the time being, I am granting you full custody of Daniel, effective immediately."

The bottom dropped out of Hayley's stomach. The room swam in her vision. "No!"

"I know this will be difficult for you to accept, Ms. Parker." The judge's stern gaze softened a little. "You are human, and cannot understand the strength of our instincts. But Daniel *must* have a pride. Mr. Ljonsson can provide him with that. You cannot."

"But, but you said," Hayley stammered out. She wanted to beg, to scream, to grab Danny and run away, *anything* but accept this judgment. "You said he needed to see both of us. He needs *me* too!"

"This is true. He does. At the moment, his need for a pride is greater, but this will change as he masters his lion." The judge turned to Reiner, who was practically glowing with satisfaction. "Mr. Ljonsson, after Daniel has integrated into your pride, you will ensure that he has regular contact with his mother. I will draw up a schedule based around school holidays."

I'm only going to get to see my little boy during school holidays? For just a few weeks, out of months?

"Of course," Reiner said to the judge, surprisingly meekly. His amber eyes gleamed as he glanced at Hayley. "I will be happy to do so...once Danny is firmly established in my pride."

"LYING!" Hayley leaped at Griff's sudden, explosive roar. He surged up from his wheelchair, his concealing sheets slipping away. "He is lying!"

Reiner recoiled in horror from Griff's bestial, snarling features. In that split-second, unguarded moment, Hayley read the truth in Reiner's eyes. He *was* lying. He had no intention of ever returning Danny.

If Danny went to Valtyra, she'd never see him again.

"Your Honor, please, you can't do this." Ignoring the shocked gasps at his appearance, Griff took a step toward the judge. His tail lashed from side to side, the feathered tip sweeping across the floor. "Reiner's lying. Every school holiday, he'll just claim that Danny isn't ready-"

"Your Honor, these are baseless slanders against my client!" Paucus interrupted. "I petition that Mr. MacCormick be removed immediately!"

Griff bared his fangs at the shark, making him flinch.

"*You're* the one who made a big song-and-dance of my eagle abilities. You can't pretend not to believe in them now. He is *lying!*"

"Mr. MacCormick!" The judge had visibly paled at Griff's twisted form, but she banged her gavel down decisively. "You are not under oath, and your motivations are suspect."

"Then *put* me under oath-"

"I am not dragging this case out indefinitely, when there is a vulnerable shifter child's welfare at stake! My decision is final. Stand down, or be held in contempt of court."

Hayley rushed to Griff's side as he opened his mouth to say something that would doubtless get him arrested. "Don't," she hissed in his ear. She could feel his arm shaking under her hand, and realized he was perilously close to a full-blown seizure. "Not now. We'll- we'll think of something, we'll find a way to fight this."

His eyes met hers, blazing with intensity. He took a deep breath, and some of the rage left his features…replaced by determination. "Yes. I will."

Then he turned toward Reiner, drawing himself up to his full height as best he could. "Reiner Ljonsson, *I challenge you!*"

CHAPTER 28

GRIFF

Reiner let out a disbelieving bark of laughter. "You cannot possibly be serious. You can barely stand."

"Then you won't have any trouble defeating me, will you?" Griff's muscles were screaming in agony at the effort of standing upright on his backward-bent legs, but he refused to show any sign of weakness. "I challenge you for your pride, Reiner Ljonsson. Face me like a lion."

"Oath-brother, what are you doing?" John's blue eyes were wide with shock. "You are in no condition to attempt this."

Hayley too had gone pale. "Griff, no! He'll kill you!"

Griff ignored them both, focused on Reiner. "Well, Reiner? Answer the challenge."

Reiner hesitated, looking from Griff to the judge as if seeking higher intervention. "This is ridiculous. I'm not debasing myself by acknowledging a challenge from that twisted freak."

The judge banged her gavel down, the sound echoing like a gunshot around the room. "Order! Mr. MacCormick, I will not have you disrupting my courtroom!"

Paucus leaped in to back up his client. "Your Honor, we petition to have Mr. MacCormick removed from court. His condition is clearly causing him to become irrational-"

"Mr. MacCormick's mental state is of no relevance," Michael interrupted. He shot Griff an *I hope you know what you're doing* sort of look. "Alpha challenges are an inviolable right, protected by law and enshrined in lion tradition. With all due respect, Your Honor, you have no power to intervene."

"*Lions*," the judge muttered under her breath. She fixed Griff with a piercing stare. "Mr. MacCormick, as a wolf shifter myself, I must respect the sacredness of an alpha challenge. Nonetheless, I will ask you to reconsider. Even if you somehow defeat Mr. Ljonsson and become Daniel's legal alpha, I will not change my ruling. Daniel needs the guidance of a true shifter, and a true pride. You cannot provide those things."

He'd been expecting her to say something like that. "I understand, Your Honor."

She narrowed her eyes at him. "Furthermore, in the unlikely event that you kill Mr. Ljonsson during this challenge, I *will* prosecute you to the fullest extent of the law. Accidental deaths during alpha challenges are protected. Deliberate murder is not."

"Is that your plan, cripple?" Reiner clenched his fists, glaring suspiciously at Griff. "What is this, suicide by lion? You think you can entrap me into a murder charge?"

"Your Honor, my client has a valid concern," Mr. Paucus interjected. "In Mr. MacCormick's state, he is highly unlikely to survive the stress of an alpha challenge. Mr. Ljonsson cannot be held responsible for that."

The judge sighed, rubbing her forehead. "Mr. MacCormick, Mr. Paucus is correct. Since you are the challenger, and seem fully cognizant of the risks you are taking,

Mr. Ljonsson will not be held liable in the event of your death. For the last time, I ask you to reconsider. Will you withdraw your challenge?"

"I will not. My challenge stands."

Hayley's fingers dug into his arm. "Griff," she whispered, for his ears only. "What are you doing?"

"Buying time," he muttered back. "I'm going to die anyway. Let me make it mean something."

He turned back to Reiner, who was still looking mortally offended by the entire situation. "Reiner, I repeat my challenge. What is your answer?"

"You're deranged." Reiner's lip curled as his scornful gaze swept Griff from head to toe. "You don't stand a chance. I refuse to take part in this mockery of lion tradition."

"I'll happily accept your surrender, if you're too cowardly to fight." Griff smiled at Reiner, aware that his bestial features turning the expression into a mocking snarl. "Get down on your belly. Show me your throat...*beta*."

As Griff had intended, the taunt raised Reiner's hackles. "I'm not frightened of you. I accept your challenge!"

"In which case, court adjourned." The judge rapped her gavel down again. "Gentlemen, you will settle this immediately. I am not having this farce drawn out any longer than necessary. Stewards, please prepare the arena."

"Mr. Griff, Mr. Griff!" Danny broke free of his social worker at last as officials started clearing away chairs. Without the slightest sign of repugnance at Griff's monstrous form, Danny wrapped his arms around his waist, burying his face in Griff's side. "Don't fight Daddy, *please*. He'll hurt you."

"It'll be all right, lad." Griff dropped down to his haunches to embrace the boy. He rubbed his furry cheek against Danny's tear-streaked one in a leonine gesture of love and comfort. "Sometimes this is just the way lions have to settle things."

"He'll hurt you bad," Danny sobbed. "And it will all be my fault."

"*No.*" Griff put a flex of alpha power into his emphatic tone. "None of this is your fault. It's mine and your da's fault, because we can't come to an agreement like grown-ups. Don't ever, *ever* feel like this was your fault. Promise me that."

Danny's shoulders shook, but he nodded.

Griff looked over his blond head at the judge. "Your Honor, I don't want him to see this. Permission to let his mother remove him until this is over?"

The judge motioned at the social worker, and at one of the security guards. "Please escort Daniel and Ms. Parker to a waiting area."

"No!" Hayley exclaimed. "I mean, yes, Danny can't see this. But I'm staying. I'm not leaving you to face this alone, Griff."

"He will not be alone," John rumbled. "I shall be here, my lady. Oath-brother, if you cannot be dissuaded from this, then I will be your second."

"No, you won't," Griff said firmly. "You're going with Hayley. I need you to make sure she and Danny are safe."

"But-" John and Hayley started together.

Letting Danny go, Griff grabbed John's arm. Under the pretext of using the sea dragon as support to stand up, he leaned in close to his ear. "I am calling in your debt. On your honor, you *will make sure they are safe*. Do you understand?"

John went absolutely still for an instant. Griff felt his muscles tense as he understood his meaning.

They will be safe. John's telepathic voice was a dirge of grief and loss and utter, unbreakable determination. **I will spirit them away. I will hide them in the wilds where none shall*

ever find them, and I will lay down my life in their defense. I will repay my debt.

Unable to respond telepathically, Griff could only embrace him briefly, fiercely. He knew that he could count on the sea dragon to get Hayley and Danny away while everyone else was distracted with his challenge to Reiner.

Hayley was still looking stubborn, unaware of what had passed between John and Griff. "I'm not leaving. John can take Danny, but I'm not leaving."

Letting go of John, Griff turned to her. For the last time, he took her in his arms. For the last time, he breathed in her scent. For the last time, he felt her soft warmth against his body as she clung to him.

"Go with John. He'll explain." He touched her face lightly, hoping that the brief, simple caress could say everything that he didn't have time to put into words. "I love you. Always."

There was no more opportunity for goodbyes or explanations—the stewards had finished clearing away the chairs, and erected the barriers that turned the center of the large, round chamber from a courtroom into an arena. Alpha challenges were not exactly common, but they happened often enough for there to be an established procedure.

To his relief, Hayley reluctantly allowed John to pull her away. Griff waited until the doors had swung shut behind them all before turning to Reiner. "Let's do this, then."

Reiner was already shrugging out of his suit. Quietly, so that the watching witnesses couldn't hear, he snarled, "In a hurry to die, freak?"

Quite the opposite, actually.

Every second he survived was another second Hayley could use to escape. Every second increased the distance between her and the officials who sought to deprive her of her child. Every second increased her chance to save Danny from growing up under Reiner's harsh, misguided influence.

Griff would do whatever he could to buy her those seconds.

He was under no illusions that he would be able to defeat a fully-grown lion with his bare hands. Reiner was going to kill him. The best he could hope for was to make him do it slowly.

Reiner shifted, leaping lithely over the arena barriers in lion form. Taking a deep breath, Griff shrugged off his sheets, though he left his pants on. It wasn't like *he* needed to shift, after all.

Rather less elegantly than Reiner, he struggled over the barrier. It was a relief to drop to all fours, having been upright for so long. Even with his right arm more wing than forepaw, his body worked a lot better this way.

He took a deep breath, ignoring the pain that shot through his chest. His erratic heartbeat steadied as he focused on his opponent.

We will not sell our life cheaply. We will make him tear us apart piece by piece. We will fight to the last drop of blood, to the last breath. We will not fail our mate.

"Begin," said the judge.

CHAPTER 29

HAYLEY

"I changed my mind, I can't just leave him." Hayley tried to stop, but John had her wrist engulfed in his huge hand. "John! Let me go. I have to go back."

He shook his head at her, his face set in grim, hard lines. He continued to drag her after the social worker and the security guard. The two had Danny between them, as if they thought Hayley might try to snatch him and run off.

"Here we are," the social worker said in a horribly fake cheerful voice as she opened the door to a small break room. "We can all have a nice little rest in here. Would you like a snack, Danny?"

He glared back up at her, scowling beneath his tousled blond hair. "No. I wanna go back to Mr. Griff."

The security guard rolled his eyes, shoving Danny forward. "Get in, kid. An alpha challenge is no place for you."

John pulled Hayley into the room too, though he had to duck to get through the doorway. Letting go of her arm at last, he shut the door quietly behind the five of them. Catching her eye, he put one finger over his lips.

The social worker and the security guard were still

arguing with Danny. John loomed over them, one enormous hand falling onto each of their shoulders.

"My sincere apologies," he said. With one quick, sharp motion, he banged their heads together.

"John!" Hayley exclaimed in shock, as the social worker and the security guard fell into limp heaps. "What-"

"My oath-brother has charged me with your protection," John interrupted. He opened the door again, casting a quick glance either way down the corridor before motioning them to follow him. "I will get you to safety. Hurry. He cannot buy us much time."

Hayley sucked in her breath as she realized Griff's plan. She grabbed Danny's hand. "Come on, baby. Sir John's taking us on an adventure."

"Is Mr. Griff coming too?" Danny asked hopefully, trotting along at her side. "Is he going to meet us later?"

Hayley couldn't bring herself to answer him. Somewhere behind them, Griff was fighting for his life, for *their* lives. Every step away from him felt like a noose tightening around her throat.

I have to get Danny away. But...I can't leave Griff.

Her head said one thing, and her heart screamed another. She felt as trapped between them as Griff did with his two animals. The conflicting instincts tore at her soul until she couldn't bear it any longer.

"I can't," she burst out, balking in the middle of the street outside the courthouse. "I can't leave him."

John sang a low, agonized chord. "We must. *You* must. He is doing this for you. Do not waste his sacrifice."

"I won't." Dropping to one knee, she took Danny's shoulders, looking him straight in the eye. "Danny, you have to go with Sir John now. Do exactly what he says, understand?"

"Are you going back for Mr. Griff?" At her nod, a smile broke through Danny's worried expression. "Good. The pride is supposed to stick up for the alpha, just like he does for the pride."

Hayley hugged him, hard. "I *will* find you. I promise, I'll find you."

"And I too swear that you shall," John said to her, as she released Danny. "I will take your son to safety, and then return for you. There is no stone, no wall, no prison ever built that can withstand my kind. I will keep my oath."

Hayley staggered as an abrupt, burning pain lanced through her chest. Somehow she knew, *knew* that it was Griff's pain that she was feeling. He'd been mortally wounded.

He needed her. *Now.*

Without another word, she ran back into the building. She'd dressed up for the trial in her nicest shoes, but now the heels hobbled her. She kicked them off carelessly, her feet slipping on the polished floor as she raced down the corridor.

Another lash of agony twisted her guts. The hallways seemed to stretch endlessly before her, like a bad dream. She charged past a couple of confused security guards, heedless of their shouts. Up ahead, she could hear other noises—bestial snarls and shrieks of rage. The sounds of battle drew her like a magnet.

She didn't know what she could do to help. She didn't know if there *was* anything she could do to help. She just knew that she couldn't leave her mate to die alone.

She burst back into the courtroom, just as an almighty crash rattled the walls. A scene out of a nightmare met her horrified eyes.

The protective barriers that formed the arena had seemed so thick and sturdy, but now two of them were overturned. Griff lay unmoving in the wreckage, broken and bleeding. A wide crimson smear marked his trail, showing where Reiner had thrown him straight through the arena wall.

Witnesses screamed, fleeing higher up the tiered levels of the room as Reiner's massive golden form leaped through the gap in the barriers. The lion had deep scratch marks on the side of his face, and his eyes were alight with savage rage. His tawny coat was splattered with Griff's blood. He left red paw prints behind him as he stalked toward his fallen opponent.

Griff stirred a little, struggling to push himself up on broken limbs. Reiner roared at him, lips wrinkling back from his dripping fangs.

Griff raised his head, meeting Reiner's glare without flinching. Despite his shattered body, he roared back, defiant, undefeated.

Reiner's eyes narrowed. His powerful muscles bunched as he gathered himself for one final pounce.

"NO!" Hayley hurled herself toward them. Her bare feet skidded in Griff's blood as she threw herself between him and Reiner. "*NO!*"

Reiner was either too blind with bloodlust to notice her… or he just didn't care.

Claws extended, he leaped straight for her.

CHAPTER 30

GRIFF

Get up! Get up!

Griff raged at his useless body, struggling to force his broken limbs to obey him. His vision was going black around the edges from blood-loss. But if he could just *move*, he could buy Hayley another five seconds. Those extra five seconds were worth any amount of agony.

It was no use. He couldn't push himself up, couldn't even roll away from Reiner as the lion stalked toward him. All he could do was roar defiance. All he could do was refuse to surrender.

All he could do was hope it would take Reiner at least five more seconds to tear out his throat.

Hayley, Hayley, Hayley.

Her name ran through his mind like a mantra as Reiner gathered himself to spring. Griff held tight to the memory of his wonderful, perfect mate. He wanted his last thoughts to be of her. He filled his mind with her beautiful face and stunning body, picturing her so clearly he could almost see her standing in front of him.

She *was* standing in front of him.

Time froze. With crystal clarity, he saw Reiner leaping toward them, leaping toward *her*. Hayley was right in his path, arms spread, protecting Griff with her own body. The lion's long, powerful form seemed to hang in midair.

NO!

Every atom of his body, every part of his soul, united with the need to protect his mate. Shattered bones reformed, muscles coalescing around them. He surged to his feet. As unstoppable as an avalanche, he leaped to block Reiner's attack, meeting the lion's talons with his own.

Reiner roared in pain as Griff hurled him to one side. The lion hit the ground hard, rolling. He staggered to his paws, snarling—and stopped dead.

Griff spread his wings to protect his mate, his tail lashing. Reiner cowered as Griff screamed at the lion in rage. Griff didn't give him a second to recover. He pounced, sinking his talons into the lion's shoulders, pinning him to the ground. His powerful beak closed around Reiner's throat.

The temptation to bite down was almost overwhelming. But...despite everything, Reiner was still Danny's father. That single fact was the only thing that kept Griff from tearing the lion's head clear off for daring to threaten his mate.

SUBMIT! Griff demanded, hurling the thought like a spear into Reiner's stunned mind. *Submit, or I will kill you!*

Reiner whimpered. *I surrender! I surrender!*

Griff dropped him, backing away. He stayed tense and ready in case it was a trick, but Reiner just fell bonelessly to the ground. The lion rolled, exposing his belly in utter submission.

Alpha. Reiner's telepathic voice shook with terror and awe. *You are Alpha. Forgive me.*

Griff's hackles settled. Satisfied that the lion no longer posed any threat to his mate, he folded his wings-
...Wait.
Wings?

CHAPTER 31

HAYLEY

One second, Hayley was staring straight down Reiner's throat as he leaped for her. The next thing she knew, she'd been hurled aside, a huge, golden form surging between her and the lion. Vast, gleaming wings spread protectively over her. For a mad moment, Hayley could only think that she'd been saved by an angel.

But it wasn't an angel.

"*Griffin*," Hayley breathed.

She wasn't sure whether she was saying his name, or naming what he was, or both. But in any event, there was no mistaking that majestic, powerful form.

He could have sprung straight from a heraldic coat-of-arms, or some medieval bestiary. He had the head of an eagle, with fierce golden eyes and an enormous hooked beak, but halfway down his chest the ruff of feathers blended into a lion's tawny coat. His front legs ended in the strong, scaled feet of a bird of prey, but his back legs were entirely lion. His wings spanned the entire width of the arena, every feather shining as if made of pure gold.

He was beautiful, and terrifying, and utterly overwhelming. And he was whole. Finally, he was what he was supposed to be.

He was a griffin. He was *her* Griffin. Her mate.

"Griffin!" she called out again, but he was too fixated on Reiner to notice. She could only stay back, out of the way, as the griffin ruthlessly pinned the lion down.

In a few short moments, it was all over. Reiner lay whimpering and defeated on the ground. And Griff…suddenly stopped and stared down himself, as if he'd only just noticed his new form. His beak dropped open in comic surprise.

"Griff!" Unable to hold back any longer, Hayley flung herself at him. She wound her arms around his soft feathered neck, half-laughing, half-crying. "You're a *griffin*. That's what you've been all along!"

A small, wondering noise rumbled deep in his throat, somewhere between a lion's purr and an eagle's call. The hard side of his beak rubbed against her cheek, tentatively, as if he didn't quite trust his newfound strength.

She hugged him tighter, burying her face in his feathered chest. He was *huge,* at least double the size of even Reiner. He had a clean, wild scent that reminded her of both snowy skies and dry, sunbaked grassland—a strange but beautiful combination, as unique as he was.

"Ah." They both looked up at the judge, who was staring down at them with a completely nonplussed expression. "Yes. Well, that seems to be quite decisive. Mr. MacCormick, it appears that you will be able to be the alpha that Danny requires after all. I shall…I shall have to reconsider my verdict."

"Oh my God, Danny!" Hayley exclaimed, releasing Griff. "John's still-"

She cut herself off, not wanting to spill the secret, illegal plan in front of the judge. Griff understood, though. He cocked his head, his golden eyes going a little unfocussed.

Then his beak dropped open in an unmistakable smile. He nudged her shoulder, rumbling.

"You talked to John? Telepathically?" Hayley guessed. "You can do that now?"

He nodded. Spreading his wings in a heraldic pose, he gestured at himself with one front claw.

Delighted laughter bubbled up in her throat. "Of course. *You're* a mythic shifter too. Just like John is. So you can talk to him. Did you tell him to bring Danny back? That everything's okay now?"

He nodded again. The feathers of his ruff raised a little, as if he was starting to get a bit agitated. She could *feel* his delight and awe, glowing in her heart where earlier she'd felt his pain...but she could also sense a growing undercurrent of frustration. And worry.

She stroked his shoulder, a thrill shivering through her at the contrast of the soft fur over the hot, hard muscles beneath. "What's wrong?"

He shuffled his clawed feet, looking a little sheepish. He gestured at himself again.

"I think he's stuck," said Michael, coming up beside her. For once, the polished lawyer had lost his air of ironic detachment. He was grinning from ear to ear. "Trust you, Griff. First you can't shift, and now you can't shift *back*."

Griff rolled his eyes at him. He let out a pained hiss.

"Can you talk to him?" Hayley asked Michael. "You're a mythic shifter too, aren't you?"

The lawyer shook his head. "Fae hound. Similar, but different enough that I can't contact him telepathically."

People were starting to emerge out from behind overturned chairs and benches, creeping back down toward the arena with staring eyes and open mouths. Michael raised his voice, addressing the room at large. "Anyone here a mythic shifter? Charades are only going to get us so far. We need a translator."

Unfortunately, none of the officials turned out to be dragons or anything similar. Hayley thought that Reiner, as a lion, might have been able to talk to Griff, but *he* didn't seem to be able to shift back either. The arrogant lion shifter was nearly catatonic with shock.

In the end, they had to wait until John finally returned with Danny. Hayley spent the time anxiously checking Griff for any wounds, but his transformation seemed to have completely restored him. He was gleaming and flawless, from his powerful beak to his tufted tail. There was no sign that he'd ever been injured at all.

"Oh." When he arrived, Danny didn't seem at all surprised by Griff's new form. He looked the griffin up and down thoughtfully, and nodded a little, as if something had become clear. "Yep. That explains a *lot.*"

"At last, oath-brother. What took you so long?" A joyful melody rippled under John's teasing words. "Come now, shift back. You are an expert in the theory, are you not?"

Griff shot him a dirty look. He growled, low in his throat.

"Can you help him?" Hayley asked the sea dragon shifter. "What's he saying?"

John chuckled under his breath. "That it turns out theory is a lot more difficult than practice."

"Mr. Griff?" Danny tugged on Griff's feathers, his upturned face serious. "Think of cookies, Mr. Griff."

Griff looked down at the boy…and shimmered.

"My boy," he said, gathering Danny up. He turned to Hayley, pulling her into his embrace as well, his face shining with joy and wonder. "My mate."

He held them both in his strong arms, and she knew he would never, ever let go.

EPILOGUE

Three Months Later...

"Mommy, Mommy, Da's here!"

Hayley froze, her pulse spiking with anxiety. By court order, she was required to allow Reiner access to Danny, but until now he'd meekly followed every condition she'd set. His visits with Danny were strictly supervised, either by Griff or one of the other firefighters on Alpha Team. He wasn't allowed to return Danny a minute late...or pick him up a minute early.

So what was he doing turning up a whole *hour* before his scheduled time?

Does he know Griff is still at work? Does he think he can snatch Danny and run before I can call for help? Has he just been biding his time all along, only pretending to be contrite and reformed?

"Da! Da!" Downstairs, Danny's feet charged for the door.

"Danny!" Flinging aside her hairbrush, Hayley sprinted for the stairs. "Don't let him in!"

She stopped on the landing, her mouth dropping open.

"I don't have to let him in." Danny paused just long enough to shoot her a single baffled glance. "He's got a *key*, Mommy."

Then he leaped up into Griff's outstretched arms. "Hi Da! Did you have a good day at work?"

From the dumbfounded expression on Griff's face, this was the first *he'd* heard of this new name for himself too.

"What?" Danny looked from him to Hayley and back again, evidently confused by their stunned silence. "You *said* I didn't have to call you Mr. Griff anymore."

"Aye, but…I thought you'd just drop the 'Mr.,'" Griff said, rather weakly.

"I thought he meant *Reiner* was here!" Hayley's heart was still hammering with shock.

"Hmm." Griff cocked an eyebrow at Danny. "Lad, I'm afraid this might get a little confusing."

Danny rolled his eyes at their obtuseness. "Katie at school has a Daddy and a Papa, and no one finds *that* confusing. So Daddy's Daddy, and you're Da. That's okay, isn't it?"

Griff looked up at Hayley, his golden eyes silently echoing Danny's question.

"Of course that's okay," Hayley said, to both of them. Blinking back tears, she came down the stairs to embrace them both. "That's *more* than okay."

"Ugh." Danny wriggled, squished between them. "Let go, Mommy. Da stinks."

A rich chuckle rumbled through Griff's chest. He released Hayley, and let Danny slide to the ground. "I bet I do. Sorry, lad. You're going to have to get used to it, I'm afraid."

Griff did indeed reek of smoke. When he'd left this morning, his firefighter's uniform had still been pristine, but now it was covered in scuffs and smudges. There were streaks of soot at his hairline where he hadn't quite managed to wash up thoroughly before coming home from his shift.

He looked tired, and sweaty…and utterly filled with a deep, quiet joy.

Hayley beamed at him, her heart swelling with pride. "First real fire?"

"Aye." He knelt to undo the laces on his filthy boots. "It's good to be back on the team."

Hayley still wasn't tired of seeing him bend his left knee casually, without even the memory of pain. She also wasn't yet tired of seeing him in his firefighter's uniform. And, she secretly had to admit, it was even sexier when he was all rumpled and disheveled from a hard day saving lives.

Griff glanced at her, grinning as he read her thoughts. "And I was worried that *you* were going to be worried." His sweeping gesture indicated the evidence of the dangerous nature of his work. "When you realized what this job actually involves, I mean."

Hayley ducked down to kiss him, an illicit thrill going through her at the taste of smoke on his lips. "I'm not worried. You *are* the Griffin, after all."

His hand captured the back of her neck, holding her close a moment longer. "Amazing woman," he murmured against her mouth. "My lion-hearted love."

He let her go again, straightening. "I'd better go shower before Reiner gets here. Oh, John volunteered to chaperone him for us this evening. You don't mind, do you?"

"No, of course not." Something about Griff's overly casual tone snagged Hayley's attention. "Why?"

"Just thought it would be nice for us to have an evening to ourselves," Griff said, much too innocently. "I thought we might go out."

She narrowed her eyes at him. "What are you up to, Griff?"

Danny chortled, his small face alight with glee. "It's a secret, Mommy. A *big* secret."

Griff mock-growled at him. Danny slapped both hands over his own mouth, his shoulders shaking with muffled giggles. Before he could spill any more hints, Griff scooped him up under one arm, carrying him firmly off upstairs.

Hayley shook her head in bemusement, watching them go. *What was all that about?*

John, when he arrived, only added to the mystery. The sea dragon turned up with an overnight bag, his sword, and an air of great, secret delight.

"I simply thought it might be wise to bring a few essentials with me, my lady," was all he would say. He held up his bag, which made an odd clinking noise, as if whatever John considered essential for a sleepover was made of solid gold. "So that I could guard your territory and your son overnight, if necessary. Just in case you found yourself…delayed."

Hayley couldn't get anything more out of him. His enigmatic silence just fanned the flames of her curiosity. By the time Reiner finally rang the doorbell, she was practically burning up.

What are *they all up to?*

"Hi," she greeted Reiner. For once, she was too preoccupied to feel her usual flutter of apprehension at the sight of him. "Are you in on this too?"

He stared at her blankly. "In on what?"

"Evidently not," Hayley stood aside to let him in. "Never mind. Griff and I are going out. John is going to stay here with you and Danny, okay?"

He nodded distractedly, as if he barely heard her words. He'd been oddly subdued over the last week, ever since he'd returned from his trip home to Valtyra. Now he too seemed preoccupied with something.

"Hayley," he burst out. He drew himself up, setting his shoulders as if bracing himself for a fight. "I have something I need to say."

Hayley eyed him warily. "Griff!" she called over her shoulder. "Reiner's here. He wants to talk to us."

"What about?" Griff had changed into his kilt, and Hayley momentarily lost her entire train of thought. He moved to stand protectively at her side, fixing Reiner with a piercing stare.

Reiner cleared his throat, fidgeting a little. "It...that is... well. You know how I'm paying maintenance for Danny now?"

"Yes, and don't think you're going to weasel out of it," Hayley snapped. "The judge set a very fair level. Don't tell me you can't afford it."

"No! I mean, that is, I can. It's just...I realized that I should have been paying before. All these years, I mean." He pulled a check out of his pocket. "So...I wanted to give you this."

Hayley blinked at him in complete disbelief. "You *want* to give us *more* money?"

The piece of paper trembled, as if Reiner's hand was shaking. "Yes. Please. If you'll accept."

Then he did something very strange. Keeping his head bowed, he knelt to lay the check at their feet.

What is this? Some sort of trick?

"If you think you can *buy* Danny-" Hayley started.

"Hayley," Griff said, very quietly. He'd gone still as stone, his expression utterly blank. "Do you mind if I handle this?"

Hayley threw up her hands. "Be my guest. I have no idea what's going on tonight. Is everyone drunk? Is there something in the air?"

"Quite possibly," Griff murmured. He looked down at Reiner, who was still crouched on the floor, head bowed. "Why?"

Reiner didn't quite meet his eyes. "Because...Danny says you are a good alpha. I, I think perhaps I do not actually know what that means." His mouth twisted, rather ironically. "But in any event, I *do* know that you are certainly stronger than my brother. Stronger than any lion. *No one* could challenge you. No one could shame me for not being able to."

Griff blew out his breath. "We'll...think about it. I can't give you more answer than that right now."

Reiner nodded submissively. "Thank you." To Hayley's complete confusion, he picked up his check, pocketing it again as he rose. "That's all I ask."

"Okay, spill," she finally demanded, after they'd said goodbye to Danny and gotten in the car. "What on earth was all that about?"

Griff glanced at her sidelong as he drove, his expression still rather thoughtful. "If a lion wants to join a pride, it's traditional to lay a gift at the alpha's feet."

Hayley could barely believe she'd heard him right. "Reiner just asked to join your pride?"

"No, he asked to join *our* pride. He was laying the gift at your feet too. He was acknowledging you as the alpha female." Griff shook his head ruefully. "Believe me, I'm as shocked as you."

Hayley chewed her lip. "Do you think it's a ploy? A way to infiltrate us, and get closer to Danny?"

"No." There was absolute certainty in Griff's tone. "From his body language, he was completely sincere. He genuinely wants to join the pride."

"Something must have happened when he went home to Valtyra," Hayley said slowly, thinking back on Reiner's subdued behavior ever since he'd returned. "Maybe his old pride kicked him out."

"No, I would have been able to tell if that had happened." Griff drove in silence for a long moment. "Reiner used to think that being an alpha meant crushing everyone else down and ruling by fear and intimidation. He got that idea from *somewhere*. I think…I think he went home to his own pride, and compared it to ours. I think, perhaps, his eyes have finally been opened."

"Mmph." Hayley folded her arms over her chest. "Well, I'm not yet ready to start feeling sorry for *Reiner*, of all people. Let alone welcome him into the family with open arms."

Griff's mouth quirked in wry acknowledgement. "That's more than understandable. And as alpha female, you've got the final say in whether he ever joins the pride."

Hayley studied his profile. "But *you'd* let him join, if it was up to you?"

Griff didn't answer for a minute, his eyes on the road. "I can't help imagining a scared little boy with amber eyes, without anyone to teach him what it means to be a real lion. I can't help wondering if that scared little boy is still trapped somewhere inside an angry, scared man."

Hayley put her hand on his, on top of the gearstick. "You'd save everyone in the world if you could, wouldn't you?" she said softly.

The laughter lines around his golden eyes creased as he glanced at her. "Comes with the job, I'm afraid. But enough about Reiner for one night. I'm not having him spoil things even when he doesn't *mean* to."

"Agreed." Hayley noticed that they were heading for Griff's house, rather than into the city center. "Hey, I thought you said we were going out on a date, not just back to your place."

"Oh, we'll go out, I promise." There was an odd undertone in Griff's voice, half-laughter, half…nervousness? He parked the car outside his house. "I just need to pick something up from home first."

Hayley had assumed that meant he would run in while she waited in the car, but he came round and opened her door. She gave him a narrow-eyed look as she took his hand. "What, can't you get this mysterious thing for yourself?"

In the darkness, his eyes glowed with a faint, warm light. "Actually, I need you to carry it for me."

Hayley was starting to have an inkling about what was going on. It therefore wasn't *entirely* a surprise when she walked through the front door and into a heady, perfumed cloud of roses and jasmine.

Fragrant blooms overflowed every surface, transforming Griff's simple house into a glorious bower. Tiny, flickering candles provided a romantic light. Even as her heart started to pound with anticipation, Hayley couldn't help being amused by the fact that they were battery-powered LED tealights, rather than real candles.

Trust a firefighter not to leave flames unattended…

"This is what I needed to get." Griff picked up a tiny box from the coffee table. He went down on one knee, taking her hand. "Hayley Parker, will you-"

"*Yes!*"

Griff burst out laughing. "Will you at least let me finish the question?"

"Sorry." Hayley tried to school her face into an appropriately serious expression, but couldn't suppress her wide, foolish grin. "You've clearly worked hard on this. Go ahead."

"Will you marry me?" Hayley opened her mouth, but Griff quickly held up his free hand, forestalling her. "*And* will you be my mate?"

"Yes! Yes! Of course!" Hayley could barely wait for Griff

to slide the stunning diamond solitaire ring onto her finger before she threw her arms around his neck. "Oh, Griff!"

Still on his knees, he caught her, easily supporting her weight as their lips met. Hayley closed her eyes, feeling the familiar sweet fire lance through her. No matter how often they kissed, no matter how often they touched…it was always like the first time.

"Will I be able to hear your thoughts, after we're mated?" she murmured against his lips. "Like Connie and Chase, or Virginia and Dai?"

"Aye." His fingers twined tenderly through her hair. His eyes burned with a deep, contented fire. "We'll be truly joined, mind and soul."

She let out a sigh of longing. "I can barely wait."

The heat in his gaze flared brighter. "Well…the wedding will take a little organizing. My clan is fairly extensive. But the mating…*that* just takes the two of us."

The growl in his voice made her shiver in anticipation. "So we could do it now?"

He grinned at her, looking deliciously feral. "I was hoping you'd say that."

"You mean, you knew I'd say that," Hayley teased, as he swept her up in his arms. "Don't think I've forgotten that John was *planning* on staying overnight."

He laughed softly in her ear, holding her cradled against his chest. "I can't help being observant."

She'd been expecting him to carry her upstairs. But instead, he headed for the back garden, carrying her easily in one arm as he opened the door.

"I did promise to take you out," he said, putting her back on her feet. "And I will. Or rather…*up*."

Hayley's breath caught. She hadn't even *seen* Griff fly yet, though she knew he'd been practicing. His eagle sisters had quite literally taken him under their wings, with much delighted teasing at finally being able to get their own back on their big brother. But he'd refused to let her watch his lessons, claiming that his fledgling attempts were far too embarrassing for her to witness.

"You sure I won't weigh you down too much?" she asked anxiously. "I'm pretty heavy, after all."

His hand slid over her curvy hips and round to her backside, lingering in appreciation. "*You* are perfect. *John* is heavy. He helped me practice this. That's why I waited so long to propose. I wanted to make absolutely certain my flying skills were up to the task."

Hayley raised her eyebrows at him. "You do realize most men don't feel the need to be able to fly before proposing, right?"

"Eagle men do. Flying is part of our mating ritual. And I *am* half-eagle." He shrugged one shoulder. "Though that's the other reason I had to make you wait a while. I needed time to puzzle out how to stitch eagle and lion rituals together."

"So what do lions do?"

He captured her chin in his hand, tilting her head up. "You'll find that out later."

Hayley's toes curled as he bent to kiss her again, slow and lingering…and utterly commanding. Her body instinctively molded itself to his, submitting to his irresistible dominance.

When he released her, she swayed, helplessly yearning for him as he stepped back. The January night raised goosebumps on her skin, but her core still burned with a fierce, hungry fire. She wrapped her arms around herself, shivering with cold and desire as he moved back until he had room to shift.

He met her eyes, and smiled. Then, between one breath and the next, the man was gone. In his place stood the griffin, as fantastical as a statue brought to life.

That's something else I'll never get tired of. Seeing him like this.

She ran her hand down the deadly curve of his massive beak, still barely able to believe that this extraordinary, powerful creature was real. Not only that, he was *hers.*

He was the only one of his kind, utterly unique. And he was hers.

With a whisper like silk, he unfurled one vast, gleaming wing, kneeling down so that she could mount. She scrambled up onto his back, straddling his neck where the feathers blended smoothly into golden fur. She had to grab at his feathers for balance as he crouched, his muscles coiling underneath her.

With feline grace, he leaped straight up into the air. Hayley gasped with delight as the ground fell away beneath them, driven away by the powerful beats of his shining wings. She'd always secretly longed to fly…but never, not even in her wildest dreams, had she'd imagined it would be like this.

There were no walls, no boundaries, no limits. She had no fear whatsoever of falling, not with Griff bearing her up. The wind whipping through her hair was frigid, but his solid warmth between her legs heated every part of her body. She was free, the normal world of rules and restrictions left far behind.

The whole glittering night sky was theirs. He bore her up so high, she felt as though she could stretch out and pluck stars out of the sky as easily as harvesting apples. She reached out a hand in awe, and the diamond on her finger glittered as if a star had indeed fallen into her hand.

When they were so high that the thin air burned like ice in her throat, he paused, stretching his wings out to balance on the wind. She felt his chest swell underneath her. He let out a single high, fierce call, proud and wild. Somehow, she knew that he was proclaiming to all the world that she was his, his mate, now and always.

Tears of joy leaked from the corners of her eyes, whipped away by the wind. "Yes," she whispered. "Yes."

Hold on.

The thought was not quite her own. Hayley caught her breath, a faint, tentative presence tickling the back of her mind, light as a feather.

Hayley. Hold on.

She huddled down against his back, wrapping her arms around his feathered neck. His delight sparkled in her head like a distant firework.

Then he folded his wings, and dove.

Hayley screamed in exhilaration and terror as they plummeted like a stone. The wind snatched at her, trying to tear her from his back. She buried her face in Griff's feathers, clinging on for dear life. Blackness gnawed at the edges of her sight. All she could do was close her eyes, hold on, and trust him.

At the very last moment, he flared his wings. They settled back to the ground as lightly as a falling leaf. The griffin's warm back shivered underneath her, shifting into Griff's strong arms.

"They say that the higher and faster the flight, the stronger the bond," he said in her ear.

She twined her arms around his neck, leaning her whole weight against his hard, muscled bulk. Her legs were still weak from the exhilarating swoop. "Then our bond will be as strong as our love."

He made a low rumble of assent, deep in his chest, as his mouth covered hers again. The hot, hungry length of his cock pressed against her stomach. But more than that, she could *feel* his all-consuming desire for her, a fire burning in the depths of her soul. She could feel how the touch of her tongue against his drove him wild, barely able to restrain himself from pushing her down and taking her there and then.

"Not that I want to wait any longer either," she said, pulling back a little to grin up at him, "but it's pretty cold out. How fast can you get us to the bedroom?"

In answer, he seized her waist in both hands. Hayley giggled as he tossed her over his shoulder in a fireman's hold, striding back into the house. In bare seconds, he'd flipped her down onto his bed.

Scattered rose petals brushed against her cheek. Hayley stretched out her arms, like a child making a snow angel, smiling as the scent of crushed petals rose from the sheets. "You *did* prepare thoroughly."

His mouth quirked in amusement. "I promise, *this* time I have condoms."

She hesitated, looking up at him. "Do we...do we really need them?"

"I'm afraid from your scent you're at the peak of fertility, so-" Griff stopped dead, his face going slack with realization. "Oh. *Oh.*"

She dropped her gaze a little, suddenly feeling too shy to meet his eyes. "Sorry, I shouldn't have said that. It's not the sort of decision you should make in the heat of the-"

That was as far as she got before his body covered hers. His bulk pressed her hard into the bed, laying claim to every inch of her. His hands found the sides of her head, holding her as he kissed her with fierce, desperate intensity, as if she was the air he needed to breathe. She closed her eyes in blissful surrender.

"There's no decision to make," he said, his voice shaking with need. "I want more children with you. The only thing I want more than that is *you*. If you're sure..."

"Completely," Hayley breathed against his lips.

He kissed her again, this time just the lightest butterfly

brush of his mouth against hers. Then he pushed himself to his hands and knees, holding himself above her. His eyes burned hotter than she'd ever seen before, swirls of fiery gold.

"Mine," he growled. "My mate."

He straddled her, pinning her hips down underneath him. His hands hooked in the neckline of her dress. With a single, sharp motion, he ripped it apart, exposing her body to his ravenous gaze. His fingers slid up under her bra. Hayley caught her breath, her pussy clenching in response as his fingers dug possessively into the softness of her breasts.

"*Mine.*" Pushing her bra up, he freed her nipples for his hungry mouth. Hayley arched against him, gasping. He took advantage of the motion to unhook her bra, jerking it roughly off. Waves of pleasure pulsed through her core as he sucked hard at first one nipple, then the other.

"Griff!" she cried out, tightening her legs around his waist as her climax surged closer.

Before she peaked, though, he released her, pushing her flat against the bed with one hand. "*Wait.*"

Unbelievably, her body obeyed the flex of alpha power in his voice. He held her on the very brink of orgasm, every part of her throbbing with frustrated need. She writhed, desperate for release, but was helpless under his strength.

His teeth gleamed in a satisfied smile. Lifting his weight off her, he ran his hand lightly down from her breastbone to the curving swells of her stomach. Trails of fire ignited on her skin. She sobbed at the unbearable pleasure, still held back from climax by his alpha command.

He worked his way lower, spreading her legs. He traced her dripping folds so lightly, she wasn't even sure he was even touching her. Even that faint, barely-there caress echoed through every part of her oversensitive body. She was blinded by need, aware of nothing except him.

"Griff, *please!*" Her fists clenched in the sheets. "Please, please, now!"

He moved away, and she sobbed helplessly, utterly bereft at the loss of his heat against her skin. His eyes still held her, demanding her complete submission. She couldn't reach for him, couldn't move, couldn't do anything except watch as he stood back.

Tantalizingly slowly, he undid the belt of his kilt. The heavy fabric dropped away, revealing his proud, straining cock. He was so erect, the swollen head brushed his rigid abs. A pearl of eager moisture glistened on his tip, showing how hard he was having to hold himself back. Nonetheless, his hands moved leisurely, stripping away his clothes with maddening slowness.

Unhurriedly, he spread her legs wide, kneeling between them. His tip pressed against her opening as he covered her body with his, pinning her wrists above her head with his hands. Hayley wanted to squirm, to slide down and take him inside her throbbing passage, but he held her absolutely motionless.

"*Mine*," he repeated, one last time.

She exploded around him as at last, *at last*, he thrust into her. That single stroke tipped her into a climax more powerful than any she'd ever known. She wrapped around him, taking him into her soul even as she welcomed him into her body. His pleasure was hers, as hers was his, until she couldn't tell the difference between them. At last, they were one.

When she came back to herself, completely limp and undone by the intensity of the experience, she could still feel him in her head. His deep, utter satisfaction and joy glowed in her soul. It was a fire that she knew would never go out, a secret warmth that would last all the rest of their days.

Oh, she thought in wonder, and knew that he heard her

as clearly as if she'd whispered in his ear. *So that's what it's like.*

His chuckle rumbled through her bones. He rolled off her, pulling her to spoon against him, her backside fitting into the curve of his body as if they'd been made for each other. *Aye. We're truly mated now.*

"Mmm." Hayley snuggled back against him, delicious tiredness weighing down her limbs. "Do you think we made a baby?" she asked out loud.

"Too early to tell. But the chances are good." He kissed her shoulder. "And if not this time…well, we'll just have to keep practicing, won't we?"

She giggled, closing her eyes in utter contentment. "I wonder what our children will turn out to be. Griffins, like you? Or will some of them be lions, and some eagles?"

"I know what they will be." His hand traced soft, reverent spirals on her belly. "They'll be loved."

∾

The rest of Alpha Team find their mates in Fire & Rescue Shifters: Collection 2 - four thrilling books in one page-turning box set! Available on Amazon and Kindle Unlimited now!

Printed in Great Britain
by Amazon